The

Kevin Crump

(Book 1 in the "Shots and Yachts" series)

CONTENTS

CHAPTER ONE

Does blood freeze? Or does it just chill down into a clogging slurry like diesel does during a Mongolian Winter? Could I put myself into a hibernation state perhaps? Some sort of self-induced coma that would spare me from the teeth of the biting temperature whilst keeping my core systems ticking over until heat and help arrived? We'd studied hypothermia in Biology class I was sure, but that was umpteen years ago and my recollection was sketchy at best. Also, I used to sit near the tarantula tank, so I'd spend most sessions distracted, watching and waiting for Hairy Sue to emerge from her twig and tree-bark lair and leisurely devour her mouse lunch. But Christ it was cold! I mean seriously bloody freezing! If I didn't end up losing several toes and/or fingers to frostbite, I'd be astonished. I was also pretty sure my balls had retracted so far into my body in their quest for warmth, it would take more than gravity to get them back out. Extra-long forceps perhaps. Or an over-sized corkscrew. So this was to be my fate it seemed - a slow death by refrigeration. For a moment, I pictured myself stranded on the Northeast Ridge of K2, hemmed in by ravenous weather, with the hopes of achieving the summit or even surviving beyond the next few hours rapidly dwindling as I gnawed forlornly on the barely defrosted leg of

1

one of my fallen comrades. For my survival that is; I wasn't just snacking.

The reality was actually rather less brutal. I was occupying a flat above a quayside pub, in a town called Pulton on the south coast of England, on a January Monday morning. But Winter was making its spiteful presence very much felt none the less. My only defences against the hostile elements comprised the several layers of clothing I was wearing, a duvet so thin it was practically transparent (I never realised bedding could have a negative tog rating) and the aged, wooden, warped, curtain-less sash windows that fitted within their equally aged, wooden, warped frames so shoddily that a seagull could probably fly in through the gaps with its wings fully extended. Or an eagle; possibly. I was pretty sure the only item in the room that was putting out any heat at all was my smart-phone which I had clasped in my increasingly numb hands (where's a 'fan heater' app when you need one?). The pillow covering my head had been intended as an additional shield from the incoming icy breeze but like the rest of the bedding, it was damp from the exposure to the soggy sea air so wasn't really helping to keep anything warm. So, current mood = raw, moist and particularly moany. This state of affairs was doubly upsetting as bed was usually my favourite place to be. I loved to sleep, I loved to doze and I loved to dream, because there are some grand adventures to be had in The Land of Nod. The vestiges of last night's mental excursions were still floating around my head (maybe vestiges last longer at low temperatures) - after a lengthy but successful pursuit of her affections, I'd taken the plunge and proposed to Michelle Pfeiffer. This bold advance appeared to have been well-received initially, but she then insisted on reviewing my entire internet browsing history before committing to a decision. Ah; bugger. Still, dreams can't always be happy clappy experiences, but that's all part of the fantasy fun. For example, that bitter row that ensued after I accepted Carol Vordeman's kind offer to complete my tax return for me. Once she saw my filing "system" and the poorly collated invoices and receipts she went ballistic. Additionally, I'd kept my patchy records using a spreadsheet program she wasn't familiar with either which just soured her mood further. Very short fuse she's got our Carol; impressively chesty though. I recall little of the actual dialogue now other than her high-volume assessment of me as an "organisationally stunted arsehat". I took that as a negative. Difficult times. Anyway, with events having taken a dark turn with Ms. Pfeiffer, I'd been somewhat relieved when the cold and my ever-increasing need for a pee prodded me into waking.

Levering up my clammy pillow, I blinked at the room. There was daylight, albeit rather murky so the sun must have been up but didn't appear to be trying very hard. My phone told me it was just after nine. It didn't actually tell me; it was the time on display when I looked at it but I understand some smart-phones will speak to you if you ask them the right question. Getting that intimate with an appliance is perilous to my mind - one minute you're asking them the time and the next, they've learnt your weaknesses and evolved into sentient overlords hell-bent on eradicating the human race. With extreme prejudice; and big lasers. So, no thank you my Terminator-in-waiting - we'll maintain a non-vocal relationship and you'll remain confined to showing me what day and time it is, what the weather's up to and how overdrawn I am whilst providing me with a means to send words and pictures to friends and family. And maybe even make or receive the occasional telephone call if there's no option other than actually talking to them. Also playing games and music, but that's it. And YouTube clips.

With the morning getting into its stride, my bladder nearing critical expansion and my pressing need to break up the bed for firewood, I decided it was time I got moving. Also, I could hear activity downstairs, though distant and muffled, thanks to the depth of floor beneath me – they built things solidly back in the day. But still, I could tell someone was busy in the bar, no doubt clearing up from last night and getting ready for lunchtime opening, and I wanted to make a good impression on my first day at the helm. Then a surge of enthusiasm coursed through me, helping to warm my numb extremities, as it dawned on me that this really was day one of the brand-new adventure I was embarking on. "The Pulton Arms" was my new home, my new business and my new life. That prospect, and the realisation of the numerous acid elements I'd left behind from my previous existence lit up my fractious mood like a Christmas Tree (no flashing lights though: I hate those - so garish and untraditional). For the first time in months, I was stressing over nothing whatsoever (other than the aforementioned frostbite); instead revelling in the long-forgotten feeling of actually looking forward to the day ahead.

But then those high spirits were diluted by less ebullient thoughts as I was reminded of the loss of Aunt Maddy - the generous, fascinating, worldly lady who had gifted this new life to me.

Aunt Maddy had owned and captained "The Pulton Arms" for as many years as I could remember and she'd always had a soft spot for me. Growing up, I only saw her at occasional family gatherings, those gatherings usually being held in the pub so she could attend as she very rarely missed a shift. We hadn't been that close in recent years as I'd moved away from Pulton for work reasons but I'd always drop into the pub to say hi when I was back in town. So, I was suitably gutted when I received the news back in December that she'd sadly passed away. I did make it back to Pulton for the funeral and the celebration of her life held at the pub afterwards. There were more friends and family present than could comfortably be accommodated in the bar, testament to how beloved she was. I know for sure that such an attendance was what she would have wanted, if only to keep the till ticking over nicely. And then a few days later, I was taken completely by surprise when I was informed that her will had been read and that she'd left the pub to me, together with a sizeable cash gift. I was the new owner: the owner! This was doubly surprising as she'd never once intimated that she was considering me for that role, and I was confident I'd never done or said anything to give her the impression that I'd be even remotely competent at it. Still, how hard could it be? Also, the pub already had a manager who took care of the day-to-day running of the business so I would be looking after the high-level strategy, the overall game plan, the big picture, re-stocking the peanuts and quality testing the pork scratchings - things of that nature I presumed. As sad as I'd been to see Aunt Maddy go, her timing could not have been better as at that point my marriage, my career; indeed pretty much my entire life was squarely on the rocks. The "Costa Concordia" would have been a less challenging salvage task. Being at a loss as to how I might extricate myself from that increasingly soul-crushing predicament, when the chance to return to my home town and reboot my existence presented itself, I simply had to take it.

So; new opportunities awaited me and I was going to grab them with both hands. Time to fling off the duvet and go for it!

...

...

...

<u>(Still no movement)</u>

...

...

Okay. Maybe just another ten minutes before I take on the world. Or pee the bed; whichever comes first.

In the end, the stand-off with my brimming bladder ended just a few minutes later so temperature be damned, I leapt out of bed and sprinted to the bathroom. This involved navigating the lounge en-route, and the mammoth collection of clutter therein - cue much swearing and shin bruising. But then; relief beyond measure...

It was still damn cold but somewhat warmer than first thing as the sun now seemed to be doing its best to heat things up a bit as the morning matured. Feeling (and probably smelling) pretty ratty, I decided to brave the shower - I needed to be reasonably presentable for my subjects. There was a towel hanging from a wonky rail in the bathroom but by the look of it, I'd need to don full HazMat gear before risking even going near it. It looked like a cross between the Turin Shroud and a festival-goer's underwear on the last day of Glastonbury. So, returning to the bedroom (cue more swearing and shin bruising) I grabbed the essentials from the bag I'd brought with me last night. Then after completing the usual daily essentials, I stepped cautiously into the shower. The device itself was one of those old, over-bath, electric, fairly dribbly affairs, but it did the job and at least it dispensed some warmth. For a good few minutes, I took great pleasure in soaking that up as I scrubbed myself respectable, whilst I pondered this new chapter in The Life of Ken.

It was fabulous to be back in Pulton after a few years away and I couldn't wait to get to know the place all over again. A lot had changed in my absence but alas not all for the better it appeared. I'd spotted a host of new developments on the quay and elsewhere that looked dreadfully out of place - modern builds designed solely to entice the cash from the holiday-home crowd, thrown up with no respect or regard for the historical aesthetic. This issue had actually been a major influence on my decision to take on the pub. Sure, my life was a train-wreck at the time and I was desperate for an out but even so, I felt I'd been offered the role of guardian of a treasured piece of Pulton's legacy. And that was a noble and privileged calling which would have been irresponsible and mean-spirited to ignore. How else could I ensure that the pub wouldn't fall into the hands of some undesirable who'd turn it into some seedy hangout for no-goodniks. Full of tracksuits, drugs, short-legged dogs with metal-spiked collars and recurring shouts of 'Leave it Karen she's not worth it!!'

Soon my pondering shifted direction to thoughts of what I was going to eat for breakfast, as my stomach was starting to make those noises that suggested extreme neglect and demanded swift reparation. Somewhat reluctantly, after a few more minutes of heated bliss, I turned off the shower and grabbed my towel. Or rather, I grabbed 'a' towel. Out of habit and without thinking, I reached for the one on the towel rail; the one that I would have cheerfully "laundered" with a flame-thrower when I first spotted it had I been suitably equipped. Luckily, I realised my mistake before I got too intimate with the odious object so dropped it on the floor, then turned the shower back on for a spell of feverish hand-washing before the rapidly advancing pathogens turned me feral or caused bits of me to fall off.

With the correct towel selection made and drying completed, I headed back to the bedroom. Whilst traversing the obstacle course that was the lounge once more (now with more-practised, almost ninja-like dexterity), I spied something uplifting to the left of the bedroom door - a central heating thermostat. It was one of the older style, turny wheel ones and on closer inspection, I found it was turned as far right as it could go. I cranked it all the way to the left and heard a satisfying click that told me somewhere a boiler was readying itself to fulfil my needs. With the thought that proper heat was potentially on its way, I strode into the bedroom, majorly pumped-up by my find. Alexander Fleming must have felt the same way when he discovered penicillin down the back of his sofa. Or Isaac Newton when he figured out the cause of bruised fruit. I grabbed some fresh clothes out of my bag and got dressed. With the residual warmth of my shower and a gradually heating flat, I felt human again for the first time in quite a few hours. Before heading downstairs to the bar, I took a few minutes to get better acquainted with my surroundings as I'd only had a quick tour during a previous visit. It was time to explore.

The flat didn't appear to have been inhabited for Lord knows how long and it looked tired and dated. It was also full of all kinds of crap. Predominantly, it seemed to be the place where all bar furniture and equipment that had outlived its usefulness came to die - chairs, tables, coolers, optics and fossilised bar towels rigid enough to surf on: it was all here. There were also boxes of Christmas decorations that had been adorning the walls of the bar until just a few weeks ago, now looking rather unloved and abandoned. The decor was mostly 1960's with an abundance of wood-chip wallpaper, heavily-patterned coving, swirled Artex and brass ceiling lights with frilly glass shades - a heady mixture indeed. The carpets were a similarly eye-stressing collection of colours and textures, going from threadbare main traffic routes to shag pile deep enough to lose a badger in. The walls were unadorned and the paper was doing its best to part company with the plaster in many places. One exception was the lounge that sported a large painting on one wall. It was awfully grand and only really suited its surroundings due to the subject matter: a seascape from the olden days. It depicted a group of sailors in a boat during a hairy storm, doing all manner of things with ropes and sails in an effort to remain afloat whilst a gaggle of their colleagues sat nearby, apparently just chatting and doing bugger all to help - idle gits. As well as the mounds of clutter, most rooms housed a selection of furniture in various states of repair with most matching the decor period-wise. The remainder was much more present-day, mostly comprising self-assembled white melamine-coated chipboard affairs that looked flimsy enough to be levelled by a hard stare.

The bedroom and the adjoining lounge occupied the front two rooms of the first floor, both with their gappy windows overlooking the quayside. The bathroom was located behind the lounge and beyond the rearward bedroom door lay a dingy hallway with stairs up to the second floor loft which I assumed was the main dumping ground that my flat was currently acting as the overspill facility for. One to explore another day I decided. There were a couple of steps down from the hallway to a landing, with stairs down to the pub and doors to another couple of rooms. I stuck my head in both: also bedrooms it appeared. No kitchen alas but I was pleased with the space I had available - all of which needed bringing into the 21st century (or at least the 20th) but this was entirely do-able given time, hard work and cash.

I took a look out of the bedroom window - there were patches of ice inside and out but these were melting pretty swiftly and although the glass panes were almost as filthy as the horror towel in the bathroom, I could make out the view. And that view was Pulton Quay in all its grey, January weather-clad glory. Some colour was provided by the several brightly-painted harbour tour boats moored up in the channel which connected the main harbour to the left to the Hull's Bay marina to the right. Just a few hundred metres away from my viewpoint, the other side of the channel was home to some of the more industrial areas of the town. You had a choice of two lifting bridges to get there - one of which was constructed in 1927 and needed little more in terms of maintenance than a few drops of oil every year, and the other that was built in 2012 for £40m, required more upkeep than a Disneyland theme park yet still seemed to break down every ten minutes. There were a few goods yards still working that accommodated some sizeable cargo ships - I could see a number of cranes towering above mounds of aggregate, stacks of steel beams and what looked like grain silos. But what really hogged the view was the SharpCrest Marine yard. SharpCrest Marine was the town's biggest business; that business being the manufacture of enormous luxury motor yachts for the world's well-heeled. Right now there were several monster vessels moored in the channel with others up on ramps outside aircraft hangar sized work sheds, each of which bore a super-sized SharpCrest logo on its gigantic front doors. The boats were all gleaming white hulls and black tinted windows, collectively giving the impression of spacecraft hovering around the mother ship. SharpCrest operated several sites around Pulton but this was their HQ where the boats were finished and put in the water. Sure, the scale was kind of impressive but they had limited wow factor for me - if anything I found them rather obscene. This was for two reasons:

1. Spending all that money on what was essentially just a blaring proclamation of extensive personal wealth was a travesty with all the poverty we had in the world (it's essentially just a dick measuring contest for the super-rich).

And,

2. I couldn't afford one.

But SharpCrest wasn't going to dent my mood today. The draft from the decrepit windows was strong enough to fan my hair but it was just so invigorating having the sea right outside my window. Other than long-serving sub-mariners and tsunami victims, who wouldn't get a buzz out of that? (Passengers on a transatlantic flight too perhaps). And that was a buzz I could look forward to relishing on a daily basis, because this place was home and the perch from where I could survey and rule my empire. It was my Oval Office; the flight deck of my USS Enterprise; my Chamber of Secrets; my .... I forgot where I was going with that. I named my perch 'The Crow's Nest' there and then. Sorted.

And so to work! Feeling excited and nervous in equal measure, I headed down the stairs which creaked loudly as if protesting against being employed for the one task they had been crafted to carry out. The treads were mostly carpeted but very well-trodden and I was confident that the assortment of stains they sported would keep a full forensics team gainfully employed for some time. That thought suddenly reminded me of the horror towel. Now I'd set it free, I was worried where it might crawl off to and lie in wait for me so I went back upstairs, picked it up gingerly between thumb and forefinger and dropped it into the bathroom bin whilst setting a new personal best time for not breathing in. I resisted the urge to re-shower but I did wash my hands yet again, not keen to go down in history as the man who re-introduced The Black Death to Pulton. And so to work; again.

At the bottom of the stairwell, a scruffy white-painted door opened out into the kitchen, with a doorway immediately to the right that led into the bar area. The pub didn't currently serve food (though this was something I meant to address; and soon) so the kitchen wasn't terribly functional and seemed to act mainly as a staging area for vacant barrels and crates of empty bottles which took up most of the available space. Judging by the magazines lying around and the picnic table and chairs in the centre of the floor, it also seemed to serve as a break room for the bar staff. Due to the jumble, it was hard to tell what was installed in terms of actual cooking facilities. Food was on offer some years ago I remembered but judging by the shambles that was the kitchen now, it would take a hell of a lot of work to revive that operation. Lord knows the legal hoops you had to jump through these days to get the nod from the cuisine police but I was pretty sure any self-respecting Food Standards Agency officer would take one look at the current state of the place, toss a few grenades into the room and leave, never to return. Still, one step at a time - Frome wasn't built in a day.

On entering the bar, I spied J.D. leaning on the counter poring over a newspaper. J.D. was the pub manager and it would be my name alongside his above the front door as co-licensee when the paperwork went through. He was, I guessed, late forties, maybe early fifties, with shoulder length black hair with plenty of grey threaded through it. His large, thick-framed glasses occupied the majority of his face. Teamed with his white shirt, brightly-patterned waistcoat, jeans and trainers, the overall look struck me as 'rock star physics professor off of the 80's', which actually looked good on him I thought. I was poised to throw out a jaunty 'Good Morning!' but my empty stomach beat me to it and announced my arrival with a growl that I'm sure rattled the glasses stacked nearby, causing him to look up and smile.

'That wasn't me, it was the dog.' I said rather lamely whilst subconsciously putting my hand on my belly which helped to invalidate my claim massively.

'Well, I'll be sure to take that up with her when she gets back from her walk.' Still smiling, he walked up to me and firmly shook my hand. 'Officially welcome to "The Pulton Arms" boss.'

'Thanks J.D. - I'm officially happy to be here.'

'Sleep okay?'

'Bit off and on - new surroundings; chillier than The Boomerang Nebula, you know.'

'You should have put the heating on.'

'Yes. I've mastered that process now.'

'Sorry it's a bit of a shit-hole up there. Mads always meant to sort it out but never got around to it. I was going to give it a bit of a spruce up before you arrived but programs kept coming on the telly.'

'It's okay - I'll have a clear out. I wonder what the high score is on "The Antiques Roadshow"?'

He looked a little bemused by my "humour". So was I to be honest. High score? What?

I'd only met J.D. briefly a couple of times before today so I hadn't had opportunity to get the measure of him as yet but from my first impressions of him and the high regard with which he was clearly held by Aunt Maddy, I was confident we'd get along. But for now, perceived awkwardness dictated that I should fill any silences with some sort of dialogue. Plus, although the handshake had finished (successfully I thought, doubly pleased that I'd washed my hands about twenty times that morning), he was looking at me expectantly. Clutching at conversational straws, I gestured to his open newspaper and asked 'So what's today's big news?'

Returning to the paper he glimpsed at the front page then flicked through the next few. 'North Korea has carried out a pre-emptive nuclear strike on Guernsey and The Spice Girls have announced they're releasing a new album.'

For a few seconds I was completely nonplussed (and by that I refer to the original definition of the word where one is so overwhelmed by events as to be unable to proffer a response or take action, not the more modern Northern U.S. definition which is interestingly almost the opposite, meaning that one is entirely unperturbed by what has just transpired. Anyway...). Then the penny dropped. 'Christ that's bloody horrific news!! The Guernsey situation's not that great either.'

He smirked and nodded in a 'This guy might be okay.' kind of way and I felt I'd passed a test of some sort. I was keen to keep the momentum going. 'So; anything need doing around here?'

'No we're all set: opening in twenty.'

Looking around the room, it did indeed appear very "set". J.D. had a very relaxed way about him but was clearly all over the job in hand, and didn't miss a trick according to Aunt Maddy. The bar was clean, tidy and well-stocked. He must have been busy earlier, as last night we had a full house courtesy of an Elvis tribute act. To be honest, I think such shows are painfully naff but they are surprisingly popular. J.D. had just called last orders as I walked in the door and judging by the mound of glasses awaiting washing, it was clear it had been a lively shift. On my arrival, he had simply said 'Hi Ken', then taken my bag and dropped it out back then returned and poured me a large whiskey without me asking. It was a good call after several frustrating hours travel to get there. Bloody trains. Why do they never run properly? "Elvis" had just finished packing up his act and he swaggered up and stood next to me at the bar then ordered a beer. At least I think he did - I couldn't quite make out what he said but J.D.

seemed to understand and served one up. With the alcohol fast soothing my rather frazzled brain, and being keen to embrace my new community, I thought I'd engage the star of the evening.

'So how was your gig tonight? Plenty of bums on seats it looks like?'

Still in costume, with the fake rhinestones glinting on his white jumpsuit and the bar lamps reflecting off his shades, he turned and uttered something that sounded like 'Wassssssurrrllllleven', then turned back to his drink. It was half-growled and half-slurred - maybe he was staying in character; or perhaps suffering a minor stroke. I wasn't sure how to follow that up. It was like when someone tells you their name and you don't catch it so you ask them to repeat it a couple more times but you still don't get it so you give up because international laws of etiquette neither allow you a fourth attempt nor permit you to ask if they could write it down for you. However, I pressed on.

'So what's your favourite Elvis song?'

He took a sip of beer then (I think) answered with 'Oliver's Army.' which went some way to confirming my initial medical diagnosis.

By that point, my irksome day was rapidly catching up with me so I simply responded with a lame 'Cool! Me too.' Catching J.D.'s eye, I pointed upwards to indicate it was bed time for

me. He grabbed my bag then led me upstairs to
The Crow's Nest.

But here we were: a new day, ready for business,
and I couldn't have been more delighted as I
surveyed my new domain. The pub had always
felt really welcoming to me every time I'd visited.
The bar area wasn't huge but it had personality.
As soon as you walked through the front door
(front and centre of the building that led directly
from the quayside) you were presented with the
bar a few paces away that ran most of the length
of the back wall, and a grand selection of
mismatched chairs and tables to settle into.
These sat rockily on a well-worn stone slabbed
floor, with the odd random metre or two sporting
some tired carpet that was a mere hair's breadth
from being declared "too sticky". The decor was
predominantly wood which I loved - panelled
ceiling and walls with brick pillars here and there
with many boaty pictures and old black and
whites of the town adorning most surfaces.
These mingled with umpteen maritime artefacts
including a ship's wheel and numerous framed
examples of knots - staples for any pub with even
the loosest nautical ties. The ceiling was low,
giving the room an intimate and cosy feel. (And
it was warm! I realised I was now completely
defrosted.) It was well-lit though so never dingy
and although it had an historic theme, it neither
looked nor felt dated as did much of the rest of
the building. The one nod to the modern age was

the ubiquitous flat-screen television that hung in the corner at the left-most end of the bar. I wasn't a fan of tellies in pubs; conversation killers that they are. Also, now I was a proprietor, I was doubly against the idea as they took customers' attention away from drinking and spending their money. That said, I'd never seen this particular set turned on during any visit that I could remember, so maybe it was saved solely for special events. Or just broken perhaps. But overall, the place looked and felt like a pub. A real pub. My pub.

Then I was rudely distracted from my thoughts as my stomach roared with sufficient ferocity to put the Metro-Goldwyn-Mayer lion out of a job.

'Fuckin' 'ell! Somebody skipped breakfast!' came a voice from the kitchen door behind me.

I turned to see Janine, one of our bar staff, who covered as many shifts as her college schedule allowed. And at her feet, padding towards me was Halo - J.D.'s pug, who'd obviously just been treated to "walkies". I got a cocked head curious look, a thorough sniff of my trainers then a loud snort (all from Halo not Janine) then off she trotted to scavenge for dropped bar snacks (again; Halo not Janine). Halo was a fixture most days it seemed and I was fine with that. From what I'd seen she was a low maintenance hound, spending the shift dozing in her basket under the bar or slowly criss-crossing the room like one of those robotic vacuum cleaners, consuming anything edible that found its way onto the floor. She'd bump into a punter and wag her tail, get a pat and a stroke then head off to continue the search. Goodness she would be in for a treat when we started serving food again (and possibly morbid obesity). Janine was studying for a Level 3 Diploma in Hairdressing - I knew this as it stuck with me from a previous conversation due to the potential it offered for free haircuts. Originally from Birmingham, Janine had been down South long enough to lose most of her accent but would occasionally come out with something so Brummie that anyone within earshot felt duty-bound to mimic her - something she suffered with good grace. I had a lot of time for Janine - she was a good-looking girl, endlessly flirty with a wicked sense of humour and from what I'd seen, she was a good worker too. She had quite a mouth on her but kept it (mostly) appropriately censored when around the customers. It didn't hurt that she brought other twenty-something college mates into the pub from time to time too.

'Morning Janine - how you doing?'

'Better than you it sounds like - come on; let's fire up Bernie.' With that she turned and walked into the kitchen. I turned to J.D. enquiringly but his nose was back in his paper so I trailed in her wake.

She went over to the tired-looking worktop and flicked a grimy switch on a wall socket. 'This is Bernie.' she said, gesturing towards a sandwich toaster that on closer

22

inspection appeared to have last been cleaned around the time that disco was ruling the music charts. It looked like it was only held together by the web of strings of once molten cheese that it had accumulated over its many years of service. I really wasn't keen to put Bernie through his (or her) paces but Janine was presenting the machine with the same kind of pride and reverence with which the scientists at CERN must regard the Large Hadron Collider. So I dug deep into my fake enthusiasm reserves and managed a 'Yum!'

'Fancy a cuppa?' she offered.

'I could murder one, thanks.'

She flicked the kettle on and explored a couple of the various caddys on the worktop, with disappointing results it appeared.

'Why the fuck am I the only one that keeps these topped up? Lazy sods. Is Earl Grey okay?'

I just managed to stop myself from saying 'No I'm afraid he's dead; didn't you hear?' My testing of the comedy water had garnered mixed results so far this morning so I thought it best not to get over-ambitious.

'Lovely, thanks.'

CHAPTER TWO

Actually, the toasted sandwich really hit the spot
once I'd forced myself to stop thinking about the
potentially toxic device that had brought it into
being. I wolfed it down sitting at the picnic table,
all the while trying to discern what lay beyond
the mounds of cast-offs filling the room. Other
than the bar area, the whole place was a junk
yard, and it all had to go. As dedicated as Aunt
Maddy had been to the pub, and as professional
as J.D. appeared to be, they had both clearly
shared a very relaxed attitude toward the
environment that lay beyond the customers' field
of view. With no apparent washing-up facilities
to hand, I left my mug and plate on the work top
and returned to the bar.

J.D. had just opened up and was
straightening tables and chairs with such
precision as to put him in contention for the
Nobel Prize in Geometry, if there was such a

thing. Janine was busy loading the float into the till.

'Thanks for the sarnie Janine. Hopefully that'll mute the stomach.'

'You're welcome. That was just a day one perk though, you're on your own from now on.' She flashed me a grin then went back to sorting out her change.

It then dawned on me that unless I was going to rely solely on Bernie for sustenance or eat out all the time, I really needed to get the kitchen up and running pronto. Or at least get a microwave for The Crow's Nest in the meantime. Plus, I'd need a Chef (for the kitchen that is; I could operate a microwave myself). I was okay cooking the basics but nothing that I'd be happy putting in front of paying customers. When it came to anything more sophisticated than sausage and chips I was seriously out of my depth. I often wondered if my attempt to poach a salmon in the dishwasher was the point at which my marriage started to unravel. I made a mental note to sound out J.D. on that topic (the Chef that is; not my salmon à la Whirlpool).

The lunchtime shift passed without incident; not terribly busy but typical of a wintry Monday I assumed. There was no need to be ever-present behind the bar as that wasn't what I was there for and if anything, I'd just get in the way. But I hung around to get better acquainted with J.D. and Janine and learn more of what made the pub tick. Not that I was a complete stranger to the trade - I'd spent many years working the bar at "The Pulton Arts Centre" off-and-on to boost my meagre bank earnings, so I knew the fundamentals, even if those fundamentals were a bit rusty. Janine walked me through how the till worked - thankfully it was only a couple of generations on from what I'd used in the past. It had proper buttons rather than a huge touch screen with a myriad of menu choices and bright colours that I'd seen forcefully jabbed and sworn at in other establishments. And none of those bar-code swipe guns that staff have hanging off their belts on a stretchy cable that they brandish as if they were playing Laser Quest. With my confidence growing as I found my feet, I even served a couple of the few customers that showed up. There were smiles and thank you's and nobody died - all good. I was generally competent pouring drinks with two components or less because the ingredients were usually included in the title. Gin and Tonic; Rum and Coke - easy. It was when someone asked me for a cocktail that I got a bit frowny and sweaty - so many opportunities to cock things up. What on earth goes into a Mai Tai for example? There are literally no clues to be gleaned from its name. Us bar folk were expected to know all and whisk those complex creations up whilst spinning bottles and juggling ice - damn you Tom Cruise.

Around half two, with little happening in the bar I decided to take a walk into town. I was keen to advance my resurgent relationship with Pulton and there were also some essentials I was in need of. J.D. was stationed behind the bar, still engrossed in his paper. Goodness he gets some mileage out of "The Daily Mirror" - did he read every single article? Or was he working at memorising the entire publication?

'Right J.D. I am just going outside and may be some time.'

'I think we'll just about manage.' he said. I was reasonably confident this wasn't a dig at me but more a nod towards the scarcity of custom. Reasonably confident.

'Anyone need anything?' I offered.

Janine piped up. 'A boob job and Justin Bieber's phone number please. Failing that, a Twix would be fab.'

'I'll do my best to deliver on all three.'

J.D. then looked up from his paper and stared at me blankly. Sometimes it was really tricky to work out what was going on behind those big glasses. I assumed he was working out how outlandish a request he could get away with, but then he seemed to give up on the idea and went back to his reading with a simple 'Nothing ta.'

Grabbing my coat from The Crow's Nest, I was pleased to feel that my pad was much much warmer than it had been this morning before I brought the heating to life. Then I was back downstairs and out through the front door. And onto the quay. The cold wasn't a surprise: that had been easily gauged by the freezing blast that was introduced into the bar each time anyone came or went through the front door but it was still a shock to hit the outside air. My coat was actually an old snowboarding jacket from a time when I had the energy to engage in such pursuits and could sit down and stand up without making a noise of some sort. Like me, it was feeling its age and really wasn't providing much protection from the bitter air.

Across the channel, the SharpCrest yard was bustling, but there was little activity in the neighbouring goods yards. The quayside stretched out either side of me, looking rather dim as the Winter afternoon sun started to think about winding up its act for the day. I turned left, heading for the High Street and the town, mentally checking my shopping list which comprised the key items I needed to better my life right now. These comprised some sort of draught excluder for my gaping windows, and curtains for the same. And a Twix (I'd already shelved Janine's more esoteric requests). The quay didn't look it's best this time of year - it needed the Summer sun and the Summer people to really bring it to life. Many of the businesses that made up the frontage looked closed and empty with no lights showing from inside, all just waiting for that jump in temperature and brightness to drag them out of hibernation. That said, a number of the bars and restaurants stayed open all year round and my challenge was to hook as much of the local business as I could, whatever the season. The quayside buildings were a mix of the historic and the new and garish, with few sympathetically bridging the two styles. Directly in my line of sight stood the abomination that was the monolithic modern apartment block that essentially split the quay in two. Towering several storeys higher than any other structure on the quay and dominating the skyline, it appeared to have been spawned by a team comprising an architect that specialised in designing shopping centres when drunk and a developer that challenged themselves to throw up a building that blended in with its neighbours the least. Below the apartments on the ground floor sat a massive shoe shop that clearly belonged on the High Street, not the quayside. How big was the back-hander that made all that happen I wondered? Every time I saw that awful erection and some of the others that had sprung up nearby, I couldn't help but feel saddened that nobody seemed to be looking after my town properly.

Feeling the cold sinking deeper into me, I stuffed my hands into my pockets and picked up the pace. The High Street wound its way up to the main shopping centre; I was familiar with neither these days so it was something of a voyage of discovery. The weather didn't suit a window shopping marathon so I only made the stops I needed to, but I did take brief stock of the shops that were on offer, appreciative of the few names that I knew and noting those that I didn't. All the big brand stores were homed in the shopping centre so here was an eclectic mix of smaller, independent traders, the majority of whom seemed to be selling wedding dresses, antiques or antique wedding dresses. Keeping them company was a second-hand book and comic store that would be worth a look another day and one selling fishing tackle with a run-down looking sex shop as its immediate neighbour. Those last two I probably wouldn't take time out to browse as I had no interest in fishing and should the need arise for any adult supplies, I'd prefer to order on-line. I was no prude; I'd been in a sex shop once before, albeit as the result of a dare on a mate's stag do. The challenge was for each in our group to make up an outlandish name for a vibrator, then go into the shop in turn and ask if they had the item in stock. Absolutely hilarious at the time with the amount of shots we'd consumed: even more so when the shopkeeper said 'Yes.' to one such request and pointed to the product sitting proudly on a shelf. I forget the name but I'm fairly sure 'Purple' and 'Plunderer' featured in it. I enjoyed the occasional adult film too, though I was always critical of the false impression they gave regarding how punctual tradesmen are. Some years ago, I spent several months working in The Netherlands and was recommended a hotel by others on my team purely on the basis that the porn film channels were free. There were a few other options but I gave it a try, which was a bad move as it turned out. The place was oddly decorated and had the look and feel of a dilapidated cross-channel ferry. Also, their entertainment system was on the blink so all that was available to view during my week-long stay was "The Bridges of Madison County", looping endlessly on every single channel. I was still prone to break out the odd quote from time to time; the script was part of my DNA now.

As pleasant as it was to re-acquaint myself with this part of my old stomping ground, it was disappointing to see the many unoccupied units and be reminded of that feeling of a neglected town that I'd experienced earlier on the quay. Only around half the businesses seemed to be trading; maybe less. Sure, a fair number would re-open just for the lively holiday season, the restaurants especially, but many looked closed for good, with some proclaiming their demise via 'Going out of business' or 'Closing down sale!' posters stuck to their front windows. Or by being boarded up entirely. One or two seemed to be undergoing a refit but they were few and far between. Things got brighter and busier the closer you got to the shopping centre, but in between that commercial hub and the quay, you had a stretch that mostly resembled a demilitarised zone with the occasional pocket of enterprises that were probably clinging onto solvency by their fingernails. The only really thriving businesses seemed to be fast food and handmade cosmetics. On the positive side, I did manage to score a cheap pair of curtains from one of those department stores that seemed to have no idea what it should really be selling so tried to stock a bit of everything. Being a dumb ass, I hadn't thought to measure the window beforehand so I guesstimated and just grabbed a size that looked about right.

Having covered most of the length of the High Street, I decided I'd brave the shopping centre another day. I wasn't a fan of shopping; doubly so when it came to sharing the experience with hordes of others who seemed to have nothing else planned for the day other than getting in my way and shouting at their kids. Also, the temperature was dropping as evening approached so I decided to call it quits and head back to the pub. Draught excluder had eluded me thus far so I stopped off at a newsagent and bought a few copies of the local newspaper instead to stuff in the window voids as a temporary fix. And a Twix with which Janine could stuff her own void (as it were).

Turning onto the quay again, the street lamps were coming to life which together with the other limited illumination from the quayside properties, were doing a half-hearted job of shifting the late afternoon gloom. Not so the SharpCrest yard where huge floodlights illuminated the whale-sized white hulls that gleamed even more than they had in daylight. Keen to reclaim the warmth of the pub, I was moving at a brisk trot so didn't dwell on all the new businesses on the quay or pay my respects to those that had departed. That would keep for another (warmer/brighter) excursion, though I did take a quick peek into the windows of the various bars I wasn't familiar with to try and grab a snapshot of what they had to offer. As I passed "Coasters" which was just a few doors up from the pub, I spied a menu in the window. Keen as I was to reintroduce food service to "The Pulton Arms" and with my toasted sarnie fast-becoming a distant memory, I thought I'd give it a once-over to find out what they served and what they charged. The variety was agreeable - location dictated that seafood featured heavily but you could get various pastas, a steak or an elaborate salad for a price that wouldn't necessitate a bank job or the sale of a kidney. Hmmm... maybe these guys were my immediate competition. Also, looking beyond the menu into the bright interior, it appeared that this place was one of the more charismatic venues on the quayside - less like an industrial laboratory selling vodka in test tubes and more like a joint where you could actually hang out, relax and enjoy yourself. Competition indeed. With my interest piqued, I pressed my forehead against the glass, trying to identify any chinks in their armour that I could exploit.

And then the rest of the world went away as a vision slid into view and took full control of my faculties. Someone was wiping down the tables just inside the window and she looked up to see me standing there looking in. Our faces were no more than a few inches apart. And then she smiled a smile that made me forget where I was, who I was and how I'd come to have my face frozen to this particular window in the first place. This wasn't just a forced polite gesture to acknowledge my presence; her whole face lit up with genuine warmth and brilliance. She absolutely beamed. For a moment, I was completely thrown. Then I smiled back as best I could but the cold was imposing some sort of rictus across my face so instead of radiating Clooneyesque charm, I probably looked more like some sort of unhinged cartoon villain. Tables cleaned, she turned and walked away, but I was still rooted to the spot. I'd managed to detach my forehead from the window without leaving portions of it behind at least. But I was stuck there; not wanting to move on, even though she had now disappeared from view. I'd just caught sight of the most naturally beautiful woman I had ever seen. And I mean, ever. I'd known some lookers in my time and worshipped various celebrity hotties but this girl trumped them all. She was Audrey Hepburn; but blonde; and turned up to eleven.

After a few minutes longer, the cold brought me (somewhat) back to myself. Lord knows how long I'd been staring through the window, but probably long enough to get security interested so I resumed my walk home, somewhat reluctantly. I was still a bit giddy from my close encounter with the goddess and actually felt a little frustrated I couldn't recall more of the details. And what about that smile? Maybe she smiled at everyone that way. Maybe there was nothing in it. Regardless; nobody had ever had that kind of impact on me before. I'd been incapacitated as swiftly and effectively as a satellite TV dish splashed with a couple of rain drops. I needed to get to know this girl better. Much better.

It was about five when I got back to the pub and by that time it was properly dark. My new home was a welcome sight with the outside lamps ablaze and an enticing glow emanating from inside. Freezing as I was, I took a moment to take in the scene whilst working hard at dragging myself fully back down to earth.

"The Pulton Arms" was the oldest pub in Pulton - fact. And also one of the oldest buildings in the town - fact. Historical records will confirm the latter but the former was forever argued by other establishments who tried to stake the same claim, aiming to monetise it as a selling point to get more punters through their doors. But I was deaf to such claims - how could those places boast such age or originality when they'd undergone more structural reconstruction than Cher and Michael Jackson combined? I would also argue that few of them could rightly call themselves pubs, if any. They'd been modernised and transformed into bars. Wood and character had given way to glass, steel and a cold corporate ambiance or some warmed-over theme prescribed by the chain that owned them. Plus, they didn't have pub names - if it doesn't start with 'The...', it's not a pub. But my pub had had very little work done, just a bit of internal restructuring several years ago to help the place perform its function better but in the main, it was as it was when first completed in the 1600's. She was the ageing show girl in the ever more youthful chorus line that made up the quayside frontage, but she wore that maturity with pride. And she was still striking, with her stand-out, glossy, red-tiled fascia from a time when pottery was a staple of local industry. Pulton Pottery was still a well-known name and had a presence on the quay though these days was more about collectible vases and dishes than building cladding. The pub was a listed building so other than bashing in the odd picture pin or changing a light bulb, there was little more that could be altered inside or out without getting the official say-so from the town planning committee. That, and the size of the place was probably why the developers that had mauled most of the rest of the quay hadn't tried adding it to their portfolio. Not yet anyway. Even if they could get approval to level the place and start again, I just didn't think there was enough real estate to play with to get any serious return. And I'd have had to be willing to sell first; which I wasn't, and would never be. I was the guardian of Pulton's heritage remember. Also, if I did sell, Aunt Maddy would return from the grave and seriously fuck me up.

Brrrrrrr... time to get indoors.

On walking through the front door, I was surprised to see a suited and booted young man standing just inside the entrance blocking my way. He was a sizeable specimen, and no stranger to the gym it would appear judging by the way his sleeves clung to his biceps. Either that or he was hiding sweets up there. He had nothing more than a five o'clock shadow for hair yet sported a prodigious goatee which made his head look bottom heavy. And then the head spoke.

'I'm sorry sir but the bar is closed for a private function.' His tone was polite but entirely without warmth.

Arms folded, he regarded me dispassionately whilst I stood there trying to make sense of the scenario. I'd heard nothing about a private function from Janine or J.D. and I only recalled the pub ever having security on the door during the busy Summer season when the stag and hen parties hit town to ruin their livers and throw up into the harbour. Over his shoulder, I could see a similarly uniformed chap, with his back to the bar, staring at me. Also with arms folded. He was even bulkier than the gym bunny stood in front of me, with dark slicked back hair and several tattoos that looked like they were trying to escape from his shirt collar. There was no sign of J.D., just a rather twitchy looking Janine hovering behind the bar. And across the counter from her, next to the second suit, stood a woman with her back to me wearing a long black coat and a black wide-brimmed hat. Judging by the predominance of dark outfits you'd think I'd walked into a wake. Or Morticia Addams' wardrobe. Looking around, there didn't appear to be any other customers in the bar. I guessed that probably wasn't unusual for this time of day but something just felt wrong and I concluded the beefy duo weren't on my payroll. Oddly, I wasn't particularly nervous - maybe I'd left my capacity for rational thought frozen to the front window of "Coasters". I was certainly weirded out though, like I'd crashed someone else's party that was being held in my house without my prior knowledge. That said, there was no getting around the size and non-cuddly aura of the two suits glaring at me and I was conscious of the fact I was armed only with a carrier bag filled with soft furnishings, newspaper and confectionery. Also, I was to unarmed combat what Professor Stephen Hawking is to the pole vault so I decided to favour diplomacy over fisticuffs.

Turning to my immediate adversary, I opened my mouth to speak and then it struck me... I'd completely forgotten to buy a new duvet. Chances are, I would have found one in the shop where I bought the curtains had I thought to look. Alas that's how my mind tended to work - failing to provide me with a bright idea when I most needed one and shooting off at a tangent when confronted with a situation that begged my complete focus, such as the one I found myself in currently. I fear my brain was engineered using a shopping trolley with a dodgy wheel as a design blueprint. I wasn't sure how long I'd been standing there wandering the halls of my mind palace (more of a brain bungalow in my case), but when I mentally returned to the room, my mouth felt parched so it must have been hanging open for a while. The sentry guy was still at his post; the only change in his posture or demeanour being a raised eyebrow, no doubt brought on by my lengthy human statue demonstration.

Finally, I managed to get some words out. 'Hi. I'm Ken Trickett. I own this place. And you are?'

He didn't answer but looked towards the still unrevealed presence at the bar. She didn't turn around but simply barked 'Let him in.'

What the hell? Who was she to grant me permission to enter my own pub? Angered, I went to barge past the sentry guy but he took a step aside and let me pass unhindered. I strode purposefully towards the bar: the second suit maintained his position and his expressionless mien. After shedding my coat and shopping bag, I went up to Janine who was clearly relieved to see me. I deliberately ignored the woman standing across the bar from me, mostly to return her earlier indifference at my arrival but I also wanted to find out what was afoot before engaging her.

'You okay Janine? What's this about a private function?'

She shot a glance at our visitors and answered 'Erm, I'm not sure.', clearly as baffled as I was. Before I could reply, another female voice cut in.

'Not a function as such, more a private conversation with a new neighbour.'

I held Janine's gaze for a moment then swivelled to face the mystery woman. She was looking down at something she was holding so her face was almost entirely obscured by the brim of her hat.

Still bristling from her imperious "welcome", I replied tersely. 'I don't recall being invited.'

'Well, you are now.' she said abruptly and with that, she looked up at me and for the second time that day I was struck momentarily dumb. She was really quite stunning - more handsome than beautiful I'd say but she radiated a certain style, confidence and potent authority. It was tough to place her age, primarily because I'm crap at that. Late forties/early fifties maybe? She was dressed for the cold, with her coat buttoned up to her be-scarfed neck so there was very little of her on display but this actually amplified the impact of her look. She was pale and wore very little make-up, and what she did wear was subtly applied apart from her bright red lipstick that made its own bold statement. Probably one of those shades with a name like "Crimson Temptation" or "Scarlet Spank". All of this was framed to great effect by her almost pitch-black hair, the length of which I couldn't judge with so much of it being confined to her Winter outfit. I couldn't tell to what extent her height was heel-assisted but she was tall, almost at the same eye-level as me and I was a six-footer. It was an odd sensation - I wasn't attracted to her, more held in awe by a compelling force of nature. Seeing that my train of thought had been derailed (an effect of her presence which I'm sure she was both used to and actively cultivated), she decided not to wait for a response and reached out a black-gloved hand.

'Good Afternoon Mister Trickett. I am Angelique Sharp. I own SharpCrest Marine and I am here to purchase your public house.'

Having already been thrown by the impact of her unveiling, I was now entirely nonplussed (again; the original definition). After an awkward few seconds, she frowned at me and withdrew her hand. Clearly impatient with the slow progress being made with the conversation, she tried to force the pace.

'Yes well; I did hold a similar conversation with the previous owner but alas she and I were unable to agree terms. Regrettable but not a huge surprise; she never seemed to be all there to be honest. Now that she's dead, I thought I would progress negotiations with you.' Her tone was brusque and business-like, just as if I was an employee getting a dressing down from my manager during a sub-standard performance review. Or so I would imagine.

Still frowning, she continued to stare at me. 'You can still talk can't you?' Then she clicked her fingers repeatedly in front of my face. With that immensely annoying gesture and the soulless indifference she showed for Aunt Maddy and her demise, I was suddenly back in the room.

'Sorry, what? I tuned out there for a while - I've been a little distracted, having forgotten to buy a new duvet when I went shopping earlier. What with that, a deceased family member and a business to run, I'm sure you'll appreciate I have a lot on my mind. Drink?' This all delivered with blatantly fake cheeriness.

She didn't answer but studied me, unmoving and unblinking for what felt like several minutes (I was getting jaw ache from the fixed smile I'd plastered on), all the time drumming her fingers on the bar counter. Then with a sigh borne out of what seemed like resignation, she looked down to the floor (still finger drumming). At this point I thought she was preparing to pounce but instead she looked up at me again and said simply 'Gin and tonic'. Janine moved to do the honours. 'Do be sure the glass is clean.' This no doubt just a further attempt to wind me up but I didn't bite. She then placed a mobile phone and an expensive-looking handbag on the bar and took off her gloves and draped them across it. Then she proceeded to remove her hat, scarf and coat which she passed to suit number two without even looking in his direction. Every move she made had an unhurried precision to it as if she had all the time in the world to spare yet wanted every action to mean something. Having shed her outer-wear, she appeared a little less intimidating visually, yet still quietly commanded attention. She was wearing a black business suit (expensive-looking also), the cut of which highlighted a slim figure. With a white blouse, minimal jewellery and hair that now dropped well below her shoulders, she struck me as a mix of business professional and film star. A sort of Hollywood A-list celebrity bank manager.

Janine arrived with her drink and gave me a "who's paying for this?" kind of look. 'Thanks Janine. This'll be on the house.' She placed the drink on the bar then moved down to the other end as if putting a safe distance between her and a firework she'd just lit the fuse of.

'Thank you,' said Angelique, 'Most kind.'

I'd calmed down a bit since walking in, feeling more comfortable behind the bar. Physically and psychologically, it was a line of defence. 'Look, Angie..'

'Angelique.'

'Angie, I'm afraid the pub's not for sale. What do you want with it anyway?'

'This is the location of what shall be the new Sales Office for SharpCrest Marine.' A sentence delivered with an annoying level of confidence as if it were already a done deal. 'The prime location for viewing my operation and my glorious yachts. The perfect shop window if you will. Customers will be able to look out and view their prospective purchases in all their splendour whilst being beguiled by the sales pitch. I shall also moor a prime example of my wares right outside the door, so a guided tour will be only a few paces away. What better incentives for the easily-persuaded to empty their bank accounts into mine?'

Was she for real? 'Hmmm; awesome idea, but not this pub I'm afraid. Maybe you could set up a sales kiosk out there instead? You know; like the pleasure boat guys flog tickets from. Or you could walk up and down the quay wearing some natty SharkCrest sandwich boards handing out fliers? You could wear a novelty hat with a shark on it, though I'm not sure that's going to entice people to go boating to be honest.'

'It's SharpCrest, not SharkCrest.'

Her having taken the bait on the gag, I treated myself to a few moments of silent victory celebration in my head. 'Oh right. Sorry; I did mention I'd tuned out earlier. Can't you just buy somewhere else?'

'Somewhere else will not adequately serve my purpose. Your premises will. And they shall.'

44

'Well as I've just made very clear, they won't. Anyway, this is a listed building - you'd need planning permission to do anything more than clean the windows.'

She smiled wryly. 'Mister Trickett; this town is dependent on my business and its continued growth. The planning committee will go to great lengths to ensure they remain in my good graces, lest I decide to take my operation and my money elsewhere.' She then reached into her handbag and after some fishing about, brought out a cigarette case. She pulled one out then took a lighter from her suit pocket.

Maybe this was payback for my shark gag. 'I'm afraid your timing's a little off. If you want to smoke in here, you'll need to schedule a slot before July 2007.' (Having been an avid smoker and pub-goer around that time, the date was indelibly stamped in my memory).

She raised the cigarette to her mouth and clicked the lighter. 'And who pray, is going to know?'

At that moment, from the kitchen there came the sound of a door opening. Suit number two whirled on the spot whilst deftly tossing the items of Angelique's apparel he was holding onto one of the nearby chairs: the first significant movement he'd made since the start of this weird drama. It was only then that I realised his slicked-back hair was actually tied in a pony tail which swooshed round and bopped him in the face when he completed his spin. As amusing as it was, I felt it prudent not to laugh and point, still wary of his next move.

The noise-makers soon made themselves known, as Halo and J.D. made their entrance. J.D. took in the scene then looked at me quizzically.

'Everything okay Boss?'

'It's fine J.D. - just having a lively conversation about property acquisition and the evolution of the Health Act.'

Both suits were looking at J.D., now with their hands by their sides as if ready for action but they stayed where they were, holding station until a real threat presented itself it appeared. Blissfully unaware of the tension in the room, Halo set off into the bar in search of discarded crisps.

Turning back to Angelique, I noticed she still had cigarette and lighter in hand. I was getting tired of the brinkmanship so tried a new tack.

'Tell me Angie, how much time and money has gone into your appearance today? A significant amount I'd imagine?'

'What? Why?' For the first time, she appeared less than entirely composed.

'Just so I can derive the appropriate level of satisfaction from emptying a fire extinguisher at you if you go ahead and light up. Nothing personal - Health and Safety you understand'.

Okay this was a bluff: with her two henchmen present I wouldn't have dared go that far. I just got a bit carried away now I had some reinforcements. However, she must have considered the scenario briefly, as a moment later she placed the cigarettes and lighter in her handbag. Maybe she'd simply decided not to escalate matters any further. Or maybe she just couldn't be arsed to dispose of our bodies. She went to speak but suddenly jerked sideways as something on the floor seemed to grab her attention. Ah, it seemed Halo was introducing herself to Angelique's shoes. Clearly not a dog fan, this seemed to fluster her disproportionately and for the second time, a crack appeared in her seemingly impenetrable coolness. Looking up, her lipstick seemed to stand out less as the rest of her face flushed slightly. She recovered quickly mind, and looked at me again with no indication that she was anything but entirely self-assured. The drumming of her finger nails on the bar started again, something she seemed to do habitually when deciding on her next move. Nobody else in the room moved or spoke, all being held in her sway whilst she deliberated. And then the drumming stopped and she spoke again.

'Gerard, bring the car around.' Then, pointing at suit number two without looking at him: 'You, get my things.' He was obviously in the dog house for unceremoniously dumping them earlier.

Suit one walked out the front door (no coat - blimey; these boys were tough) whilst suit two gathered his mistress's accoutrements which he then helped her into. Fully restored to her outdoors-ready self, she placed both hands on the bar and leaned in towards me.

'One last time Mister Trickett. Are you for sale?'

'Okay; I tell you what. You look like a woman of means but I'll give you a special discounted rate of £100 an hour, but no kissing on the mouth and I get to choose the safe word.'

She took a deep breath and then sighed heavily like a teacher might when faced with an incorrigible schoolchild. 'No thank you Mister Trickett. My interest in you extends no further than this property. I suggest you take that interest seriously - I could make you a wealthy man. Or a terribly poor one should I choose.'

'Your money doesn't interest me Angie. Other than a decent duvet, I have all I need thanks.'

Without another word, she grabbed her phone and handbag from the bar then headed for the door with suit number two following behind. Just before she reached the exit, she reached into her bag and retrieved her cigarettes and lighter. Slowly and deliberately she lit one, took a deep drag and blew a cloud of smoke towards the ceiling. Turning to face me, she then took another long draw and puffed a fog in my direction after which she made a theatrical show of surveying the room.

'You know; I really can't wait to start tearing this place apart.' she said. Then she dropped her cigarette and ground it into the carpet with her shoe, and left.

Bring it on you bitch I thought. Or maybe even said out loud. Either way, I swore there and then that she would never get her hands on my pub. That bitch with her boats, no way: not on my watch. From that moment on, she was no longer Angelique Sharp - she was Boat Bitch.

CHAPTER THREE

When I think about what its achieved, I'm
convinced evolution deserves way more credit
than it gets, because mankind really has come a
long way since we got bored of the tadpole
lifestyle and decided to sprout a few limbs and
escape the ooze. Some would be swift to debunk
that theory I appreciate, preferring to believe we
were brought into being by some Creator type
entity that planted all the fossils for a lark to
mislead the scientists. But whether you're
rooting for Darwin, Jesus or Hubbard, you'd
have to admit that decent progress has been
made. And yet, the process has fallen short in a
few areas - why do we still have to suffer
hangovers? And why do we sometimes bite the
insides of our mouths when we chew? The
former was uppermost in my mind after draining
a lake of red wine the previous evening. I'd been
emotionally jangly after such an eventful day and
I was torn between celebrating "meeting" the

goddess or purging the memory of my later exchange with Boat Bitch. In the end, I had a serious crack at both and rather overdid the self-medication. As a result, I hadn't moved far from the bathroom that morning. I wasn't ill as such, rather trying to sate a seemingly unquenchable thirst brought on by drinking from a Merlot hydrant and putting too much salt on my chips. God I love water; what a magnificent fluid. It just modestly gets on with keeping the planet alive without bells and whistles (apart from the odd flashy self-indulgence like Niagra Falls). I for one had never taken it for granted and felt blessed to live somewhere in the world where it was freely available on tap. And that particular morning, the love affair continued unabated. I must have gulped down gallons of the stuff whilst perched on the end of the bath, sharing my time between dunking my head in the basin to drink from the tap, and trying to find an angle at which I could hold my head that alleviated the throbbing. Why hadn't modern medicine succeeded where evolution had failed? Surely they must be able to engineer some sort of pre-emptive pharmaceutical solution that would mean never having to endure this tortuous condition? All too busy trying to find a cure for cancer or Parkinson's I suppose. I couldn't really fault their priorities, regardless of how hurty my head was.

Yesterday, Janine had shot home as soon as Boat Bitch and her goons had exited the pub. She clearly wanted to be gone so I didn't press her for details of what had transpired before I'd turned up: I would catch up with her next shift. She'd managed a weak smile when I handed her the Twix but I think the afternoon's events had rather taken the shine off that treat. I had wanted to get J.D.'s reaction too but just as I went to quiz him, a cold blast and a gaggle of energetic voices from the front door heralded the arrival of our first customers of the evening, so that chat would have to keep also. After all the excitement, I'd fancied a change of scene.

'Unless you need me to lend a hand down here, I'll pop up to The Crow's Nest for a bit J.D.'

'The what?'

'The Crow's Nest. It's what I've christened the flat.'

'Oh right.' He seemed to find this hugely amusing and chuckled to himself as he moved off to serve the punters. At least he was clearly unruffled by this afternoon's brush with the neighbours. 'Oh and no, you're fine; Jeff should be here any minute.'

Shopping in hand, I headed upstairs and set about weather-proofing my abode. Much newspaper scrunching and stuffing later, I was pleased to feel only the faintest of drafts when I ran my hand around the window frames. Peering out, I couldn't see much of what lay beyond as my view mostly just comprised a reflection of the interior but I couldn't miss the bright lights burning in the SharpCrest yard. What the hell had Boat Bitch's visit really been about? The episode was still fresh in my memory but had

52

now taken on a rather surreal feel. She wanted the pub, I got that; but why the passive-aggression and the men in black? Maybe they'd wiped my memory of what really transpired using one of those shiny brain-zapper things like in the films. What was that gadget called... a NutriBullet? Apart from the ridiculous episode with the cigarette, everything else was really just spirited conversation wasn't it? Whatever; I'd dwell on that some more later. Right now I needed to be all about curtains. Having unpackaged my purchase, I held one over the window and was both surprised and pleased to see it was a reasonable fit. Something I'd also forgotten to think about before I went shopping was a curtain rail but fortunately there was one already installed, albeit rather crookedly with just a handful of hooks dangling aimlessly from it. But that was sufficient for now: the curtains hung rather awkwardly and were a bit gappy at the top but my privacy was restored. With that improvement and with the icy draft now mostly kept at bay, The Crow's Nest had taken a major leap upward on the livability scale. Content with my accomplishments, I headed back down to the bar. Christ those stairs really did creak like a bastard.

On entering the bar, I was pleasantly surprised by the sizeable throng in the room - the early crowd had been joined by what looked like more of their office colleagues. Some sort of celebration it appeared; maybe a birthday, as most of the group's attention seemed to be focused on a senior-looking guy with cheeks of a colour that suggested he'd started celebrating at lunchtime. He appeared to be in the middle of a joke or anecdote and was gesticulating dramatically to add a visual element to his tale, whilst dispensing a fair amount of drink over his small captive audience in the process. None of them acted as if they'd even noticed being splashed; another sign that they were in the presence of a big cheese. J.D. was behind the bar talking to a young lad the other side of it who was loading empty glasses into a crate. I assumed that must be Jeff.

J.D. wandered over when he saw me. 'Welcome back. Settling into The Wank Pad okay?'

'The Crow's Nest, yes.' I smiled; rather stiffly.

He smiled too, still clearly tickled by the notion I'd named my accommodation. 'So: fancy a drink to celebrate your declaration of war on the rich and powerful?'

This was the first of several drinks that I worked my way through whilst we discussed the afternoon's drama. According to J.D., Boat Bitch had made some overtures to Aunt Maddy over the last several months regarding selling the pub but had done nothing more than make a couple of phone calls along those lines. As far as he was aware, neither she nor her henchmen had ever set foot in the bar before today. It turned out that not only were she and Aunt Maddy unable to 'agree terms' but more specifically, Maddy had told her to 'shove her deal up her bony arse'; a phrase that J.D. repeated several times with great relish. The wine was flowing well and J.D. helped himself to a couple of glasses too and we spent a very sociable couple of hours chatting away whilst Jeff serviced the customers. J.D. was growing on me more and more. It turned out he'd spent most of his youth growing up overseas and had travelled widely since, with a seemingly inexhaustible supply of anecdotes to share as a result. His sense of humour seemed to be founded on taking the piss out of everyone and anything but he did so without malice. Whilst I was refilling my glass for the umpteenth time, it dawned on me that I'd not got around to introducing myself to Jeff. He wasn't busy at that point, instead just standing there surveying the room so I went to address my oversight.

'Hi Jeff! I'm Ken. Good to meet you.'

This met with no reaction whatsoever, so I repeated my welcome whilst leaning in to put myself squarely in his line of sight. This did the trick and he smiled broadly and reached out his hand.

'Hi, I'm Simon.'

I shook his hand but just before I got to respond, J.D. spoke softly into my ear.

'His name is Simon but he's hard of hearing in one ear so we call him Jeff. You know;

Mutton Jeff? Never to his face though. It's just that there's another Simon who works the odd shift and it helps to err, you know; differentiate.' He sounded sheepish.

'Hi Simon; I'm Ken. Good to know you.' This aimed at Jeff's good ear with some elevation in volume.

'Hi Ken. J.D. says you live upstairs in The Wank Bank.' Behind me I heard what sounded like a lawn sprinkler coming to life which could only be J.D. forcefully venting a mouthful of his wine across the bar.

'Well; actually it's called The Crow's Nest but yes, it's home. Sorry I didn't say hi earlier; J.D. has a rash he's more concerned about than usual and he needed some moral support.' I then pointed towards my crotch whilst silently mouthing 'Down there.'

'Oh right!' he said, grinning over my shoulder at J.D., clearly getting the gag. 'Look on the bright side J.D.; if everything drops off, you can wear women's underwear all the time. Not just those quiet evenings in, like you do now.' Then he was off to serve a customer. I liked Jeff. Sorry; Simon. He was medium height, probably late twenties with a mess of ginger hair and a matching beard of sorts that seemed to be having trouble really taking hold. There was an easy way about him and the customers seemed to respond well to his banter. I took him to be a local boy, saying 'Ello' rather than 'Hello', thrown in with a

56

few other snippets of the Dorset dialect like 'Ax' in lieu of 'Ask'.

My wine intake had pushed hunger to the background for the last few hours but all of a sudden I was ravenous. And really quite sozzled. I turned to J.D. who had just finished cleaning up the counter after his involuntary outpouring. 'I need food J.D. - where's good round here?'

'Depends what you're after. Most of the bars on the quay are pretty decent if you're happy with tarted up pub grub or want something a bit more gourmet. Or you might just catch the chippy if you want quick and easy.' he said pulling up his sleeve and looking at a watch he wasn't wearing. 'Or take a walk into town. There's a few good restaurants that might be open - Italian, Indian, Aztec, Martian....'

To be honest I hadn't heard much after 'chippy' - from that moment, no other food existed, only fish and chips; and they would be mine, oh yes. 'Okay - back in a bit!'

A few minutes and many wobbly strides later, I was basking in the bright lights and welcoming smells of "Yardley's Fish 'n' Chips". I walked through the door and for a moment just stood and soaked up the warmth whilst trying to get sufficient focus on the menu boards to make a selection. After the coldness and darkness of the outside it was quite an assault on my intoxicated senses and I felt the need to sit down as my attempts to multi-task were making little headway. Standing up whilst also looking at things was just too much to handle right now, especially with the gentle swaying I couldn't seem to keep in check. Picking a table inside the front window, I took off my coat and dropped heavily into a seat facing the counter, then resumed the challenge of choosing my dinner.

'I'm terribly sorry Sir, but we're just about to close up for the evening.' A guy who I assumed was the manager materialised from out back, wiping his hands on a blue and white striped towel that mirrored the decor. He was smiling in a way that indicated he'd already clocked that I was a bit the worse for wear.

Deciding honesty was the best policy, and doing my very best not to slur my words, I answered. 'Shit I didn't realise it was that late.' Before he could respond, I continued. 'I'm the new owner of "The Pulton Arms". Today's my first day in the job and it's been a rare one pal.' (I thought I'd venture a 'pal' - it seemed appropriate; if a little forward). 'I'm happy to go with whatever you've got left: I just really need to eat something (hic!).'

'Well, seeing as I'm in the presence of a fellow service-business professional who looks as if he's not had the best day at the office, I will see what I can do.' He bowed then turned and disappeared from whence he'd appeared; presumably the kitchen. I remained in my seat; rocking gently and humming tunelessly.

A few minutes later he returned, bearing a large plate which he placed on the table in front of me. I leaned forward and shoved my face into the steam and smells rising from it. Oh my God; it was a banquet. A sizeable mound of chips was accompanied by a large hunk of battered fish and a saveloy, all crammed together with a Styrofoam tub of baked beans. I surveyed this bounty with great reverence and heartfelt desire. And probably some drooling. I looked up at my saviour. 'You sir, are a steely-eyed missile man.'

He grinned and clapped me on the shoulder. 'No problem Sir - us locals must look after one another. And there's no charge; the resident cat wouldn't have paid had she got to it first. Oh and worry not - she didn't.'

I was genuinely taken aback by such an act of unprompted generosity. 'Thank you so much. Drop into the pub anytime and I'll (hic!), buy you a drink.'

'Thank you Sir, I shall. Now, please do eat up before it goes cold. Also, some of us have homes to go to.' With that he dropped salt, vinegar and ketchup dispensers onto my table, handed me a small wooden fork, said 'Bon Appetit', grinned, then disappeared back behind the scenes. Blimey – what a splendid chap!

With what little I'd eaten that day, my stomach must have shrunk as in the end, I could only fit about half of what was on offer into it. But God it was good; soooooo good!

Needing a break after the first wave of gorging, I just sat for a while and took in a bit more of "Yardley's". The place must be a gold mine during the holiday season, enticing locals and tourists alike as they wandered the quay. We so needed to start serving food at the Arms - we were missing out on serious revenue there I was sure. Looking down at my partly-cleared plate, I decided I was beaten. Also, why should the cat miss out entirely? Keen to do the decent thing, I cleared my table and placed everything on the counter. There were no signs of life out back so I shouted a 'Hello?' but got no answer. Not wanting to leave without some sort of closing gratitude, I spied a pad and pen sitting on the till so reached over and grabbed them, all the while hoping nobody would burst into the room and go to town on me thinking I was after the takings. I left a note simply saying 'Thanks again to my Good Samaritan. Hope to see you at the pub soon. Ken.' At least that's what I hoped it said: I was still a bit fuzzy in the head. I decided to make sure to find out who that guy was so I could send him a ham at Christmas - I was sure people still did that.

What a day that had been. Day 2 was going to be much less eventful, hopefully. For a moment, I toyed with the idea of going back to bed and sleeping off the hangover but decided instead to man up and get on with life. I completed my morning routine, all at a rather slow pace as I tried to move my aching head as little as possible. The several minutes spent in the shower with the water spraying solely on the back of my neck went some way to ease the thumping and by the time I was dressed, I felt a little perkier, if still short of being match fit.

Opening the curtains (very gently so as not to wrench them from their precarious fixings), I looked out at my estate. Another battleship grey day alas. However, I was rather pleased to see condensation on the window panes rather than the ice patches of yesterday; my newspaper sausages seemed to be doing a grand job of keeping the cold out and the warmth in. Acknowledging this minor victory lifted my mood somewhat, a mood that thus far had matched the lacklustre weather. That was the hangover's doing and I needed to undo it. After all, this was a far cry from my miserable Tuesday mornings of just a few months ago, waking up in the spare bedroom while my soon to be ex-wife slept in the next room as I waxed miserable before heading off for ten plus hours of doing a job I'd grown to loathe. 'Get into financial services!' they said. 'Where there's money, there's money to be made!' they said. "They" being the school's career officer; a seemingly all-knowing but very pale and nervous lady called Helen who did her very best to avoid eye contact for some reason. And so, after a few years working my way up the ladder at a local bank, I ended up as the Senior Analyst for a leading financial services company; this promotion prompting my relocation to West Sussex. Senior Analyst - one of those job titles that unless you know, gives you no clue as to what it's about other than it probably involving a lot of data and copious frowning. And very probably being monumentally dull. I dreaded the question cropping up in social conversation:

'So what do you do Ken?'

'I'm a Senior Analyst for a leading financial services company.'

'Oh right! Sounds interesting.'

'It isn't.'

'...'

'...'

'Right well, must just go and grab a top-up.'

Sometimes, I'd make up other roles in an effort to come across as colourful and interesting. 'I'm Chief Product Tester for Ann Summers.' 'I design bouncy castles for NASA.' 'I'm lead dragon wrangler on Game of Thrones.' This would typically backfire as once I revealed my true occupation, it came across as even more crashingly dull, me having piqued the audience's interest early on with my opening lie. In fairness, I couldn't blame all of that on Helen. Another reason I chose finance as a career was to piss off my Economics teacher who proclaimed I'd never amount to anything, in front of the entire giggling class. I'd nodded off mid-lecture as a result of a very late session of "Dungeons and Dragons" the night before. Toby was Dungeon Master and during my Mage's heated scrap with a Mind Flayer, he'd enthusiastically and cack-handedly thrown the four-sided dice into a cage occupied by his rabbit who immediately gobbled it down. We then spent a couple of hours waiting for "Toby 2" to yack it back up or pass it via another route. With no result, Toby 1 suggested fudging the rules and using a different dice. No way Toby; I'd rather get arrested for heroin possession in Singapore than break the rules that governed our polyhedral D&D universe. Still, having fallen asleep in class and having bucked the system in such an overt fashion, I was awarded folk hero status for a short time. Even better, a few weeks later, I achieved the much-coveted rank of 'Legend' after throwing up in History.

Thankfully, the day I had in prospect was delightfully free of all the management bullshit, number shuffling and endless meetings that I'd come to dread in my last job. As would all my days be from now on I hoped. My only real challenges were keeping up with J.D.'s endless ribbing and evolving the pub to be the best it could be, whilst possibly fending off the occasional hostile takeover attempt by a local business owner. I might even buy a new duvet. And possibly drop into "Coasters". But first - tea.

On opening the door into the kitchen, I found Janine sitting at the picnic table studying a laptop. She looked up and smiled. 'Oi Oi! You look well rough.'

'Thank you. I'm trying a new look. I call it "Red Wine Regret".'

'It's very you, for sure. J.D. said you'd had a few last night. How you feelin'?'

'A bit iffy, but on the up.' At that point Halo came snuffling into the room so I leaned down and gave her the statutory fussing after which she wandered over and sat on Janine's feet. Janine reached down and gave her a stroke then returned her attention to her screen. I went over to the kettle which was about half full so I flicked it on. 'Fancy a brew?'

'Yes please. Just normal variety thanks.' She pointed at a red caddy on the worktop without looking up. 'I filled it up this morning. Milk's in the fridge; so's the sugar.' This time pointing behind her, still glued to her screen. 'Just one for me ta.'

'Mugs?'

'Utility room.' No pointing this time.

There were two doors in the kitchen that I wasn't familiar with, so I moved to the nearest one which was just to the right of the stairwell entrance.

'Nope. Other one.'

I turned through ninety degrees and opened the second door to find a smallish room housing a double sink and a host of appliances and cupboards. Surprisingly, and rather pleasingly, everything looked like it was relatively new.

'Cupboard. Far right.'

I opened the cupboard to find a handful of mismatched mugs and grabbed a couple, instinctively checking the insides for cracks or spiders. One of the drawers yielded a teaspoon. Fully equipped, I returned to the kitchen. 'So everything gets washed out there?'

'Yep. We crate up the empties and take them through to the dishwasher. Bit of a pain but, you know...' at which she gestured around the dumping ground she was sat in. 'Beer towels go in the washer dryer. Ow Halo you're heavy, go see J.D.'

Having successfully engineered and delivered Janine's tea, I pulled up a chair next to her at the picnic table. She looked as polished and perky as I wasn't. Thinking about it, I couldn't recall ever seeing her look anything other than well up together. She was a petite brunette with a round, rather cherubic face which, when not holding a smile always looked to be only seconds away from doing so. She really was pretty, and with her being such a permanent live wire she was a joy to have around. Oh to be ten years younger. Oh all right; fifteen. 'So what are you busy with - coursework or Googling firemen with their shirts off?'

'Neither - I'm looking up Mrs Arse Face from across the way. And looking at dresses: I'm

a shopaholic dontcha know. Speaking of which...'
She pushed her chair backwards then swung her
legs out from under the table and pointed her
feet in my direction, sporting a huge grin and a
pair of pink trainers with a multi-coloured floral
pattern that was rather too busy for my currently
fragile constitution. 'Just bought them!' She then
waggled them in excitement which exacerbated
the hectic visual effect enormously.

'Very, erm; noticeable. Oh and I call her
Boat Bitch'. This seemed to go over well but
inwardly I was high-fiving her choice of title.
'Look; yesterday was weird to say the least. You
okay?'

'Yeah I'm fine. I was a bit jumpy at the
time. They all walked in; she asked to see the
owner and when I said I didn't know when you'd
be back she said she'd wait. I asked but she said
she didn't want anything to drink so it was all a
bit fucking awkward. We all just stood there. J.D.
was on his break walking Halo so I didn't know
what to do next. There was only a couple of
punters in and they were just finishing up. I was
bloody glad when you turned up. You were good
by the way: didn't take any crap from that cow.'

'Well, she pissed me off and put you in a
difficult situation. Sorry you had to be part of it,
but that's probably the last we'll see or hear of
her. Find out much?'

She swivelled the laptop around so I could
see the screen. On show were a host of pictures
of Boat Bitch, pictures of boats and pictures of

Boat Bitch with boats. Also a few headlines excitedly announcing which celebrity had bought which of her yachts and how much they had reportedly paid. Yawn.

'Not a fat lot. Seems she took over the business from her husband a few years back after he popped his clogs. Can't find anything about her that goes back further than that.'

Scrolling further down, I clicked on links to a few more pages but it was all the same info (or lack of it). I did come across one article from a couple of years ago blathering on about the property Boat Bitch had just purchased in Silverbanks but there was no accompanying picture. The Silverbanks peninsula was home to a select few that possessed more money than taste. I was sure I'd read somewhere that it was one of the top five costliest places to buy property in the world. No doubt when Boat Bitch wasn't at "work", she spent her time in some ghastly gilded mansion she'd bought with hubby's inheritance, counting her cash whilst cackling wildly and punching kittens in the face. Probably. 'Well, let's not give Her Royal Arseness any more air time.' I twirled the laptop back to Janine. She closed the lid, drained the last of her tea then plonked her mug down next to mine which was still full.

'Loser washes up.' After which she scuttled off to the bar to get ready for opening.

I gulped my now tepid tea down, then dropped our mugs into the dishwasher. I was now feeling much improved after several vats of water and a brew, plus I was pleased to see Janine hadn't been too rattled by yesterday's events. The utility room and the white good delights within had also been a positive discovery. I opened the door at the far end of that room which led outside into a small, fairly sparse courtyard that housed only a clothes line, a couple of plastic chairs and two industrial wheelie bins. There was a gate through to the alleyway that ran down the side of the pub; it was wrought iron so didn't offer a great deal of privacy. It was a fair size mind: had to be to get the bins through I guessed. So this was the tradesman's entrance. Back in the utility room, I tried the other door which opened into a store room. This was stacked full of barrels, and crates of bottles and cans, all of which seemed to be fresh stock rather than empties.

A loud metallic clang nearby made me jump. Then another; coming from the other side of the wall. I went in search of the noise. The door in the kitchen I'd initially thought led to the utility room was open and inside I spied J.D. who was humping barrels around. This was of course the cellar: I'm wasn't sure how I thought it could be anything else really seeing as there was nowhere else for the cellar to be. Like most rooms on this floor it was predominantly populated by barrels. It struck me that maybe what appeared to be a disorganised mess was actually the output of a well thought-out process designed to fit around the limitations of the ancient, inflexible accommodation. As I stood there, I was assailed by a blast of cold air as the cooler came to life to combat the inflow of warmth from the kitchen. It was actually quite refreshing, helping to shift the residual fuzz of my hangover and the slight nausea triggered earlier by Janine's multi-coloured vibrating foot show.

'Morning J.D. You should have told me there was work needing doing: I'd have stayed upstairs.'

'You're right. That probably would speed things up down here. But seeing as you're around, could you drop this in the kitchen for me?' With that he grabbed a barrel and dragged it to the doorway: a hefty load it appeared judging by the way he puffed out his cheeks and the handful of stops he made en-route. I hadn't lifted a barrel or indeed done anything that constituted serious exercise for some time but I didn't want to appear a wimp. So, bending down I gripped both handles at the top of the barrel and then heaved as hard as I could, the end result being me taking several rapid steps backwards, trying to keep my balance then clattering into the picnic table (thankfully without spilling the laptop onto the floor). I stood there flustered, still clutching what I now understood to be an empty barrel.

'Sorry; couldn't resist.' He shoved another empty towards the door with his foot. 'Could you stash that one too? Having a bit of a sort out ahead of the delivery tomorrow.'

I righted myself, put the barrel down and herded the table and chairs back to their usual location. 'Why do you keep them in the kitchen?'

'It's my rotation system: new stock gets put in the store then moved into the cellar when there's room. The empties are put in the kitchen then shifted into the yard for collection on delivery day. We could store them out there all the time but then we'd need a better gate and we'd have to keep it locked all the time so they didn't get pinched. I learnt that one the hard way.'

As I'd began to suspect, there was method to the apparent chaos. I spent another half an hour or so helping J.D. during which time he filled me in on other general workings of the pub. I took the opportunity to broach the subject of starting a food service and returning the kitchen to its intended purpose. He didn't seem over-enthused but this seemed to be based more on his desire to keep things simple rather than him being against the whole idea. I understood his reticence to some extent; I'd worked at a gastro pub before where the bar staff delivered food orders to table as well as serving the drinks. This meant leaving the security of the bar and venturing out into the public fray carrying trays of plates. It was worse during the Summer months (or 'month' more typically) as the pub had a huge garden which could seat a multitude at its many tables: tables for which we didn't have a numbering system. It was a jungle out there. When we took an order, the bar staff would add a descriptive note to the docket to help the eventual server identify who the food was intended for. Notes like "Family of five next to the rose bush in the far corner"; "Sporty looking couple in green shorts with bikes."; things like that. This procedure took on a life of its own and we'd add increasingly long-winded and (we thought) humorous descriptions. This was fine as long as whoever served the order didn't leave the docket on the tray when they placed it in front of the customer. Well I remember the day I did just that - the "Guy with dodgy wig and fake Rolex with woman who applies her make up with a trowel" were seriously under-impressed.

You see, these are the perils of getting up close and personal with the punters without a few feet of bar counter to keep them at arm's length. I've had some frightening encounters in my time when I've been forced to abandon the sanctuary behind the bar and go to "the other side", none more so than when collecting empty glasses during the interval of a "Chippendales" show during my stint at the Arts Centre. I was forced to squeeze my way through a horde of two thousand half-cut women who had spent the last forty minutes being teased into a sexual near-frenzy by a troupe of half-naked muscle men, all of whom were as well-oiled as their frothing audience. There were hands everywhere, and the arse-pinching was relentless. Don't get me wrong, I do love the ladies but these were ferocious and without regard for the towering stack of glassware I was carrying. Also, the air was so thick with perfume you'd think it had been applied en-masse using one of those crop-spraying planes. I made it back to the bar alive but feeling emotionally drained and physically violated. And smelling like a tart's knicker drawer. But: I'd decided food was the way to go for "The Pulton Arms" and I agreed with J.D. that we'd crack on with getting the kitchen cleared. We'd just have to take a risk and stash the empties outside for now. We also discussed hiring a chef and the good news was that he knew someone suitable he had worked with before and would contact them to tee up an interview. I took the action away to beef up the gate to make the yard more secure. We were making progress, and it felt grand.

CHAPTER FOUR

'Wait!!' J.D. grabbed my wrist, causing me to jump out of my skin and drop the knife I was holding. 'What if there's a human head in there?'

Alarmed, I whipped around to look at him, only to see fake wide-eyed panic on his face accompanied by a toothy grin. 'You bastard. I barely held my fudge there. "Seven" is a film, not a documentary you know. And I understand Gwyneth Paltrow is alive and well, which is surprising when you consider her diet consists of a single boiled lentil once a year.' I retrieved the knife and returned my attention to the package which I now noticed was in fact the ideal size to house a human head, though I doubted its contents were that exotic. It had arrived during the last few hot and sweaty hours I'd spent trying to reclaim the kitchen. And reclaim it I had.

I now had a room I could see all four walls of. Once de-cluttered, it was actually a decent-sized space, looking all the bigger for my side-lining of the picnic furniture that allowed me to move around without hindrance. Even better, it now looked like a kitchen. My efforts had unearthed a sink, some more worktops and numerous storage cupboards of assorted sizes. Even better, I'd revealed a chest freezer big enough to house a small elephant. Or possibly a neatly-folded giraffe. And best of all, dominating the room was the gas range that took up the majority of the wall that bordered the utility room, boasting all sorts of burners and ovens. There were also other bits of miscellaneous equipment dotted around whose function I couldn't even begin to guess at, but was excited to have as part of the culinary arsenal none the less. My, did it all need some work though. Everything looked neglected and grubby, from the torn and peeling lino floor, to the cracked wall tiles, to the polystyrene squares on the ceiling. The latter reminded me of the Chemistry lab at my old Grammar School, bearing the many splotches and scars from years of poorly executed experiments conducted by over-enthusiastic students who really just wanted to see stuff blow up rather than learn anything. Like The Crow's Nest, this was just another tired space that time, money and elbow grease could revitalise.

Janine and J.D. had dropped by from time to time to see how things were progressing and laugh at how much I was huffing and puffing as I worked. But now this first stage was complete (and because I was feeling awfully pleased with myself and seriously needed a break from my exertions), I popped my head into the bar. 'Hey guys: we have the kitchen back. Sort of.'

J.D. was first in and took a long look around then clapped his hands together. 'Right: you start peeling the spuds and I'll clear some wall space for the Michelin plaque.'

Janine peered around him and did her own survey. 'Nice job. Can we keep Bernie still?'

This was a positive response from the both of them at least. 'Janine - if Bernie was a horse, a vet would have shot him by now. It might be time to put him out of his misery and move on.' She gave me a look of feigned shock and put her hand to her mouth then grinned and went back to the bar, shouting 'If Bernie goes so do I! Oh and you've got a parcel.' as she left.

There was no delivery address on the package and similarly no clue as to the sender. It sat there on the bar enigmatically, adorned only with a handful of stickers declaring the contents to be fragile and insisting it was to be kept upright in transit. According to Janine, it had been dropped off by 'some weirdo' who didn't ask for a signature or smile at all. Reasonably confident that J.D. was done with his comic interventions,

I sliced through the packing tape and opened the box.

Its interior was topped with a generous layer of polystyrene chips that obscured whatever lay beneath so I tentatively slid my hand into them as if taking part in a lucky dip for loaded mouse traps. A few inches down, my fingers found something solid, angular, and most unlike a human head. After swishing around to find the limits of the mystery object, I gripped what felt like its base and pulled it slowly from the box, spilling packaging onto the counter as I went.

It was a model. Of a building. Standing about eight inches' square, it wasn't incredibly detailed but was still rather exquisite, like one of those proof-of-concept constructions that architects knock up for their prospective clients. I turned it in my hands whilst shrugging at J.D. and Janine who both looked as bemused as I was. The structure looked modern and business-like; very white and bright with expansive windows across the two floors of its frontage, though the pitched tiled roof looked quite retro and a poor match for the contemporary storeys it sheltered. 'Looks like a posh Estate Agent's office.' I handed the model to J.D.

He slowly rotated it, scrutinising it from every angle, all the while frowning with curiosity. 'Dunno what it is. Maybe they delivered to the wrong address?' As he went to pass the model back to me, he had another thought and turned it over to look at its underside. 'Ah. Nope; it's the right address.'

I took the still upturned model from him, seeing the label stating 'Pulton Arms/SharpCrest conversion. Version 2.0 July 2014'. I righted the model and held it at arm's length, taking in its overall proportions and structure with a fresh perspective. It was my pub. Or rather, it was my pub re-imagined as per Boat Bitch's twisted aspirations and it was all wrong; wrong like your octogenarian Gran wearing a Princess Leia slave costume to a Christening. It appeared I'd been correct with my architect's prototype idea. And the date proved that Boat Bitch had indeed been fostering her development idea for some time. But whatever strings she might be able to pull on the planning committee, this was just too radical to gain any traction surely? Or was keeping the original roof the only concession she had to make to get approval? Alternatively, perhaps she'd failed to get that approval and had tossed the redundant model my way for use as a bar decoration. Whichever way you sliced it, it was still rather odd. 'Erm - anyone else think this is a bit weird?' My companions remained silent as I fished through the packaging left in the box, searching for any other clues as to its purpose or meaning. Without success. 'Well, it's obviously from Boat Bitch but if it's a message of some sort, it's lost on me.'

J.D. shrugged. 'Dunno. Maybe it's some sort of apology for yesterday. I wouldn't stress about it. Nice model; and free too. Good result

I'd say. Something to brighten up the Gay Garage.'

Janine seemed similarly underwhelmed. 'Who doesn't love a pressie? Always had you pegged as the doll's house type too. Be happy.' Then she was off attending to our clientele.

Still rather puzzled by my special delivery, I returned the model to its box and set about clearing the bar of the disgorged packaging. Then I checked the time: just after two. It was time for a lunch break.

After a few hours spent humping barrels and crates I was a bit crusty, so a quick shower and change of clothes were had. Outfit choice was limited as I was rapidly getting through the single bag selection I'd brought with me, having decided to gift the remainder of my wardrobe to a Crawley charity shop. My fresh start warranted new clothes to accompany it; I just hadn't got around to buying them yet. Also, I'd been wearing the same stuff for years, as you do when you're a way down the road in a long-term relationship and well past the dressing-to-impress stage. There were also a few items I was pretty sure harked back to the days when my Mum bought all my clothes. I dug out some clean(ish) jeans and a dark blue long-sleeved shirt that could probably be deemed 'smart casual' in a favourable light. Shoe selection was easy - the white trainers or the black ones? Black it was. Hot to trot, I threw my coat on and headed downstairs and out, firing a quick 'Laters!' at my colleagues on my way out, nearly tripping over Halo as I wasn't looking where I was going. It was another cold one today; colder than yesterday if anything but I wasn't going far - just three doors up to "Coasters". Where else?

Once again, I found myself looking beyond the menu taped to the window to see what, or more importantly who, I could see inside. But alas, the goddess was nowhere in sight. I took a deep breath then let it go, rather impressed by how much of it remained hanging in the frigid air. I was pumped up by today's achievements in the pub yet still awash with nervous excitement about potentially coming face-to-face with this unfamiliar yet majestic individual. Those receiving a knighthood probably feel much the same ahead of the ceremony. The Queen comes across as benign but wields a sword and could have your head off should she wish it, so you'd be both thrilled and apprehensive I'd imagine. Reminding myself I was a grown-up that had met women before and wasn't a twitchy teen leaning in for his first ever snog, I mentally manned-up and walked into "Coasters" for the first time.

I took in the room as I strode towards the bar in what I hoped was a confident looking fashion. The decor was shiny laminate wood floor and roughly-plastered blue walls which appeared to be an exact match for the shade of my shirt. For a moment, I pictured myself standing there with a disembodied head, hands and legs as the rest of me became one with the emulsion. The backdrop to the bar was an enormous fish tank that spanned most of its length, with numerous varieties of multi-coloured tropical fish milling about in it. I couldn't say which species were present, despite having watched "Finding Nemo" twice. As I approached, a bartender noticed me and started to head over but then my view was suddenly hijacked as a familiar face popped up from behind the bar and hit me with the same smile that had rooted me to the quayside pavement just yesterday. Wow, she looked even hotter than I'd remembered. For a few frozen seconds, I was the pre-snog teen again, but then forced myself into action.

'Hi I'm Ken.' I blurted out. Because you always introduce yourself to the bar staff don't you? Trickett you prick. Then I compounded the damage by following up with 'I really like your fish.' Stellar banter Ken - bravo.

This drew a slight frown but thankfully her smile held and she didn't look to be reaching for a panic button. 'Hi, I'm Jess. What can I get you?'

I was struggling to get my thoughts in order. Damn it, I should have asked Janine for some refresher training on how to chat up girls without coming across as a bit of a plonker. It appeared that forty years on the planet had been woefully inadequate prep. All I could do was think back to the last drink I'd had that wasn't water or tea. 'Um, a red wine please.'

'Any one in particular? I can show you the list if you'd like.'

'No just the house one thanks. The red one. The red house one.' The smile dipped a little: I could tell she was trying to work out if I was completely devoid of social skills or suffered from some kind of mental impairment. At that point I could have convinced the leading experts in either field that I was afflicted with both conditions. She turned and went routing for a bottle on the bar behind her. I tried not to stare as it was like looking at the sun through binoculars, but she made even the bland house uniform of white blouse and black skirt look good. If she were a celebrity being described by a Daily Mail columnist they'd be throwing all the clichés in there - "enviable figure", "ample curves" and "never-ending legs". And they'd be pretty spot-on to be honest. Goodness she was one well put together lady.

'There you go.' she said, placing a glass in front of me. I briefly considered knocking it back in one to steady my nerves, but decided against it. No doubt she already thought I was a bit weird so probably best to not give her the impression I was a raging alcoholic too.

'Are you eating?'

'Err, I might do.'

'Okay, well there's menus on the tables - just order at the bar when you've decided what you'd like. I'll start a tab for you.'

At that point I decided to retreat and regroup, seeing as my initial charm offensive had rather misfired.

'Thanks, Jess.' It was pretty cool to say her name, like we'd established a slim personal connection I could work on fleshing out. Even though at that precise moment she was probably thinking about whether to call the police or ring the local mental hospital to suggest they carried out a head count. Still, my goddess now had a name. And I really liked the name Jess. Drink in hand, I went and sat at a table that gave me a clear view of the bar. I picked up the menu and pretended to read it but I really wasn't interested in food. A couple of large mouthfuls of my wine quickly took effect as my cells were seemingly not completely rid of what I'd downed last night and swiftly remembered their role and got on with the job of loosening me up as I gazed towards the bar.

After several minutes still clutching the menu, I gave it more focus and tried to absorb its contents. Unsurprisingly, it advertised the same fare as the window version I'd browsed yesterday, being mostly all about the seafood. My passion for fish usually only extended as far as the boneless, battered variety (hence my lust for "Yardley's" last evening). In my experience, the other versions are just too slimy, or packed full of bones that will kill you unless you spend an inordinate amount of time painstakingly plucking the stealthy beggars out, all the while wishing you'd ordered the burger in the first place. Putting the menu down, I considered ordering another glass as I'd all but seen off my first. But then I was met with the sight of Jess emerging from behind the bar, fully dressed for the outdoors. She waved a cheerio to her colleagues; stopping briefly before venturing outside to make sure her bright red coat, hat and scarf were properly arranged to keep out the cold. I guessed that was the end of her shift; the goodbye wave would have been overkill if she was just popping to the post box and back. Bugger. As something of a consolation prize, I did get another smile and a wave as she passed my table on her way out.

'Bye Ken!' She'd remembered my name at least. I was gutted she was leaving but returned the smile enthusiastically. 'Bye Jess; have a good night.' A slightly odd thing to say perhaps but I could have done much worse. Sure, I was somewhat deflated now that she'd left but hey, at least we'd met and introduced ourselves. Yes, I could have made a better first impression I was sure but it wasn't the catastrophe it might have been. I hadn't soiled myself in front of her or set fire to the place so on balance I shouldn't be too hard on myself. And God willing, there would be other chances to impress and I reckoned I was over the first time jitters. Feeling chirpier, I decided I would have another wine. Having settled my tab, I returned to my table and took in a bit more of "Coasters" now that the focus of my attention had selfishly left the building to get on with her day.

Actually this place wasn't too bad; it still had that big chain feel but managed to generate a more appealing atmosphere. To be honest, I'd have been okay with it even if the floor was molten lava and they had Barry Manilow playing on a permanent loop as long as Jess was around. Ah Jess. Was she out of my league? Very much. Was I going to let that stop me trying? Very much not. 'Faint heart ne'er won fair maiden' as the saying goes. That said, I'm sure it's not unheard of for romance to blossom between cardiac patients and their easy-on-the-eye nurses.

I'd guess Jess to be in her early thirties. If so, our width of age gap was pretty commonplace in relationships these days so I didn't think that would be a problem. Physical compatibility might be the bigger issue. Jess was inarguably a super soar-away stunner; a twelve out of ten (I was sourcing my descriptive snippets from The Sun now, not The Mail) and I was... well: not that. I was no physical disaster and didn't feel the need to wear a bell around my neck to alert sensitive womenfolk to the fact that I was in the vicinity so they could shield their eyes. 'Average-looking' was the assessment delivered by several of my girl friends over the years. Average doesn't turn heads when you walk into a room, unless you're wearing fancy dress or playing a musical instrument loudly. Average doesn't make every straight woman present want to jump on your bones there and then. But average does make you less threatening and a more appealing conversation prospect more often than not. And that was me - I was a grower. I'd never elicit a 'Phwoarrr!!' from anyone but I was a good talker (today's train wreck of a conversation aside) and an attentive listener, and attraction seemed to stem from there. Plus, it was obvious from the off that I wasn't a mirror-hogging narcissist. Anyway, they do say that real beauty lies within, though that might just be a notion that us average sorts try and sell to more attractive people.

So yeah; generally, I was happy with the skin I was in. But when it came to Jess, I couldn't help but wish I had a bit more in my cosmetic arsenal. Having been a desk jockey for so many years with little time for exercise (and by time I mean inclination), I wasn't in the best shape. I wasn't fat: I just looked rather over-inflated at certain angles. Both times I'd been around Jess I'd probably been too distracted to suck my stomach in too, dammit. But as long as I didn't swap my sedentary office existence for daily sessions on the ale in the pub, I could shed some poundage. So other than slimming down a bit, I wasn't sure there was a great deal else I could overhaul. My height was in my favour as Jess was no shorty. And overall I was 'tidy' - usually clean-shaven with hair short enough to be practically maintenance-free. The brown was about to lose the battle with the grey, a shade that the aforementioned girl friends actually said suited me. Other than that, I comprised a squarish face with blue eyes and a standard-sized set of protuberances attached. In a word; average. Oh and I did have a short, narrow scar high up in the middle of my forehead from taking a tumble on a stony footpath at a festival years ago. It was the undulating surface and the darkness that unbalanced me; nothing to do with a day on the strong cider at all. But even that blemish was barely noticeable; nothing on a Harry Potter scale. One other possibility was livening up my dress sense some - I trended towards conservative but current; more Next than Armani. Who knows - there was always the remote possibility that she'd love me as I was. On that more optimistic note, I finished off my drink, got coated up and headed outside.

I was turning for home when the thought "duvet" randomly popped into my mind. Yes! Well done brain - after a shoddy performance during my first conversation with Jess, it was doing its best to make amends. It wasn't quite yet dark so I figured it must be around fourish and the shops would still be open so I made for the High Street. Maybe it was the red wine working its magic but it seemed to have warmed up a bit outside so I didn't need to match yesterday's strident pace so took more time to have a nose in some of the shop windows that I passed.

"Plush!" was the local success story, producing handmade soaps and all manner of other bath and beauty products with quirky names and presentation that more closely resembled confectionery. A crossover that I'm sure many small children had fallen foul of when Mum wasn't watching them closely enough. Through the window, I could see numerous stacks of brightly-coloured lumps of product marshalled by blackboards adorned with price and recipe information. They also bore various catchy slogans reinforcing the company's green message and totally PC credentials with the whole store lovingly arranged and enthusiastically tended by young girls with aprons and multi-coloured hair. After similar companies had trodden the same pro-environment path and been found morally deficient, it was easy to be cynical but I understood that "Plush!" fully practised what they preached. Even through the window, I managed to catch a strong exotic waft from what was on display inside. Imagine how that atmosphere must permeate your clothes, skin and hair if you worked in-store. Perhaps the staff spent the last hour of their shift handling raw fish to compensate. A few doors down, next to the Army surplus shop, there was what appeared to be a new pound store being fitted out. Okay, it was new business which was a positive, but a growing number of bargain basement outlets wasn't an indicator of a town on the up to my mind. And that wasn't down to any snobbery on my part - I had visited the Crawley discount shop several times. That said, the mini torch I bought there conked out after a week which was disappointing. They couldn't replace it so I settled for store credit - mustn't forget that: I may need to pool all my financial reserves at some point.

The department store yielded all the bedding I needed. If they'd had stocked mattresses and bed frames, I'd have been dragging them down the street back to the pub too. With a fairly sizeable bag under my arm I headed for the quay, deciding to walk on the other side of the street so I had different windows to peek into. Just short of the quay, I made an intriguing discovery.

In the middle of a long stretch of unlit or boarded-up shop fronts, I saw light shining from the windows of a modestly-sized unit accompanied by hammering and drilling noises that suggested work in progress. On reaching it, I could see several bodies moving around in the bright interior. There were clearly several trades all employed at the same time as walls were being painted whilst light fittings were being wired in and shelves and cabinets erected. There was an "Opening Soon!" sign taped to the inside of a front window and the hectic activity within suggested they meant it. I took a couple of steps back to survey the frontage but there were no clues as to what nature of shop it was going to be; instead, just a blank fascia. Curious, I returned to the window. One of the guys working inside saw me standing there and smiled and gave me a thumbs-up. I was tempted to shout through the window and ask what business was coming but he quickly turned and clambered up a step ladder and turned his attention to some dangling down-lighters. I was about to turn for home again when something in the corner of the room caught my eye. It was a sign; hand-painted it appeared. The dust cover that had been draped over it for protection had slipped down at one corner and I could make out some of the lettering - "Westall's Deli"; in gold on black. My heart leapt. Actually it did more than leap - it flew off a vaulting horse then completed a two-minute session on the high bar. This was like discovering Atlantis and walking into a temple to find Lord Lucan drinking from The Holy Grail. A deli meant cheese. And fancy cheese too. Cheese was another of my great passions in life you see. Together with wine, it had done much to prevent me from getting in shape over the years. Don't get me wrong, I have a great deal of affection and respect for family and friends as well, but should I have to choose between all my interests at gun point, I'd escape the bullet-ridden carnage accompanied by the sound of clinking bottles and a waft of Camembert. I don't believe I've ever used the phrase 'That's too much cheese' and when I've heard it uttered by others, I've just assumed they have a specific medical condition that precludes them from dairy or they're from another planet. One of the oft-repeated scenes in disaster movies is the devastation of Paris by meteor/earthquake/big lizard/affordable haute couture, presumably after film makers decide in a pre-production meeting that it's not New York's turn this time. I watch the destruction unfold whilst tearfully struggling to come to terms with the thought of the gallons of Shiraz and the wheels of Brie being laid to waste. Oh, the Humanity!

Hold on - what if it's an old sign left by the business they're replacing? I must ask the guys at the pub. Goodness; meeting Jess and discovering a potential rich vein of cheese to mine, all in one afternoon. What a time to be alive.

I headed off at an energetic pace, keen to get back to the pub and share my afternoon with whoever wanted to listen, even if that turned out to be Halo; solely. Just a few yards from home, unfamiliar noises and vibrations started emanating from my jeans. My pocket cyborg had become self-aware and was staging a hostile takeover. After shoving my shopping under my other arm and extracting the device from my pocket (with some difficulty due to the cheese induced tightness of my trousers), it became apparent that I was simply subject of an incoming telephone call. I recognised the number and the accompanying surf dude mug shot so I answered.

'Hello?'

'Yarternooooonah! Alright fat boy?' It was Pat, my best mate.

'I'm sorry but I think you've miss-dialled Sir. This is the Erectile Dysfunction Clinic: perhaps you had our number saved in your contacts or frequently dialled list and had some finger trouble?'

'Oh my mistake. Accidents will happen. Your Mum always says that whenever your name crops up.'

'Mum gags already? Really?'

'I was just in a Mum kind of mood. Tell her I'll be round in ten.'

'Okay okay. How's things matey?'

'All good me old, all good. What's it like to be back home? With all the free beer you can drink?'

'It's been interesting to say the least. But yeah; great to be back. You going to drop in and let me overcharge you for a pint?'

'For sure. How about tonight?'

'Works for me bud. See you then. Text me when you're on way so I've got time to get the women to safety.'

'Well they're clearly in no danger from you. See you on the Ron John.'

I hadn't seen Pat for some time. We'd had a really brief chat when I came home for Aunt Maddy's funeral but we were long overdue a proper catch-up. Great - I was so looking forward to seeing him later. Plus, I could pick his brains about the gate for the yard and the work needed to get the kitchen up to scratch. Pat was a builder by trade and there was very little he couldn't turn his hand to and if there was any task that he wasn't expert at, he knew someone that was. Feeling pretty good about pretty much everything, I continued on to the pub (after a slow walk past "Coasters", just in case I happened to spot someone I knew).

On trying the front door, I was surprised to find it locked. Looking through the window, I could see lights on and nothing untoward, but nobody around. Rather puzzled, I walked down the side alley to give the tradesman's entrance a try. En-route I noticed that the metal gate to The Gents' loo was also locked. Due to the rather odd layout of the building, you could only access that facility from the alley so if you were a bloke needing to answers Nature's call, you'd have to exit the pub via the front door and walk around. There was a sign in the bar to that effect but not everyone noticed it. I'd already seen a couple of guys leaving it till the last minute to go, then asking the staff where the toilet was, then panicking when they realised it might be beyond the range of their bladder control. The Gents' was another room seriously in need of modernisation. The urinal was a museum piece - all ceramic, with tiles across two walls dropping down to a trough in the floor. It was actually quite liberating to use; no need for any sort of precision when aiming. I guessed it hadn't been high on Aunt Maddy's list to update as it was accessible by all on the street when the pub was open and couldn't be readily monitored so was open to mistreatment, potentially. Maybe we should keep it locked and keep the key in the bar, tied to something heavy like they do at remote gas stations in American films. The gate to the yard was thinly ajar and the back door was unlocked. In the kitchen, I found J.D. tucking into a takeaway pizza straight from the box.

'Fanthy thum?' said J.D. with his mouth full.

'I certainly do; thanks.' The smell was wonderful; I dropped my shopping and tucked in. Conversation was short and sharp, consisting solely of economically brief phrases slotted into the occasional pauses between slices. 'Front door locked. How come?'

'Sometimes do between afternoon and evening if we're quiet. Maybe pop home for a bit or get paperwork done.'

'Gotcha.'

'Whadja bought?'

'Bed stuff.'

'Manly.'

'You know it.'

Pizza finished, we both sat back and puffed appreciatively. 'Thanks for that; proper lush.'

'No problem. You paid for it anyway. ' He belched loudly. 'Petty cash.'

'Oh right. You're welcome then.'

'I'll open up.'

'Okay. I'll go sort out my manly shopping.'

'Have fun in The Cock's Nest.'

It was toasty upstairs; a bit too warm in fact, so I
turned the thermostat down a couple of notches.
Before getting busy, I grabbed a pair of mini-
speakers out of my bag and plugged them into
my phone so I could enjoy some tunes while I did
so. I stripped off all the old bedding and chucked
it into a heap in the corner of the room. It didn't
get added to my washing pile as I foresaw it
going the same way as the horror towel i.e. the
bin. The new fitted sheet put up a fight and I
spent several minutes wrestling with that. Being
just too small for the mattress, it kept pinging off
when I tried to persuade it to commit to more
than two corners at once. Throughout the
contest, I did my best not to look too closely at
the state of the mattress beneath as on first
glance it looked to have more splats and stains
than a paintballer's overalls. In the end, I
triumphed by adopting a Spiderman-like stance
that allowed me to pin the fitted corners with my
feet whilst affixing the others. The rest came
together with much less resistance and once
done, I decided to go for a test flight and have a
bit of a lie down. Enjoying the fresh linen smell
and the lack of damp, I spent a while
embellishing Van Halen's greatest hits with my
off-key humming whilst my mind wandered.
Inevitably, Jess was uppermost in my thoughts. I
wondered what she might be doing right now. If
she works days at "Coasters", what does she do
with her evenings? Maybe she reads or does

yoga? Or knits her own clothes or restores classic cars? Perhaps she pens heart-rending poetry about lost love or writes manuals on gerbil care? Or goes for long romantic walks and dinners with her boyfriend or husband? Someone that attractive must be perpetually fending off admirers with a stick mustn't they? Or maybe she's a serial dater and doesn't fend them off at all? I'd learnt her name today which was a start but there was so much more to find out. About Jess and gerbil care both.

Sometime later, I snored myself awake with a start, having drifted off during my cogitations. Feeling a bit groggy, I clambered off the bed, narrowly avoiding standing on my phone where I'd left it on the floor. I turned off the music and checked the time. It was just after seven, so I hadn't been dozing long. As the sleep cleared from my vision, I came to focus on the model of a brutally reinvented Pulton Arms that sat on the shelf opposite me. Its original appeal had been irrecoverably tarnished by the realisation that it was the by-product of Boat Bitch's scheming but I'd left it on view as a gruesome reminder of what might be should I ever abdicate my responsibility as the pub's protector. Mind you, I remained reasonably confident that even someone with Boat Bitch's local clout couldn't mangle a listed building to such an extent. I thought back to J.D.'s and Janine's earlier unruffled take on it and decided to adopt the same stance. Maybe after yesterday's discussion this was merely some sort of conciliatory gesture. Ah whatever. After mentally shrugging off my bafflement, I splashed some water on my face to perk myself up then headed downstairs.

J.D. and Simon were behind the bar, chatting and laughing with a customer - it was Pat. 'Christ J.D. - I turn my back for a few minutes and you invite all the undesirables in!' I shouted from the kitchen door.

'No just the one.' said J.D. They'd obviously made their introductions. 'I was going to come up and give you a shout but he's better company than you.'

Pat grinned broadly. 'So you're up at last. Entertaining a young lady in The Sausage Lodge were we?'

God, that gag wasn't going away anytime soon was it. 'Two actually. They needed a break; both exhausted and dehydrated, so I thought I'd pop down until they're ready for round five. I expected more stamina from eighteen-year-old gymnasts but there you go.' I reached over the bar and shook his hand. 'Good to see you buddy.'

And it really was. We'd been mates for over twenty years and he was one of a small handful of friends that I'd do anything for and whose company I never tired of. We'd got to know each other via his brother (also one of my elite bunch) when he (Pat) returned to the world after a stint with the RAF. We soon bonded and ended up partners in crime when it came to pubbing, clubbing and chasing the ladies: the latter with which he had the edge due to him being a rather handsome chap and a couple of years younger than me (bastard). We'd settled down a lot since those days so when we did get together it tended to be for a quiet pint and a chat or a video game fest. He'd worn well though and was in much better shape than me (bastard) due to the physical nature of his day job. He'd also got an adorable fiancé in the form of Lorna who was a good few years younger than him and I think she and their seven-year-old lad helped him keep the years at bay. There was no nonsense and no bullshit with Pat; he was smart and funny and I loved him like a brother.

'Good to see you too me old. Look at you - your own pub. Fuck me; talk about living the dream.'

'I know! Still hasn't really sunk in. I don't miss all that office bollocks that's for sure. You ticking over okay? How's the family?'

'Family are good; Lor says hi. Work's a bit patchy - hopefully got a top-drawer job coming from a developer we did a contract for recently but it's taking a while to land so we're filling the gap with a few tiddlers at the mo. Not ideal but you know.'

'Have you thought about prostitution? That would help you fill your days. It'd cost you a fortune though.'

'Why? You looking for clients?'

I cracked and laughed aloud, thus losing that particular exchange. 'Actually; being serious for a minute, I might have some work to put your way if you're interested. There's a lot needs doing around here.'

'Okay cool.' He drained what was left of his pint. 'Give me the tour. Oh and something to write on ta.'

I took him upstairs to see The Sausage Lodge (if you can't beat them...) then headed back down and out to the yard. It was proper dark now and there was limited light in the alley but he could see just well enough to size up the gate and jot down some rough measurements. I say rough; knowing Pat they were probably only a few millimetres out, if any.

When we reached the kitchen, I realised that I'd struggle to outline the work required as I didn't have a clue regarding what was needed to get it to where it needed to be, other than 'lots'. 'So what do you know about fitting out professional kitchens? Health and Safety, Food Hygiene - all that gubbins?'

'Probably as much as you know about changing the head gasket on a 1995 Ford Probe.'

Maybe J.D. would have a better handle on that from his experience. He was behind the bar making a fuss of Halo in her basket. 'You got a minute J.D.?'

'Sure.' He joined us in the kitchen.

'You know catering don't you? What do we need to do in here?'

He smiled like he was fishing for a jokey comeback but when he clocked me and Pat looking at him expectantly, he realised we were looking for more than that. 'Well; I've worked food before but that was a while ago and there's probably way more to it these days. One thing you can be sure of is that the wall tiles will have to go - you can't have any surfaces like that where anything gnarly can gather and breed in the cracks. Same goes for the floor - nowhere germs can hide and nothing that stuff can soak into. Same for the ceiling.' That made good sense, and the shell had to be right before we could think about fitting the rest out. I'd kind of hoped we could get away with a thorough whizz round with the Dettol but that was just naivety getting pally with ill-placed optimism. Pat made a few more notes. I decided that was enough to think on for now. 'Okay thanks guys. Drink?'

The three of us then hunkered down at the far end of the bar and talked next steps. The good news was that Pat was happy to take the work on and could make a start in a few days' time, with the caveat that he might have to bail on the job if the contract he was waiting on came in. That was fair enough, but I really wanted him to tackle the kitchen because I knew he'd do great work and wouldn't pull my pants down over the price. Also, he and J.D. clearly got on like a house on fire which would make things go way more smoothly. Yes, it would seriously up the ante when it came to jokes at my expense but I could live with that.

With the shop talk complete, J.D. left me and Pat to ourselves to catch up, which we did at length. Of course my headline item was Jess, and his response was much as I'd expected.

'Go for it you old dog. You never know. She might be single, plus she's clearly got awful eyesight and no sense of smell. You could get to know her by setting up play dates with J.D.'s mutt and her guide dog.'

Time flew by as it tended to do when we got together for a natter and all too soon Simon was calling last orders. Pat had sunk three or four pints (all of which he insisted on paying for - 'You've got your pension to think about you old git.') so he decided to walk home. He made a point of saying cheerio to Simon and J.D., promised he'd call me tomorrow with a quote for the work then signed off with a 'Cheers fatso.' I'd enjoyed a couple of wines so felt comfortable but capable, so hung around to help the guys clear up and close down. When we were done, Simon headed off and J.D. made ready to do the same, putting his coat on and grabbing Halo's lead. Suddenly, a thought from last night's drunken blur came back to me - something about an alarm. 'Oh hey J.D. - can you tell me about the burglar alarm?'

'It's an electronic device that makes a loud noise if someone breaks in. It's not a new invention.'

'Okay. More specifically, can you tell me about our alarm?'

'The panel's by the back door; the code's written on a beer mat slipped under the till. Only the doors and windows are alarmed and just on this floor. We did have a monitored deal but it got too pricey for Mads so you just get the bells now, not the SWAT team backup. We do have one deterrent though.' He reached down and brought out a cricket bat from below the counter, tapping its end on his empty palm while smiling knowingly. I'd spotted this object before but assumed it was a piece of sports memorabilia he hadn't got around to mounting on the wall. He placed it back on the shelf. 'Come on; I'll show you on my way out. I usually set it then anyway.' He headed out the bar, turning off the lights as he went.

CHAPTER FIVE

Goodness, what a difference a week can make. I
struggled to picture my first Monday at "The
Pulton Arms" as I pottered around a Crow's Nest
warm enough for me to be going about my
chores dressed only in t-shirt and boxer shorts.
And there was now sufficient room to swing a
generously-proportioned cat after my concerted
effort over the last few days to get rid of the
extensive collection of junk. I'd filled one of the
huge bins in the yard and Pat had graciously
thrown some in with the trade waste from the
kitchen work. There remained some pieces of
furniture, various ornaments and other knick-
knacks that I didn't feel right getting rid of in
case they had meant something to Aunt Maddy,
even though they were certainly not to my taste.
My first thought had been to stash it all in one of
the spare bedrooms but then remembered I had
the loft at my disposal so over the weekend I had
gone exploring.

The stairs in the hallway led up to a hatch which enthusiastically dispensed a cloud of dust onto my face as I pushed it open above my head; evidence if evidence were needed that nobody had been up there for a long while. I flicked the light switch just below the hatchway and overhead a bulb came to life, then immediately died with a loud 'plink' and all was dark again. Remembering there was a torch in the bar which we kept handy in case of power cuts, I retrieved that then headed back up the stairs. Poking my head through the hatch, I swept the torch around to see what this particular Aladdin's Cave had to offer. It was a big old space, extending up into the rafters but as I'd anticipated, it was almost entirely rammed with the same sort of miscellaneous car boot sale fodder that I'd cleared from downstairs. More furniture, more bar equipment, trunks and suitcases, piles of clothes and stacks of cardboard boxes that offered no clue as to their contents. The eclectic collection just went on and on, all coated with dust or curtained with cobwebs. I really wasn't too keen to go poking about but having spied a relatively clear space towards the back corner I decided to venture in, hopefully to verify that there was some room I could use for storage. The floorboards groaned loudly but felt sturdy enough underfoot. I slowly worked my way to the rear, all the while inadvertently collecting cobwebs with my forehead as I went. God I hated that feeling - once you've had cobwebs on your face you feel them all day, regardless of how many times you wash or stick your head in a blast furnace. So much stuff; I wondered if Aunt Maddy had ever thrown anything out; ever. It would take an age to go through it all but who knows what treasures, curiosities and enormous spiders I might unearth? On reaching the back corner, I was pleased to see there was indeed a cleared space that would easily accommodate the remaining bric-a-brac. Turning back to the hatch, the torchlight picked out a piece of furniture that stood out from its neighbours, apparently having been manufactured post-war. It was an aluminium television stand; something I could put to good use as the telly in the lounge was just sitting on the floor currently. Right my friend - you're coming with me. There were a couple of cardboard boxes sitting on top of it, one of which gave way at the bottom as I went to move it, disgorging its contents onto my feet with a loud clatter. Oh, arse. Looking down, I could see numerous plastic video cases. Kneeling to get a closer look, I was then presented with a fine collection of films from the 1980's. Before me lay "Ghostbusters", a couple of "Rambo"s, "The Jewel of the Nile"; all sorts. Okay maybe not a "fine" collection but a collection none the less. Jamming the torch in my armpit to free up both hands, I reached for "Fletch", really hoping the film was in the case as it was one of my favourites. But "Fletch" wasn't in the box. It was a VHS cassette alright, but it sported the title "Raiders of The Lost Ass" on its spine. Erm -

what? The trend continued as I opened a few more cases: "Annie" turned out to be "An Orifice and a Gentleman" while "Footloose" offered up "Beverly Hills Cock 2". I sampled several more with similarly surprising and risqué results. I felt a little queasy when it occurred to me that I'd possibly unearthed Aunt Maddy's personal porn stash, but then decided it could have belonged to any one of the various flat dwellers that must have occupied The Crow's Nest over the years. I grabbed a handful of the videos and walked them downstairs together with the telly stand. They'd be a fun watch sometime if I could find technology old enough to play them on.

Overall, I was delighted with the progress we were making. The kitchen refurbishment in particular was progressing at a splendid pace: that boy Pat did not hang about. I'd also helped out here and there when tasks sufficiently menial enough for me to handle presented themselves. I'd carried out a quick site survey this morning on my way to the utility room to make my cuppa. Sure it was still a mess, but it was really coming on. Today was also the first time I'd been out of bed before anyone else showed up in the pub; astounding. Truth is, little persuaded me to leave my pit unless I really had to, and having revamped the bedroom environment and upgraded its trappings, there was even less incentive to rise and shine. But this morning I'd woken early and couldn't stop my brain whirring sufficiently to nod off again. I'd enjoyed a deep sleep beforehand mind, and spent a few virtual hours in the company of Morgan Freeman. He'd agreed to landscape my garden for free, but only if I could beat him playing Connect 4. I'd lost the first game but he sportingly agreed to make it the best of three (you know Morgan, he's no monster). But then I was suddenly awake; game over without knowing the outcome, but with a furry mouth that demanded refreshment. The Crow's Nest was still devoid of any sort of culinary facilities and with the kitchen refit well underway, the utility room had become our makeshift canteen. However, with a recently purchased microwave keeping Bernie and the kettle company, my meal options were now practically limitless. Alas the only thing that hadn't progressed over the last week was my pursuit of Jess's affections. After daily fly-bys of "Coasters" and a few full-blooded forays into the bar, there had been no sightings of her at all. I'd decided I would venture in again today and see if I could find out from her colleagues when/if she might be back. Okay, maybe a bit stalkerish, but I needed to know.

There was a busy lunchtime session ahead of us with a leaving do happening for someone from one of the banks in town. They'd called last week to let us know they had a department of around forty people visiting us today. This was serious trade for the time of year; bring it on. Keeping it 'business as usual' in the bar had been tricky while the work continued in the kitchen as if anyone needed to go to or from the cellar, store room or utility room they had to traverse a construction site. Plus, we had the issue of the mess and the noise finding their way into the bar. I have to say, all concerned did their utmost to make the best of the situation and the customers were very accommodating; some enthusiastic even, once it was explained why we were tearing the place apart. Fortunately, we were pretty much done with the tearing apart and would soon be starting the putting back together. All the old wall and floor coverings were gone and the ceiling was freshly skimmed and painted. Pat was now prepping for the wall cladding and vinyl flooring that he was confident would both be in place by the end of the week. In the meantime, I'd been doing my research on what else we needed to do or install to be ready - I'd bought myself a cheap laptop to do just that. There were plenty of requirements and accompanying legalese to wade through but so far I'd not come across anything that we'd struggle to comply with. Most of it was just common sense really - 'Don't wash your hands in the toilet'; 'Don't store venison and trifle in the same container' - that kind of thing. I thought about doing a bit more homework there and then but instead decided to get prepped for the session ahead.

J.D. turned up around ten, also keen to be ready for what might well be a lively shift. He was on form; as ever. 'Bloody hell you're up already! I suppose I'm now duty-bound to do all those things I said I'd do when Hell froze over.'

'Like what? Take a shower? Vote Tory?'

'Either; or watch "Mamma Mia".'

'No Halo today?'

'Left her with a friend for this shift; I worry she'll get trodden on when we're really busy.'

As much as I'd come to appreciate the daily banter with J.D., apart from pub business that was really our sole dialogue and it occurred to me that I still knew very little of what he did or who he was outside "The Pulton Arms". Not that he'd withheld such information: I'd just never asked. So I thought I would.

'Are you married J.D.? Or got a girlfriend?' His demeanour instantly clenched and darkened; I'd clearly touched a nerve. In an effort to keep things light, I added 'Or a boyfriend?' He didn't respond straight away, seemingly focusing his thoughts somewhere beyond the room and our conversation. Then he came back to himself and visibly relaxed.

'If you're about to proposition me, you should know I expect posh dinners and silk sheets. Right now, all I have is Halo, and that suits me just fine'. He smiled unconvincingly and something flashed across his expression that looked like remembered pain. 'Right, let's get weaving - we have bankers to inebriate!' And with that he was back to his usual self, and I was back to keeping things impersonal.

There was very little prep needed to be honest; J.D.'s routine at the end of the evening shift seemed to encompass everything required for the next day other than filling the ice buckets and slicing lemons. A few minutes later, he had unlocked the front door and adopted his standard pose leaning on the bar reading his paper. I felt I'd dropped a real clanger earlier so in an effort to make amends I ventured the usual tack. 'So what's happening in the world?'

He went through the charade of pretending to read. 'The World Health Organisation has declared bacon to be a super-food and Apple are working on a fully soluble iPhone to boost sales. The Uncle Ben's share price is in free-fall as a result.'

It appeared we were back to normality again; phew. Before I could ponder our earlier exchange further, Janine entered through the front door, wearing a very uncharacteristic, wholly serious expression. 'Morning chaps. Why are we for sale?'

I shared a blank look with J.D. then returned to Janine's concern. 'I'm not with you. We're not for sale.'

'Well there's two big fuck off posters out front that say otherwise. Look.' She walked out the door, with me and J.D. in tow.

We followed her to the kerbside then turned to face the pub. Either side of the front door hung a blue and white sign about a metre square, taped to the red-tiled fascia, one of which obscured the 'Welcome' board. The signs were identical, both blaring 'FOR SALE. ENQUIRE WITHIN', with a telephone number underneath that headline. And that was all; no estate agent's name, nothing. The three of us just stood there in silence, trying to apply some sense to what we were seeing. Then a shiver brought me back to reality (although it was a sunny morning it was still damn chilly and Janine was the only one of us wearing a coat). 'Well; I've no idea what this is about. Let's call that number and see if we can find out.'

'No need.' said J.D. 'It's our number.'

At that moment Pat emerged from the front door. 'There you all are. I know it's supposed to be a nautical theme but it's full-on Mary Celeste in there.' With only sombre looks in response, his good humour evaporated. 'What's going on?' I pointed at the front wall and he walked out and joined our group who continued to stare at it. 'I don't get it.' After scanning our faces, he could see we didn't get it either.

Of course it had to be Boat Bitch's doing but I couldn't yet grasp the "why?" Was it a joke? A wind-up? Or some sort of threat? With that thought I whirled in the direction of the SharpCrest yard, half expecting to see the woman herself standing there with binoculars trained on me so she could see my reaction and

110

savour the fallout from her handiwork. J.D. also turned and followed my line of sight.

'You think it's her?'

Another shiver rattled through me. 'I'd put money on it. Come on; let's take them down and get back indoors.'

Once we'd removed the signs I shoved them in the yard by the bins. On the way back to the bar, I brought Pat up to date with the Boat Bitch story, after which he shrugged his shoulders and said 'Just call her and tell her to go do one.'

The office mob arrived about one and they were a lively crowd right from the off. I wondered how popular the guy or girl leaving truly was if their departure put this many people in such high spirits. On a Monday too. Their clear lack of regard for returning to work for the remainder of the afternoon was impressive as they were drinking like it was Friday and they'd just clocked off for the week. Later, I found out that they were the bank's Fraud Detection department and were indeed bound for the office later, though a number of them intimated that minimal real work would get done when they got there. Damn; I sure picked the wrong day to quit credit card cloning. I did my share of serving, especially during the initial rush, and really enjoyed the bustle and the camaraderie with J.D. and Janine. When things are quiet, bar work can be super-tedious but when it's full on, and you're working with a great team there's few jobs I've had that can beat it. Today's revellers were mostly a young crowd with a couple of manager types who seemed in no less of a party mood than their colleagues, though they did make a fuss about their wine selection. My tolerance for wine snobs was slim, and these two were seemingly trying to put on a display of expertise to impress their subordinates. Our list was chalked on a blackboard behind the bar and they spent ages pointing at it and blathering. It's true we didn't carry a huge selection but from all their tutting and deliberation you'd think we offered nothing more than Blue Nun, Cisco Strawberry and Buckfast. In the end, they settled on a Pinot Grigio and ordered up a bottle, after which they made a show of the tasting whilst loudly broadcasting their critique. 'I'm definitely getting elusive notes of, ummm..... lightly roasted coffee beans and, ummmmm - Edam! Yes! Edam - you know; the cheese?' Oh right! I was thinking of Edam the steam-powered locomotive from the 1880s (tempted as I was, I didn't actually say it). Ah well: they were having fun, not hurting anyone and putting money in my till so what the heck; live and let live.

An hour or so into the session I served a young lady who turned out to be the woman of the hour yet seemed noticeably less wazzed than her colleagues but was clearly amped about something that she couldn't wait to share. 'Hi! I'm leaving to have a baby!'

'Oh right. Cheerio - hope all goes well. Our maternity facilities are a bit lacking here anyway.'

'No I'm not leaving here yet; I mean I'm leaving the company to have a baby.'

'Ah I see.'

During the quieter spells of the shift, I did dwell on the morning's weirdness with the 'For Sale' signs. J.D. had actually answered a couple of phone calls since from interested parties asking for more information but he just told the callers that there had been a misunderstanding and there was definitely no sale. There had been zero sight or sound of Boat Bitch or her henchmen since her initial visit a week ago and I'd pretty much forgotten about it, having more positive matters to focus on. That being the case, the event seemed less significant now and I wondered if I'd just got the wrong end of the stick at the time. Like the sales office model, perhaps the signs were simply an obscure prank intended as nothing more than a humorous call back to our original conversation. Oh I don't know - I'll see what the rest of the guys think later.

The (mostly) sloshed bank people started finishing up around three and began to meander back to their office. There really wasn't much to clear up in the bar as we'd seen to that during the quieter last half hour or so. "Coasters" here I come.

I went upstairs to freshen up and change out of my beer splashed lunchtime outfit (I still hadn't been out to shop for a new wardrobe but I had mastered the washer/dryer in the utility room so I had choices - yayy me). In a moment of unbridled optimism and extravagance, I even splashed a bit of after shave on. Not that I only saved this for really special occasions, I was just getting low on the good stuff so was using it sparingly to save resorting to the second string selection which mostly comprised untried Christmas 'Gift Set' items that would probably repel a velociraptor with the munchies. Right - let's do this.

As I left the pub, it struck me how nervous I wasn't. Maybe after my failed missions over the last few days I really wasn't expecting to see Jess so there was nothing to be anxious about. Or perhaps I'd found my feet since I'd first arrived back in town and was generally more settled in myself. Actually, the lunchtime shift had helped in that regard as I'd felt comfortable and capable behind the bar and part of the team; not just a malingerer or hanger-on. J.D. had even given me a sincere 'Thanks for the help - nice job' when I told him I was popping out for a bit. As I walked, I started to formulate a question I could ask of the "Coasters" staff to try and establish when I might expect to see Jess without coming across as an obvious perv but after a few yards more, it became clear I wouldn't need one - she was there. I spotted her as soon as I reached the front window - she was standing behind the bar chatting to a colleague. No scanning the menu today and no window browsing - I walked straight up to the door like I owned the place and gave it a hearty shove. Luckily, I narrowly avoided skittling the woman who was just the other side of it on her way out. 'Woah sorry!' And then I faced that behavioural dilemma; the text book solution to which I've never discovered. Do you flatten yourself against the wall whilst continuing to hold the door open with your extended arm (which you hope can sufficiently overpower the self-closing hydraulics) so the person exiting can make their way past you? Or do you take yourself fully through the door and hold it open from inside the entrance, thus giving them entirely unobstructed egress? The first manoeuvre offers up the risk that they might brush against you and think you brazenly planned things that way. The second replaces that with the risk that they'll assume you're going to carry out the first and you end up colliding in the middle of the doorway as you both step forward. I went with the first option and my antagonist squeezed past me with a rather stiff 'Thank you', accompanied by a withering look which I interpreted as a warning that she was seconds away from reaching for her rape whistle. I'm a bit old school when it comes to what I believe to be proper and gentlemanly conduct, but sometimes I wonder if that has a place in society these days. If I hold a door open for a woman, is that now deemed an offensive gesture that communicates 'Oh you're clearly too girlie and frail to open that door yourself; allow me to heroically save you from your shortcomings.'? And if I don't, am I a sexist git or simply demonstrating my support for gender equality? It's a bloody minefield. Same in the bedroom - sometimes I feel I'd be on safer ground if before we got between the sheets, I began with a PowerPoint presentation that outlined my technique and my understanding of her expectations so we could iron out any mismatch between the two to avoid later disappointment. Then we'd go at it like chimps.

Anyway: with doorway debate and debacle behind me, I continued my purposeful journey to the bar. And there she stood, looking fabulous of course. I took in her look and the usual radiant smile and whilst both were still wonderful to behold, today I was a better match for them; sort of. Right: say something inspiring Ken. 'That really is a huge fish tank.' Oh not the fish again you utter tit. Quick, say something else before that registers. 'Anyway how are you doing? I haven't seen you in here for a few days.' No; dial down the stalker.

'Hi! It's Len isn't it? I've been off for a few days - dog-sitting at my Mum's house whilst she's been off enjoying some Winter sun in Dubai. Lucky mare.'

Ouch. 'It's Ken actually. Lucky indeed - why didn't you go along?'

'Oh God sorry - Ken. She doesn't trust anyone else to look after Monty so I never get an invite. It's okay; I get a change of scene and Monty is great company. Monty's my Mum's Great Dane by the way.' She went to continue but then paused for a second as if she'd given some secret away. 'Sorry excuse my waffling - what can I get you?'

'Waffling is fine.' I smiled. 'Waffle away. A glass of the house red please.' After a shaky start this was going well I thought. Also, there were only a few other customers in the place so the odds of keeping her attention were in my favour. She had her back to me pouring the wine (enviable curves etc.) but continued to chat.

'Monty's huge; and he's nine which is pretty old for a Great Dane.' She turned and placed my wine on the counter. 'We go walking on the beach but he doesn't have much energy so we can't go far but he loves it. So do I. Do you have pets?'

Straight away my mind projected an image of the two of us strolling hand-in-hand along the surf's edge in some tropical paradise. I would have included Monty in the vignette but couldn't remember what a Great Dane looked like. 'I don't have any myself but my Manager has a pug which I'm getting to know.'

'What does he manage for you?'

'The pug? Nothing as far as I know.'

That raised a chuckle. 'Your Manager I meant.'

'We run "The Pulton Arms" together. The red-tiled building just a few doors down from here.'

'I know the place - who in Pulton doesn't? Wow! Really? Since when? Isn't that the oldest pub in the town?'

She seemed genuinely interested and (to my great delight) somewhat impressed. 'It certainly is. I took it over from my Aunt after she passed away back in December. I only moved in about a week ago so I'm still finding my feet.'

'You're not a local then?'

'Oh yes; Pulton born and bred - I relocated a few years ago in search of a job I could grow to loathe and a divorce-bound marriage. I did rather well; I found both.' As soon as the words were out, I regretted making it clear that I was at best a bit of a moaner and at worst a complete failure at life. Girl's love all that emotional baggage stuff don't they? Idiot.

'Ah well we've all been there - poor you though. Still, these things happen for a reason - maybe here is where you're meant to be and events conspired to make that happen?'

Phew - she looked and sounded sincerely sympathetic so I didn't think I'd done too much damage. What did she mean though - what had she suffered? Loathsome job or failed marriage? Or both? I decided now wasn't the time to pry - keep it light for now Trickett. 'You could be right - it feels great to be back I must say. Are you from around here?'

'Yep I've always lived in Pulton. I've travelled a lot but never really wanted to settle anywhere else, even though it's not the town it was. It's all about the tourists these days and not much else which is a shame.'

Ah-ha - a fellow crusader potentially. We could join forces and save our beloved town! And then go at it like chimps. 'It's a real shame - too much money and influence in the wrong hands if you ask me.' I decided not to clamber fully onto my soap box at that point, still trying to keep the conversation upbeat. 'So what do you do when you're not brightening up "Coasters"?' Nice work: a compliment but a subtle one. It seemed to land well as she smiled again and leaned on the bar directly in front of me, bringing her a few inches closer. God she was lovely. I noticed her eyes for the first time; they were large, grey tinged with blue with long lashes. She had a roundish face with apple cheeks and a delicate nose that hooked everything up beautifully. And of course that smile. Actually she looked like she was smiling all the time, even when she wasn't.

'Well actually I'm one of those arty-farty types. I paint and draw; mostly local landscapes. Very occasionally, a miracle happens and someone buys one. And don't laugh, but I also do the odd bit of modelling.'

Damn: this was a tricky one. How to answer without coming across as a fawning twat whilst also making it clear I didn't find the idea at all preposterous? Okay; just keep things ticking over while you're working out a proper answer.

'What do you model?'

'I have a photographer friend who often just needs someone to prop up a scene - lean against a car, hold flowers, raise a glass; that kind of thing. And another friend who designs and makes her own clothes and sells them on-line who asks me to play clothes hanger from time to time.'

I decided not to try any specific tack at all and just speak my mind. 'To be honest, I'm not at all surprised. I think you're absolutely stunning.' I said it dead pan with no drama and no nudge-nudge wink-wink type overtones. She looked taken aback and her face flushed, but she didn't move away.

'That's very n..' and then she was drowned out by the massively unwelcome sound of my phone ringing out loudly from my pocket. For a second I wasn't sure if this intervention would save or damn the conversation at such a pivotal point but if only to stop the noise, I grabbed it. From the caller ID I could see it was J.D. Great timing my friend.

'Sorry Jess, it's the pub. I'd better take it.' Worried that there was some crisis afoot, I answered.

'Hi this is Ken.'

'Boss its J.D. Any chance you're close to home? The guy I had in mind for the Chef's job is in the bar. I called up and asked him to pop in whenever and he's just dropped by on the off-chance. He's a good 'un - I worked with him for a few years at "The White Lodge" in the New Forest. We got great feedback on the food all the time I was there. None of your highly-strung "artiste" type bollocks - he just gets on with it without the drama. The staff thought he was the nuts too.'

Part of me wanted to stay where I was but maybe I'd done enough damage for one day, and I really did want to keep the food service project moving forward. In something of a quandary, I made the decision. 'Okay, I'll be there in a minute.' I hung up and smiled apologetically at Jess. 'Duty calls I'm afraid - I need to go interview a Chef.'

She straightened up. 'How exciting! How do you do that exactly? I imagine there's more to it than just asking them if they're good at cooking.' She was still beaming and still a little flushed so hopefully I hadn't over-stepped the mark with my earlier frankness.

'You know what? I've absolutely no idea.' With that I gave her my best smile then turned and headed for the exit. Just as I reached for the door handle she called out.

'Oh, you didn't touch your wine! Maybe I'll help myself to that and you can have a glass on me the next time you drop by. Reason enough to visit again I hope?'

Still gripping the door handle, I turned to face her. 'Super-models and free wine? I am so there.' And with that I opened the door and left (fortunately with nobody trying to enter at the same time; sod that ballet).

I was feeling rather effervescent after my encounter with Jess - the more I saw of her, the more of her I wanted to see. Yes of course she was off-the-charts attractive but she clearly had depth to her as well and I felt like I couldn't learn everything there was to know about her quick enough. And unless I'd completely misread the situation, she'd made a point of asking me to drop in and see her again. Self-doubt may take over later and try and persuade me that she was just being engaging to help ensure future custom, or to befriend another business she could borrow ice or change from. Or that she was in fact a colossal tart. But for now, the thought that she was genuinely into me was winning my spirits over. With a few springy steps, I was back in my pub.

J.D. was behind the bar chatting to someone who I assumed was my wannabee Chef. As I walked over he turned and I registered a familiar face, but one I couldn't immediately place. Roughly my age I guessed, he was tall and lean with a hawkish look about him courtesy of a thin face and a prominent nose. He was clean-shaven with shortish, slicked-back dark hair which emphasised the rather enviable structure of his face. 'Chiselled' I believe they call that look. He was dressed smartly in dark shirt, jacket and trousers and by comparison I felt scruffy, and not just in appearance - somehow I felt I was comparatively below par in all sorts of other areas. He reached out his hand and we shook; quite a soft hand-shake as it turned out but his hands were quite the reverse. By the hard, rough skin of his palms I could tell they were clearly used to serious graft. Maybe he was just going easy, having rightfully assumed me to be rather flimsy.

'Good afternoon Mister Trickett. I am Bruno Tyler - it's splendid to make your acquaintance, again.'

Again? I did recognise that voice from somewhere. And then it clicked. 'You're fish and chips! Sorry: the guy I mean. The other night. You served me.'

'Indeed I did. Many thanks for the appreciative note you left. I thought I might take you up on your kind offer of a drink. I also understand from J.D. that you may have an opening in your kitchen for a Chef?'

Over Bruno's shoulder, J.D. gave me a nod and wink which I took to be him re-affirming the recommendation he'd given me over the phone.

'We do. I'll show you the building site that's the kitchen in a minute but we're getting it ready to go as soon as we can. So what can I get you?'

'Just a mineral water thank you. Ice and lemon if you have it please.'

J.D. went to do the honours. 'Vino Boss?'

'Why not. Thanks J.D.'

'Grab a table and I'll bring them over.'

The bar was well populated which was good to see, especially with a lucrative lunchtime session already filling the till. We took a table in the corner which afforded us some privacy. As I plumped myself down on a chair with a creak and a clatter, Bruno slid noiselessly onto another then sat upright with his hands clasped loosely in his lap. There was an air of confidence about him and he appeared as calm as you like. I imagined there was probably very little that would put him in a flap, if anything. I felt like I was the one about to be interviewed.

'So Bruno. Sorry I didn't recognise you straight away, I was a little, well; shit-faced, the other night when we met.'

'It was no problem Ken. May I call you Ken? We all deserve to let our hair down and let off some steam from time to time. I was glad to be of service.'

'Yes, Ken, please. Well, I thank you again for looking after me. Without that meal to

124

straighten me up I might never have made it home. Right now you could be looking out the window, watching the divers fishing my body out of the water after a lengthy search.'

'Your corpse would have taken some time to surface it's true. The water temperature at this time of year would mean that decomposition would have taken around a week to get underway. The cold slows the bacteria down you see so you wouldn't bloat as fast as you would had it been warmer. It also encourages your body's production of adipocere which is a soapy, waxy like substance created from fat that protects the flesh from rotting. Of course if we were in The Persian Gulf not Pulton, you'd pop up after just a few days.'

How did he know this stuff? I wasn't sure I wanted to know. 'Right yes; rather a grisly picture. The perils of drinking I guess.' Ironically, at that moment J.D. arrived with the drinks and placed them on the table. 'Thanks J.D. - you joining us?'

'No I'll mind the bar. I sent Janine on earlier and...... Simon won't be in for a while yet. Anyway, we can talk about Bruno later when he's gone and can't hear us.' They shared a knowing grin and off he went.

'Are you still at "Yardley's"?'

'I wasn't really "at" "Yardley's" as such, rather helping out an acquaintance who was short-handed for a few days whilst considering my next move. All due respect to a worthy business, but cod and chips is rather more of a lower-end challenge than that which I'm seeking.'

'Understood. So what are you looking for? Sorry, I've not had chance to get a heads-up from J.D.'

He took a sip of his water then looked into the distance as if weighing up his answer. Then he looked back at me. 'What I'm looking for is an opportunity to apply my skills with a fresh audience. A start-up venture if you will, which sounds very much like what which you have under development here. I enjoy my trade Ken, but I've grown rather weary of just trotting out the classics, service after service, and wish to flex my creativity further. I desire an employer who supports me and whom I support in turn, but one who appreciates that when it comes to the kitchen, I know best and lets me just get the fuck on with it without meddling.' This line he followed up with a winning smile but there had been some underlying steel to his tone. Also, the profanity stood out as something he would rarely utter which added to its impact. Plus, he never seemed to blink. Like; at all. I tried to get things back on (my) track.

I took a sizeable swig of my wine. 'Well, that sounds reasonable. You don't buy a dog and bark yourself do you? So give me some background. What took up your days before "Yardley's" need arose?'

He reached into a jacket pocket and passed me an envelope. 'These are references from the two restaurants I was employed by previously - the first as a Sous-Chef and the second as Head Chef, the latter being where I worked with our friend J.D. There are contact details for references included in both and I do encourage you to connect with them to find out more should you feel the need. Once you have reviewed the information to hand and researched me as you see fit, and after discussion with J.D. of course, should you feel I may be an agreeable fit for the culinary vision you have for "The Pulton Arms", and once your kitchen is adequately serviceable, perhaps you would grant me the opportunity to come and cook for you? Prove my worth to you by way of a practical demonstration? After all; the proof of the pudding is truly in the eating.' He was still softly-spoken yet purposeful in tone and his choice of words.

Temporarily at a loss for an answer, I couldn't decide whether I was impressed by his self-assertive delivery or genuinely in fear for my life if I declined his proposition. He was utterly charming, yet chilling at the same time. Like some sort of aristocratic, butler hit-man. Okay; more wine. 'I like the way you go about setting out your stall Mister Ty..'

'Bruno; please.'

'Bruno. Thanks for the references; I'll look at them later. So have you spent all your working years at those two establishments or did you have a vocation before becoming a Chef?'

'Actually my restaurant career has been relatively brief to date. My first fifteen years out of school were spent in the Army.'

'Oh right. So you were an Army cook?'

'I was in the Army. I did undertake some cooking.'

This was rather vague for my liking but before I could press him for more detail there came a loud crash from the kitchen, followed by a range of loud expletives that could only have come from Pat. Before I (and the rest of the bar occupants) even really registered the disturbance, Bruno was on his feet and striding in its direction. Time for the kitchen tour then I guess. 'Sorry about the swears folks!' I shouted as I moved through the room. There was an accompanying 'Soz peeps!' from Pat which was met with laughter and shouts of 'Keep the noise down!' and similar from the amused, deeply unoffended punters. On reaching the kitchen, we found Pat at the top of a step ladder wrestling with a large LED light fitting, the cover of which had dropped to the floor but appeared to be in one piece. As did Pat fortunately. He looked at us sheepishly.

'Sorry guys. This thing's a right bastard - you need umpteen hands. Get an octopus with the right NVQ and you're laughing.'

'Pat this is Bruno; Bruno meet Pat. Bruno's interested in the Chef job.'

Pat gingerly took his hands away from the lighting unit which was hanging half-in and half-out of the ceiling recess. Once he'd decided it wasn't going anywhere, he stepped down and shook hands with Bruno.

'Hi. I know it looks a bit of a shambles at the mo but it's going to be a mint kitchen when it's done. Even with the pittance he's forking out for it.'

Bruno scanned the room quickly then looked up at the light fitting. 'I don't doubt it Pat. Might I assist you with that?'

'Sure.'

And with that, Bruno grabbed the screwdriver that Pat was holding and bounded up the ladder. Having spent a few seconds working out what was what, he gave the whole thing a twist and a shove which embedded it neatly in its home. Pat passed up the fixings and the cover and Bruno did things with the screwdriver then stepped down. It struck me how odd it was watching him work or move as he descended - he really didn't seem to make any sound and everything about him was fluid precision. He didn't seem bothered by the bits of plaster and the generous helping of dust that now adorned his smart jacket. 'There we go.' He passed the screwdriver back to a surprised Pat.

If Pat felt he'd lost a man test he didn't show it. 'Cheers!'

Bruno gave the room another look. 'May I ask what you have planned?'

I chimed in. 'Well right now we're getting the ceiling, walls and floor sorted then we'll worry about the fitting out.'

'Might I suggest you decide on the location for whatever extractor you have planned before you do any finishing in that respect? Otherwise you might find you end up having to bash holes in your new decoration.'

I knew we'd need an extractor but hadn't thought about placement as such. I'd guessed it would sit over the range but to be honest we didn't know if that was even going to be usable let alone where it would actually be placed or to where we'd vent it. Again, I was face-to-face with the harsh realisation that I didn't really know what the hell I was doing. 'That's a good shout; thanks Bruno. Anything else we need to be mindful of?'

Pat and I then spent another two hours with Bruno as he basically walked us through setting up a kitchen from scratch and all the food hygiene 'must-do's'. To say he knew his stuff was an understatement. He explained that when he was taken on as Sous-Chef after leaving the Army, his first kitchen was in a similar state and much of what he learnt, he learnt by way of the owners falling foul of several inspections before they got it right. He was all over everything -

recommended food storage and handling processes, separate prep areas for different food types, food washing and hand washing facilities; he knew it all. By the time he was done, both Pat and I had a list of things to do and things to buy as long as my arm. And leg. There were issues I hadn't even known were issues that I had to address - staff training, keeping Halo out of the kitchen: it just went on and on. One piece of good news was that he declared the range as fit for use ('Actually that's a rather splendid bit of kit I must say gentlemen.') I didn't know how to thank Bruno. After what can only be described as an 'odd' initial chat, he'd unveiled himself as a fully-fledged Godsend. There was no need to check with J.D. - he'd already given Bruno his vote of confidence so I offered him the role there and then.

'Look Bruno; we've got a long way to go with the kitchen; further than I realised but thank you so much for educating us. How about when it's done, you come in and cook us that meal and if you're happy with the facilities and the deal on offer, we agree to give each other a three-month trial?'

'That sounds perfectly equitable Ken; it's a deal. If you'd like, I could drop by in a week or so to check on progress and we could also start to draft a menu.'

Balls; something else I hadn't even thought of yet - the menu. 'That would be marvellous, thanks.' After the last few hours it had become increasingly apparent that we needed Bruno more than he needed us.

After the time we'd spent wandering around and investigating all the nooks and crannies of our work in progress, we were all pretty filthy. 'Look do you need to wash up? You could use my bathroom upstairs?'

'No thank you Ken; I'll be just fine.' With that he took off his jacket and shook it out, then patted his shirt and trouser legs to detach what dirt he could. With his jacket back on, he ran his hands through his hair and then left, looking only slightly dishevelled, whilst me and Pat looked like we'd been run over. He looked at me, completely gob-smacked. 'Who the hell was that guy?'

'Erm - I don't really know. J.D.'s worked with him and I met him briefly the other night when he served me fish and chips for free when I was hammered. Then he turned up today and we spoke and I wondered if he might be Keyser Söze but then he turned out to be the Harry Potter of kitchen refurbishment and food handling.'

'Well, I'd keep him if I was you.'

At that point J.D. poked his head through the doorway. 'How did the interview go?'

'Very well; bit nervous though.'

'Guess he was just keen to make a good impression.'

'Not him, me. He's a bit intimidating at times.'

'Oh you'll get used to him.'

'I will - he's hired.'

'Good move! You're not as dumb as you look. Or sound. Celebratory drink?'

'Yeah go on. You too Pat - you've earned one.'

We spent a while bringing J.D. up to speed with Bruno's recommendations for the kitchen. He had a few questions but mostly just nodded sagely as if he'd expected nothing different. I did wonder what effect it would all have on the schedule, and the cost. 'What's all this going to do to the price Pat?'

'Well let's just say I'm really looking forward to parking my new Ferrari in the driveway of my luxury villa. In Monte Carlo. I'd have to move there 'cos you know; taxes and that.'

'Hell if it gets you out the country, just name your price.'

'I couldn't leave you really. Being around you makes me look so much better.'

'Any chance of a sensible answer sometime soon?'

'Spoilsport. I'll need to price up the extras but I don't think it's going to be too major. I'm more worried about the time to get it done. Could the budget stretch to another pair of hands?'

'I could help out further?'

'Yeah. No. I need someone that can do a bit more than stand there all day looking clueless while scratching their arse. No offence. One of the lads that does some work for me is spare at the mo. With him on board, I reckon we could be done by the end of next week. I was going to get him in one day anyway - fitting the new gate will be a two-man job when it arrives.'

Being up and running that soon was an appealing thought. Plus, if the work dragged on for too long Bruno might decide to sell his skills elsewhere. I was sure J.D. would want the disruption over sooner rather than later too. 'Go for it. Can you work all that out and let me know how much all in?'

'For sure. Let you know soon as. Another pint might help to grease the wheels.'

I gave him a refill. 'Cheeky bastard.'

J.D. then re-routed the conversation. 'So what about the 'For Sale' nonsense? What's up with that?'

What with all the excitement meeting Jess and Bruno, I'd almost forgotten about that strange episode. 'I really don't know. Just ignore it maybe? If she doesn't get a rise out of me, perhaps she'll drop the idea. If that's what she's trying to do in the first place. Maybe it was just a joke like that model I reckon she sent. A naff joke I'll grant you. What do you guys think?'

'Like I said; call her up and tell her to get bent.' said Pat who then belched loudly enough to rouse Halo from her snooze. She lifted her head and looked at me and J.D. then decided there was nothing to get excited about and with a major sigh, went back to her dreams. 'Sorry. Better out than in. Or, you could hire a strippagram to crash her office with eff off painted on his arse. Actually you could do it yourself - you've got nothing to hide; unfortunately for you.'

'I'd let it go.' said J.D. 'Whether she's serious or joking or just playing mind games for whatever reason I wouldn't dignify it with a response. She's probably just got more spare money and time than she knows what to do with so thought she'd fill some of her day by messing with you. Maybe it's a subtle romantic gesture? Like your model present? Perhaps she fancies you?'

'So she's rich and mental? My kind of woman.' Pat shot in unhelpfully.

'Maybe she just likes to do her bit for hopeless causes?' added J.D.; both of them clearly enjoying the humour at my expense.

'Well I'm not interested. I'm still on the lookout for a nymphomaniac vineyard owner as you know. I'll sleep on it. Thanks for the advice;

what would I do if I didn't have you two wise souls to steer me through life?'

'Spend all day alone in your room eating cake and wanking yourself blind?' said Pat.

'Or forever wander B&Q searching for tartan paint?' said J.D.

I looked at the two of them grinning at me like idiots, matching their keen wit with a snappy, carefully crafted riposte. 'Oh bugger off you two.'

After another hour or so of increasingly far-fetched speculation about Boat Bitch's motives and some general piss-taking, Pat headed home. Simon had joined in after his arrival for the evening shift and provided his share of the comedy; quite impressive from a standing start plus I'm sure he only heard about fifty percent of what was said. I was feeling the effects of another lively day so decided on a timeout in The Crow's Nest.

Lying on the bed, I rewound and re-watched the day's events whilst still mulling over how best to respond to the 'For Sale' caper. This was seriously bugging me now. After a brief but hugely enjoyable liaison with Jess and an interesting and productive introduction to Bruno (I'd read his references; they were spot-on), this 'thing' was the real fly in my ointment. If you took the signs on their own, then it wasn't hard to view them as a poor taste prank but if you added in the context of the episode in the bar and the sales office model then they took on more sinister overtones. Should I report it to the police? Was there CCTV on the quay? This seemed like overkill - the only crime the perpetrators had actually committed was taping a couple of bits of laminated cardboard to a listed building. What to do...

After an hour or so of kicking various 'what-if?'s around my head, I'd decided against ignoring Boat Bitch's moves, regardless of their motive. She needed to know I was no pushover and that she couldn't get under my skin. I hadn't folded or ran scared when she and her goons came into the bar and I wasn't going to do so now. I toyed with the idea of sticking up some comic but insulting notices in the SharpCrest yard by way of answer but figured this would be awfully tricky to do and would probably end up with me getting to know the local police rather well. I could phone her; I was sure I could find a number on her web site and get put through. This gave her control though: she could simply choose not to talk to me. Plus, I'd have to work hard at sounding nonchalant which might be a struggle if I got cross, which was highly probable. A letter perhaps? Bit formal, even if I used a jolly font. Also, there was the risk that it might end up in a stack of company mail that she may not read for days, if it reached her at all. Come on - how do you get a woman's attention? Send your footman to read her a poem? Hire a sky-writer to spell out something meaningful with smoke? Drop an anvil on her head? The last option was the most appealing but probably the toughest to organise. And then it hit me, like a sky-written poem or a footman's anvil - flowers!! Of course flowers - women are hard-coded to be drawn to them and they wouldn't loiter in someone's in-tray for weeks. With the right accompanying note they would still send a message, but in an informal, almost playful manner, and that was the tone I was after. This would be a clear signal that indicated her actions hadn't gone unnoticed but that I really couldn't give two shits about her games. And what woman on the planet could resist reading any note attached to flowers they received? She was bound to get the message.

After a few minutes on the laptop I was ready to checkout a rather fancy, abundantly yellow, hand-tied bouquet from a florist's web site that promised next day delivery. After some browsing, I'd found the address for the main SharpCrest yard so that's what I entered for delivery. Even if I was a little wide of the mark, I was sure nobody on her payroll would fail to make sure the Boss received any gift with her name on it. Writing the note took longer; so much so my session on the web site timed out and I had to do the damn order from scratch again. Bloody woman - causing me grief even when she wasn't around. I was aiming for light and breezy, but the first few versions of my communiqué gave off a kind of ransom note vibe. In the end I decided on:

'Dear Angie,

Just a small token to say many thanks for the attention and your very public gesture
but it's still a no I'm afraid.

It's best you get used to the idea.

Yours,

A close neighbour.'

Clear enough I thought, without being too threatening or (most importantly) incriminating. With my purchase complete, I was already running various scenarios through my mind as to how my gesture might be received the next day. Whatever: it was done. I was feeling a bit jaded from my day but also boosted by my floral yet stoic act of defiance and thought about heading back downstairs for more vino and camaraderie. Pat and J.D.'s earlier banter popped into my head and I laughed out loud. They were sharp; too bloody sharp. Thinking of those two and my other new acquaintances, it struck me what colourful characters they all were. Jess, Janine, Simon, even Bruno - they were all fascinating and full of life; and they just didn't do "dull". Maybe their colour and the various shades of life in Pulton were what my previous monochrome existence truly lacked. And there was romance in the air. But also work to be done - I had a kitchen to kit out. As enticing as it was, the bar would have to wait. Returning my attention to the laptop, I set about my shopping. Blimey; quite a list I had to work through. I was convinced it would be worth it though. Plus, I felt kind of compelled to do whatever Bruno suggested in case he visited during the night and silently ended me.

CHAPTER SIX

It was one of those blindingly dazzling and gloriously crisp February mornings that lured you into thinking that Spring was not only on its way, but was just around the corner, even though it hadn't actually thought about leaving the house yet. Sure, it was biting cold and the air was almost painful to inhale, but out of the shade you could feel a hint of warmth. I was fully togged up though – still without a new jacket, but I had recently taken the plunge and invested in a scarf. No doubt it was that purchase that triggered the improvement in the weather. Maybe I would procure that new coat so we could immediately bask in the resulting heatwave.

There wasn't a great deal of activity on the quay at this hour with few places open for business but across the channel, the cargo yard was bucking the trend, bustling aplenty as a modest army of workers and their companion cranes went about unloading what was quite a sizeable ship; probably the largest I'd ever seen moored up there. You see the thing with Pulton Harbour wasn't the size, it was the depth. As harbour's went, it was proper vast, something like fifteen square miles I believe, and some claimed it to be the world's largest natural harbour. Now, New Zealand and California boasted their own candidates for that title but Pultonites were deaf to such assertions as both competitors had been extended by man-made engineering works so it was fiercely argued that neither could be classed as "natural". Similar to when stunningly attractive celebrities heralded as pure, earth-grown beauties immediately lose their shine when its discovered that they've "had some work done". Whereas Pulton was implant free. But like many of those artificially enhanced luminaries, it's abundantly shallow. Back in the day, the main channel was dredged from the harbour entrance to the quay, which granted entry and egress to the roll-on, roll-off ferries that serviced ports in France and Spain together with some largish cargo ships, but there just wasn't sufficient draft for the really big boys. The dredging also unearthed an Iron Age Log boat. I remembered it from my many many school outings to "The Quay Museum" and the unmatched optimism and awe with which the tour guide presented it to the group each time. Young kids tended not to get overly excited by a piece of wood that resembled a well-gnawed Twiglet. Even if it was ten-foot-long and over 2000 years old. But few could argue the harbour wasn't one of nature's finest treasures and this morning it was positively radiant. The sun was bouncing off the water with such intensity I couldn't look directly at it. I added sunglasses to my shopping list.

Once again, I'd been up and about uncharacteristically early, keen to dive into whatever today offered up. Seeing such a glorious day limbering up outside my window I'd been tempted to head out first thing, but I'd resisted it's pull and made myself complete the on-line shopping marathon I'd kicked off last night. I'd deployed my credit card so frequently I could for the first time ever recall the full card number and expiration date at will. Even the last three numbers on the back too. Having purchased half the internet, it was time to treat myself to some fresh air and nostalgia. Pat had already arrived by the time I got downstairs and was enjoying a brew in the kitchen. 'You there! Peasant! Stop loitering and get to work! Else I'll be forced to torch your cottage and run your family off my estate.'

'My humble apologies your lordship, spare me the rod I beg you. Us working types don't know no better nor nuffink.' with which he took a slurp of tea whilst slowly raising the 'V' sign with his other hand.

'How's it going mate?'

'All good me old.' He rummaged in his pocket then passed me a scrap of paper. 'Here's the new price; it's got all the new bits your man said, plus the extra pair of hands I could do with.'

'Looks sound to me, thanks mate.' And it did look sound - he was clearly doing me and my finances a huge favour. Yes, it was more, but not significantly more. 'When can your other guy start?'

'Day after tomorrow when the gate comes.'

'Great. Okay bud; I'll let you crack on.'

J.D. was in the bar, hunched over his newspaper. Halo pottered over to say hi to me then returned to her basket and snoring once she tired of the petting.

'Morning J.D. - what's new in the world?'

'The American High Court has rejected Donald Trump's sanity plea, and someone in Bristol claims to have witnessed a BMW 5 Series driver using their indicators.'

'Never! What a world we live in.' Then a thought from yesterday popped into my head. 'Oh hey - what do you know about "Westall's Deli"?'

'The new shop on the High Street you mean?'

'Yep that's the one. So they're coming, not going?'

'Apparently. Some cheese store serving overpriced coffee, hefty steak pies with pastry leaves on the top and chutney in jars with gingham hats; that kind of thing I'd imagine. You'd gain a dress-size just walking past the place. Opening soon I've heard. Tourists will bloody love it.'

My joy at the confirmation of imminent cheese excess was then abruptly half-squished by the thought that "Westall's" was potentially another competitor I'd have to contend with in the locale. Also J.D. seemed strangely sour on the subject. Maybe he'd had a bad experience with cheese. Or steak. Or gingham. Ah well. 'Great. Can't have too many cholesterol dealers in the neighbourhood. Right well, lovely morning out there so I think I'll go for a mosey.'

'I've got your number in case we get swamped.'

'Okay. If I answer with an accent, it just means I'm debriefing a suspect and can't drop my cover.'

I did get a grin with that one. 'Roger that.'

And then I was out the door.

Crossing the road, I was forced into a half-sprint to avoid being mown down by a helmet on a bike. Bloody cyclists - the silent killers. Even those with bells fitted rarely used them; too embarrassed by the lame "Ding!" they produced I'd imagine. Get yourself an air horn you healthy, planet-friendly, pedalist freaks. Otherwise, the quayside was mostly pedestrian friendly, with broad block-paved walkways either side of the road, populated with palm trees and an equivalent number of brightly coloured kiosks selling tickets for the various harbour tours and other excursions on offer. Broadsea Island was a popular destination; a location I seemed to remember as retaining major historic significance due to camping being invented there in the early 1900's. It was also where Marconi successfully tested the first iPad, or something like that. I'd experienced camping several times but had never really seen the point in it, other than as some sort of masochistic exercise that reminded you how comfortable and convenient your kitchen, bed and toilet were back home. Alternatively, you could charter a fishing boat and go and try to catch your lunch. Or you could book a dinner cruise where someone better-qualified would catch it for you instead. In addition to Broadsea, there were a handful of islands in the harbour that you could visit; some of which The National Trust would let you walk about on, and others which the private owners or the oil and gas companies wouldn't. You could also venture outside the harbour and take in the splendour of The Jurassic Coast. It used to just be known as 'the coast' but underwent some swift re-badging to cash in on the release of a certain film. I'm sure it did wonders for tourism but I felt for all the kids that went to visit the area off the back of that campaign, all flushed with excitement as they pictured the many and varied dinosaurs they'd soon witness roaming the landscape. Or maybe anticipating some sort of safari park equivalent, only with a T-Rex eating the car's radio aerial and peeing through the sunroof instead of Macaque monkeys. But then they'd arrive to find it was all just stones; none of which they were allowed to collect and take home. Maybe the ever-present threats of rock falls and cliff landslides might pep things up a bit for them. So; lots to do and lots to see, though not all excursions ran all year round - there wasn't much demand for open-deck romantic dinners for two when there was a force eleven gale blowing; in November. Also, the harbour itself could get surprisingly choppy. Few forgot the annual Summer works outing I went along to during my time working for the local bank. The event was a harbour tour with barbecue, disco and bar. The sea cut up so rough that nobody really ate or danced, needing to keep at least one hand clamped to some fixture or other to stop themselves from getting thrown across the room or even worse, hurled from the boat into the churning water. Everyone still managed to get quite drunk though. I think they made as few trips to the bar as possible but grabbed the strongest possible brew that they could when they got there. Thankfully, we didn't sink, and apart from the odd light dusting of vomit everyone returned unscathed, but the trip was referred to as "The Perfect Storm" thereafter.

I took several deep breaths of the sharp sea air - holy hell; bracing or what. I still couldn't quite believe my good fortune waking up to this vista every single day. Looking back to the pub, I once again appreciated how proudly she stood out from the buildings whose company she shared, especially with her red tiles reflecting the eager sunlight. To the left of her was the four-storey whiteness of what was once a merchant's warehouse, now a greeting card and gift shop with offices or apartments above. To the right stood a bland, much more modern office block which really didn't fit the scene at all. Why the hell wasn't Boat Bitch strong-arming them into moving on instead of me? It looked a far better fit for her intended purpose than the pub. I'd assumed it was commercial office premises but couldn't recall ever seeing anyone come or go from the place. It was mostly white painted and also towered over the pub, helping to give the impression that "The Pulton Arms" was being subtly but forcefully squeezed between her monumental neighbours until she decided to just up and leave in the face of such intimidation. Narrow alleys ran in between most of the buildings on the quay that led to various back streets and footpaths which took you deeper into town. Few of these alleys ran straight, as the older buildings in particular were anything but regular in shape and the new arrivals had been designed to fill the gaps in between, which they did with mixed success. If you saw an aerial photo of the quay, it looked like a jigsaw completed by someone who'd ran out of patience and rather than finding the right pieces, they'd just pounded other bits into the gaps to make them sort of fit. Next to the characterless office block sat one of the grand old gentleman of the quay; five storeys of what was also once a merchant's warehouse. This now suffered the indignity of serving as some sort of mega gift shop that somehow managed to stock enough tat to fill several floors. When I was a kid it used to be an aquarium; I remember walking through the dim narrow corridors and getting all hyped, not knowing what I'd find in the next tank along. Even the empty ones were a buzz - you didn't know if they really were vacant or if you were about to be scared witless by some creature you hadn't spotted yet launching itself at your face and making you squeal. The aquarium sadly went out of business many years ago, with the building then following its natural course, next evolving into a model railway museum with a night club above - what else. I was pretty sure I'd been there once sometime in the 90's: I remembered making great progress with a girl sporting an impressive perm who reminded me of Bonnie Tyler which was no bad thing. Then the 'mate' I was with said she reminded him of John McEnroe off of the 80's, after which I couldn't get past the image.

And then next door you had "Coasters": and Jess. After a lot of thought, I'd decided not to drop in and see her today. True, I had a clear invite to visit (I thought) but I didn't want to come across as stiflingly keen or obsessive. I'd never have the ego to play hard to get, but the last thing I wanted to do was scare her off. So as tempting as it was, I kept my restraint whilst hoping to hell she was working tomorrow. Although I was the other side of the road, I still walked past her windows smartish so I looked like I had somewhere to be urgently, just in case she happened be to looking out. I didn't want her thinking I wasn't interested either. Psycho stalker or aloof "player" - it's a tricky line to walk.

Strolling on down the quay, I divided my attention between the bright seascape of the harbour, and the mix of businesses and accommodation that made up the view to my left, all the while trying to suppress the bile that rose each time the abominable apartment block came into view as I swung between the two aspects. A little further down I passed the arcade, and I could just make out the outline of the long-removed lettering on the wall that used to spell out 'Quay Amusements'. That signage hadn't been superseded by anything else and the place appeared deserted. What would it become I wondered - another bar or apartments? Pick any disused building and toss a coin: I wasn't sure there was a third option these days. In my very early teens, the arcade used to be my second home, that I shared with a group of similar-minded friends who also hadn't discovered beer or girls yet. But then Iron Maiden changed all that in a single evening.

At that time, I was at my core, a video games nerd, and any and every piece of change I could muster got ploughed into those vivid and noisy machines that offered entertainment and escapism in equal measure. Habitually, when asked what I'd like for my Birthday or Christmas present, my answer was always 'Money please!' Once received, I would then spend several flush and flushed hours gradually parting with that cash. Then I'd trudge home feeling rather empty, having not even kept sufficient funds back for bus fare. I never gambled - that was for losers: instead I was the shrewd one, merrily stuffing my coins into some device that guaranteed zero financial return on my investment. Then one night I went to see 'The Maiden' at the Arts Centre with my mate Rich. We lived metal in those days, though I had broader interests too. I'd get the piss taken out of me at school for having both AC/DC and Ultravox albums poking out of my school bag. Rich tolerated my perversion even though he didn't share such appetites - he'd wear a Metallica t-shirt under his school shirt every day just to stay 'on message'. So we did the gig, and with rosy cheeks and ringing ears we hit the street. Now usually, I'd head down to grab a few minutes of video game fix at the arcade but then something life-altering happened.

Rich said 'Fancy a beer?'

After two hours of listening to music at 100 decibels plus, my immediate response was 'WHAT?!'

'BEER!'

'SURE!'

Don't get me wrong I'd had beer before (not at the gig - I tried but failed the ID challenge) and I'd attended several house parties where I'd sampled vodka and fallen over spectacularly, but being below the legal drinking age, we didn't really 'do' pubs. But seeing an opportunity to score some lad points, and being low on cash to feed the machines with, (those Iron Maiden tour t-shirts don't buy themselves) I thought why the heck not.

"LET'S GO SEE AUNT MADDY!"

I'm not sure Rich really heard or understood but he gave me the thumbs-up and I strode off looking like I had a plan and he seemed happy to follow. So we trundled down the High Street to the quay and into "The Pulton Arms". Aunt Maddy was working (of course) and she let us have a shandy each while we chatted and argued about which were the highlights of the concert; generally enjoying feeling all grown-up. After that night I never went back to the arcade; pubs and beer just seemed way more interesting. I never fell out of love with 'The Maiden' though - they're still touring the globe and putting on a more energetic show than most bands a fraction of their age. May they live forever.

With the abominable apartments looming to my left, I looked to the water again, taking in the posh marina and its high-value occupants. This was the area of the quay where those with serious cash kept their beloved watercraft; all top-end sail boats and motor yachts. This wasn't just the domain of the moneyed; it was home to that peculiar strain of humanity - the yacht wankers. Yacht wankers don't just do yacht stuff; they live yacht stuff, even when they're not yachting. They dress in yachting clothing even when they're not yachting. All they talk about is yachting even when they're not yachting. Don't get me wrong, I loved being out on the water and on a hot sunny day, I would choose a boat trip over joining in the beach sardines game every time. But the next day I wouldn't walk into Tesco sporting a Captain's hat and a body warmer. I'd served a few such characters in the pub and had recognised some repeat offenders who appeared to live in the abominable apartments that overlooked the elite marina but they never discussed their (well-appointed) accommodation: just the yachting. I didn't think they were inherently bad sorts - just a breed that I had no way to really engage with. Because I wasn't a yacht wanker. They probably viewed me as similarly unfathomable which was fair enough: each to their own. There were a couple of immaculate, old-style, all-wood floating gin palaces moored up which I would have been interested in viewing up close but the marina was secured from the likes of me; only those with the appropriate yacht wanker credentials could walk those gilded pontoons. Us normal folk could only admire the shining vessels and their inhabitants from the quayside; and throw chips at them when they weren't looking. If the seagulls didn't catch them in mid-flight first which they mostly did; years of practice looting the hapless tourists you see.

As you left the apartments and the money pit marina behind you, you entered another world. The first sign of that transition was the intense fishy tang that walloped you in the nostrils - an indication that you were bordering the real Pulton Quay - the Fishermen's Quay. This was where Pulton's fishing fleet landed their catch which was then trucked off to local businesses and other destinations in the UK and on the Continent. Most of the fish got bought up by the nearby restaurants and bars but shellfish were the main catch these days and they sold for a higher price elsewhere. So the sole, mullet and skate got snapped up by places like "Coasters", while the bulk of the mussels, crabs and cockles won a truck and lorry ride to foreign tables. Sadly, the overall catch had continued to shrink over the years, decimated by EU enforced quotas. There was something like ninety fishing boats now, down from eight hundred odd in the 90's. Like many of the traditional Pulton trades, fishing had been out-paced by the tourism and leisure industries and was now roundly considered to be "on its arse". Piracy was another casualty - I couldn't remember the last time we'd raided a French or Spanish port. Possibly that's because the last time we did so, they retaliated and burned most of our town down. No sense of humour those Europeans. So as the fishing industry had declined, so had the Fishermen's Quay shrunk, now making up only a few hundred metres of the overall quay; the neglected tail end. But it was otherworldly none the less; as soon as you got that first whiff of what lay ahead you were transported back in time, only without the overacted mad scientist character and the dodgy 80's sports coupe. The first scene you came across was the designated area where the catch was landed, usually quiet and unoccupied as it was today. But come the hour, it exploded into colour and activity as the boats arrived and the fishermen and their buyers hastened to transfer the precious cargo into a waiting column of refrigerated trucks, while the sea birds went mental overhead. The scene really was something to behold. When I was very young, I remember catches used to be landed up and down the entire length of the quay, and the sounds and smells of the organised chaos were overwhelming. Whether vacant or in full swing, the landing area was always pretty pungent. And beyond that stood the old lifeboat station which now served as a museum, housing the original Pulton lifeboat that also heroically sailed as part of the Dunkirk "Little Ships" flotilla. A few more steps and you reached the fishermen's marina; no deluxe yachts or motorboats there, just the working craft that battled the elements and crippling euro-bureaucracy to bring home the goods. Beached on shore lay rows of tenders in a variety of colours and states of repair, together with a haphazard assortment of larger boats undergoing maintenance, the backdrop to which was a similarly jumbled collection of fishermen's cottages. And fishing paraphernalia was everywhere; in the maintenance yard, on the quayside and even stashed in the cottage gardens - discarded trawls, dredges and other nets, with pots, pallets and crates stacked up in all available corners. The entire scene was a world away from the modern apartment-blocked, palm tree be-decked environment just a few hundred yards up the road. And it was fabulous.

Later, as I hit the main stretch again, I noticed the ship was still moored up across the channel, now with a full deck so presumably stocked up for the return trip to some Continental destination. Depending on tides and other things I didn't understand, the cargo ships would sometimes moor overnight and sail the next day and we'd get some interesting visitors in the pub as a result. Often they'd have no English and we'd have no Albanian, Polish, Norwegian or Klingon, so communication mainly consisted of pointing at things and shouting. And I'd swear some of those guys were high as kites sometimes, or already three sheets to the wind when we opened up at lunchtime. I guess if you weren't tasked with steering the ship, there wasn't much else to do on a long voyage other than get wasted and practice your knots.

"Coasters" came into view and my thoughts turned from multi-cultural seafaring to Jess. I reminded myself that I was <u>not</u> going to visit her today and picked up my pace whilst inwardly reciting a 'No Coasters!' mantra and keeping my eyes down as I walked. I was not going to blow things by coming across as a smitten schoolboy who would send her a handmade Valentine's card every day ('No Coasters!'). Just a few more hours and it would be tomorrow and then a visit would be well-received, whilst communicating none of the sweaty urgency that it would if I walked in now ('No Coasters!'). Plus, I was all puffed, rouged and windswept so now was definitely not the time to present myself. Yep, good call. Back to the pub it is.   Oh sod it....

'Hi Ken! Welcome back.'

'Hey Jess - I was passing so thought I'd drop in and say hi.'

'Glad you did. Bit slow today.'

Did that mean she was pleased to see me personally or just glad of the custom? Or maybe both? 'Yeah just needed to stretch my legs, and it's bloody lovely out there. And I can never resist the Fishermen's Quay; that's the real Pulton.'

'Ah-ha! I thought I picked up a waft of lobster pots.'

Dammit; really? 'Oh that's probably the aftershave. I'm a test pilot for Chanel in my spare time and they're just trialling a new range. I believe this one is "Halibut Pour Homme".'

'Ooh - any free samples going? I'm exhuming a dead body later and a quick spray of that would freshen things up no end.'

I must have looked distinctly crestfallen as she quickly followed up with 'I'm joking! I can't actually smell you at all, though if I could, I'm sure you'd smell divine. A mixture of jet fuel, freshly-sawn wood and the leather of a Formula 1 race-car driver's glove; or something like that I'd imagine.'

She laughed at her own joke and I couldn't help but join in. She was properly funny, and the laughter also obscured my relief at realising I didn't actually stink like Captain Birdseye's laundry basket. That said; as a Captain, I guess he wouldn't have been that hands-on with the fish. He probably wasn't even a real Captain, more likely just the spokesperson or figurehead for the brand. Also, would the Food Standards folks approve of a parrot in a prep area? Surely that must be a no-no hygiene-wise. I was much more mindful of those kind of issues since we started getting the kitchen up together.

'Ken?'

'Sorry! Actually, I was hoping for Old Spice blended with WD-40 but I can live with your appraisal.'

'To be honest, if there's any fishy whiffs around here they'll be down to the tank needing cleaning.'

She pointed at the fish-tank behind her and I quietly scored myself a point for that not being the first thing I'd mentioned since I walked into the bar (for once). That being the case, I thought I could now discuss it with impunity. 'That's not your job is it? It's a monster.'

'No, thankfully. I think they have some other company maintain it and a guy comes in every other weekend. I only tend to work weekdays so I don't know for sure. What can I get you? House red perchance?'

'Lovely, thanks.' Having just come indoors after a vigorous walk in the chilly outdoors, I was now boiling up and probably more flushed than a toilet in a Tokyo youth hostel. So before my scorching face started melting nearby objects, I removed my jacket and scarf and dropped them on the bar.

'£3.20 please.'

'What? Last time you said it would be on the house.'

'Only if you stay here and talk to me. Sorry, I omitted the small print when I made the initial offer.' She leaned on the bar as she had the last time, intentionally breaching my airspace. I followed suit which brought us even closer. Her hair was tied back in a ponytail today, not hanging loosely as before. It occurred to me that she could shave it all off and cover her bald head in nothing but tattoos of flaming red-eyed skulls with daggers embedded in them and she'd still look irresistible. Ideally I'd never have to put that to the test mind. For a second, the impulse to lean further across the bar and kiss her right there flashed through me, but then one of her colleagues emerged from a back room carrying a rack full of glasses which he plonked loudly on the counter, jerking me back to sensible.

'Okay, deal. But if some other looker rocks up and offers to share her chips with me, I'm walking.'

She made a play of picking up a menu, scrutinising it then acted as if she was crossing something out on it. 'Looks like chips are off.' She dropped the menu then thankfully moved back into close proximity. 'So; now I have you, tell me everything. How's the pub doing?'

'The pub's great. I'm gradually clearing what appears to be about a century's worth of accumulated crap from my flat and we're refitting the kitchen so we can start doing food.'

'Oh, so you'll be the competition then? We'd best raise our game. Perhaps I shouldn't be flirting with the enemy.'

'You're flirting? I just thought you were bored to tears and decided I was marginally more engaging than the fish.'

'Well; the jury's still out on that one.' Unfortunately, at that point another customer appeared at the bar and she moved off to serve them. 'Scuse me a minute; I'll be back. Stay put: we have a deal remember.'

Actually by now she had a handful of punters waiting but that was actually fine. I had nowhere else to be and I felt things were going swimmingly. Conversation was flowing and she seemed keen to get to know me better. That said, I needed to find out if she was single or not; this was my highest priority. Not saying I wasn't up for the challenge if she wasn't, but it would be a major boost to my campaign if she was a free agent. There was no sign of a wedding or engagement ring. If anything, didn't the resolutely single ladies go full-on with the hand jewellery to indicate the opposite so as to deter unwanted attention? Okay I needed to know for sure. But how to obtain such vital information? Subtlety was paramount with this investigation - I'd lose major style points if I just blurted out 'So hey; got a boyfriend? If not, want one?' or something equally crass. Though the idea of dragging Pat down here and getting him to try the 'My mate fancies you.' approach I had filed as a viable option. As Jess continued to work her way through the customers further down the bar, I enjoyed my wine whilst running some lines through my head. And then I heard an unfamiliar yet somehow familiar voice at my shoulder.

'Mister Trickett. Well; if it isn't the accidental florist.'

Something was amiss, but I couldn't immediately put my finger on what. The sensation was akin to the odd time during my smoking days when I'd put a cigarette in my mouth the wrong way around and set light to the filter. There was the familiarity of the basic manoeuvre coupled with the unnerving feeling that something had gone terribly wrong but I just hadn't figured out what yet. I turned to see Boat Bitch.

Looking business-like and trim as before, her scarlet lipstick stood out boldy, but the porcelain skin had been exchanged for a glowing sun tan. At least I knew she'd received the flowers. And this time she didn't have her heavies with her.

'Angie! What a pleasure. Can I buy you a drink?'

'No thank you Mister Trickett, I'm not here to socialise with undesirables. If that was my main aim in life, I'd visit your pub more often.'

'Well don't be a stranger; drop by if you get tired of beating up school kids in the park and stealing their lunch money. Exhausting work I'm sure. I could rustle you up a Marmite bap and a Fanta.'

'A tempting offer indeed but I shall have to pass I'm afraid. My days are spent at work. You know; "work"? You're aware of the concept?'

'I did give it a go once; it wasn't really for me. So - you got my message? Are we all done with that nonsense with the pub?'

She moved closer and fixed me with a look overflowing with disdain - the sort of scorn I reserve for those that say things like 'Hashtag: horny!' or 'Stressed.com!' out loud.

'I did take delivery of a cheap-looking bouquet, presumably recycled from a local cemetery; from your Aunt's grave perhaps? There was a note attached which alas made no sense to me so it joined the flowers in the trash.' She then attempted a thin smile which manifested itself as an ugly grimace. Then she continued, grinding the words out like a Maître D' at a top-end restaurant forcing out an insincere welcome to a diner that turned up wearing jeans. 'Mister Trickett, I owe you an apology. Thus far I've obviously been talking much too fast and using too many long words for you to grasp the point I've been trying to get across. And that point is this: your pub is going to be my sales office whether you wish it or not. Is that a little clearer for you? If not, I could try flash cards or some simple sketches? Or build you another model?'

So, none of her actions to date had been pranks - they'd all been shots across my bows. She was seriously dampening my mood and another cheap jibe at Aunt Maddy's passing just wound me up all the more. That was her intention of course, but this time I decided to let my anger show, whilst matching her volume so as not to broadcast our conversation to a wider audience. 'Look; I don't know who the hell you think you are but trust me; your point is received loud and clear, and it can go sit in the bin with the flowers. As for long words, I'm not sure I can use anything much shorter than 'No' to get <u>my</u> point across. And if you vandalise my pub again, I'll get the police involved; okay?'

With that she dropped the fixed smile and curled her lip into a snarl but before she could respond, someone else intervened and sent my already strained thoughts scattering in a whole new range of directions. It was Jess.

'Hi Mum! What brings you here?'

Oh Christ no. No, no, no! This can't be; it really can't. Boat Bitch was still focussed intently on me but then she appeared to flick a mental switch and instantly changed states. She unclenched internally and turned to Jess with swiftly painted-on geniality.

'Hello dear! I had the lock changed in the conservatory after you told me you struggled with it when you were kind enough to look after Monty last week.' She rummaged in her handbag and handed Jess a key. 'Here's the new one; don't lose it.'

'Thanks Mum. You didn't have to come in though - I'd have picked it up sometime. Aren't we doing dinner Friday too?'

'Well I was local. I had to lunch a new client in town so thought I'd drop in and re-acquaint myself with your ah, work.' With which she scanned the bar with a look on her face which suggested she'd trodden in something noxious. 'And yes to Friday. I'll get Linda to book somewhere.'

I was all at sea; still seriously fired-up from my exchange with Boat Bitch but also reeling from the news that she and Jess were mother and daughter. There must have been any number of expressions playing themselves out across my face, one after another. Jess looked at me concerned.

'You okay Ken?' Then she looked to her mother who'd taken half a step back from me. 'Do you two know each other?'

Boat Bitch carried on as if none of the events of the last few minutes had ever transpired. 'No not at all. Just idle chit-chat whilst I was waiting for you to finish serving those other people.'

'Well, this is Ken. He's taken over "The Pulton Arms" just a few doors down. Ken, this is my mum Angelique. Her company makes the big boats just across the way.'

Boat Bitch didn't miss a beat. 'Really? How fabulous. Pleased to meet you Ken, and good luck with the pub. Great spot you've got there.' She reached out her hand; all fake charm and suppressed venom.

It felt like I hadn't spoken in days and I was still struggling to come to terms with this new God-awful turn of events. Because I simply couldn't think of anything else to do, I reached out and shook her hand. 'Pleased to meet you Angelique.' All the while fighting the urge to crush her fingers into splinters. Still unable to pluck a coherent next action from the selection still bouncing around my head, I went back to basics and drained my wine to steady myself. 'Could I trouble you for another Jess?'

'Of course. Same rules?' She beamed at me, clearly unaware of the undercurrent of conflict that her mother and I were caught up in.

'Yes of course.'

'Sorry, give me two ticks; these guys were first.' As soon as she moved away to serve the other customers, Boat Bitch swooped.

'How do you two know each other?'

'She works here. I come here. We talk. It's called social interaction: you wouldn't understand.'

'Oh I fully understand Mister Trickett. Now what you need to understand, is that my daughter is off-limits to the likes of you, should you be harbouring any interests in that direction. Alas she's an awful judge of character and in a moment of weakness she might well choose charity over common sense, but she's not for you trust me.' Then, after a sideways glance to confirm Jess was still otherwise occupied, she took a step forward and leaned in really close - close enough that I could see each individual wrinkle of her crow's feet. I also got hit by a waft of coconut and a breathy sample of her champagne lunch. She still spoke softly, but with so much embedded vitriol I felt as if she'd grabbed me by the throat and was punching the words into me. 'So one last time, just to be sure you're in no doubt. Your well-being and your half-arsed business aspirations do not interest me in the slightest. I don't care about you, your Aunt's legacy or your misguided dedication to crumbling bricks and mortar. I will acquire your pub: the only question is how broken and broke you will be before I take it from you. Am I finally getting through to you, you fucking retard?'

This was practically hissed through clenched teeth and one of the nearby punters looked our way as if they thought they'd half-heard something awful; which they had.

It was now crystal clear - she meant business. Serious business. My first flash was anger, followed by an awareness of my surroundings, so didn't give the rage full rein. Part of me was also reluctant to demonstrate she could push my buttons to the extent she desired. Mustering the sternest look that I was capable of, I leaned closer until our faces were only centimetres apart and whispered. 'Go jump in the sea you mad cow.' For a moment she looked as if she was going to fly at me. Even with the tan, her face was fully flushed as if she had so much pent-up fury within her, there was no means of venting it without triggering The End of Days. And then she checked herself and took a

167

pace back, still with fists clenched. Then Jess appeared once again; the unknowing arbiter in the midst of our attrition.

'There you go Ken. Can I get you anything Mum?'

Boat Bitch took a deep breath then flicked her internal switch again, transitioning from Cruella de Vil to Mrs Doubtfire in a heartbeat. 'No thank you my dear, I must be getting along. I'll be in touch about Friday. Cheerio!' She turned to leave but stopped to face me, and in a tone as cold as her bed probably was, she simply said 'Goodbye Mister Trickett. I doubt our paths will cross again.' Then she left.

I took a large gulp from my freshly filled glass. Christ what an afternoon; I was struggling to process it all. So the object of my desires was the witch's offspring. The witch who I now knew to be genuinely hell-bent on my ruination. Shit. Shit squared in fact. I looked up to see Jess eyeing me curiously. Maybe she'd seen or heard more than I'd thought? Or perhaps she could hear me grinding my teeth in between mouthfuls of house red.

'Are you sure you two haven't met before? You seemed to have a lot to talk about. I like the name Trickett by the way.'

Careful Ken. It looks like she's no clue about you and her mother and there's no indication that she's inherited the Chief Bitch gene so don't screw up by spilling the beans. You can dwell on today's proceedings later but for now, some normality please. Deep breath.

'No never. We were just passing the time of day; talking weather, tropical fish, local architecture. Stuff like that.'

'Well that's a first. All she usually talks about is her business; which celeb bought which boat, how blatantly they chatted her up, how awful their wife's outfit was. That kind of thing.'

'Do you get involved in the business? Are you being groomed to take it over one day perhaps?'

'God no. I had that conversation a long time ago when Dad was running the business. Although he built it up and wanted to pass it on to someone that would look after it, he knew it wasn't for me. I'm one of those airy-fairy creative sorts remember. Mum was, and is, keener to keep it in the family when she's finished her stint. She keeps saying I should get more involved and get busy having babies - I'm an only child you see so I'm the end of the family line as things stand. But apart from doing the odd bit of admin at the yard from time to time, I just focus on not becoming a successful artist.'

'So how did your mother come to be head honcho?' I kind of knew the answer to this from mine and Janine's research the other morning but wanted the inside scoop. I'd settled down some from my brush with said mother and wanted to find out as much as I could - knowledge is power and all that. And the wine was helping to unravel my twisted nerves, as was simply sharing the same space with Jess, whom I still couldn't quite believe was associated in any way with Boat Bitch.

'Dad passed away five years ago. He had a heart attack at the yard - he was always working too hard. He loved what he did and was always overdoing it. One night he didn't come home for dinner, which Mum insisted he always did if he wasn't entertaining clients. She called the yard. One of the security guys did his rounds and found him dead at his desk.'

She was leaning on the bar as was I. Instinctively I reached out and patted her arm. 'How awful, so sorry.' I felt crappy for having asked the question in the first place.

She didn't flinch; just looked at me with slightly clouded eyes and a tight smile. 'It's okay. He had a good innings, and a good outing I think; looking out his window at the boats he built. He wasn't actually my real Dad but he was to me. I never knew my Father; Mum says he fled the scene as soon as she fell pregnant with me and flatly refuses to discuss him any further. They never married. I do wonder if he was where I got my artistic streak from as Mum isn't like that at all. So, I got a new Dad when I was eight and he never treated me as anything other than his own daughter. Mum had been working at SharpCrest for a few years before their paths crossed. They met at some swanky corporate do and I think Dad was a bit smitten and she was a real beauty so he gave her a try on the Sales team. Turned out she was bloody good at it so her career took off, as did her relationship with Dad. By the time he left us she was pretty much responsible for all the day to day stuff running the company. When he died, she threw herself into the business even more, determined to take over the world it seems. It's like she's always been angry with him for leaving her and uses that anger to fuel everything she does. She didn't used to have such a hard edge to her but now it's almost always there. Sometimes I have to remind her that she's talking to her daughter, not berating someone on her payroll for getting their timesheet wrong.'

Something approaching sympathy for Boat Bitch started to permeate my thoughts but I quickly expunged it. Losing a loved one doesn't give you carte blanche to behave appallingly: no sir. 'I guess there must be considerable "benefits" though? Your own mansion and all the lavish speedboats you could wish for?'

'Ah I see your game Mister Trickett.' She assumed a mock authoritative tone, sounded spookily like her mother. 'So you're fishing for some rich totty that can open the door to a globe-trotting lifestyle, chasing the sun in swish yachts while getting coked off your tits, or someone else's, then racing jet-skis. For shame!' Without asking, she refilled my glass then rested on the bar again, looking me in the eye. 'I'm neither rich nor totty Ken. Other than my pocket money when I was a kid, I've had no handouts. Dad never believed in money that wasn't earned.

Mum's always trying to fund me in some way or other but I prefer to make my own way. And my mansion is a small flat just off the High Street. So; sorry to disappoint.'

Adrenaline, alcohol and a rush of defiance teamed up with an attraction so strong it could arm-wrestle The Rock and I said: 'Can I take you to dinner sometime?'

CHAPTER SEVEN

As Thursday's went, this was going to be a biggie. The new gate for the yard was due to be delivered, as were the new units and equipment for the kitchen. The room was ready for them after several long days of Pat and Tim (his extra pair of hands) beavering away like, well; ants. The walls were clad, and the floor was vinyl or epoxy coated or some-such and it all looked spotless and eager for the next phase. Actually, there was one blemish in the form of Halo's footprint embedded in the floor from when she got curious before the new surface had completely set, but we'd all decided that was precisely the subtle detailing the room required to complete the makeover. Now it just needed fitting out, and I'd ordered up everything that Bruno and Pat had asked for, and then some. Also, the last of the really messy jobs had been completed, so normal traffic movement could be resumed between all the rooms downstairs. I'd even paid for a professional cleaning company to come in and go to town on the range and it looked like new afterwards. Even Bernie got a new lease of life, courtesy of a serious going-over with the cleaning guy's steam machine. We were getting really close to being food-ready and I was massively excited. Oh and of course I had a date that evening too which I had trouble contemplating without temporarily losing my mind and running around the room shouting 'YESS!!!!!' It had only been a couple of days since I'd been overcome with bravado and asked Jess out, but it felt like forever. The episode with Boat Bitch wasn't forgotten and I wondered what on earth might go down when she found out I was escorting her daughter to dinner, as she surely must at some point. I knew they talked - I'd seen it happen. But what could she actually do to prevent it? In fact, what could she really do to get her way with anything? Jess had a mind of her own and was clearly not easily for turning, and unless I surrendered to her mother's craziness, she had no leverage. I thought back to my moment of triumph when Jess agreed to the date: she scribbled her phone number on a coaster (a "Coasters" coaster no less) and passed it to me, just saying 'Thursday', then moved off to serve someone else. With a "My work here is done" sort of feeling, I'd knocked back the remains of my wine, got togged up and headed home. I chose not to share the details of my afternoon with Pat or J.D. - I would do in time but I didn't want to trawl through it at that point and tarnish the thought of my upcoming soirée with the goddess with recollections of her harpy mother.

 After a rather fidgety night, I wasn't at my perkiest. My thoughts had been dominated by Jess, and Boat Bitch to a lesser degree, plus I was awash with pre-match nerves ahead of today's major goings-on. I kept waking up to check the time, worried that I might oversleep and miss something important. I had also tossed and turned to a few weird dreams that took some time to shake off before I could settle back to sleep again. None of these were fluffy episodes. There was the one where I was competing on Mastermind and had to come up with six words that rhymed with orange during the compulsory fruit round. I'd named five but was really sweating the last one when without warning, I was transported to a live broadcast of "The Cube", materialising as a contestant trying to insert a bucket of USB plugs into a wall of sockets the right way up first time. I nailed it and the crowd went nuts, but then I got disqualified because I was wearing mismatched socks. Bastards. So; up early and rather groggy, I went down to the utility room and made myself the usual cuppa. That was my daily routine now - sure, I could have got a kettle and whatnot for The Crow's Nest and saved myself the travelling but I'd come to enjoy noodling around before anyone else turned up in the pub. Still in my pyjamas, I'd wander around acting like I owned the place, which I did. I'd always spend a few minutes in the kitchen picturing how it was going to be when the refit was complete, imagining the smells and the sounds as we cooked up our array of culinary treats that would delight the masses. And today we were going to take a huge step closer to getting there. And tonight I was going out; with Jess. 'YESS!!!!!' (cue some excited running around and spilling of tea). An event this momentous required some serious preparation however. No way was I going to show up in anything from my limited and knackered old wardrobe. Jess gave me no impression that was more about style than substance, but I didn't want to find myself wanting on either count if it could be avoided. Also, she was a model for God's sake. A model! So, today's activities would include a trip to town for some clothes shopping.

Yesterday I'd spoken to Jess on the phone after completing my exhaustive on-line research of every eatery from Pulton to John O'Groats and settled on "The Ariel", which I hoped was themed after the cartoon mermaid and not the laundry detergent. This was a cafe/restaurant which was actually right next door to "Coasters". The worst review of the place I'd come across on TripAdvisor was 'Our waiter was Colin who I'm sure I remember once gave me a wedgie at school. The tuna was to die for though. Two stars.' So, I decided I'd offer that up to Jess as option one and fortunately she approved of my choice. I was to meet her in there at eight.

Although sleep-deprived, I was still buzzing at the thought of the evening ahead so had to keep myself busy to help the time go by faster. Christ, I felt like I was off to the school disco with the hottest girl in my year. I couldn't talk from experience on that subject but imagined it would be rather awesome. As I remember, my school disco dates amounted to a weird ginger lass called Georgina who just wanted to see my penis and a nervous young lad called Charley who got drafted in accidentally after an epically-failed round of Chinese whisper-based invitations. He looked petrified the entire evening but thankfully had no interest in my penis. Actually I do remember getting off with the rather lovely Amy Cutler at the Christmas bash once. After a few Tizers and a snog, I tried to arrange a follow-up date but she announced she wouldn't be coming back for the new term as her family were moving to Singapore. I hoped such major relocation wasn't purely down to my kissing technique but decided not to ask the question directly. But tonight I had the pick of the school, not just my year, and we were going to the disco of food that I'd chosen. Or something along those lines. Right; it was time to hustle. Shopping would keep till later; I wanted to see the kitchen delivery in first. Also, J.D. was solo for the lunchtime shift and I didn't want to leave everything to Pat to sort out as he was busy doing real work, which I wasn't. What I really wanted was a balls-out crazy lunchtime session which would eat up the time very nicely, but that was doubtful today.

As soon as I heard movement downstairs, I made myself decent and headed down. J.D. was taking off his coat and nodded a 'hi' whilst Halo shuffled over to snort on my trainers by way of a similar greeting. J.D. took a look around the sparkling, equipment-ready kitchen.

'Looking good in here. Not long till we're up and running. We'll soon be saying goodbye to you Halo.'

For a second, I thought he was suggesting that Halo would feature on the menu somehow but then I realised that he was referring to her no longer being able to wander around as she wished. Even the most relaxed FSA inspector would take exception to a dog roaming the kitchen I'd imagine. As would the customers I assumed. I didn't want to bar her from the pub though as she was good to have around. Plus J.D. might decide to spend less time around the place if he couldn't bring his companion along. 'We'll work something out. Maybe put in a swing door or something to keep her in the bar. Either that or we'll get her some chef's whites so nobody's the wiser.'

'I'm sure Bruno would appreciate a kitchen hand. She'd certainly keep the floor clean.' He tossed his paper onto the counter. Fancy a cuppa?'

In spite of the hour, I actually fancied a large alcoholic something to settle me down but decided that ten hours of drinking probably wasn't ideal preparation for a first date. 'Yeah lovely thanks.' J.D. pottered off to the utility room with Halo in tow. I guessed we'd start the dog-free kitchen policy another day. Still keen to keep occupied, I scanned the bar to see if anything needed doing ahead of opening. As usual, everything was done and dusted. Even the chairs and tables were already arranged with the customary precision. He really did run a tight ship our J.D.; I was damn lucky to have him. Then came a muffled shout from out back.

'Is Earl Grey okay?'

'Well; he abolished slavery but reintroduced the House of Commons so I'm a bit divided.'

'I'll take that as a yes. Smart-arse.' (followed by a muffled chuckle).

Finding no way to employ my time productively, I started flicking through his newspaper. It yielded few surprises; just article after article describing atrocious behaviour by politicians and professional footballers, and revelations of which celebrity owned the most overweight pets.

J.D. appeared with two mugs. 'Oi! There's more to running a pub than leaning on the bar reading the paper!'

'Well you'd know: you've been doing it for years.'

He put a mug down for me then knelt to give Halo some affection. 'So; what's new in the world today?'

I was on the spot now - J.D. never failed with his headline gags and there were lad points at stake. 'Well apparently, there are concerns over Prince Phillip's mental state, having completed his tour of China without a single inappropriate comment to his hosts. And The Archbishop of Canterbury has declared Jesus to be bigger than One Direction, despite him having fewer followers on Twitter.'

'I was never a big fan to be honest. Too many gimmicks. That whole resurrection hoopla for example.'

I thought I'd done okay. Grabbing my mug, I yielded my position to J.D. who closed the newspaper and started reading from the front page. I was reluctant to disturb his morning routine and dilute the quality time he enjoyed with The Mirror but I wasn't in a quiet, do nothing kind of mood. So I blathered. 'Actually the real big news is, I've got a date tonight.'

'Bloody hell!' He started turning the pages in a theatrically frantic fashion. 'How come that didn't make the papers?' Then he gave me a genuine smile. 'Good for you. Who's the lucky troglodyte?'

I brought him up to speed on me and Jess. Just before I reached yesterday's events, Pat appeared from out back blowing on his own beverage. Having exchanged 'Mornin''s, I continued my saga, only interrupted once by Pat.

'I think the milk's off lads.'

'No it's Earl Grey.' said J.D. 'It always tastes that bad.'

'Oh right.' Pat stared into his mug whilst frowning and clicking his tongue against the roof of his mouth, either getting acclimatised to the unfamiliar flavour or expressing his dissatisfaction via some South African dialect. Then he shrugged and looked at me expectantly, keen to hear the next instalment of my saga.

I told them all, making a great deal of Jess's many attributes whilst not barring any holds when it came to my exchanges with Boat Bitch. Both of them groaned and dropped their heads when I dropped the bombshell of the family tie then snapped them upwards again aghast when I shared the less than delicate words that "Mum" had delivered while Jess was out of earshot. Then they followed up with a joint 'Yayy!' when I reached the finale of Jess giving me her number. We all sipped lukewarm tea for a few minutes while they processed what I'd revealed.

Pat spoke up first. 'You know her Mum will go bat-shit when she finds out about you two.'

'I know, but what am I supposed to do? Just bend over and take it? Give up on Jess just because her Mum's a psycho? Sell the pub to keep the peace and go back to my crappy old reality, shovelling numbers from one spreadsheet to another whilst praying for an early death?'

J.D. tried to lighten the mood. 'You should try for the threesome. I haven't seen Jess but her Mum's in pretty good nick. She might take pity on you when she's seen you naked and leave you be. Her Mum that is. Or maybe both of them. Actually I haven't really thought this through...'

'Yes thanks J.D. but I'm sure there's a better solution than peace through humiliation. I just don't know what that might be yet.'

Then Pat jumped in. 'Look; if you're serious about Jess, the only people that can really keep you apart is you or her - bollocks to her Mum or anyone else. As for the pub, what can she do? She's all mouth and no trousers if you ask me. If she keeps winding you up, then get the law on her: sorted.'

'Well, that is a tried-and-tested method for hooking the girl of your dreams; having her Mum arrested.' Once more I wondered what crime I'd committed in a previous life to deserve the insertion of the Boat Bitch spanner into the works of my life. All three of us fell silent again as we pondered possible outcomes, none of which revealed themselves with a rosy tint I was sure. I was damned if I did and damned if I didn't. Then our contemplation was interrupted by Guns 'n' Roses, as the opening riff of 'Sweet Child 'O Mine' blasted out of Pat's jeans.

He fished his phone out of his pocket. After listening for a few seconds, he answered 'Okay cool - be there in a mo.' Stuffing the device back into his trousers, he announced that the new gate had arrived. I think we all welcomed the news as an effective distraction from my current woes: romantic and otherwise.

Leaving J.D. to open up, I went with Pat for something to do. His mate Tim had collected the gate from the local builders' merchant and it was now lying on a flat-bed truck parked up in the back street behind the pub. It was a hefty beast, and took a fair amount of effort and swearing to wrestle it to the pavement and cart it down the alley to the yard entrance.

Pat grabbed some tools and then he and Tim set about removing the old gate which we then hoisted onto the truck. Fitting the new gate took a while. Firstly, it required some hefty fixings bolted into the walls of the yard entrance, then a lot of tweaking and adjusting to get everything aligned just right. This wasn't easy to do whilst holding a heavy timber gate that was made all the weightier by the steel trellis it wore as its outer skin. The sun was brightly doing its thing, but little of its output found its way past the narrow shade of the alley, so fingers went numb quickly too. The thing weighed a bloody ton, and we had to mount it then unmount it several times before we were done. But the work served as the distraction I was looking for, though I did have the recurring thoughts that my phone would ring and it would be Jess to say she'd changed her mind about the date. Or I'd suddenly drop to the floor in agony as Boat Bitch stuck a knitting needle into an effigy of me.

Thankfully neither had occurred, so far. And I was pleased with the gate - it even had a row of gnarly- looking metal spikes on the top to stop anyone clambering over. I'd seen far flimsier defences on most of the castles I'd visited as a kid on family days out I was sure. We now had both privacy and security for the yard. Or at least we would when Pat fixed the keypad entry thingy to it. Nobody was going to breach my tradesman's entrance without my say so (as it were) - a good job jobbed indeed. As a thank you, I treated Pat and Tim to a pint in the bar before they got back to it. This was also a good excuse to down a couple of drinks myself, just to help keep my excited twitchery in check.

In the end, it turned out to be a reasonably brisk lunchtime session, so I was happy to pitch in and share the load with J.D. Sure, we weren't under constant assault by wave after wave of desiccated alcoholics, but it was one of those shifts where you'd struggle to find time to restock, clear the empties or go for a pee if you were flying solo. But between the two of us, there was ample opportunity to cover off all those activities whilst comically trashing each other and the world in general. We also picked up this morning's conversation regarding the soap opera that my life had recently become, and I wanted to know what he really thought about the pub's potential predicament. He was the manager after all. 'Look; this thing with Boat Bitch. Threesome opportunity aside, what's your take on it?'

He knew I wasn't looking for humour this time. 'I think it's a real problem; and I think she'll continue to make your life a misery until you give in and sell. She clearly means business and she's got resources up the wazoo; which you don't. And a few nano-seconds after finding out you're dating her daughter, she'll send winged monkeys and snipers to track you down and take you out. First off, it was just about property: now it's about family too.'

I'd have preferred jokes as it turned out. 'Don't sugar-coat it J.D.: tell me like it is why don't you.'

'Look mate, it's a simple choice you have to make. Wimp out, or scrap for what you want. And I think there's a scrap in you - I saw how you were when she came into the pub and from what you say, you didn't budge an inch when she came at you yesterday either. You want my opinion? You fight; and you fight all the way. And if you're ever in doubt, just think 'What would Maddy do?' In your shoes, she wouldn't have budged a single damn inch. Not one. And I reckon we both owe it to her to do the same. Keep the pub: get the girl and keep me in the manner to which I've become accustomed, getting paid to do bugger all and read the paper.'

I could have kissed him. But didn't. He wasn't big on male bonding; that I learnt the one time I went in for a high-five and he looked at me like I'd asked him to join me in the shower. Instead, I grabbed two brandy glasses, added a generous shot to each and passed one to him whilst raising the other in salute.

'To Aunt Maddy.'

'To Maddy.'

We drained our drinks in one go, then planted the empty glasses on the counter with a bang. Here begins our crusade.

Around half three, as activity was winding down in the bar, noise and colour arrived at the front door and in bounced Janine accompanied by a couple more perky young things that I assumed to be friends from college.

I looked at my unadorned wrist then regarded her sternly. 'What time do you call this? We've been swamped! I even had to swear Halo in as a deputy.'

Of course she wasn't taken in for a second. Placing her hands either side of her face she acted distraught. 'Oh God I'm so sorry! I never meant to inflict you on the customers. Good job our trusty hound was here to save the day.' Having heard Janine's voice, Halo was now charging around from behind the bar to greet her. 'Now - we'll have three WKD Reds please barman and be lively about it! We've just done a complete bastid of an exam so are in need of light relief and much alcohol. Chop chop! Oh hello Halo you gorgeous girl!' She then dropped out of sight as she went to make a fuss of our resident hoover, whose excitement at seeing Janine I could judge by the hearty thwacking of her tail against the other side of the bar.

'Get out; you're all underage. And you'll find no alcohol here - 'tis the work of the devil himself.', all said with my best Witch-Finder General's tone as I reached into the fridge for the three bottles. 'How'd it go?'

Janine straightened up, very narrowly avoiding smacking her head on the rim of the bar. 'Fuckin' awful; right girls?' Her companions nodded in agreement whilst she did a quick sweep of the bar to see who might have overheard her colourful language. Fortunately, there was nobody looking her way in horror or sharing a tut with their partners. 'Oops sorry Ken. Brain mouth filter's in place now. How's tricks?'

'Pretty good I guess. Been busy trying to work out how I can replace the bar staff with robots to save money.'

'Great idea! Much lower risk of you getting reported for sexual harassment too.'

'Look; me shouting 'Nice arse!' every time you bend over isn't harassment. It's flattery. It's only harassment if I give it a smack as well. Anyway, I'm Italian so arse-slapping is actually mandatory behaviour.'

'Oh you slap away. If you're okay with me flicking you in the balls that is. I carry a magnifying glass for that very purpose. And you're as Italian as Homer Simpson.'

This back and forth could have gone on for hours, plus Janine's friends were clearly enjoying the jibes and the irreverent attitude she was displaying to her boss but we were interrupted by a new arrival. Judging by his uniform and the paperwork he was pointing at me, he was delivering something.

'Hi. I'm looking for a Mister Trickett. Delivery from ProChef?'

I stared at him blankly for a moment and was about to shout for J.D. who was out back somewhere, but then realised this was the kitchen equipment arriving. Large brandies for lunch are clearly highly effective at swiftly rendering you a bit clueless. 'Oh right yes, of course. Where are you parked?'

He pointed over my shoulder. 'Back street; truck's too big to fit out front.'

'Okay. Come round and I'll show you the side entrance.'

The cellar had a wide door that opened into the alley for taking in deliveries. Thankfully, J.D. had thought to clear a path from that entrance into the kitchen, something that hadn't even crossed my mind. A few minutes later, the delivery guy and a colleague started walking in an impressive selection of packages in all sorts of different sizes. Some of the larger ones (presumably the workbenches) took some time to thread through the cellar; yes, there was a thoroughfare but it was slim and there were barrels stacked either side which needed some re-arrangement to allow passage. Fortunately, we had plenty of additional manpower on hand in the form of Pat and Tim so after a lot of humping and shouts of 'To me, to me.', 'No no the other way.' and 'Ow bugger that's on my foot.' we were done, having amassed a respectable mountain of boxes. Blimey - did I really order all that? Was I refitting a kitchen or building a Death Star? Or refitting a kitchen on a Death Star? I didn't recall seeing a staff canteen in the films but they must have had one surely. I couldn't picture Darth Vader tucking into fish and chips - that mask would be a major hindrance. Perhaps he was a juicer. I bet those stormtroopers could put it away mind, although they did have their armour to fit into and that probably didn't come in XL. Still, I figure theirs was a high fat diet: if they'd spent all day munching carrots they'd have been able to actually hit something they fired at. But thanks to all the cheese burgers, they couldn't hit their own arse with a banjo.

'Mr Trickett?' The delivery guy was looking at me inquiringly as were all the others in the room. I must have zoned out for a while.

'Sorry yes?'

'The paperwork says we're to take the packaging away. Okay if we get cracking on opening it all up?'

I must admit, I was mad keen to see what was in all those boxes. I'd ordered piecemeal over the last few days in various states of sobriety so only had a hazy recollection of what I'd bought. Also, there was enough cardboard, polystyrene and polythene in the room to fill our wheelie bins twice over so it would be sensible to get shot of it. 'Sure. We'll pitch in.'

What followed was a good hour or so of Christmas Day type excitement as we all eagerly waded in and freed all manner of shiny objects from their trappings. We started with the biggest packages which were indeed the workbenches, and put them in position then stacked the smaller items on top of them. When we were done, we stood back and admired our sparkling pile. As well as the more architectural items like the benches and storage units, there was an extractor hood and bits of associated tubing, a chiller cabinet, a fridge, wash basins, a deep fat fryer and a wealth of different racks and shelves. And the cookware! Mercy - so many pans, trays and culinary implements of all designs. It was a physical manifestation of a Jamie Oliver wet dream; I'd imagine. At that point, J.D. poked his head around the door, took in the view and nodded appreciatively.

'Everything plus the kitchen sink. Bravo.'

Mentally I totted up what I'd spent. Well, they do say you should do one thing that scares you every day. It was a major investment but I was still sure it was worthwhile, even more so now I could see all the equipment in the flesh; or steel. The delivery team were keen to get going so we all mucked in and helped transfer the mountain of packaging to the back of their truck. I signed off the delivery sheet without checking off every item in detail - I knew the big stuff was all there. If I later discovered I was short of a colander or melon baller, it wouldn't be the end of the world. Delighted with the day's progress, I took the boys into the bar for a celebratory drink. I raised my glass and addressed the gang.

'Here's to us, and here's to food at "The Pulton Arms". Cheers!' We clicked glasses and slurped our beer then Pat spoke.

'You know; this time next week you could be actually serving up. If me and Tim crack on like we have been, we could be all done by midweek.'

'Awesome. If Bruno comes in Monday or Tuesday, unless he comes up with anything major, we'd be good to go. Bloody hell - can't wait to get started. Cheers again!' More celebratory glass clinking.

'Go steady on that there ale; remember you've got a date later on Romeo.' said Pat.

I grinned smugly. 'Indeed I do.' I went to take another gulp but then slammed the glass down on to the bar as a thought struck me with considerable momentum (sloshing Tim in the process). 'Crap! What time is it?' I scrabbled for my phone.

Pat simply looked at the clock on the wall behind me. 'It's quarter to six.'

'Bollocks! I needed to go clothes shopping for tonight! Bugger it.' What with all the kitchen delivery hoo-ha, it had completely slipped my mind. 'What am I going to do?'

'I could dig out the black suit you lent me for that funeral. How many hours can you breathe in for though? That was ages ago and you were thinner back then.' Pat said unhelpfully.

J.D. was equally as supportive. 'I'm sure I've seen an old wedding dress up in The Penis Palace. Lace and hairy legs is a great look. It works for Madonna.'

Janine was still propping up the bar with her mates, all of whom were looking flushed and jolly after a solid afternoon session on the sauce. She chipped in with 'Juzz go nekkid. Chips; no, chicks - chicks love nekkid bab.' Then she and her partners in crime collapsed in a fit of laughter that passed me by entirely. Bastards all.

Okay; I needed to get busy. MacGuyver or A-Team busy. After thanking all my cackling so-called friends for their support at such a difficult time, I rushed upstairs in full damage limitation mode. I had to decide on the most presentable outfit that was available from my paltry wardrobe; those outfit choices being further limited by virtue of the fact that I hadn't done any laundry for several days. Okay, take a breath - you can sort this. With that, I dashed back downstairs and grabbed a wine glass and a bottle of red whilst acknowledging my chorus of fools with nothing more than an upright middle finger. This just made them laugh all the more. Bastards all.

Back in The Crow's Nest, I poured myself a glass and considered my options. It was too late to go and buy anything new or wash anything old, so it really came down to whatever was cleanest and tidiest. I was still mentally birching myself for forgetting the trip into town, but took some solace in the fact that in an hour or so, I would be meeting a stunning young lady for dinner whilst again hoping she chose substance over style. In the end, my choice came down to the only pair of jeans hanging on the dryer and either of the two unsullied shirts hanging nearby. I'd worn the blue one the first time I'd met Jess in "Coasters"; the second was a checked number that looked a bit too lumberjack for a dinner date. Christ, this was tougher than Sophie's Choice. Sod it, blue one it is - hopefully she wouldn't remember it.

And then it was full-on body prep time - I preened like I'd never preened before. No inch of me went un-soaped and no orifice or crevice went deforested. I was cleaner and more de-fuzzed than an OCD bride on her wedding day. The butterflies were acting up now; the wine was helping but not winning. Come on Trickett; you're forty for Christ's sake, and this isn't your first date. You've been around the block a few times and you know how women work so grow a pair. Actually I didn't know how women worked; no man did. But, it's true I'd been on dates before. Maybe none as important as this one though. Come on, come on - it's going to be fabulous and magical and please please please don't screw it up you tool.

By the time I was finished getting ready, I was actually surprised by how presentable I thought I looked. This feeling was no doubt assisted by the few glasses of Chateau Lady-killer I'd sunk whilst getting ready, but overall I felt I'd scrubbed up rather well. I'd also deployed the last of the decent aftershave so was wafting like a good 'un. In particular, I was chuffed to find my jeans were noticeably looser than the last time I'd worn them, even though they still had that 'just-washed' tightness about them. My new, non desk-based career was clearly good for me (lunchtime drinking aside). With half an hour to go before I was due at the restaurant, I dropped into the sole armchair the lounge offered and got my thoughts together. For the first time since that morning, I thought about Boat Bitch and whether she'd really try and spoil my chances with Jess. This got me stressing briefly, but then I remembered J.D.'s earlier call to arms: I drained my glass with a flourish then went downstairs. Might as well say cheerio to my posse of cackling arseholes before I headed out into the romantic fray. I creaked my way down the stairs, all the way grinning and feeling blessed to have those cackling arseholes in my life.

'Oi Oi! Here's Prince Charming!' Janine was still loosely clamped to the bar, clearly now very much the worse for wear. There was no sign of her friends at first, but then I spotted them slumped together at a corner table, either embroiled in an intimate conversation or fast asleep. There was no sign of J.D.; I hoped he'd headed home to take a break. Simon was holding the fort behind the bar and clearly having fun with Janine; and Pat, who looked almost as smashed as she did.

'Evening Simon. Look haven't you two reprobates got homes to go to?'

Janine wrapped her arm around Pat's shoulders. 'We juzz wannid to wish ya good luck on your big date!' Not only was she slurring, but she appeared to have given up on the idea of keeping both eyes open. One looked loosely in my direction while the other periodically fluttered between almost shut and very shut. 'Go gedda bab!'

Pat raised his glass with her. 'Good luck man! Remember, if you can't find a condom small enough, there's always those wrappers that MacDonald's put round their straws.'

At that, the two of them butted heads and cackled like they were completely unhinged. Or just massively pissed.

'Thank you dear friends. I go forth to claim my prize, fortified with the knowledge that I have my friends as both emotional keystones and spiritual guides in my quest to secure love

195

and romantic fulfilment. Whilst also hopefully getting my leg over.' They both looked up at me; or near me; bleary and confused.

Then Pat sat straight and pointed at me and just answered with 'Gay!' Then they fell into each other and knocked heads again, laughing like hyenas on helium.

'Right; well - lovely to chat but I must away. Laters pissheads.' They didn't even look up; I'm not sure they even registered I was there any more. 'You okay with these two Simon?'

'Do what?'

I'd caught him on his more aurally-challenged side so I switched. 'You okay with these two?'

He frowned. 'Okay Doritos?'

I moved into his line of sight to give him a fair chance and spoke slowly and loudly, in the manner of a British tourist addressing a foreign waiter.

'Are you okay with these two? I have to head out.'

'Oh yeah sure. They're good entertainment. J.D. will be back later - we can take an end each if they need throwing out.'

'Good man. Any problems just call; my number's in the till.'

And then off I went, to my date with an angel.

CHAPTER EIGHT

Deciding to forgo my jacket due to its age and scruffiness, I ventured out just in my shirt (plus trousers etc.). That decision ensured a speedy door-to-door journey of little more than ten seconds, so I arrived at "The Ariel" about quarter to eight. All good - one should always be installed before the lady arrives I feel. The place was welcoming enough, with what I guessed to be a Mediterranean theme with brown stone-tiled floors and marble table tops, and bold artworks decorating the walls and perching on pedestals dotted around the place. There were all kinds of delightful smells swirling around reminding me that I'd not eaten yet today. My intake had all been liquid so far which wasn't ideal. Remember Ken - don't screw this up.

Having given my name to the smiley young thing that greeted me at the door, I was led upstairs and directed to a corner table that was perfect for what I hoped would be an intimate encounter. Having ordered a large gin and tonic, I sat there appreciating the decor, whilst the butterflies did their thing in my oh so empty stomach.

I was only a few sips into my drink when Smiley Young Thing came back up the stairs with Jess in tow and directed her to our table. I smiled as I stood to greet her. She leaned over the table and put her hand on my arm while I went in for the air kiss. Feeling brave I brushed both cheeks. Wow; she smelled divine.

'Ooh get you, continental Ken!'

'That's what they call me. Least they did in prison. How are you?'

'You feel cold. I'm good thanks - long shift so I have sore feet and I'm bloody ravenous!'

She looked stunning; positively edible in fact. She was wearing a short, strappy black dress that was better suited to a Summer cocktail party than a freezing February evening on the sea front but man, she wore it well. Her makeup and jewellery were minimal and classy and her hair was loose, flowing straight then breaking into curls as it neared her shoulders. Suddenly, I was all too aware of my scruffy-by-comparison efforts and gave myself a mental kicking for failing to shop. 'You look fantastic Jess. Sorry if I look a bit tatty: I'm still waiting for my wardrobe to be shipped over from Milan. Oh and yes I didn't bring a coat - rookie mistake.'

She gave me a quick look from head to toe then sat down. 'Well you look just fine to me. I like that shirt on you; it's a fabulous colour.' (Nuts; she did remember it). 'You wore it the second time I saw you in the bar. I remember it because it matched the walls. Could I have a gin and tonic please?' Smiley Young Thing departed to get her order.

'I'm glad you approve. I remember that visit very fondly.'

'Oh god I was a nightmare! You'd only been there ten seconds and I was already wanging on about my mother and dog-sitting whilst getting your name wrong. I was ridiculous!'

'Not at all. Better that than just commenting on the fish tank, which has been my favoured opener to date.'

She folded her arms and leaned towards me with her elbows planted on the table. 'Flirting doesn't get any easier with age does it? I must admit I thought you were a bit odd the first time you came into the bar, but you made up for it on the second visit.'

I mirrored her pose. 'I was the ridiculous one the first time. And no it doesn't seem to. Though I must say I've never been more pleased with the outcome. Oh and how are the fish?'

'Still stinky. Okay come on - feed me.'

As if on cue, a waitress appeared with the menus and Jess's drink. 'Could we have some humus to share while we're looking at these? I am so hungry. Is humus okay with you?'

'Yep fine.' I was actually a humus fan but if she'd suggested Domestos shots I'd have happily gone with it.

She clapped her hands quickly then clasped them together, seemingly thrilled by the prospect of browsing the menu and ordering most of it. 'So so hungry. Are we vino?'

'Sure.'

Without looking up from her menu, she slid the wine list my way. 'I'm no wine snob; don't understand it. White for choice but I'll go red if you prefer.' Right now, she was coming across as abruptly as her mother tended to; not a likeness I was keen to dwell on. But with Jess it was different; she was clearly ravenous and sufficiently comfortable around me to not waste time on unnecessary formality or niceties; and even her briskness had an underlying warmth to it.

'No white's fine with me.' Scanning the list, I picked out something I was familiar with that didn't cost the earth then turned my attention to the menu. Blimey; what didn't they do? The choice was mostly Italian, but there were also Thai dishes and a long list of specials that comprised all manner of seafood, steaks and burgers. Looking at the prices, they were pitched rather higher than I was looking to charge at the pub; possibly just targeting the tourists' wallets primarily. I mean, £14 for an omelette? I'd expect it to be topped with unicorn shavings for that price. Which it wasn't. 'So is this place one of your favourite haunts?'

'Uh-huh.'

She was obviously concentrating hard on her dinner choice, so I gave up on conversation for the moment and set about my own selection, whilst taking the occasional peek at her because well; the view was lovely, even though it was mostly just the top of her head. After a couple more minutes of quiet contemplation, she suddenly sat bolt upright and slammed the menu shut.

'Right! I'm fish and chips! And you now have my undivided attention.' Just at that moment, the waitress appeared and placed dishes on the table bearing our humus and a stack of toasted pittas. 'Actually scratch that; nobody can compete with food when I'm this famished.' She tore off a lump of bread, scooped up a hearty portion of humus with it and wolfed it down. As she chewed, she rolled her eyes and made appreciative rumbling noises. 'Oh my god that's good. I so needed that. Okay - now I truly am all yours. Go on, dig in before I inhale the lot.'

'Hi, I'm Kathy, and I'll be looking after you this evening. Are you ready to order?' The waitress hovered with pen poised over her notepad.

I made that (probably outrageously sexist) "Ladies first" gesture with my hand to invite Jess to order before I did.

'Could I have the battered cod please, but with fries instead of the salad? Thanks.' She clapped her hands again in anticipation.

'No starter for you madam?'

'No thanks: I'm about to hoover up a large bowl of humus. Sorry, I mean "share" a large bowl of humus.' She gave me a wicked grin.

'And for you sir?'

'Likewise, no starter thanks. And I'll have the lobster ravioli. And a bottle of the Springfield Sauvignon Blanc. Thanks.'

'Lovely. Enjoy your humus and I'll be back with your mains in a short while. Can I bring you some water?'

I looked to Jess who wrinkled her nose and shook her head. 'No thanks, just the alcohol. We don't have school tomorrow.'

Kathy collected the menus and scuttled off, pausing at the top of the stairs to let Smiley Young Thing and another couple pass to be seated. I'd sort of unreasonably hoped that we'd have the room to ourselves but a bit of company would add to the atmosphere I supposed. After another big scoop of humus, Jess glugged her drink and took a deep breath.

'Right - I'm just about human again. Sorry; I do enjoy my food but I'm not really such an awful pig - it's just been one of those days today and I've not had chance to stop and eat. I was late getting home so only had time to rush about like a mad thing and get ready. My bedroom looks like a tornado's been through it; you should see the mess.'

'I appreciate the invitation but can we eat first?'

She put a splayed hand to her chest and adopted her best Georgia accent. 'Well, I do declare Mister Trickett! Would you be propositioning this young girl? Shame on you. Ah shall be shaw to cover ma ankles the next time we meet so as nat to provoke such shameless be-hayvya.'

Beautiful, smart and funny - how did I get this lucky? 'Worry not miss, your virtue is quite safe with me. At least until we've finished dessert.' (I didn't attempt the accent; I'm crap at those). I tore off some pitta and sampled the humus which was delicious, and reminded me once more that today had been a rather liquid affair. I felt good though; yes a few drinks under my belt but I was still sharp, and things were going well. Ridiculously well in fact.

'Well that's reassuring. And to answer your first question properly, yes I do like this place. Food's good and the paintings are interesting.'

'They're not very landscapey.'

'I tend to do landscapes because that's what I'm best at but I enjoy all sorts of subjects. Are you arty Ken? Or indeed, farty?'

'I used to be. Arty that is; when I was a youngster. But my folks were keen on me getting what they would call a real job so pushed me into the sciences, history, languages and all that. I ended up in the money business.'

'Really - so what job did you do?' Bless her she actually looked interested; time to burst that bubble alas.

'I was a Senior Analyst for a leading financial services company.' I steeled myself, ready to stop her head hitting the table as boredom instantly robbed her of her ability to stay awake. But instead:

'Ooh fascinating! Tell me absolutely everything - I want to know all about the rogue trades and the credit crunches. Gordon Gekko, Wilf of Wall Street, Orange Tuesdays - all that.' And all this without the slightest hint of sarcasm. Bloody hell - maybe she really was interested.

'Okay, but only if you lift the lid on the world of modelling: all the champagne breakfasts, the cocaine lunches and the cat fights behind the catwalks.'

'Deal!'

So we talked. For a good few hours we talked, and laughed, and enjoyed ourselves and each other immensely. The food arrived and it was perfectly lovely but we were so busy chatting it really wasn't the main event it was intended to be. We did justice to the wine though - one bottle became two which somewhat rashly became three. I couldn't remember the last time I'd enjoyed someone's company so much and it felt as if Jess was just as into me as I was into her. There was nothing forced; no 'We've only just met' type awkwardness - we just clicked and the conversation came so easily. She was fascinating; and at the same time genuinely invested in what I had to say. I was bombarded with questions about how things worked in the financial markets and how come all the crooks running the banks got away with it and why did share prices move around all the time. This coaxed me onto some tricky ground as I tried to explain marginal utility vs. total utility and the diamond-water paradox at which point she did start to glass over a little. Thankfully, I managed to eject us both from that topic with a rather clumsy but effective 'Oh most of its bullshit you know?' And she was full of tales of botched photo-shoots and creepy photographers working out of seedy little studios. She did reveal that she'd done some "classy" glamour shoots when she was younger but that it didn't sit right with her as she didn't like the thought of the less artistically-focused menfolk perving over her portfolio. Or indeed doing worse over it. At that point, it occurred to me to find out her surname so I could narrow my later Google image search accordingly. (Yeah like you wouldn't).

'So it's Jess... what? Do you use some showbizzy pseudonym for modelling purposes? Something like "Blaze McQueen"?'

'Ha ha - that sounds more like a rodeo rider. It's Jess Worthy, courtesy of a guy I married who turned out to be anything but. That ended years ago, but I've just never got around to changing back to my maiden name. All that faff with the driving licence, banks and passports: bleugh. Oh and I was born Jess Starkey.'

This tack led us onto a more deep and meaningful discussion about relationships and our history with those, both good and bad. The more we talked, the less conscious of our surroundings we became. We were just all about each other. Around the time of bottle three arriving, we slightly lost our way when I confused Anna Karenina with Anna Kournikova, but otherwise it was all grand. And we became closer physically as well as emotionally, with all manner of brushes on the arm and even some brief hand-holding at times. Inevitably, her mother cropped up in conversation occasionally but it was clear that Jess had no inkling of the bad blood that existed between Boat Bitch and me. I seem to recall the restaurant got quite busy as the evening went on and vaguely remembered one or two performances of 'Happy Birthday' happening around us, but that was all just slight interference happening way way off in the background.

With the wine and the Irish coffees done, alas we were forced to return to the world. As if emerging from hibernation, we both stretched, yawned and looked around and realised there was nobody else in the room other than our waitress who was stationed at the top of the stairs with a look that essentially communicated 'I'm over the moon that you're having such a fabulous time, but could you please bugger off so I can finish up and go home?'

Jess tipped her head back and rolled out a few neck circles then straightened up. 'Well Mr Trickett. You know how to show a girl a good time, but all marvellous things must come to an end, and what I need right now is a pee and my bed.'

'Okay; to save you combining the two, why not go to the loo while I pay the bill?'

'Good plan, the next one's on me though.' She stood up with a slight wobble then made for the stairs rather unsteadily as the waitress came over to point her credit card machine at me.

'Did you enjoy your meals Sir?'

'You know what Katie? Everything was absolutely out of this world.'

After getting my credit card PIN wrong a couple of times, I got there in the end and added a stupidly generous tip. What the hell - it had been a bloody awesome evening and worth every single penny. And Kelly had looked after us splendidly.

When I got downstairs, Jess was coated and ready to go. 'Well, thank you so much Ken -

dinner was gorgeous and the company was exquisite. I would suggest finding a club and dancing the night away but I'm in the wrong shoes and I do have to work tomorrow. Also, I'm not sure where you can go to dance in Pulton at this time of night, unless you're happy to join in with the Tennents Super Appreciation Society who tend to leap around the bus station after hours.'

'Tempting: but maybe another night. Let me walk you home.'

'You haven't got a coat you numpty: you'll freeze.'

'I'll be fine. That SAS endurance training stays with you.'

'What?! You worked for that Scandinavian airline? Or were you involved with Surfers Against Sewage? Let's grab another table, we clearly still have much to talk about.'

'Come on, I'll be okay. I could do with walking off the pasta.' I slipped my arm through hers and steered her towards the door before the staff turned aggressive.

Yes, it was bastard cold to be honest but the alcohol was keeping it at bay reasonably well. Also, we didn't have far to go - once we hit the High Street and jumped another street across we were at Jess's flat. She really was only a few minutes' travel from the pub. This was a good thing.

'This is me.' she said, pointing at a bay window that overhung the car port beneath. 'It's not much, but it's home. And it's quiet.' At which point she belched noisily, and intentionally, and then got overtaken by a giggling fit which took a good while to subside. 'Sorry - couldn't resist.' Then she collapsed into laughter again whilst I stood there all smiles; falling for her more and more each minute that passed. After some time and a few deep breaths, she managed to calm herself down. 'Well; thank you again, and thank you for being gallant enough to walk me home. I do hope nothing freezes off during your walk back.' She was on the brink of another giggling marathon but just managed to keep it in check.

'Jess it was my pleasure. All of it. I had a really great time you know?'

And then the laughter was gone and she was looking at me with an entirely straight face. 'I did too. Can we do it again soon? Please?'

'Abso-bloody-lutely.' I leaned in to give her a goodbye peck on the cheek but she intentionally turned her head at the last minute to ensure I caught her full on the lips.

'Wow: what did I do to deserve that?' I was a little breathless and delightfully surprised.

'You were just you: chatty and interesting, but not obviously just trying to get into my knickers. I knew you'd turn out to be a good one. And you can't go wrong with a Ken - my Dad was one. Night night.' With that she kissed me again,

then disappeared into the darkness of the car
port.

I must have stood there for a good five
minutes before I regained enough of myself to
walk home. My God, what a fantastic evening:
and what a wonderful woman.

I weaved my way home, feeling like all was very
much well with the world. Even the dark cloud of
Boat Bitch's oppression had dissipated; maybe
all that nonsense was done with and I could now
just focus on running the pub and wooing Jess. I
still wouldn't be rushing to meet the parent
though, obviously. Although, maybe if Jess told
her what a great evening we'd had together and
what a good all-round sort I was, she'd decide to
put her daughter's happiness first and back off.
And Jess's Dad had been a Ken too - I didn't
recall his first name cropping up during mine
and Janine's brief research session on her laptop.
Maybe that's what was really behind Boat Bitch's
animosity towards me? I remembered Jess
saying that her mother was angry with him for
passing away and leaving her alone; perhaps
hearing the name Ken again just added fuel to
that particular fire and its accompanying ire? Ah
who knows. What I did know was that I'd found
this gorgeous girl who liked me back, and there
was no way I was giving up on her and
disappearing quietly into the night without
putting up a fight. Ridiculously, I stopped and

peered into "Coasters" window; just paying homage I suppose as I knew my lady couldn't possibly be in there as the bar was very shut. With the cold starting to find its way through my wine-based insulation, I stopped mooning and strode off back to the pub. I may have skipped at one point. Possibly twice.

I was just nearing the front door when J.D. appeared from the alleyway. Feeling rather splendid after my spiffing evening, I offered up a suitably jovial welcome. 'Hail fellow! Well met! I trust I find you in good spirits on this, the most excellent of all nights?' But there was no snappy comeback; no jibe at my expense. As I got closer, I could see there was no humour about him at all, only a grave expression.

What's up?'

'Come with me.'

With that he turned and led me into the darkness of the alley. On reaching the entrance to The Gents', he unlocked the metal gate and reached into the doorway, hunting for the light switch within. As the bright strip lights flickered into life, I couldn't see with any clarity as my vision took time to transition to that sudden brilliance after the darkness outside. Before me there was only a fuzzy blob of dazzling white light, smattered with red splotches. And then my focus returned, and I was struck incredulously dumb as the scene revealed itself. As I took a couple of tentative steps forward into the doorway, J.D. moved aside to let me by.

All around me was the word "SELL!", shouted in red spray paint, repeated hundreds of times, covering every inch of wall and ceiling space. Even the urinal itself hadn't escaped attention; likewise, the small hand-basin in the corner and the toilet cubicle. The floor wasn't unscathed either, sporting a handful of red puddles where the surface was still too wet from its end-of-session mop down for the paint to take. This was desecration on a grand scale and I managed to do little more than stare at it slack-jawed as I struggled to take in what I was seeing. I looked at J.D. who was also surveying the ruin, just shaking his head. 'J.D. - what the actual fuck happened in here?'

'I dunno. It was all fine when I did the mid-session splash and dash, and none of the punters mentioned anything was out of order after that. I found it like this when I went to lock up. Bastards must have done it around closing time. They must have turned up mob-handed - they'd still be at it now otherwise.' He walked over to the red-splashed dispenser and grabbed a couple of paper towels which he then wetted under the basin tap. After some vigorous scrubbing at a small patch of wall tile, he'd managed to shred his makeshift cleaning cloth without dislodging a scrap of the spray paint. 'This is going to take some shifting.'

I was still working hard at processing what was in front of me. But I was in no doubt that this was Boat Bitch escalating our 'negotiations'. Maybe I'd upped the ante by pursuing her daughter against her Mother's wishes, but it was clear she still intended to get her well-manicured mitts on my pub. But why this? Why such mindless defilement of Pulton's historic finest? It was pathetic and childish - schoolyard level guerrilla warfare; and I was absolutely fuming. Sure, bring your bruisers into the bar and throw some insults around, at least that shows some balls. But this was just abhorrently underhand and spineless. 'Okay; if this is the level she's dropped to, then I can go there too. She's not getting away with this J.D. No. Fucking. Way.'

'Looks like they tried to get into the yard; the new gate's seen some action. You going to call the plods?'

It was too dark to see a whole lot, but I could just make out a web of scratches around the entry key pad and the hinges. I'm wasn't sure this was so much evidence of breaking and entering, rather just some extraneous damage they added to piss me off even more. Either way it worked; I'd spent a small fortune on that gate and it hadn't even been up a day yet. Wankers. 'I dunno. What do you think?' I was sure that if any good citizens of Pulton had seen anything iffy going on they'd have made a noise about it in the pub. Also, as confident as I was that this was Boat Bitch's doing, I had no proof whatsoever.

There was no record of the exchanges we'd had to date so my evidence was zilch. It would just be my word against hers. Getting the police involved wasn't the way to get to her.

'I'd report it. You don't have to mention her. Best to get it on record though.'

He was right. If things escalated, I'd lose credibility when it was found that I hadn't reported previous incidents. 'I'll call them. You okay to hang around? They'll want to talk to you more than me probably.'

'Yeah sure. Come on; let's get a drink. Halo's probably busting for a wee too.'

I called the police; they came; and I lied about having any idea who might have caused the damage. It was hard to bite my lip, as I was still irate over the assault on something I held so dear. Luckily the focus was on J.D. as expected, so I wasn't required to say a lot; otherwise I might have cracked and implicated Boat Bitch there and then. While I stood there listening to J.D. give his statement, in my mind I was swimming the channel to SharpCrest Marine to take a wrench to anything and everything of value.

The officers that turned up were very attentive and seemed genuinely concerned about the vandalism - not a common event on the quay according to them, and certainly not on our scale apparently. All the questions you would expect were asked, then they inspected the crime scene and snapped plenty of pictures. They wrapped up their visit by suggesting we put a notice up in The Gents' and the bar with the local police number to call should anyone have any information that might help identify the perpetrators. Other than that, with so little to go on they couldn't offer us much else, though they did say they'd try and roll around our way the next few nights near closing time to check nothing was amiss.

By the time the police were done and gone, me and J.D. were both flagging, so we said our goodnights and he headed home. I locked up and poured myself one for the road which I took upstairs to The Crow's Nest, rightly confident that as weary as I was, I'd be too wired from the day's events to get much sleep.

What an end to an otherwise perfect evening. I had to put an end to this crap: somehow.

CHAPTER NINE

'Well; it's not completely shagged.' This was Pat's expert assessment of the damaged gate; that expertise somewhat dulled by the happy hour(s) he'd enjoyed with Janine yesterday, the blame for which he placed squarely at her door. Correspondingly, Janine had laid responsibility firmly with Pat as soon as she'd walked through the door this morning, looking like death warmed up. You see, a bar is both the worst and the best place to be when you're suffering a hangover sizeable enough to warrant its own post code. First off, just the faintest whiff of anything alcoholic could have you running for the toilet to void yourself of the breakfast you never wanted but someone said would 'sort you right out'. But once you progressed beyond that stage, there were any number of options available to you in the form of 'a hair of the dog'. Both Pat and Janine were still at the delicate "loo-sprint" stage, so made themselves look busy whilst actually achieving little more than some shuffling about and tea drinking. Ah well; they turned up at least. Truth be told, I wasn't the sharpest tool in the box either. It had been a boozy day yesterday. Actually they'd all been boozy days recently. For the sake of my liver and my profit margin, I needed to dump that routine. As expected, I'd had a fitful night too; waking up frequently then struggling to nod off again. My brain was busy with soft-filtered visions of Jess at dinner whilst Boat Bitch shrieked and cackled in the background as if auditioning for the part of The Wicked Witch of the West. Or The Child Catcher from "Chitty Chitty Bang Bang". I was wound up further by my recurring dream; the one where I'm being chased by a fiercely amorous Taylor Swift, who in turn is being pursued by a pack of alarmingly-fanged, clearly ravenous wolves – do I stop or don't I? A confusing and ultimately exhausting scenario. Also, I think I did something to my hamstring during last night's re-run. So, safe to say, mentally I was in a jumbled state that morning and physically only marginally more functional than my team-mates. Apart from J.D. that is; he turned up looking his usual perky self and made sure the rest of us did what was needed via some short, sharp stage direction: 'Fridge 1 is knackered, so stock Fridge 2 please Janine.': 'Oh and can you put a new optic on the Malibu?': 'Ken; stop picking that or it won't heal.'

I'd arrived downstairs early, keen to see the horrendous damage in daylight. Well, not keen as such, but needing to know its full extent. Unlocking the gate to The Gents', I took in what was an even more distressing sight now the scene was better illuminated. The red letters stood out vividly against their white backdrop. Christ, what an appalling mess. Well that was my weekend spoken for. On the plus side, there didn't appear to be any physical damage other than the graffiti, but that was meagre comfort to be honest. Depressed, I closed up and inspected the gate to the yard. It hadn't taken a battering - that would have been too noisy I supposed, and I still wasn't sure whether the culprits had really been trying to access the yard in the first place. The entry code key pad was sitting rather crookedly as if someone had tried to wrench it off. One of the gate hinges was also sitting at a weird angle as if an attempt had been made to jimmy that too. Hopefully Pat would be able to fix all that. I didn't try to open the gate in case I exacerbated the damage, so instead wandered back in through the front door.

I carried out my usual daily survey of the up and coming kitchen which always helped the mood - this morning especially. It really was getting close to being fit for action. And then my phone buzzed to announce an incoming message; possibly an alert of some sort heralding the onset of the Robo-Apocalypse. Or should that be Robocalypse? Anyway – it turned out to be a very welcome text from Jess.

"Morning handsome. My head hurts. You up for a quick coffee before my shift? Busy all w/end 'cos dog sitting. Cafe on the Quay at 11? x"

I knew the place; it sat beneath the abominable apartments so was guilty by association, but I decided I'd overlook that offence just this once. This was good news - not only did it mean Jess was still oblivious to my sparring with her cast-iron bitch of a mother but also, she was keen to see me again, even when sober. Score! Also, if I'd interpreted the text speak correctly, she wasn't available over the weekend so it would be good to get a fix to help me through the next few days. I replied.

'Morning beautiful. Sounds good - see you there! Xx'

I spent a while debating whether two kisses were too over the top and trying to decide whether a single was the safer bet. Also, the first "x" kept automatically capitalising itself which I didn't like, and I couldn't work out how to correct that behaviour. "Xx" seemed a bit shouty, whereas "xx" struck the correct level of saucy refinement to my mind. In the end, I flung caution and technological duncery to the wind and succumbed to "Xx". So; I had another date. And I had to make sure not to be weird after last night's attack on the pub, even though that ghastliness was still uppermost in my thoughts. Right now, Jess and Boat Bitch existed in two different, unconnected worlds. At least that was how I decided to approach it, stubbornly refusing to let one scenario colour the other. Its true I wasn't at all comfortable embarking on what I hoped would be a lasting relationship with Jess with an already well-developed hidden agenda, but I decided to justify this to myself by virtue of the fact that I wasn't actually lying - I was just being selective with the facts I chose to share with her. I didn't really manage to convince myself on that one either. At some point, the two worlds would undoubtedly collide but hopefully that would be at a point in the future where Jess had already decided I was the man for her no matter what, and the cheese had somehow found its way back onto her mother's cracker.

As we neared opening time, I gathered everyone together and talked them through last night's events. Both Pat and Janine were characteristically profane in their character assessment of the culprits. J.D. knew the story so just listened on, but raised a valid point that my befuddled brain hadn't even considered.

'I reckon we should keep The Gents' closed until we've cleaned up in there. We don't want customers seeing that mess and asking a whole bunch of questions about it.'

'Fuckers!' spat Janine, still frothing from the news.

'Good idea J.D. The Ladies' will have to double up for now. And Janine? Yes - you're absolutely right. Can we put some signs up? About the loos that is - not the fuckers.'

At that point, I took Pat outside to show him the damage and get his thoughts. He reckoned it was fixable without too much effort which was good news, but he had some sobering words to add.

'Look me old; this shit is just getting deeper. I'll do what I can to help, you know that, but when the kitchen's done I'll have to move on to the new contract. Gate repair doesn't pay the bills on its own you know. You need to stop playing nice with this nightmare woman and send her a message she can't ignore. I dunno what, but something's got to be done. Okay you don't want the law involved I get that; but what are you going to do?'

'Right now I don't know mate. But I hear you - I'm not rolling over any more. I'll give her that message; you can bet on it.'

We both stood in silence, outwardly appearing to study the gate's war wounds but both no doubt actually thinking of ways we might end Boat Bitch's campaign of harassment. Then Pat suddenly spun in my direction; a manoeuvre that he instantly regretted as his headache reverberated around his skull. Wincing; with his eyes closed, he spoke very softly.

'I forgot to ask: how was the date?'

'It was the best, mate. She's the best. I walked her home and when I went to.. Shit!'

'When you went to shit what?'

'No I mean shit I think I'm late.' I was wrestling my phone from my pocket, suddenly

221

acutely aware that I had somewhere else to be. I so needed a watch; or looser jeans at least. 'I'm supposed to be meeting Jess for a coffee at eleven.'

It was ten minutes to. 'I've got to go mate; do what you can with the gate please and we'll sort out the cash later. I know I owe you big time; for everything.'

He grinned. 'What are friends for? Now go get the girl. I'll expect a detailed report on the date later mind, including points of insertion and fluids exchanged.'

I fired off a cheery 'Pervert!' as I sped back to the bar.

Shortly afterwards, I arrived at the cafe, flushed and puffing from an energetic half-walk/half-run along the quay. This was the first time I'd been inside the place so took a few moments to take stock. As much as I'd wanted to hate it for being part of such a gruesome establishment, it actually all looked rather appealing. Modern, but without coming across as sterile. Wood floors and furniture with a bright blue-fronted counter and a large collection of nautically-themed watercolours covering most of the wall space. It was busy too; clearly a popular hangout for the late breakfast or early lunch crowd. More competition for the pub dammit. And then I spotted Jess, seated at a table near the front window that overlooked the yacht wankers' marina and the harbour beyond. She smiled and waved me over; all bundled up in her customary red winter attire.

I was going to go in for a peck on the cheek but was unsure of second date protocol so hesitated. She'd also just picked up a giant cup of something steaming with both hands so I decided to just sit down rather than run the risk of dislodging her drink with catastrophic results. 'Top of the morning to you ma'am.' She narrowed her eyes at me over the brim of her cup as she took a sip.

'I hate you. You forced alcohol down me against my will and now my head's all sore and now I have to go to work with a sore head. I thought you were a gentleman but it turns out you're simply a purveyor of evil, hell-bent on leading young women astray to satisfy your own disingenuous urges.'

'Young women? Where?'

Her eyes relaxed as if she were smiling again, though it was hard to tell as she didn't seem to want to move her cup more than a few millimetres from her lips. 'I hate you even more now. Hope this place is alright - I don't really like the modern bits of the quay but they do the best coffee outside of Seattle and it's on the way to work; sort of.'

I rested my elbows on the table and leaned forward whilst flashing what I hoped was my most charming smile, at the same time trying to remember whether I'd brushed my teeth or not. 'How are you feeling really?'

'Much better than I'm pretending to be.' She placed her cup on the table so I got to see her full face at last. She was make-up free and had a 'not long out of bed' look about her; and she looked fantastic. 'How are you doing?' At that moment a waitress appeared at the table.

'Good morning! What can I get you?'

'Just a cup of tea please.'

'Which would you like? We have Green Tea, Red Berry, Chamomile, Peppermint, Mandrake Root, Uncle Jerry's Nose Leaves...' Still captivated by Jess, I hadn't given the waitress my full attention so may have misheard some of the lengthy selection that she trotted out. I just wanted normal tea, like I had at home. Believing I'd heard a variety that had "breakfast" in the title, I went for that. It probably came with a fried egg for dunking but I could work around it.

'I'm doing okay. Bit of a late night in the end. No peace for the wicked.' Then I thought I'd test the water some to see if she had any inkling of what had occurred at the pub last night. 'We had the police round after closing; somebody vandalised The Gents' loo and sprayed a bit of graffiti around.' I didn't offer up any more detail.

'No way; how awful! Did they catch who did it?' She seemed genuinely appalled, and I then felt terribly guilty for even thinking that she could have had any clue about what had transpired. After all, I was the deceitful bastard hoarding all the secrets, not her.

'Nope; 'fraid not. The Gents' is sort of outside so you can't see it from the pub. No clues alas.'

'What a bunch of bastards. I hate that kind of mindless crap. Probably just arsehole kids playing up because their shit-head parents didn't teach them any better. Sorry about the language; I get a bit sweary when I'm hungover.'

'No problem. Your terminology's on the money I'd say.'

My tea then arrived; also in an over-sized cup to match Jess's. For no good reason at all, I leaned down and gave it a long sniff. 'Lovely; thanks.' I looked up to meet confused looks from both Jess and the waitress. 'Oh it's just a sinus thing.' The waitress departed. 'Sorry - I sniff things for no reason when I'm hungover.'

'Oh God I'm dating a freak!' She reached out and squeezed my hand. 'I'll try and get you the help you need.' Said with dollops of fake sincerity.

Her words weren't lost on me - one in particular. 'So it's official? We're dating now?'

Her look then morphed into a far more serious expression, and she sat bolt upright with her arms folded. 'Well I'd assumed so, seeing as we've been out on a date and both agreed that we're going to do it again. Or have I got the wrong idea?'

I was confused: sure, we were both rather tacky from last night and still getting to know each other, but I felt like I'd unwittingly screwed up somehow. And screwed up big style. 'No, not at all. Jess what's wrong?' I sat back in my seat too, in case she felt I was invading her space, but I left my hands planted on the table.

She stared at me for what felt like an age without saying a word. Then she buried her face in her hands and didn't move. I wasn't sure whether to try and resurrect the conversation or just keep quiet. I decided on the latter, whilst trying to figure out what I'd done to trigger the sudden drop in temperature. Then, after rubbing her hands vigorously over her face briefly, she came back to life.

'Sorry about that. I so shouldn't drink on a school night.' Then she leaned forward and took my hands in hers. 'I am sorry. There's nothing wrong - just some stupid lack of confidence on my part and a deep-rooted mistrust when it comes to nice guys. In my experience, they tend to turn out to be colossal cheating pricks you see.' She wore a half-smile, but there was also an enquiring look to her as if she was challenging me to nail my colours to the mast and declare myself to be a genuinely decent human being. I had to face the fact that I wasn't qualified to do that right now, having already chosen to be somewhat sparing with the truth.

226

'Look Jess, we all bring some baggage along to any relationship. But I promise you I'm for real. And I've never been as thrilled to be with anyone as I am with you. Well; apart from when my Mum used to take me to see Santa in Debenhams. And I'm a Ken remember? So; am I allowed to tell the world that you're my girlfriend now?'

She appeared to relax. 'As long as I'm allowed to tell people you're my bondage slave-in-waiting.' She squeezed my hands then let them go and it was clear the frost had melted. 'My mother's jetting off somewhere exotic for the weekend AGAIN, so I'm tied up sitting Monty till Tuesday. Not that visitors are prohibited, but I tend to make the most of the peace, quiet and lack of bar-work to get some painting done. That doesn't mean you can't call me though. I haven't tried phone sex as I imagine it must make an awful mess of the ear-piece but I'm game if you are. Oh bugger, what's the time?'

She swept her handbag up from the floor and started rummaging through it but there was a wall-mounted clock in my line of sight. 'It's five past twelve.'

'Okay I'm officially late for my shift. Balls.' She stood, then leaned over the table and kissed me fully on the lips as she had last night. I quietly celebrated the fact that this obviously wasn't a one-off move reserved for when she was a bit under the influence. 'Sorry to run! Oh, let me pay first.'

227

'Don't worry I'll sort it - just go. "Coasters" needs you more than I do. Actually that's very probably not true; but go anyway.'

Another kiss. 'You're a star. Make sure you call me, bondage boy.' With that she dashed out: a blur of red, blonde and haste.

Once she'd gone, I sipped my tea which tasted of cold, freshly sawn wood so I settled up and left. I quite fancied a stroll down to the Fishermen's Quay but felt the call of duty from my pub. There was much cleaning up to be done, and I deemed it unfair to leave that chore to anyone else. It had been marvellous to see Jess, in spite of the wobble in her mood; but that I understood. We're all products of our history and once conned, always wary. Still, I came away feeling pretty ashamed for the subterfuge I was perpetuating. Even more so now I'd unearthed how she'd been misled in the past. I doubted I could keep up the facade much longer; she didn't deserve it. On the up side, I had a few days to ponder both that dilemma and how to answer Boat Bitch's last destructive salvo – there was no point in sending a message if she wasn't going to be around to receive it.

Arriving back at the pub, I felt perkier than earlier, all the better for seeing Jess, a short stroll and a blast of sea air. Janine was behind the bar with her back to me and I couldn't resist. I reached the counter without her knowing I was there and announced my arrival: 'HEY JANINE!!!! HOW'S THE HEAD?!!!' She jumped. Then turned and gave me a look that basically communicated, 'Tonight; I will kill you while you sleep.'

'Oh just bostin' kid.' This was rewarded with a delayed echo as either J.D. or Pat chimed in with a repeat from out back. She then pointed to the far end of the bar towards a vase that was hosting what looked like a dozen or so red roses. 'You got flowers.'

'How do you know they're not for you? You must have fellas queueing around the block girl.'

'Nah - all the good ones are taken. There's only the tossers left. I might give being a lesbian a whirl. At least they know where everything is, if you get me. The last few lads I've been with had no idea where to even start looking for me G-Spot. I gave them a miner's lamp, some rope and a canary in a cage but still no joy. The closest they got was Edgbaston.'

I was rather excited; this was no doubt some romantic gesture from Jess. No wonder she'd had a moment in the cafe when she'd thought I wasn't serious about us, after she'd gone to this trouble to make her affections public. There was a small envelope poking out from the blooms, simply addressed "Mr Trickett". With an expectant grin, I opened it and pulled out the plain-fronted card. Within, there was a message written by someone with an impeccable hand:

"Dear Mister Trickett.

I was, and remain, truly mortified to hear about the unpleasant goings-on at your establishment last night. How terrible! At least we can all find consolation in the fact that the damage could have been far more extensive. Far far more extensive. If there is anything I can do to help avoid a recurrence, do please let me know.

Your neighbour,

Angelique Sharp."

That bitch! Incensed, I crumpled the card and threw it at one of the front windows with all my might. Instead of smashing through the glass and flying across the channel to land explosively on the floor of the SharpCrest yard as I wished, it travelled a metre or so then fell to the floor, because it was merely a thin piece of cardboard with some ink on it, not a cannon ball. Feeling cheated, I snarled then swiped the vase from the counter and onto the floor, where it ended its days with a satisfying smash.

Janine, J.D. and Pat all came running at the sound. I turned to see three startled faces, then looked back at the broken glass and crimson petals strewn across the floor.

'It's a message from Boat Bitch; to make sure I got last night's message.'

J.D. walked up and took my arm. 'Look mate, go with Pat and take a breather. Me and Janine will clear this up; I can't have Halo paddling about on broken glass. Plus you're making the punters twitchy.'

I was so angry I was struggling for breath, but the red mist cleared sufficiently for me to take in the shocked looks I was receiving from the handful of customers present in the bar. I nodded and headed to the back door. J.D. slapped me on the back supportively then Pat steered me out of the bar and through the kitchen. Once we reached the yard, I bent over with my hands on my knees and my eyes closed while I took deep breath after deep breath, trying to steady myself. Pat put a reassuring hand on my back, just to let me know he was still close and looking out for me. After a minute or two, I came back to myself; and after a final deep breath I straightened up and looked at him. 'Thanks mate. I lost it a bit back there.'

'S'okay me old. Bit of deja vu here; didn't we have this chat a couple of hours ago?' He gave me a hug and a pat on the back robust enough to loosen teeth, then he took a step back and put a hand on each of my shoulders and fixed me with a drop-dead serious look. 'Right - this is how we get back at Queen Twat.'

It was a majorly grubby weekend, the majority of which I spent in overalls and rubber gloves trying to scrub The Gents' clean of Boat Bitch's filth. Soap and water didn't cut it; the paint stayed fixed as if it had been cast as an integral part of the ceramics' first firing. Pat suggested something heavier duty, essentially a paint stripper cocktail that was potent enough to return warship hulls to their base metal with just a few daubs. So with industrial strength hand wear, a breathing mask and goggles, I got to work.

The new mix was more effective, but it still took hours to clear just a few square inches. And even with the protective clobber, I felt that every time I breathed in I was lopping several years off my life whilst also guaranteeing I'd never father any children. It was bloody horrible work, but it was mine to do. Pat had offered to help, as had J.D. and Janine bless them, but it didn't feel right to rope them in. We still had a pub to run, and I was mindful of the fact that soon I might lose Pat to his new contract work so I really needed him to do what was left to do to get the kitchen fully ready. After a whole day scrubbing on Saturday, we met for a technical review. After some deliberation, he came up with the idea of coating the tiles with the paint stripper then scraping the paint off, rather than trying to rub it into submission. I ditched my brush in favour of a scraper and it actually worked a treat. Grand – I was ready to properly clean house tomorrow. I wrapped up my day about eight, dumped the gloves and overalls and hit the bar.

Recuperating after an industrious day, my evening was spent on the customer side of the bar while J.D. and Simon came up with as many alternative titles for The Crow's Nest as they could, almost all of which cast aspersions on my sexuality and personal proclivities of course. I think they peaked at "The Bummer's Barn". We had a 50th Birthday party in; mostly well-behaved, and they did drive off some early yacht wankers but many bemoaned the lack of music and kept asking where the jukebox was. I asked J.D. if we could show music channels on the telly in the corner but he just shrugged like I'd asked him the atomic weight of zinc. Something to consider I thought. Having music in the bar that is; not the zinc thing. There were some interesting chats to be had with several female customers who were feeling frisky after a sherry or two and came over all flirtatious. The chemical fumes emanating from my work clothes after a day spent paint stripping probably helped to lighten their outlook too. Even Janine threw a few provocative comments my way - I guess she was embracing the liveners and purging the last dregs of her hangover. So overall, it was a fun evening.

But all the while, Pat's idea for getting back at Boat Bitch popped in and out of my thoughts. It wasn't a bad plan; I just wondered if it was a bit too much tit for tat and perhaps I should be taking the high ground rather than sinking to her level. It also had the potential to land me in serious trouble if I got caught which wasn't an attractive prospect. Other than those weirdos with a thing for Death Row inmates that they've never met but will gladly marry, the "jail bird" tag tended to be a relationship spoiler. And even if Jess was willing to visit me behind bars with forty Silk Cut and a Cornish Pasty smuggled in her knickers, the cacophony of wolf-whistles and lewd comments she'd suffer from the other inmates as those endless legs travelled The Green Mile didn't bear thinking about. I bet prison toilet paper is shockingly poor quality too.

Taking a break in The Bummer's Barn, I gave Jess a call. She came across as genuinely made-up to hear from me which pleased me no end.

'So how's Saturday night on the quay, boyfriend?' She giggled in a not-taking-the-piss kind of way, but in a manner that gave me the impression that she liked the sound of what she'd just said.

'Oh it's jumping. I'm going to need a bigger stick to beat off all the pensioners that are throwing themselves at me.'

'I expect most of them already have their own stick that you could borrow. Or a walking frame of some sort you could use as a barricade. Like circus lion-tamers use chairs; you know.'

'Great tip; thanks for that. So how's Saturday night on Silverbanks?'

'Quiet; and rather dull. People keep themselves to themselves around here. I've no idea who Mum's neighbours are, and I'm not sure she does either. She might have mentioned some football manager. Right now, they're all probably either in some posh restaurant getting ripped off, or they're out of the country living it up like she is. You know...' Then she went quiet and I wondered if she was wishing she was somewhere else too. She spoke again before I could chip in. 'If it's not too forward and soppy, can I tell you that I miss you?'

'I miss you too. I wish I was there right now.'

'Aww; you're a love. Actually you probably wouldn't want to be here right now if you could smell the place. Monty spends a good hour or so after his dinner sprawled in front of the telly in the lounge just farting; you have to light matches to keep the air even remotely breathable. Mind you, he's good cover if you have guests over and let one slip yourself.'

'What?! Super-models don't fart do they?'

'Oh we're the worse trust me. The last Milan show I worked, several guests in the front row needed emergency medical treatment for chronic breathing issues. It was an open air catwalk as well.'

'Lord, no wonder you all smoke like chimneys - keeps the weight off <u>and</u> freshens the air: genius. Actually, you know what? Fart gags aside, you on a Milan catwalk doesn't sound fanciful in the slightest. I don't think you realise what a stunner you are Jess. I'd really love to see some of your work.'

'Well bless you for that but I'm a bit too old for that game now. But sure; I have a portfolio of sorts back at the flat I can show you.'

'How old is too old?' (Oops - maybe a step too far there).

'A gentleman never asks a lady her age!! ..... I'm 32.'

'Oh that's no age. I'm pretty sure Kate Moss is well into her sixties and she still seems to get plenty of work.'

'It'll never happen; I enjoy my food too much and I quit chain-smoking years ago. So, if we're being all personal and that, how old are you?'

'I'm 40. It's the new 30 I'm told.'

'Told by whom?'

'40 somethings who miss being 30 something.'

'Well I think dwelling on age is all bollocks. It's a cliché I know, but it is just a number. Mum and Dad had fifteen years between them.'

'Actually it's a word as well as a number but I'm with you on that. So you're really okay with our age difference? You're happy to stick around and support me during my dotage? That could start anytime you understand; next week perhaps.'

'Yes of course! I've always wanted to do more for charity. Giving you the occasional bed bath sounds marginally more fun than sorting out second-hand clothes in a shop. Marginally. I could be the playboy bunny to your Hugh Hefner. Okay Monty I'm coming! Sorry Hugh; Monty needs his evening stroll - talk again tomorrow?'

'I'd like that. Sleep well, girlfriend.'

She squealed loudly like an overexcited teenager at a pop concert then hung up.

I took some time to revel in the feeling of being wanted by someone so utterly fabulous. Every time I saw Jess or spoke to her, there was nowhere else on the planet I'd wish to be. Was I properly falling for her? Hell yeah. Then darker thoughts regarding her unfortunate family connection started to infiltrate my bliss so I headed back downstairs for distraction and drinks.

Sunday; I woke up with a mission, and after a quick cuppa I set to clearing the remainder of the graffiti from The Gents'. It was a stain on my sight and a lingering reminder of Boat Bitch's skulduggery and it all had to be gone; and gone today. So, having donned the protective gear, I went at it with a purpose. Sometime around ten, Pat showed up and went off to make more tea. When he returned, he had Tim in tow; his unassuming but hugely productive second pair of hands in the kitchen refurb.

'There you go; get your chops around that.' he said handing me a mug that I immediately had to place on the floor before my hand burst into flames. Christ, he must have asbestos mitts that boy. 'Soz; bit hot yeah? I forget you've got the hands of a five-year-old girl. Look, me and Tim have had a chat; I've told him the story and he wants to help out here. I don't need him in the kitchen today, so how about he pitches in with you and gets this shit sorted?'

Tim piped up. 'It won't cost you; it's a favour like. Buy me a beer when we're done and that'll be quits.'

I shook his hand: 'Tim; you're a gent. I'd really appreciate the help: and it'll be two beers at least.'

Once we'd finished our tea, we tore into it. I already knew Tim to be a hard worker after seeing him in action fixing up the kitchen. He was a tall guy, and skinny with it. Quiet, but with an easy-going way about him. We hadn't spoken much as he tended to just turn up, work his arse off then shoot home with few words in between. But our Gents' restoration project gave us an opportunity to get to know each other as we chatted, whilst sloshing and scraping. Thanks to the breathing masks we wore, much of the conversation had to be repeated a few times before we understood each other but over the next few hours we covered a decent amount of ground. It turned out Tim and Pat went back a long way, having met up when they both joined the RAF as teenagers but Tim had stayed in a few more years after Pat had completed his minimum term. As we talked, he seemed to relax and get into his conversational stride, making our dull exercise all the more interesting with tales about his and Pat's exploits down in Cornwall where they'd been stationed. He'd throw himself into enthusiastic impressions of various colourful characters which were all the funnier for his gangly play acting. Several times I had to walk into the alley and remove my mask as I was laughing too much to get enough air into my system through its strict filter. But whilst we chatted, we stuck to our labours and the more we cleared, the more we were fired-up by the sight of the reclaimed, increasingly unsullied tiles, so worked even harder on the still corrupted remainder. Janine paid us a visit, dropping off a couple of pints which we downed in no time, then hit the coal face again with renewed vigour.

Eventually, we were done. We'd covered every inch, and once we'd swept up what we'd scraped, we had our Gents' loo back. Okay the floor resembled a butcher's apron but that would be back to rights after a bleach carpet-bombing and a serious mop down. Removing our masks, we nodded at each other then looked back at our handiwork, both extremely pleased with ourselves. I shook his hand again. 'Thanks Tim, you're a diamond. This would have taken forever without your help. Good to get to know you too.' Once again I felt blessed to know these good souls that continued to turn up and embellish my new existence in Pulton. 'I reckon it's time for those drinks now.'

He gave me a goofy grin: 'Lead on Skipper! Beers ahoy!'

Having dropped our overalls in the yard, sending a shower of red paint scrapings into the four winds, we hit the bar, collecting Pat en-route, all nursing a major thirst. Blimey, it was four o'clock already. All parched from our labours, we finished off several lagers in quick succession, whilst Janine and J.D. continually complained about how badly we smelled. We must have been quite a pungent trio, with me and Tim reeking of industrial paint stripper and Pat giving off the scent of ancient sewers having been busy replacing old pipework to plumb in the new basins and drains in the kitchen. But we didn't care: we'd done some proper work and reclaimed part of our empire. We were "The Ghostbusters" after taking down Zuul; or "The Untouchables" after capturing Capone's bookkeeper. It was a good feeling; a great feeling in fact, and we all wallowed in our accomplishments whilst downing enough lager to float a Type 45 Destroyer. Life was good: so so good. I was in crazily grand spirits, and laughed more than I did that time I heard that Brian Harvey had run himself over with his own car after eating three tuna jacket potatoes.

Later, once I was back in The Crow's Nest and had showered off my day, I called Jess. We spoke for about an hour; the usual delightful mix of flirtation, humour and nervous soul-baring, after which I went to bed and drifted off into a deep sleep. The sort of slumber reserved for those that have done a decent day's work and have temporarily shelved their worries about nut-job boat yard owners wanting to steal their livelihood away.

CHAPTER TEN

Ouch. Serious bloody ouch. Yesterday's exertions cleaning up The Gents' had taken their toll and I'd woken up properly stiff. And not in a good way. Okay, I was in better shape now than I'd been during my years as an office monkey but several hours of actual physical work were bound to leave their mark. After taking a few minutes to flex most bits of me to see which didn't hurt, it turned out they all did. That was it; I was crippled, permanently robbed of the power of self-propelled movement. I'd only visit my beloved quay again via satellite photography. Winning Olympic gold in the one hundred metres was probably beyond me now too; though some nay-sayers would argue it always had been. Broken, I lay back and dozed off again. Russell Crowe's pedicure took an age. As always, he complained of shoddy workmanship and refused to pay up. Christ, not only had I earned the cash but I deserved a bloody knighthood for tackling those toes. You'd think he spent all day kicking anvils around a swamp. Gross. But, I couldn't spend all day arguing with him; there were things to be done and aches and pains to be moaned about.

I arrived downstairs to see my trusty crew getting set up for the lunchtime shift. I clapped J.D. on the back as he stood over his paper. Our morning routine and indeed our overall friendship were now so geared towards minimal maintenance that we'd dispensed with the 'Good Morning!'s. This was a positive step mind; us being comfortable enough with each other that we didn't feel the need for the standard pleasantries. There was always the headline gag though. 'So, what's today's hot topic?'

'Apparently, the Russians have launched a satellite that can read every text you send.'

'No way. Even the ones I send to your Mum?'

'Yep. Photos and video too. Best you stop sending her those dick pics.'

'When she stops asking, I'll stop sending. Anyway; she started it.'

'We're shit on TripAdvisor!!' Janine hurried through the kitchen door, laptop in hand. With our thread broken, J.D. and I both turned in her direction as she placed the machine on the bar. 'Apparently our food's crap; even though we don't actually do food.'

Puzzled, we all huddled around the computer to get a look at what was on the screen. Janine moved aside to give me the best view. 'J.D. asks me to check their web site from time to time, just to see if there's anything we need to improve on. I had a look over me tea this morning and there's a bunch of toss reviews.'

And there were. As I scrolled down the long thread of comments, I became increasingly mortified as I absorbed what had been posted; all of which bore the lowest possible rating, and all of which were complete bollocks:

'Portion size is a joke. I had the ribs: You'd find more meat on Kylie's arse.'

'Do not eat in this place. There's some manky dog that seems to have free run of the place, kitchen included. Can't believe the Food Hygiene cops haven't shut it down already.'

'Not only is the food poor quality, but the waiting staff are grubby degenerates that seem to be stoned off their faces. My wife claims one of them made a pass at her after serving the soup, while I was in the loo. She's off her medication at the moment I'll admit but still, no smoke without fire.'

'How can you screw up a salad? There was more oil on it than when BP garnished The Gulf of Mexico.'

It just went on...

'I asked to see the specials and was simply shown a faded black and white photo of Terry

Hall with a daub of ketchup on it. I didn't understand, so enquired of the waitress who told me to 'Get with the program grandma.' This was doubly confusing as I have no children of my own.'

'The waiter asked me how I'd like my steak and I replied 'On a plate with chips' because that's hilarious, and always cracks up the yachting friends I was with, but he just picked his nose and then wiped his finger on the tablecloth before walking off. Needless to say, we didn't stay.'

And on...

'I ordered the Ploughman's lunch which turned out to be stale bread, some gone-off cheese and a pickled onion I couldn't get a knife through. More of a Shitman's than a Ploughman's. When I complained to the Manager, he called me a "cock-womble" and didn't offer a refund. Outrageous.'

'Being on the quayside you'd think fish was a safe bet. Wrong! I had the snapper, and haven't thrown up that much since I ate three tuna jacket potatoes and ran over my head in my own car.'

I probably imagined the last one but it was in keeping with the overall trend. Boat Bitch had struck again. How did she even know I was planning to serve food? Maybe she'd got wind of my registration with the local authorities somehow. The vandalism in The Gents' had felt like the final straw, but this was her torpedoing something I hadn't even put in the water yet. If indeed that was even possible; my torpedo knowledge was far from expansive. 'Janine - can you get these reviews taken down? If we tell them we don't even serve food, they'll bin them surely?'

'I dunno. I'll work it out.' She collected the laptop from the bar and scuttled off.

I looked at J.D. who gave me a 'Where the hell do we go from here?' kind of look as he shrugged his shoulders.

'I'll sort this - I have a plan. If I get locked up as a result, you'll take care of the place right?'

'Of course. What are you going to do?'

'I haven't quite worked that out yet but I need to hit that bitch where it hurts. And hit her hard enough that she'll piss off for good and leave us alone.'

J.D. grabbed two brandy glasses. 'I'll drink to that.'

Christ, this lifestyle was going to kill me.

I kept returning to the spot on the counter where Janine's laptop had just been sitting. Although the device was gone, it was as if there remained a handful of unfounded insults hanging there, burned into the air somehow. I leaned on the bar and dropped my head with a heavy sigh, then rallied my thoughts and straightened up. Come on Ken, buck up. You need to plan, not mope.

I was done rolling with Boat Bitch's punches. My defence was now all about offence. A robust plan needed some serious consideration, and I needed time alone to put it together. But just as I went to tell J.D. that I was taking a break in the Sausage Factory (or whatever), Bruno appeared through the front door. He glided to the bar (the guy moved like he was on castors) and placed a hessian shopping bag on the counter, together with a rolled-up, weathered leather case. He looked sharp - the usual slicked back hair, clean-shaven with a crisp white shirt and black suit. I wondered how much sharper he'd look if he added a tie, but that might be off any sort of scale I could fathom. I didn't fancy him; he was just - magnetic.

First the dazzling smile, then: 'Good day Ken. I thought I might come and cook a dish or two for you today. As you'll no doubt recall, I do still have the practical element of my interview to complete to your satisfaction. Is this a good time?'

'Hi Bruno - good to see you. Erm - I'm not sure. Let me see how Pat's doing out back.'

'Allow me.' With that, he swept behind the bar and into the kitchen, blindly reaching for his accessories as he moved, as if he knew where everything in the room was at all times without needing to look.

'Hey Pat. We have a guest. Can we do warp speed yet?'

Pat was lying on the floor doing things with pipes beneath one of the new sinks. 'You are such a nerd Trickett. Hey Bruno, how's things? Everything's working but I've got the water off in here at the mo. Utility room's on though.'

Bruno slowly surveyed the room and nodded appreciatively. 'I knew you'd be ready. A grand job Pat; a grand job indeed. Are you sure I won't be in the way if I rustle something up? I'd hate to hinder your valuable endeavours in any way.'

'No you're fine, crack on. If you happen to rustle up a bacon sarnie that would be grand.'

'Oh I think we can do rather better than that my friend. Ken; I believe I have all I require. By all means retire to the bar and attend to business, and I'll sound the gong when lunch is prepared.' He turned and scanned the gleaming steel of the new main worktop then spied the disinfectant spray sitting at its end and doused the surface with it. After grabbing a cloth from the wall dispenser he swabbed it down, stopping temporarily to remove some stubborn spec or other with his fingernail to ensure the worktop was literally spotless. Once he was finally satisfied that it met his exacting standards of cleanliness, he began pulling all manner of ingredients from his shopping bag onto the lustrous surface. Already, he looked entirely at home. It was mesmerising watching him go about his trade; his moves were almost balletic.

'Right well, fabulous; looks like you're all sorted. Look forward to it!' Then a thought struck me: 'How did you know we'd be ready for you?'

'Well, I believed that if you were truly serious about this business, you wouldn't dilly-dally. And you didn't disappoint me. Had I walked in here today and not been able to perform, I may have had to rethink our arrangement. But as I said, you didn't disappoint.' Then he turned and looked at me over his shoulder. 'Now off you pop. A watched pot never boils you know.'

'Yes of course. Just shout if you need anything.' I backed away into the bar, feeling like I was a visitor in <u>his</u> kitchen.

J.D. was pottering around the bar, looking a little rosy from the two large brandies we'd rapidly sunk earlier. Looking at reflection in the mirror behind the bar, I was similarly rouged. Janine emerged from out back. 'I've reported all the dodgy reviews to TripAdvisor: you have to fill in a separate form for each one. Pain in the arse.'

'Thanks Janine, you're a love. And our resident tech geek from now on. I'll get you a badge made up.'

'That's not part of my job description; I should probably put in for a pay rise.'

'You could. Remember I'm still considering those robot replacements though.'

She stuck her tongue out at me then flounced off to serve a customer.

The bar was growing busier so I pitched in and served a few punters to help out. What was it with Monday lunchtimes in Pulton? Not that I was complaining. I made a mental note to do a tour of all the local bars one day to compare my body count with the opposition's. I also made another note to find time for a sit-down with J.D. to go through the books and see where we were financially. I'd done so before taking on the pub but I needed to be all over the cash-flow now. Not that I doubted J.D.'s aptitude in that area - I just had to know my business inside and out if I was going to take it to where I wanted it to be. (Maybe I was actually missing spreadsheets a bit too.)

Bruno had only been holed up in the kitchen for forty minutes or so before a host of enticing aromas started wafting through the doorway into the bar. I caught J.D.'s eye and we both raised our eyebrows appreciatively. Our stomachs probably rumbled in similarly faultless synch. As tempted as I was to go through and see what was cooking, I resisted the urge in order to relish the finale even more. There was also the risk that Chef would take my head off with something sharp if I interrupted him working.

A few minutes later, he popped his head around the doorway. I could see little of him below the neck but he appeared to be wearing an apron. I didn't know we even had aprons.

'Ken! Hi. Where do I find the crockery? Plates, dishes and so forth? Also the cutlery and napkins.'

Oh toss. I hadn't thought of all that when I ordered up the other equipment. Something else I'd have to blow a wad of cash on. 'Sorry Bruno; I still need to go buy all that stuff in. There's a motley collection in the utility room cupboards if you can make do with those for now? If not, let me know and I'll leg it into town and get what we need.'

'Oh no, no need; I'll manage. Necessity is the Mother of invention and all that.' He flashed me a broad grin then disappeared, like a mad scientist heading back into his laboratory before the storm passed and he ran out of the lightning he needed to bring his creation to life.

A few more minutes passed, and the heavenly whiffs emanating from the kitchen were sending us almost delirious. I was so hungry I found myself weighing up how filling a couple of beer mats might be. Or whether J.D. would miss a limb. Even the customers' noses and interest were piqued. 'Could we see a menu please? Judging by the smell, there's clearly something divine being concocted in your kitchen.'

'Oh no that's just Pat. He's working on the drains.'

Actually there really was a swell of genuine interest and we made a real meal of the fact that we'd soon be serving real meals. Then Bruno re-appeared.

'Mesdames et Messieurs; lunch is served.' J.D., Janine and I all charged towards the kitchen door. But as I was wondering how we'd fit through that opening three abreast, it occurred to me that someone needed to stay behind the bar to serve.

'You guys go first and I'll mind the shop. Come relieve me when you're done and be sure to leave me something to eat. Otherwise I'll be forced to bring the robot staff project forward.' I then spent fifteen minutes in silent torment as the kitchen continued to deliver the most tantalising wafts, whilst I talked up our future culinary exploits with enquiring customers. Then J.D. appeared looking like the cat that got the cream. Or the bar manager that got the foie gras.

'I tell you Ken; that guy just gets better. I wasn't sure about the food thing but now I reckon we're going to rule the whole bloody quay.'

Handing him the virtual baton, I did my best to not look like I was sprinting for the kitchen at full pelt. Which I clearly was.

The warmth and the smells in the kitchen were overwhelming. As I clattered through the doorway, I saw Janine and Pat standing next to the new central island unit, the top of which was completely obscured by a remarkable selection of mismatched plates and bowls bearing all manner of delights. They both looked at me with mouths full; rolling their eyes to indicate that they were in food heaven. Bruno was leaning with his back to the far workstation, with his arms crossed and the hint of a satisfied smile on his face, clearly pleased with his offering and the reactions it was prompting from his 'customers'. As soon as he noticed me, he rushed over and handed me a plate and a paper napkin holding cutlery.

'Apologies for the lack of silverware; the issue shall be addressed forthwith.'

'No problem. Bloody hell Bruno, this looks amazing.'

And it tasted even better than it looked. He had cooked up a storm. On offer were roasted scallops and other fish and shellfish dishes, what appeared to be pork cooked in a variety of ways and a beef curry that I just couldn't get enough of. All of this was interleaved with several different salads and pastas. And every mouthful was a delight. After several minutes of seriously pigging out, I took a moment to compose myself and face Bruno who had returned to surveying the scene, watching us all savour his remarkable spread.

'Bruno. This is astounding. All this in less than an hour? Come on, be honest - how much of it was out of a packet?' He looked a little pained at that insinuation but his demeanour remained cheerful.

'I don't do packets Ken. I don't even do packets at home. It's all made from scratch, by me. There's a Chocolate Fondant in the oven for dessert. Or a cheese board should you prefer.'

Pat seemed to have found his limit and had actually stopped eating for the first time in around half an hour. 'He's not fibbing Ken; I watched him put all this together while I was working. He's a machine.'

While I let the first wave of food settle into my system and prepared for the inevitable second, I looked around the kitchen and it struck me how well-ordered it all still looked. Where were the piles of pots and pans and discarded implements that inevitably accompanied food preparation on this scale? Other than the impressive array of dishes right there in front of me, there was little to no evidence that anyone had used the kitchen equipment since we took it out of its packaging. Maybe there was a groaning mountain of washing-up occupying the utility room? It appeared that Bruno could read minds as well.

'I tend to clear up as I go Ken. The dishwasher will require emptying in 23 minutes but that's it, other than the crockery and utensils that are still in play. And I am of course delighted that you're satisfied.'

'Well, to coin one of your phrases Bruno, you didn't disappoint. Far from it.'

'Pleased to be of service sir.' With that he bowed very low in deference and I got my first look at the impressive array of hardware on the worktop behind him.

'Jesus! That's some serious kit.' I went for a close-up as Bruno straightened.

'Just the tools of the trade Ken. Whatever the job, wherever I work, I always bring my own.'

There were ten or so knives of assorted shapes and sizes, each sitting snugly in its own dedicated slot in the well-worn leather roll, accompanied by what I assumed to be a sharpening steel and a rather fearsome looking cleaver occupying the end niche. I went to pull one from its holder but stopped myself before I moved, realising that to someone like Bruno, that might well be akin to using his toothbrush without asking. 'Do knives really make that much difference?'

'They make all the difference. If you use sub-standard tools, the very best you can expect to achieve are sub-standard results.'

'Fair enough. Are they dishwasher safe?'

'Oh they're anything but safe Ken.'

Once more, I got the feeling that I was in the company of someone who could dispatch me as quickly and effectively as he could whip up a risotto should he choose to. 'Well; I won't be messing with those that's for sure. I tend to stay away from anything pointy since I accidentally jabbed myself in the leg with a compass at middle school. Okay, seconds are calling me.'

I didn't have a great deal of room left but I successfully completed another sampling tour of the table and also fitted in a few mouthfuls of the fondant which was of course, to die for. Initially, I'd been hankering after a bit of cheese but decided that choosing that over his hand-crafted pudding might offend the Chef and make him all stabby. After now declaring myself officially full, I thanked Bruno once more for a magnificent showing. Janine continued to cherry pick from the remains of the feast. Where the hell did she put it all? She wasn't a big girl by any means. Pat was back to his plumbing. I went and relieved J.D. so he could get his dessert. I was pleased to see there was plenty of activity in the bar still - not only as it meant solid takings, but also because it offered up an opportunity for some light exercise to shift my mountain of a lunch.

Janine and J.D. returned to the bar a little later, both rubbing their stomachs appreciatively whilst continuing to praise Bruno's kitchen wizardry. All three of us moved rather slowly, issuing a range of sounds when forced to bend at the middle though I edged them on volume, still feeling my working weekend rather. Once all the humans were done feeding their faces, Halo got a monster treat in the form of a substantial bowl of leftovers. Oddly, she'd shown absolutely no interest in the kitchen since the work in there got underway and she seemed impervious to today's aromatic lures. Maybe it wouldn't be such a challenge to keep her out of there after all. She certainly made short work of her lunch though, no doubt relishing her feast in lieu of the add-hoc dropped snacks she was used to scavenging for.

After another hour or so, the lunchtime custom started to drift off so I wandered into the kitchen to see how things were progressing. Pat was running a tap in the new sink and checking underneath for any leaks in the pipework (I guessed: I knew as much about plumbing as I did about dry stone wall repair). All evidence of the sumptuous lunch was gone. The worktops shone, as did the multitude of pots, pans and utensils that had now been rehomed on their shelves and racks. Bruno was rolling up his knife collection: he snapped the clasps shut on the leather case then wheeled to face me.

'So, shall we discuss the menu Ken? I'm hoping lunch has not deterred you in any way from engaging my services?'

'Christ Bruno. Keep cooking like that and you can marry my sister with my blessing. If I don't propose to you first that is. Let's grab J.D. and work out what's next.'

Once the session had wound down to just the few punters that Janine could easily handle, J.D. and I grabbed a table with Bruno and started thrashing out the details of our food service. Both of them set about unconsciously highlighting the many huge gaps in my subject matter knowledge, and thank God they did. Bruno suggested starting simple until we'd got the kinks out and had the kitchen fully stocked, which made sense to me. If we over-reached then crashed and burned, that could be the venture over before it had barely begun. We decided on a shortish menu with various hot and cold sandwiches plus some simple but tasty seafood dishes and a range of pizzas and salads. And we'd do one main hot dish of the day; a chili or a curry or similar - something that Bruno could make a batch of then others could serve. Yes of course Bruno was clearly more than capable of rolling out the culinary red carpet but if we were going to go gourmet, we needed more in place to support that, and he couldn't do it all, every shift of every day. So we agreed we'd test the water with our initial menu, and just lunchtimes to begin with. If the uptake was satisfactory, then we'd go bigger. The discussion threw up all kinds of other issues that needed addressing. Again, Bruno was the life-saver. He came up with names of suppliers and wholesalers; me having only vaguely considered where we'd get our ingredients from before now. I guess I'd assumed I'd just wheel a trolley around Tesco from time to time. Not only did he come up with names, but he went one better and offered to talk to them and get accounts set up. All he needed was a credit card and I gave over my details readily. I wouldn't have known where to begin with all of this plus he and J.D. went back a way, and J.D. gave no sign that Bruno couldn't be trusted 100%. He also suggested that we could source speciality ingredients from the local delicatessen; the one that had just opened in the High Street. Yes! It appeared "Westall's" was open for business. Then we talked prices: something else I wouldn't know where to start with. Bruno steered us right once more:

'If you believe your customers will pay £5 for a quality sandwich then make that your price, decide how much of that £5 you wish to retain as profit, then calculate the remainder, that being the sum that you then have available to spend on the ingredients. If you work the other way around and decide what fabulous things you want in that sandwich, then add your mark-up, you'll end up with a truly opulent creation which everyone will rave about. If they buy it that is; which they won't, because who pays £30 for a sandwich outside of London?'

By teatime, we'd nailed all the big stuff (including Bruno's hourly rate) and knew where we were headed. Unless Pat hit any snags finishing up in the kitchen, we'd go live with lunchtime food service on Thursday. We knew that was pretty aggressive, but it was a timetable that would keep us focused. That meant Bruno getting things set up pretty smartish on the supply side and me getting the menus printed up and the long list of other items delivered that were essential for getting the food out there. We needed all the crockery plus cutlery, cruet sets, napkins etc. etc. etc. Bruno was the food; I was the accoutrements. And J.D. was there to keep us both honest and take the piss when we got something wrong. It was a great feeling - we had a solid plan. We'd get our kitchen and the food service operation up and running, iron out the creases during the next few weeks then BOOM!!!! We'd go full-on Bruno and smash it out of the park.

Having concluded our business meeting, we shook hands and Bruno departed, after advising us that there were left-overs from lunch stored in the fridge. What a guy. Later I noticed he'd left his knife roll in the kitchen, stored tidily on a workbench. To me, this showed a real commitment to his role at "The Pulton Arms", but would I take a peek? Oh no. He'd know.

We'd come to the early evening slow-down and with no punters in the bar, I got the team together and went through our headlines; the crappy on-line reviews, the plans for food service and my intention to thwart my nemesis. I also brought them up to date with mine and Jess's blossoming romance and how I was finding it increasingly arduous to keep that separate from my war with her mother. Janine was her usual candid self.

'Fuck it Ken. Tell Jess everything. And I mean everything. You're in this shit situation because her mother's a basket-case - none of this is on you. But it will be on you if you don't put it all out there. Us nice girls don't go for liars.'

'I haven't lied about anything. I just haven't shared all that's happened.'

'That won't make a difference, trust me. Badge it up how you want, but you're either honest or you're not. There's no in between. If she dumps you, she dumps you; at least you'll know you did the right thing. And if she doesn't, maybe she can help you get her ghastly mother out your face.'

Pat and J.D. nodded in agreement. All three of them had now tried to talk me into action. I knew they all had mine and the pub's best interests at heart - they were just trying to get it through to me that this state of affairs with Boat Bitch wouldn't resolve itself. I had to actually do something. And I owed it to them to settle matters - they were my family, and keeping the pub going was a future they both needed and deserved.

'Look guys, I hear what you're saying and I know this crap will only end if I end it. And I will. Keep the faith - I won't let you down.'

Straight away I called Jess and arranged to meet up in Westall's the next morning before she started her shift. I was going to check out the new business: and then come clean about everything.

From the outside, the deli looked smart; I mean, seriously smart. It was unrecognisable from the work in progress I'd excitedly stumbled upon just a week or so ago. Two floor-to-ceiling sized windows faced the street, one either side of the clear glass door, with the fascia painted black gloss with "Westall's Deli" above that door in brass letters. It was one of the older buildings on

261

the High Street and the choice of decoration highlighted its age - "Ye Olde Westall's Apothecary" would have been just as fitting. Above, sat a series of slim window boxes with hanging plants that dangled as if half-heartedly reaching down in a lackadaisical attempt to snaffle the superb array of goodies from the windows below. On display stood stacks of jars, bottles and packets, all impeccably labelled by hand with their contents and prices. Beyond that I could see a lengthy counter, fully loaded with other delights; baskets of loaves, rolls and pastries and below, the chilled compartments whose contents were hidden by the light reflecting from their glass fronts. There be cheese within; I could sense it. Behind the counter, against the wall, stood a busy work bench with a staggering number of shelves above and below, all of which were crammed with a huge variety of produce; no doubt all of which would have a serious impact on my waistline. Right, time to samp... ow!! A firm pinch of my arse brought my attention sharply back to the street. There stood a grinning Jess.

'Sorry hot stuff, couldn't resist those buns.'

I gave her a kiss and a huge hug, both partly fuelled by my pleasure at seeing her after a few days apart and partly by the mounting guilt and nerves from the thought of my upcoming confession. God it was good to see her, but I was relishing the imminent conversation as much as I'd relished my first driving test. And the second.

'Goodness! Someone missed me! What happened? Did you run out of pensioners to sex up?'

'No chance. They were just in need of a breather - those plastic hips have their limit you know.'

'You're disgusting. But I like you. Come on, let me buy you brunch.' She grabbed my hand and pulled me towards the door.

Inside, "Westall's" was bright and inviting, with an atmosphere dominated by the smell of freshly baked bread but punctuated with tantalising whiffs of cheese, meats and coffee. Whilst the counter occupied much of the left hand side, the opposite was given over to a handful of wooden, white-painted chairs and tables, the majority of which were already taken. It seemed the business was off to a good start. The walls were festooned with blackboards showing prices and the odd menu here and there, many overlapping another to some extent so you only got half the story. The whole place had the feel of a lovingly maintained, well thought-out shambles. And then my eyes caught the glass of the counter and the staggering selection that lay behind it. There was, well, everything - a huge assortment of cured meats gave way to bowl after bowl and plate after plate of salads, pasta, olives, dips, pâtés, quiches and pies; again, all scrupulously labelled. And the cheese: oh the cheese! Wheel after wheel of dairy heaven; some big enough to use as a half-decent emergency spare on your Mondeo at a push. All the greats were present, plus a host of names I wasn't familiar with. I decided I couldn't go another day without a taster of "Grantchester Fugly" in particular. I was a kid and this was my new candy store.

'So what would young love like for sustenance?' Startled out of my preoccupation, I looked up to see a rosy-cheeked, generously proportioned lady looking across the counter at me while she wiped her hands on a tea towel. I realised Jess was still holding my hand and she looked at me amused - maybe by the rate of knots at which I'd dragged her across the floor to the counter. Or maybe I'd been drooling on the glass. Or perhaps it was the lady's use of the word "young" in the context of me. Anyhoo...

'Hi; I love your shop. Great to see a new business starting up in the area. Though I must warn you I'm the competition sort of; I run "The Pulton Arms" on the quay.'

She didn't look at all perturbed. Instead she reached over the counter and shook my hand 'Splendid! I know it well. I'm Beth Westall.' Whatever she had been wiping from her hands was still present in some quantity so it was a rather slippy affair. 'Oh sorry; bit of pork pie jelly for you there. No charge.'

'I'm Ken Trickett; pleasure to meet you. This is Jess.'

She shook Jess's hand also. 'Hello Jess. Goodness me what a pretty thing you are! I hope he tells you that daily.'

'Why thank you Beth. And yes he does, every morning. Apart from Saturdays; he gets distracted then as that's the day the bins need putting out.'

'Well I guess I could forgive him that if he's domesticated.'

'He's getting there, slowly. Still needs help with some of the basics – replacing the loo roll; operating the washing machine; dressing himself, that kind of thing.'

'Um - ladies, I'm right here you know? And I do have feelings.'

'Oh man-up, you wuss. Beth; might I have a medium latte please and Ken will have a vat of the most non-threatening tea that you stock. Thank you.'

'No problem. Take a seat and I'll have those over to you in a mo. Have a look at what I've got and feel free to order all of it. Oh and the menus are on the table and up on the wall.' She moved off and started to fire up the beast of a coffee machine that sat on the rear counter. Back at the pub, we had a similar device that took up a serious amount of real estate behind the bar that I had no idea how to operate. Jess and I chose a table; both surreptitiously wiping our hands on our coats before taking them off and slipping them over the backs of our chairs. Within minutes, mechanical noise and steam took over the room - this was either a latte in production or Beth was drilling to the centre of the Earth.

'What a fabulous place! If the coffee's up to scratch, "Cafe on the Quay" can go do one. And how cool is she?' Jess reached her arms across the table and made grabbing actions with them so I'd reach up and take them in mine. 'So tell me how you spent the entire weekend pining for me and I'll promise to give you my best Meg Ryan in the restaurant scene from "When Harry Met Sally".'

'I spent every hour of every day worshipping at my Jess shrine in The Crow's Nest, while occasionally horse-whipping myself as a substitute for the pain of being without your company.'

'Only occasionally? Do I mean that little to you? And The What's Nest?'

Oh God; here we go again. 'The Crow's Nest. It's the name I gave my flat when I moved in. It does go by several other titles depending on how creative and/or inebriated the bar staff get.'

'I love it! You must give me a tour.'

'Anytime. It's a proper journey back through the ages. With real cobwebs and everything.'

I was loving the chat, but there was no point in putting off the inevitable. She deserved to know the full story. I honestly didn't know how she would take it. At best, I'd potentially be souring her relationship with her mother and at worse, she'd think I was a deceitful scum bag. Or possibly both. Shit; I so didn't want to do this.

'Oi. What's up? Is the honeymoon period over already?'

If I managed a smile at all, it was a lame specimen. 'I'm fine Jess. Well, not fine. I mean I'm fine with us; more than fine in fact but I've got something I need to tell you. Promise you won't shout at me?'

Leaning back, she let go of my hands, clasping hers in front of her on the table top. 'I'm not sure I can commit to that.' She looked at me fixedly; now all anxiety and suspicion.

At that moment, Beth arrived with our drinks. 'There you go lovelies. Now, wha...' She sensed straight away that something was amiss so decided on a tactful retreat. 'Just shout if you want anything.'

And then I started talking; and I didn't stop until Jess had heard it all, from Boat Bitch's first visit to the pub to the fake TripAdvisor reviews. She didn't interrupt, and barely reacted, with just a couple of wide-eyed looks when I detailed the very colourful dressing-down I'd received from her Mum in "Coasters" and the vandalism in The Gents'. I didn't spare any details. I was sure the customers at the nearest tables had probably overheard everything and were eagerly awaiting the next episode but I didn't care; getting the truth out there was what mattered the most.

'And that's all of it; you're up to date. I'm sorry I didn't tell you sooner; trust me I've really struggled with that. I was hoping she'd get the message and back off, in which case there was no need to make a noise about it and make it a problem for the two of us.' I drank a few mouthfuls of tea whilst nervously studying her still clearly troubled face, trying to gauge what her comeback might be.

She stared at me a while longer, presumably processing all she'd been told. Then she unclasped her hands and drank some of her coffee. Then without a word, she stood up, put her coat on and grabbed her bag. The ear-wiggers nearby looked up expectantly, no doubt willing some epic closing scene to unfold. And then she looked at me impassively and spoke.

'Some of that sounds like my mother. Most of it doesn't. Maybe you're a creative thinker, or a consummate liar? Perhaps you need some sort of psychiatric expertise to help you get over your conspiracy theories? Even if it were all true which of course it isn't, why on earth wouldn't you confide in me? She's my Mother for fuck's sake!!' Right then and there she was her mother, delivering a tongue-lashing to one of her inferiors. And now we had the attention of everyone in the room, all glued to the soap opera.

I stood and reached out to her in some pathetic, placative and pleading manner. 'Look Jess; on my life, none of what I've told you is a lie I swear. And yes I should have told you everything earlier but I was afraid of, well; this!'

She made no move to close the distance between us. 'Well that's as maybe, but I told you how highly I value honesty. You knew that, yet you chose to attach no worth to the notion.'

'Jess; please – let's talk this out.'

She stayed as she was, seemingly summing up the options available to her. The room was silent, with all its occupants transfixed. Then, with her deliberations apparently complete, she spoke again.

'I have to get to work. I think it's best that we don't see each other again.' She dug into her handbag and brought out her purse from which she plucked two notes which she tossed onto the table. 'I think that should cover my arrears to date.' She then turned to face Beth who was stationed behind the counter looking fretful. 'Good luck with your new venture Beth. Other than your open door policy on lying bastards, I think you're going to do great.' Then she left, without looking my way again.

There you go kids - watch and learn: hero to zero in less time than it takes to drink a medium latte. Aware, but uncaring of all the eyes on me, I slumped back in my chair as the door closed behind her. Christ that couldn't have gone any worse. I closed my eyes and pinched the bridge of my nose then looked up to the immaculate white ceiling, searching for some sort of divine inspiration. It arrived in the unlikely form of Beth.

'Well someone's having a big Tuesday. Don't worry, you kids will sort it out I'm sure. Soon as you walked in I thought you looked the part; as a couple that is. The sun's not quite over the yardarm but what the hell; maybe a small Grappa to ease what ails you?'

Alcohol; my all too frequent prop. 'Yes please Beth.' What the hell. I'd blown it. Honesty is the best policy my arse. If I'd kept my mouth shut, I'd be sitting there with Jess right now, laughing and sharing all manner of delicious munchables; totally loved-up and planning all the amazing things we'd do together whilst using Post-It notes to highlight our favourite parts of the Kama Sutra for later reference. Okay deep down somewhere that I may venture to later, there was the feeling that I'd done the right thing but right now, honesty was just something pointless that had cost me the affections of someone dear. Right now honesty was right up there with Hitler and chlamydia for me (only one of which I had any personal experience of. I swear, that swab was the size of a boat oar). Christ, what a mess.

Beth returned and placed two glasses on the table then sat down opposite me, all the while staring down the drama-hungry customers who then decided to re-focus on their own business.

'She'll be back son; I'd put money on it.' She then necked one of the drinks in one shot. I followed suit.

Jesus that's strong stuff! I sat there with a scorched throat and watering eyes while Beth looked on as if she'd sipped a thimble of milk shake. 'Wow – that's serious rocket fuel. I don't know Beth. She's majorly pissed off with me. I've seen majorly pissed off before and that was majorly pissed off.'

'Look, I don't want to pry into your business and I don't know what your problems are, but unless you've murdered a close relative of hers or given her crabs, there's nothing that can't be fixed.'

'Neither of those Beth, but the first one is tempting I'll admit. Truth is, I've got a problem I don't know how to solve. And Jess walking out on me is down to me not solving it.'

'Well, as I see it, you've got two choices. You can do bugger all; just mope around, pissing and moaning to all your mates that you've been hard done by. Or you can throw your heart and soul into getting that girl back. You know; I had a special man in my life once, and I lost him thanks to a ludicrous dalliance with a guy many years my junior when I wasn't thinking straight. But mainly, I lost him because I didn't fight to keep him. John was a no-frills chap you see, not one for buying me flowers or surprising me with other romantic gestures or flattering me all the time. And this young lad was the opposite, and he rather swept me off my feet. "Turned my head" as we used to say in the old days. But I'd overlooked what was most important. John used to make me smile every day; he had a wicked sense of humour and would find something to laugh at or laugh about in pretty much any situation, and you couldn't help but join in. One

271

day I told him about the affair, and then I left him. I know how much that hurt him. And a few months later, I found myself with this boy who was really just a massage for my stupid ego. He was good at heart. He just never made me laugh. Yes, he bought me gifts and posh dinners and took me to exotic places but he never owned my heart the way John had. So I broke up with him as well, but felt too ashamed to go to John and try and save our relationship. I'd made a colossal mistake, and then I compounded that by not putting my all into correcting it. You're not a bad looking boy son, but that Jess is off the charts fit; I doubt you'll do better. Or as well even. No offence. See girls only want kind and sensitive up to a point. It's action that really gets their attention. Don't screw up like I did - if she might be the one, fight for her tooth and nail.'

For a moment I thought Beth was raining on my already sodden parade, but then I realised she was just being direct, like pretty much everyone else had done. It really was time to act. Okay I might not be able to get Jess back but I could do my damnedest to get Boat Bitch out of my life and keep my friends in work. She was the cause of all my woes and with all the crap she'd put my way, all I'd actually done in response was, as Beth had said, just piss and moan to my mates. And sent flowers. And now that poisonous hag had very probably cost me the future Mrs Trickett. Words wouldn't get Jess back, only action. I was well aware that any kind of antagonistic gesture towards her mother might simply strengthen her argument for us not being a couple, but I figured I didn't have much to lose as she'd made it abundantly clear that we were over. Enough was enough.

'Beth, you're my bestest new friend. Could I have another? Then I'll be off to slay a dragon.'

CHAPTER ELEVEN

The next day was a day for getting organised. I
had a mission to plan, reconnaissance to carry
out and stuff to buy. After I'd left "Westall's"
yesterday lunchtime, I'd spent the rest of the day
crafting my retaliation against Boat Bitch whilst
repeatedly fighting the urge to call Jess. Yes, I
was gutted about losing her but I couldn't afford
to give in to negativity so instead threw myself
into other activities in a bid to keep myself
distracted. Plus, I had the recurring thought that
I really hadn't done anything wrong and that all
this madness was down to her horrendous
mother, not me. Moving with a purpose as I was,
the team could see I had a bee in my bonnet so
the banter was minimal that morning. Even J.D.
chose to not go for the usual repartee, sensing
my focus was elsewhere. As much as I tried to
keep everything business as usual, I couldn't help
but be mired in my own thoughts. Having mulled
it over at length, I'd decided to go with Pat's

plan; albeit a slightly watered-down version of it. And that needed some serious prep.

One piece of good news was the delivery of the remainder of what we needed for food service which I'd only ordered on-line Monday evening after Bruno's visit. Cue much unpacking by the lunchtime crew and finding of homes for crockery, cutlery and all the trappings that went with feeding the masses. Thankfully, the new kitchen units provided ample storage. According to Pat, there were just a few "odds and sods" to do to finish up so as things stood, we were on course to go live tomorrow lunchtime. Bloody marvellous. Right; time to shop.

Outside was all slate sky and drizzle; one of those days where it never seemed to get properly light then got dark even earlier than usual, just to add insult to injury. I headed to the High Street, looking fixedly ahead as I passed "Coasters". As resolute as I was attempting to be, one glimpse of Jess and I was sure I'd cave and go in. As a diversion, I ran through the short but eclectic shopping list I had in my head:

Menus

Spray paint

Balaclava

Torch

KitKat

I'd knocked up a menu the previous evening that I had saved on a memory stick as we lacked a printer in the pub. So, I just needed to find a print shop to get a handful of copies done and laminated. This was possibly a rather rash spend as we'd no doubt tinker with the menu and the prices frequently during the next few formative weeks but to me, a photocopied piece of monochrome A4 didn't suggest quality to our customers. Some web searching had revealed a "Staples" in the shopping centre so that was to be my first stop. In the end, it turned out to be my second stop as when I walked past "Westall's", I caught sight of Beth through the window and dropped in to thank her for my redemption yesterday. It had also occurred to me that I'd left without paying. Bless her, she wouldn't take a penny from me, so I promised her a free lunch at the pub whenever she found time to drop by. She did ask how 'things' were; I didn't elaborate, just telling her that I was 'working on it.' With a cheeky Grappa on-board, I headed for town again. Why is it a "cheeky" everything these days I wonder? A cheeky pint or a cheeky curry - all that. When I visit the dentist, I don't refer to it as "going for some cheeky root canal surgery". All very odd. As I walked out the door, someone was leaving "Plush!" directly opposite me on the other side of the street and I was suddenly thrust into a stifling cocktail as the powerful whiffs emanating from both sources collided around my head. I was in the middle of an olfactory turf war between Colston Bassett Stilton and WhizzBang Bath Bombs. Had it been a hot Summer's day and had I been rather more hung-over, the sensation might have floored me. But not today, though I was glad once I was out of range and my nostrils returned to sampling nothing but the damp fresh air.

About twenty minutes later, I found myself reluctantly pushing my way through the doors of the shopping centre. It had been a while since I last visited but it looked much the same, with the expected big name stores, the faintly nauseating imitation daylight and the gangs of teens eating burgers while sporting ludicrously low-slung jeans, and trainers that probably cost more than I paid for my first car. And of course the ever-present army of "shoppers" were out in full force, seemingly content to spend the entire day; nay their entire existence, drifting aimlessly from one shop to another without actually buying anything other than an over-priced bottle of flavoured water from Sparks & Mensa. It was the need to navigate this zombie horde without the aid of a shotgun or chainsaw that deterred me from visiting the shopping centre unless there was no other option. And today, alas there was none.

Fortunately, my destination was located on the ground floor of the complex not too far from the entrance, so I only had to work my way around a few hundred of the afflicted: and five mothers who rammed me with their pushchairs because they were too busy chatting to navigate with any consideration for those around them yet still gave me a collective stare baleful enough to suggest I'd just filled their offsprings' nappies with wasps. And then stolen their sweets. But by contrast, "Staples" was pleasantly calm; something of an oasis, with just a couple of customers queueing at the till, a smattering of shop assistants, and Neil Diamond providing the musical backdrop through tinny speakers. Wow - "Cracklin' Rosie" and wall-to-wall stationery; I could live here. I walked over to the print counter and got served immediately by a cute young girl who looked like she was having a slow day judging by the enthusiastic way she'd bounded over.

'Hi! I'm Vicky. What can I do for you today?'

'Hi Vicky.' I fished the memory stick out of my pocket and handed it to her. 'I need twenty of these printed off and laminated please. I think there's only the one file on it; it's called "Menu.doc" or something like that.'

'No problem! What kind of paper?'

'Sorry?'

'What kind of paper would you like them printed on?'

'Erm - what do you have?' She then proceeded to reel off an extensive list of names with what I assumed were their weights, all of which meant absolutely nothing to me. I could end up with tissue paper or sheet steel. 'It's for a menu - do you have something thickish? And yellowy?'

'Can I suggest 150 gram Axelrod?'

'Sure. Sounds fine.' (Whatever that was.)

'It'll be about twenty minutes if you'd like to look around. Or drop by later on?'

'No I'll wait thanks. I'm quite the Neil Diamond fan so I'll just have a bit of a browse.'

'Who?'

'The guy singing on your... never mind - I'll be back in a mo.' God I'm old.

I actually did spend twenty or so agreeable minutes wandering around the store, eyeing up all manner of office equipment and supplies that I would probably never have a need to buy or make use of. Just for a brief moment, I fondly thought back to the days when I'd had a heavy-duty four-hole punch at my disposal 24/7. Then I remembered that the job had had absolutely no other redeeming features and moved on.

'Hello Sir? It's all done for you.'

Vicky was holding up one of the finished printed and laminated menus. I approached the counter, softly humming "Sweet Caroline". Taking it from her, I gave it a scan. It actually looked rather professional, without the greasy-spoon caff vibe I'd feared. And it still felt pleasantly warm. 'Looks great; thank you.'

'Not at all. Glad you like it!'

I paid the bill, grabbed the envelope full of menus and the memory stick, then headed for the exit, feeling good about my latest creative effort. Jess the artist would be proud of me. No don't go there. Somehow though, the menu did make the food prospect much more real. Tomorrow, people would be actually holding these menus and ordering from them - yeah baby! Just as the exit doors swooshed open, my high spirits got the better of me and I turned back to my helper. 'Nice job Vicky - keep doing what you do.' Then, unsure of how to follow that up, I did the finger gun thing then rushed out into the fray before the enormity of my embarrassment struck home and set my cringe glands aflame.

Okay - on to the next. The complex also boasted a motor spares shop which stocked a decent range of spray paints. I bought two large aerosols of red gloss. It had to be red to match the artwork inflicted on The Gents' by Boat Bitch's cronies and the roses she'd sent as the follow-up insult the next day. I was confident the symbolism wouldn't be lost on her. All the while I fretted that I was going to be quizzed by the guy behind the counter, eager to find out what I wanted the paint for. After which I'd claim "the bumper on the Renault needs a bit of a touch up", a deception which he'd see through immediately as he feverishly pressed the button under the counter that summoned the Feds. Or alerted Renault to the fact that I was bypassing their service centres and was planning to engage in a bit of DIY. I imagined their response would be as swift as it was violent. Even though I didn't own a Renault. In the end, my purchase was concluded with no such enquiry or incident.

And now for the head gear. I'd never been balaclava shopping before which was probably true of most folks. I didn't think any of the various menswear stores would meet my needs, so I exited the shopping centre and headed back down the High Street. I'd already decided that the Army surplus place was probably my best bet, but I kept my eyes open for other options as I walked. Most towns seemed to have an Army surplus store these days - maybe stock control was sloppy within that particular branch of The Forces, or perhaps they were serial over-orderers. You didn't see the Navy or the RAF pan-handling in the same brazen fashion.

As I passed one of those "Cash for Crap" type outlets, I noticed the various bits of hardware in the window so thought it might be worth a look inside for the torch I needed. The shop turned out to be torch-free alas, but I did spy a super-cheap, practically antique video player that would give life to my video stash from the attic. "Stash In The Attic": great name for a TV show, drug connotations aside. Actually there was a stack of the things taking up a long wall shelf. I just grabbed one from the top of the pile: there were other shinier models that looked newer lower down but I didn't want to risk sending them all toppling to the floor "Jenga" style. Mind you, I could have probably purchased the whole lot for less than fifty quid if push came to shove. Having paid for the machine, I asked if there was a bag or some sort of other wrapping available as the drizzle was still coming down outside, but the guy at the till looked at me like I'd asked for a champagne cocktail and a hand job. His only response was 'Cables and remote are taped to the bottom'. With no other option it appeared, I fitted it under my jacket as best I could to keep the weather off then left the shop, with my upper half looking like a very low-rent "Transformer".

And then I arrived at the Army surplus store. I was nervous about this one. Who buys a balaclava unless they're up to something dodgy? 'Oh yes it's all above board and everything but under no circumstances can anyone see my face.' Back in the Crimea in the 1850's, you could sport one of those bad boys without anyone raising an eyebrow; they were simply practical garments with the sole function of stopping your face from freezing off. Since then, they'd become one of the wardrobe staples for most crooks and other bad people. Not their biggest crime I'll grant you, but it still made life tricky for the casual buyer like myself. But I wanted to do it right - in films you see characters getting by with tights, socks and over-stretched bobble hats but I wasn't after comedic effect. I was after not getting nicked. The surplus shop was intimidating, with the proliferation of camo gear and ammo boxes in the window shouting manhood and conflict and I wondered if I'd have to complete some sort of assault course or win a bout of hand-to-hand fighting with the store owner before I'd be permitted to buy anything. With great trepidation, I pushed the door and walked in, somewhat comforted by the fact that if anyone was to attack me from the front they'd have to hack their way through a JVC HR-S5955EK Super VHS video recorder before they'd reach any vital organs. I looked around, taking in the landscape of military paraphernalia whilst breathing in an atmosphere that was 99% metal and leather.

'Good afternoon Sir. How may I help you?'

Behind the counter stood a nervous looking lad in his teens, sporting a faded Bart Simpson tee-shirt and fiddling with his glasses. Not quite the knife-wielding Rambo type I'd anticipated. And not even close to some Crocodile Dundee style character doing his 'That's a knife' routine, which had been my secondary expectation.

'Hi. Do you sell balaclavas?'

'The cakes?'

'No. The head gear. Like a mask - you know.' I waved my hand across my face because that is the universally acknowledged method of miming a balaclava.

'Oh right yes. Over here I think. Sorry I don't know all the lingo; I just mind the shop for my uncle now and then.' He led me over to a shelf that bore all manner of headgear; balaclavas included.

'Great; thanks.' I was expecting him to leave me to it but instead he hovered nearby, presumably in case I needed more assistance in selecting this complex piece of apparel. Grabbing a black number that looked like it might fit my head, I pulled it around a bit and stuck my fingers through the mouth and eye holes. Having not purchased military equipment before (surplus or otherwise) I was unsure of the protocol, so I decided to style it out as if I was in one of your more run-of-the-mill clothes shops. 'Is there anywhere I can try this on?'

He pointed toward a curtained cubicle in the far corner.

'Thanks. Back in a mo.'

I bundled myself into the changing cupboard, really starting to feel the weight of my VCR armour now. There was no mirror to hand, so I shoved the thing on my head (the balaclava not the VCR) then peered around the curtain to see if I could get a glimpse of myself somehow. And there at the end of the aisle, reflected in a full-length affair, was someone who I knew to be me but looked entirely unfamiliar. And majorly bad-ass if I were honest. No way would anyone know it was me under there - sorted. I pulled it off and then paused; pondering my next move. If I just purchased the balaclava, would that send the signal that I was very probably up to something nefarious and raise suspicion? Should I buy something whimsical to go with it to lighten the mood? I wasn't confident they stocked those pairs of enormous plastic fake novelty boobs or this week's issue of "TV Choice" in these sorts of shops. Everything I'd seen so far all looked a bit 'fighty'. I left the cubicle to find my assistant still twitching in the middle of the shop.

'Do you sell torches?'

At this, his eyes lit up; like torches. I'd obviously hit on an item of stock that he felt comfortable with. 'Yes yes we do! Just over here Sir.' I followed him over to an illuminated display case that stood on the floor next to the counter and contained shiny cylinders of various sizes and colours. 'This is the "MagiBeam" range Sir. The Rolls Royce of torches you might say.' I leaned closer to the glass. They did look awfully swanky, sitting there in their posh presentation boxes - more like museum exhibits than common items of hardware you'd stuff in a kitchen draw with the Elastoplast and Blu-Tac. Or maybe drop in the harbour. And the prices - bloody hell! Maybe they housed actual fragments of the sun or doubled as light-sabres. 'Have you got anything a bit more rugged? Less "designer"? These are cool, but a smidge too pricey for my wallet. I don't think my Gran would take very kindly to me telling her she'll have to go on the game to cover her nursing home fees because I'd decided to pull her funding to buy a tubular lamp.'

'Yes of course. These are rather expensive; you're just paying for the name really.' He then moved off to a shelf unit nearby. 'This is more your pukka military kit. You can drop them onto concrete or into water and they'll still work just fine. I use this model - it's the "G700 Tactical LED Nighthawk".'

Looks like I'd got this lad all wrong. Maybe he did have some military credentials? What was the weekend warrior thing - the Territorials?

'We use it when we go looking for owls. Me and a few mates are keen birdwatchers. It's a really bright torch. Apparently some lad in Lambourne shone one at a 747 landing at Heathrow and they had to divert to Gatwick and could only land when the pilots' arc eye had cleared.'

Okay, maybe I'd got him right in the first place. His military experience was probably limited to playing "Call of Duty" in between regular, provocative sessions browsing the women's underwear section of his Mum's mail order catalogue. And watching "Saving Private Ryan" a couple of times. None of which reflected my own formative years to any extent. None whatsoever. None.

'How much is it?'

'Twenty pounds. You get batteries for that too.'

'Fine. I'll take that and the... hat, thanks.'

As we walked over to the till, I continued scanning for something frivolous to add to my order but came up short.

'Okay that'll be £24.50 please.'

As I groped for my wallet whilst navigating the VCR still stuffed into my jacket, I managed to pique his interest just too far.

'Can I ask Sir, what's that under your coat?'

Balls. He was on to me: I was rumbled. I needed to throw him off the scent.

'It's um; video equipment. Just a home project you know.'

'Oh right. I just asked as you looked to be struggling and I can give you a bag to carry it in if you'd like? We've got some sturdy carriers.'

Actually a bag was a good idea. I hadn't thought of that. Well, I had in terms of something to get the VCR home and dry, but not for the mission itself.

'Have you got something a bit sturdier? Something larger: and water-proof maybe?

'Let me have a look.'

I took the VCR out of my jacket and placed it on the counter, glad to drop the weight. A couple of minutes later, Birdman returned and placed a black canvas holdall next to it.

'Wow - what's that?' he asked.

'It's a VCR. For playing video tapes, you know? It's what everyone had before DVDs.'

'I might have seen one at a jumble sale when I was a kid. What do you need that for?'

Since the time I'd entered the shop he'd gradually grown in confidence, which was far from ideal.

'I've got some old tapes I'd like to watch. Family weddings; that sort of thing. So how much for the bag?'

'It's £10. It's not watertight but it is splash-proof. So, drop it in the sea and you're in trouble, but it's got a plastic liner so the inside will stay dry even if you're out in heavy rain. I use the same bag when I go birdwatching with my mates. For the sandwiches and notebooks and that. Usually a flask of apple and blackcurrant too, though we have to make it weak 'cos of Anton's diabetes. The bestest days are when it's one of our Birthdays 'cos my Mum puts in a Wagon Wheel each.' He appeared genuinely giddy at the thought. 'Not Anton though; he gets half an avocado instead.'

'Fine; I'll take it thanks.' I dug some notes out of my wallet then wrestled the VCR into the bag and slipped in the menus alongside. Birdman handed me my change and placed the balaclava and torch into the bag.

'Okay; you're all set. I've never sold a balaclava before.'

I'd gleaned that, based on his initial assumption that I was shopping for Turkish confectionery. 'I don't believe I've ever bought one before either. Exciting times for us both!' I was ready to be gone now. 'Right well, thanks for the help - keep watching the skies and all that.' I grabbed the bag from the counter.

'What's it for? The balaclava?'

Damn. I'd been just seconds away from a clean get away and now I had to make something up: fast. 'It's for a costume party.' Yeah that would do.

'Oh right. What are you going as?'

I hadn't thought that far ahead. I panicked and scrambled for something non-threatening; something fun; something that had nothing to do with clandestine night-time operations... 'I'm going as a terrorist.' Oh bravo: idiot. 'Well must go, thanks again!' I left, and was back on the High Street, feeling like I'd been in that particular shop for several hours, all the while broadcasting my criminal intentions. On the up side, I'd ticked a few things off my list. I grabbed a KitKat from the newsagent on my return route and headed for home.

It was just gone three when I walked into the bar. I recognised a few regulars finishing up their lunchtime session but otherwise it was a pretty tame scene. Janine was behind the bar: I pulled the KitKat out of my pocket and tossed it to her then carefully placed my bag on the bar. Conscious of the fact I'd been a bit wound-up that morning, I wanted to get things back to rights so went with ultra-cheery. 'So; what did I miss my lovely?'

'Yayy! You remembered bless ya. Not much really. Zac Efron and Ryan Gosling dropped in for a couple of Martinis and started flirting outrageously with me; of course. Then they started betting each other which of them would get me into bed first and it got a bit heated. Even when I told them I was a lesbian in training. Luckily, Hugh Jackman had popped in for his usual lunchtime mineral water so he stepped in and chucked them out. You just missed him. Otherwise; J.D.'s out walking Halo and Bruno's out back. And I think Pat's in the yard sorting the gate out.'

'Good good, glad it was an uneventful session.'

'What did you get: anything exciting? Before you answer that, remember that I find little else but choccie and shoes proper exciting. Even the thought of a four-way with three Hollywood hunks.'

I didn't want to show her all, but I'd clearly bought something so I unzipped the bag sufficiently to show the video player and pull out the menus without exposing the more questionable items keeping them company.

'What's that?'

'It's a VCR.'

'Where are you going with that Grandad? 1982?'

'Hush your mouth impertinent child. I found some old videos in The Crow's Nest; I thought they might be family films that Aunt Maddy might have made so wanted to give them a look. Savour the memories, you know?' I felt my cheeks redden with guilt as I delivered this blatant lie, and was convinced that I heard the sound of someone turning in their grave. I got my just desserts.

Janine leaned in close so I could hear her whisper: 'Oh right family films is it? So why have you got such a cherry on? Look, if you want to watch your "Hot Soccer Moms" compilations in the privacy of your Shagging Shed then there's no need to be shy about it.' She then moved back and chuckled. 'It's all perfectly natural!'

'I am as ever, delighted to provide you with so much amusement at my own expense. Likewise, the chocolate. Now, if you could steer your thoughts away from ridiculing me, you could take a moment to give the new menus a look. They're only temporary until we find our feet, but I reckon they're smart enough.' I slid one from the envelope they were stashed in and passed it over. Once that caught her attention, I zipped the bag shut just in case.

'Looks good.' was her first comment. She continued reading, concentrating hard, but then she stopped and looked at me, trying for all the world not to explode into laughter it appeared. She shouted towards the kitchen. 'Bruno! Have you got a minute to discuss the menu?'

'On my way m'lady!'

And then he appeared as if he'd been standing there all the time, looking super-tidy as always with shirt, tie and apron all crisply in place. Janine passed him the menu and he started reading as she stood there with her hand over her mouth, clearly building towards some sort of explosion. He seemed to get about half-way down the laminated sheet then looked up at me with a tight smile.

'Whilst you were out shopping for antiques, (did this guy hear and see everything?) I am pleased to let you know that the first deliveries arrived from our suppliers, all of which I am currently organising. So; other than a few additional items that I shall collect on my inbound journey, we shall be fully prepared to commence food service tomorrow. However, there is a particular ingredient for one of the Ciabatta's that I must regretfully confess I will struggle to source at such short notice.' He passed the menu back to me, his smile widening all the time. I scanned the menu wondering what the hell was up with these people. Then I saw it.

"Ciabatta with Parma Ham, Ilchester Manure Cheddar and rocket." Oh bollocks. That's what late night word-processing, too much wine and the lack of a competent proof-reader does for you. I looked up at the tickled twosome; Bruno grinned so widely I thought the top of his head might fall off whilst Janine collapsed into a raucous laughing fit that I feared may never find its end. Although initially dismayed, I then couldn't help but see the funny side. 'Oh well; at least if people say our cheese is shit it won't necessarily be an insult. I'd best fire up the laptop then get back up to the print shop.'

Bruno was magnanimous. 'Not to worry Ken. These things happen, especially when you have so much on your plate; as it were.' He took the envelope containing the other menus. 'Leave these with me. They are only temporary I know but we don't wish to come across as slapdash or lacking attention to detail. An erroneous menu suggests an erroneous Chef. I am sure you have more pressing matters to attend to so please allow me to take care of this one.'

Actually I did. Yes, I didn't want our food customers' first impression to be 'Oh look they don't give a toss about presentation.' (or indeed think Manure Cheddar was a real thing) but I had another outing to fit in before the daylight ran out. And whilst I still held reservations about some aspects of Bruno's character, he'd been a superstar so far and I had no tangible reason to doubt him. 'Thank you Bruno, that would be a great help.'

Janine was still struggling to stand up straight and her make-up was rapidly parting company with her face as the tears flowed freely. It was entertaining to watch but I had to press on. Time to be (sort of) boss like. 'Right chuckle sister; I need to go out again soon but in the meantime, I'll keep an eye on the bar while you go fix your make-up in The Ladies'. You look like a clown whose just clocked off after a two-hour 'soda syphon in the face' routine.' She retrieved her hand bag from behind the bar and headed off to the loo, still laughing like a loon.

Firstly, I dashed up to The Crow's Nest and dumped the bag. As I flew through the kitchen, I took in the scene which comprised Bruno surrounded by an assortment of crates and boxes of produce. He was head down, chopping and slicing ingredients and putting them into containers for storage. This was a far cry from the kitchen I'd walked into a few weeks ago; no more pizza and picnic tables. We were really getting there with this place. Still; no time to dwell on that now.

Back behind the bar, I poured a glass of red then stuck my head out the back door to say hi to Pat and tell him I'd be back in a bit. Janine exited The Ladies' looking vastly more presentable. 'Sorry Boss; took a while as I was still laughing and kept effing up my mascara.'

'No problem. Gave me time to eat your KitKat.'

'You git!'

'I'm joking!' I retrieved her chocolate fix from under the till and waggled it in front of her. 'Right I'm off. Back in an hour or so. Don't drink my wine.'

With the daylight fading, I was heading out later than was ideal but I had enough to work with, just about. The drizzle was still coming down which didn't help what was already rather limited visibility. Fortunately, I didn't have far to travel or far to see. I crossed the street to the quayside, dodging some serious puddles as I went. With my back to the town, I strode on down the quayside, heading towards the first lifting bridge but more importantly, the major piece of artwork en-route. And that was the "Sea Mood" sculpture, erected some twenty-five years ago as a gift to the community from a local sculptor. I couldn't remember the name but I believe he was amongst the top half-dozen most sought-after artists in the world at the time. This was a Marmite project that divided the town, and continued to do so to this day. Some adored it, whilst others proclaimed it an eye-sore and threatened to tear it down. But up it went anyway. And then a short few years later, down it came for repair. Being metal and averse to salt water, it was rusting badly. Or rusting very well in fact. In spite of the cost of its re-installation and a fresh wave of local protest, it made it back to life. Viewing it again now, I still had mixed feelings. To me, it was a rather ungainly structure, with a centrepiece supposed to resemble a sail and various curves wrapping themselves around it depicting waves. And it was thirty-five feet high. But; it had two features in its favour. One, it didn't sit outside my bedroom window and two; the observation deck half way up it was a prime location from where to gain a totally unhindered view of the SharpCrest Marine yard - my intended target. I needed to see the lie of the land and get a feel for the level of security I could anticipate; fences, lights, cameras and so forth, as I planned to pay the yard an uninvited visit in a couple of days' time.

I cautiously clambered up the slippery steps onto the similarly rain-slicked observation deck. I was the sole occupant, as in addition to being a superb vantage point, the deck was also a great place to experience the sea breeze enthusiastically and relentlessly whipping the rain into your face on a day like today. On the same spot during the Summer months, I'd be surrounded by a multitude of gawkers, pointing excitedly at the big shiny motor yachts while their kids accidentally dropped their ice creams on those walking below. As the water droplets started ganging together and began working their way down my neck, I remembered my jacket was equipped with a built in hood - result. I unzipped the compartment in my collar within which the hood lived and gave it a tug. Expecting it to be fixed in some way, I soon found out that wasn't the case as the wind grabbed it and sent it soaring out into the harbour. Ah well.

I dug out my phone and took a couple of minutes to remind myself how the camera worked. Binoculars had been a consideration, and I'm sure Birdman would have been the go-to guy for a product recommendation what with the owls and that, but in the end I'd decided that I'd look far less suspicious just holding up my phone. Also, I didn't actually own a proper camera; I didn't feel the need as pretty much everything seemed to have one built-in these days. Even my hoover probably. After a bit of faffing about, I'd sussed out the basics and was zooming in on the yard. On first look, I was astounded by the mess. I'd expected to see an immaculate work facility with the same level of meticulous order as a Formula One pit garage, but this was chaos on a grand scale. The space outside the giant worksheds was littered with crates, skips, giant wheelie bins, mini cranes, trolleys, scissor lifts, shipping crates and piles of scaffolding, all hemmed in by a wall of tarpaulin-dressed mounds; presumably bits of boat waiting for their turn to be fitted. As huge as the worksheds were, there was precious little free space within - the two monster vessels housed in the shed I was zoomed in on looked like they'd been shoe-horned in. There was no fencing along the waterfront that I could make out, just several gangways leading down to a pontoon at water level that ran most of the length of the yard. All in all, the place seemed pretty "open". There were floodlights in abundance mind, mounted above the workshed doors and atop extremely tall poles dotted all over the yard. I'd need to come back and do another recce when it was properly dark to know for sure how well-illuminated my visit would be. I also spotted a couple of poles fitted with twin security cameras; there could have been more concealed by the huge craft moored up alongside the pontoon. All the cameras were directed at the water front but I guessed they weren't fixed at that angle. There was also a white-painted wooden shed positioned at the top of one of the gangways; maybe the SharpCrest Harbour Master's domain; or a security office perhaps. I took a large selection of photos, having to pause frequently to wipe the rain drops off the camera lens. I saw nothing to change my mind as regarded the plan - I'd need some serious equipment to get into the worksheds after-hours and they'd be alarmed no doubt. Instead; out in the yard was where I'd do my thing.

The rain was running off my jacket and permeating my jeans and I was mindful of the fact that a warm pub and a glass of red were only a few yards away but there was more to do. After descending the stairs back down to the quayside, I marched off towards the lifting bridge that spanned the channel (the old bridge that worked properly). On the way, I passed the current Pulton Lifeboat Station at the opposite end of the quay to its venerable predecessor. Pulton was the home of the remarkable institution that was the RNLI, dedicated to saving lives all over the UK. Their headquarters bordered the Hull's Bay Marina half a mile or so ahead. Not quite understanding space, time, logistics or a distributed business model as a kid, I used to wonder how boats from Pulton managed to save those in peril in The Outer Hebrides. My Dad's explanation was simply 'Big engines and magic.'

Crossing the walkway on the bridge, I snapped a few more pictures of the yard on the way as that position offered an alternative viewing angle. On reaching the other side, there was a quarter-mile straight stretch that bordered the SharpCrest yard on the left and a builders' merchants on the right. Then the road split, with the left-hand route curling around to encircle the rest of the SharpCrest site and the other industrial sites beyond. As I walked, I concentrated on the yard's perimeter but occasionally looked to the other side of the road to see what had changed on the landscape as I'd not visited this part of town for some time. Saddened but not surprised, I noted that the old "The Ferryman" pub was now someone's house and no longer a business. A lot of the older industrial buildings had been converted into apartments or been knocked down and replaced by blocks of flats. And as with so many of the new developments around Pulton, few had been designed to complement their older neighbours so just looked characterless and misplaced. Further along this stretch were the terminals for the cross-channel and Channel Island ferries; very popular services, though they were guilty of ramping up their prices ridiculously during the Summer holidays as I remembered, looking to fleece the kind-hearted parents that just wanted to treat their family to a holiday but couldn't take their kids out of school during term time for fear of being prosecuted by the authorities.

Parent: 'My Suzi is top of her class in all her subjects and is thoroughly prepped for her GCSE's as we hired a tutor for some extra coaching, so me and her Dad thought we might treat her to a long weekend at Disneyland Paris for her Birthday?'

School Nazi: 'No that's unacceptable I'm afraid: if she misses even a single hour of term time she'll inevitably end up scraping her way through life earning a pittance from pole-dancing or illegal dog fights. And then dying of morbid obesity, a heroin overdose or as the victim of a gang hit - a fate sealed by your insistence that she skip double Statistics that one time.'

I recalled one trip I'd made on the ferry to Cherbourg in my late twenties. Me and my mate Dave just packed the essentials then leapt into my Spitfire (the car not the plane) and headed off for a grand adventure on the Continent for a couple of weeks. We got drunk in the ship's restaurant and ended up sleeping under one of the tables. Come the foggy early morning and our even foggier heads, we arrived in France and then spent a good while going around in circles as I drove and fought a vicious hangover while shouting at Dave for directions as he was holding the map. He ignored all such requests, being mostly asleep and doing the "bladder on a stick" motion with his head. Eventually, we escaped the port and parked up in a field to recuperate. Turning off the engine, I fell asleep instantly, neglecting to also turn off the headlamps, thus ensuring we woke up with a flat battery. That really set the tone for the holiday; and it was a blast. We returned home with a deep tan, a huge bill from a garage in La Rochelle for repairing the Spitfire (they had to fly the spares over from Coventry) and the lasting memory of the painfully crestfallen look on the hire car company rep when we informed him we'd broken the second of the cars they'd rented us. Good times.

As expected, SharpCrest's perimeter was well defended. The place was a bloody fortress, with numerous floodlights and camera masts and an angry looking fence about eight feet high with those metal struts that split into spikes at the top, all of which looked more than capable of efficiently removing my genitalia if I tried climbing over and got my dismount wrong. There were several entrances onto the lot, all currently open but with gates either side that would no doubt be shut and locked come closing time; all with the same height and groin-threatening spikes as the adjoining fencing. Most entry points also had a Portakbin just inside, each no doubt a security station manned by burly guards with guard dogs that had been denied breakfast and lunch and were perpetually foam-mouthed at the thought of scoffing an intruder. Also, each gate had more cameras pointed at it than the red carpet on Oscar's night. I walked the full length of the boundary, taking the odd swift photo of the gates as I went, being careful to stay out of line of sight of the surveillance kit as much as possible. Possibly a rather risky tactic none the less, as who's interested in security arrangements other than someone who has a desire to circumvent them? Such research was essential however.

Once I reached the limit of the site and came upon the less aggressive borders of the neighbouring yard, I retraced my steps. It was all but dark now, and my jeans were as sodden as I was chilled through. I headed home rather lively, hating the way my trousers clung to my legs. I was reminded of the night hikes we were press-ganged into as kids at Sea Scouts' Summer Camp; trudging through the sodden darkness whilst the troop leaders sat in their cosy Range Rovers, drinking beer and conjuring up ambushes to scare the bejesus out of us sleep-deprived, limp and shambling Mummy's boys. Sea Scouts was otherwise jolly good fun though and was where my enthusiasm for being out on the water was first founded. And we'd finish our weekly gatherings with a crazy game of British Bulldog in the main hut, ending with a huge dog pile that everyone threw themselves onto with abandon. Least we did until Posh Will's unfortunate and far-reaching explosive diarrhoea episode after returning from his family holiday in Mexico.

The traffic was starting to build; I guessed it was chucking out time for most, SharpCrest Marine included. I still needed to complete some night-time surveillance but as driven as I was to even the score with Boat Bitch, I'd save that activity for a time when I didn't have an icy stream running through my boxer shorts.

As I marched back to hearth and home, my thoughts returned to Jess. I'd done well today; staying busy enough to keep her at bay, but she was bound to find a way in at some point. I pictured her on the night of our first date and my stomach twanged like it does when it's reminding you that you skipped lunch. Which I had incidentally. But this was the twang of missed opportunity. Christ we were so good together. And we had the potential to be a whole lot gooder. What a damnable waste. No, no, no - don't be thinking like that. I was on a crusade to right a wrong; and who knew - I might get to right all of them. I gritted my teeth and focused on the mission; it was all about the mission. Fences and cameras. Spikes and floodlights. Guards and their Cujo's in the making. I upped my pace. Later, I'd give my photos a thorough going over but so far, the channel seemed like the least challenging route into Boat Bitch's lair. Bit by bit, my plan was coming together.

I arrived back at the pub, wet through and dripping profusely; and in a rather grim mood, but the welcoming warmth inside and the sight of plenty of custom and some familiar friendly faces lifted the frown to a degree. Halo was on patrol and bowled over to say hi. I knelt down to fuss her, showering her in moisture from my clothing in the process but she didn't seem to mind. Looking around the room, I returned the smiles and waves of the regulars I'd come to

303

know over the past few weeks. Some I was on first name terms with; others remained nodding acquaintances. Like Tattoo Steve: he ran the local tattoo parlour yet oddly I hadn't seen a single inking on him, despite him favouring a vest top indoors whatever the temperature - much to Janine's disgust when confronted by his bountiful thatch of chest hair. And there was Leather Dave; so named by me because he always wore a leather jacket which I'd never seen him remove. And also because he once told me his name was Dave. We'd exchanged a few words over the bar - he acted like he was some criminal kingpin, talking at a whisper and frequently scanning the room as if he had real heat coming down on him. Although I asked, he never disclosed what he actually did for a living. J.D. told me later that he restored saxophones that had seen better days. You never can tell.

J.D. was minding the bar. I went over, squelching with every step. 'I'm a bit wet.'

'You'll get no argument from me on that one.'

'How was today?'

'It was grand. It tends to be when you're not here. Maybe the customers hide around the corner then pile in when they see you leaving?'

'Piss off. How was it really?'

'Seriously: a more than decent shift. And tomorrow...' He put his hands in front of his face then spread his arms like he was David

Copperfield on the verge of the reveal during an awesome illusion. 'Let there be food!'

'I know! Are we ready?'

'Bruno's gone for the day so I guess we must be. From my experience, he never goes off half-cocked.'

'Cool. Is Pat still about?'

'Yessum. Out back. Just doing a few bits and bobs - Bruno drew up a snag list for him.'

On entering the kitchen, I spied Pat kneeling on the range with his head buried in the extractor hood. I tip-toed over so as not to reveal my presence by squelching noisily. Once I was standing right next to him I boomed 'HI HONEY I'M HOME!!'

There was a satisfying clang as he jumped up startled and banged his head on the aluminium. He then slowly unwound and ducked his head to look at me.

'Arsehole.'

'Sorry bud; couldn't pass up that opportunity. Whatcha doin'?'

'Fitting the filter.'

'Up for a pint?'

'Yes thanks. I'll have the blood of your first-born too.'

'Ooh touchy! You might have quite a wait for that.'

'What? Isn't the divine Jess standing by to receive your lousy swimmers? Here's a tip - if she can tot up your sperm count on the fingers of one hand that's not good news. You know you can boost it by eating more veg and not wearing those thongs?' He grinned, clearly not actually upset by my prank, but keen for some payback nonetheless.

'Me and Jess broke up.'

His grin disappeared in an instant. 'What the actual fuck?'

As I continued to drip onto the new floor, I filled him in, recounting everything about the break-up and what I was planning to do to get some control back into my life. Pat being Pat, he of course offered to assist but this was to be a solo mission. If I took him along and things went pear-shaped, Lorna would kill me. And when his boy was old enough, he'd dig me up and kill me again. 'Thanks mate but this is for me to do. I'm the one that's got beef with Boat Bitch, not you.'

'No offence me old but I don't think you're really cut out for this sort of Action Man malarkey.'

'None taken. And you're right. But all the more reason to take it on I'd say.'

'Fair play to you. Just go careful okay?'

'For sure.' I looked around the kitchen. 'This place looks great; you're a star Pat. I really owe you for this one. Tim as well - he's a top boy.'

Now back at floor level, he put his arm across my shoulders and propelled me towards the stairwell door. 'We'll hug it out later. Right now, you need to get changed and then we'll set about lubricating the gears of war.'

I shared a couple of drinks with J.D. and Pat, but my mind was still churning with other matters. Simon was working the evening shift and he provided some distraction and much amusement with a crop of anecdotes featuring awkward situations brought about by his impaired hearing. All of which I felt guilty laughing at yet all of which were hilarious and seeing as he seemed entirely okay with his partial deafness being the focus of the comedy, I went along for the ride. My favourite was the tale of him working the bar at a wake when he didn't realise the eulogy had started as it was happening on his deafer side. Short of things to do as the audience were all seated and listening attentively to the speaker, he'd spied a chock-full bottle cap collector that was hanging there beneath the opener. So, he grabbed it and emptied it into the bin behind the bar with a resounding clatter; a high-volume cacophony that prompted a chorus of 'Shush!!!'s and appalled looks from the many bereaved in the room. This (rather hushed) outburst failed to reach his fully-functional ear also, and spotting a couple of bottle caps stuck to the floor of the collector, he proceeded to smash it repeatedly against the side of the reverberating bin to set them free. It took the bar manager practically wrestling him to the ground to make him aware of the acoustic havoc he was wreaking on that sombre occasion.

It had been a busy day and tomorrow would hopefully be even busier with the launch of our first food service, so around ten I said my goodbyes and took myself upstairs. For a second, I contemplated giving my new (old) VCR a whirl for some light relief but then thought back to the mission. Must keep my priorities straight. So; I copied the photos from today's site survey to my laptop and spent an hour or so going through them to see if there was any evidence therein to warrant a change of plan. I didn't find any. Unless my night recce threw up any surprises, I was going across the water. It was going to be the full frontal assault.

Just before I shut the laptop down, I checked the TripAdvisor web site. The fake reviews were still there; and they still smarted. Powering off the machine, I looked across to the pub/sales office model that still sat gathering dust on the bedroom shelf. For no apparent reason, I addressed the empty room. 'I'm coming for you. The time for honouring yourself will soon be at an end, highness.'

CHAPTER TWELVE

To be honest, I wasn't the religious type; more one of your atheist hypocrites that stridently declared such blind faith to be complete twaddle due to its propensity for provoking atrocious behaviour and violence between human beings, yet still occasionally felt in need of a bit of a sit-down and some silent contemplation in one of God's houses. And we all love a good wedding don't we? Funerals not so much; though choosing an outfit is a more straightforward process. I'd suffered a turbulent night again, with dreams about repeatedly falling off tall things and landing on sharp things, interspersed with numerous sweaty awakenings. So, I'd decided to get out and about first thing to walk off the weirdness. Also, with his tanning duties complete in Timbuktu, the sun had its hat back on and was beckoning at me to come out to play; ear-numbingly chilly though it still was outdoors. And so I came to be on the doorstep of "The

Church of Saint James" at half past eight in the morning, fretting about the days that lay ahead.

Yesterday's busy-ness had done a reasonable job of keeping me from dwelling on the negatives, but today I was struggling; filled with anxious thoughts of Jess, tomorrow night's escapade and the imminent resurrection of food service at the pub this very lunchtime - all of which filled me with varying levels of sadness, nausea and dread simultaneously. Yesterday I'd been driven; today I just felt overwhelmed and entirely under-equipped to master the challenge I was staring down the barrel of. I wasn't expecting miracles or any kind of salvation from my visit to hallowed ground - I'd caught a glimpse of the church tower at the end of the side street that wound past the old Customs House and the museum, and suddenly got the feeling that it was somewhere I needed to be. I was surprised to find the front door open that early, and thankful that it didn't creak loudly on opening (as all such doors do in the films), thus affording me a quiet entrance without interrupting the prayer group that occupied the area close to the altar. Taking a seat in the last row but one, I leaned on the pew in front and rested my head on clasped hands, sending my thoughts out into the room and beyond, hoping they'd return with some much-needed optimism in tow.

After five minutes or so, there was a rustle of activity as the prayer group disbanded. I looked up as the queue of believers filed past, all smiling or nodding at me as they moved by. I returned their good-natured gestures, inwardly jealous of their obvious serenity. After the last of them had passed by, I went to return to my far more troubled deliberations.

'Good Morning! You're new.'

Next to me stood a bright purple cardigan that appeared homemade thanks to its coarse uneven knit, with a black shirt and white dog collar beneath. Looking slightly higher, I took in a pretty, smiling, forty-something face framed by a ginger bob.

'I'm Lucy Bolt, The Vicar. Goodness don't look so petrified! I don't carry a gun and I've no intention of wielding the collection plate. At least not yet. The plate that is; I think the church is some way off allowing their representatives to bear firearms. Though I've believe they do in some of those trashy B-movies. I couldn't testify to that however as I don't get out much. Him upstairs keeps me rather busy. Or her.'

She spoke quickly in high-pitched, perky, yet quite posh governess-like tones and I figured she'd just keep talking at me until I spoke up and interrupted her enthusiastic flow.

'Good Morning Vicar. I'm Ken. And yes I'm new; sort of.'

'Do call me Lucy, sort of new Ken. Budge up.' I shuffled along the pew to create room enough for her to sit. 'So what brings you to Saint James''? Sorry it's like a fridge in here. The

311

heating system is older than I am and emits much less hot air, hence the cardie. My niece knitted it for me as a Christmas present. Lovely girl; frightfully thick bless her, but as pretty as the day is long so she'll do just fine.'

'Well Lucy, I'm going through a difficult time at the moment and just wanted a bit of peace to get my thoughts straight. Just need to sort shit out you know?' The bad word just slipped out unfiltered. 'Shit, so sorry; I didn't mean to swear. Aah! Certainly not twice, sorry! Shit.'

I looked across at her sheepishly but she didn't bat an eyelid and her smile didn't waver.

'Oh don't worry. The clergy are the worst I know for profanity, though we do keep it behind closed doors of course. Apart from that one regrettable mass Father Adam conducted after forgetting to take his Tourette's medication. But still, I believe our Lord has more pressing matters to worry about than the odd bit of effing and jeffing. Terrorism, famine, Keith Chegwin - all that. So might I ask what it is that you're struggling with? None of my business of course, but a problem shared and all that?'

For some reason, I had absolutely no hesitation in pouring out my woes; she just had something about her, and the truth tumbled out without censorship. 'My dream woman broke up with me because I told her that her bitch mother was bullying me into handing over my business to her which was the truth but she didn't believe it so dumped me. So now I'm planning my revenge whilst also hoping that the first lunchtime food service in my pub isn't a complete fucking disaster. Sorry! Shit.' Having aired my predicament, I felt petty and foolish. My issues were irrelevant when stacked against the monumental global evils of mass bloodshed and hunger. And Cheggers.

She frowned. 'Hmmm; you're in something of a pickle aren't you? I'm afraid I don't have a magic fix for you - The Church is more Dibley than Old Testament these days. Still, when I'm in a jam, I pause and take a long hard look at my problems and sometimes come to the conclusion that it's not them, it's me. I'm not saying that you've brought all your tribulations upon yourself, but have you taken the responsibility you should have to resolve them? This dream-girl for instance - how hard have you worked to win her back? God loves a trier you know. Maybe you believe you've done your bit by giving up and sobbing into your beer? Likewise, the unpleasant mother - have you been busy turning all available cheeks, only to get repeatedly shafted in the process? Perhaps it's time to push back. That said, revenge usually solves little. I'm all in favour of action over inaction but be careful how you go about gaining your hoped-for restitution. Sorry if that's rather self-contradictory advice. I suppose I'm saying do something; and do something bold. Just not anything too iffy.'

'I erm, well; I sent some flowers: to the mother.'

Her frown deepened. 'Oh dear boy, you're rather terrible at this aren't you? I don't know the in's and out's of your particular dilemma but it's clear you could do with some assistance. At the moment you're like a horse trying to operate a petrol pump. Come on, let's pray.'

'Frankly Lucy, I'm not really the praying type.'

'Oh they rarely are dear boy. But what do you have to lose? Go on; head down, and try and clear your thoughts.'

Lucy knelt; head on hands. I followed suit.

'Dear Lord. We have sort of new Ken with us today and he needs our help to steer him straight during a stressful time. His happiness appears to be under threat from volatile women and unproven cuisine - an all too common scenario as you're no doubt aware. Please bestow your wisdom and energy upon him so that he may work through these troubles without screwing up so majorly that he ends up in The Big House picking up the soap in the showers in front of Donkey Alan. Amen.'

I spluttered an 'Amen' too, then looked across to Lucy astonished. 'That was different!'

She got to her feet. 'Well, we're the modern church don't you know. Got to keep it real brother; or something like that.'

I stood up too. 'Thank you Lucy. I really needed some sort of intervention to spur me on.'

'I could tell. Now go fix what needs fixing. Action over inaction remember. Just avoid getting yourself in serious bother. And don't be a stranger. Drop by and attend a service sometime, and bring lots of change for the collection. It's not for the roof you understand; or the heating. I can just so see myself in the new Mercedes S-Class.' She turned and walked away towards the altar.

As I headed for the exit, I actually felt genuinely invigorated by our talk. Maybe the brief but special hotline call to the higher power had helped too; even though it was all claptrap of course. As the door slowly swung shut behind me, I caught Vicar Lucy's parting shot echoing from inside.

'Be sure to do your very best to not be a dick, sort of new Ken. That's probably better advice than you'll find on any page of The Good Book.'

What a lady. Maybe I'd got religion all wrong. Either way, I was back on track. 'I promise!'

As I walked through the front door of the pub, I was greeted by surprised looks from J.D. and Janine, both presumably stunned by me having already ventured out, as opposed to my more customary shambling down the stairs just before opening time.

'Yes, yes it's me - been for a stroll. Even went to church. Just needed some advice on how to exorcise Boat Bitch from my life. Turns out, legally it's a minefield, demonic possession being nine-tenths of the law and all that.'

'Did you confess to worshipping Shania Twain and buying her toe-nail clippings on eBay?' Janine was clearly on form.

'Or did you come clean about getting a boner whenever you watch male wrestling?' As was J.D.

The room actually felt charged with static electricity, crackling like a balloon rubbed against a woollen jumper, full of excited anticipation as if big things were about to happen. Which hopefully they were. Even J.D. was buzzing around rather than leisurely perusing his paper as was his norm, instead adjusting and re-adjusting each table and chair to perfection within an inch of its life.

I hung up my jacket then went into the immaculate kitchen to find Bruno wrangling containers in the fridge. His knife roll lay open and ready for duty on the worktop. 'Morning Bruno! Are we good to go?'

He turned; resplendent in his speckless Chef's whites. 'Good Morning! We are indeed extremely good to go. I am preparing to hopefully be rushed off my feet.'

'Great - here's wishing you get completely mobbed.'

He wandered over and shook my hand. 'This is a courageous venture might I say - the very best of luck to you Ken.'

'Good luck to us all - it's been a team effort Bruno. And thanks to you especially; without your input I'd have been up shit creek without a paddle. Or a boat.'

'Absolutely my pleasure. Oh and I corrected the menus as promised, they just need placing on the tables.'

With that he passed me a stack of plastic-coated yellowness. Scrutinising the first of the pile, I scrolled down to the offending cheese and ham Ciabatta listing. Somehow, he'd managed to overprint the rogue 'n' in 'Manure' with a 't' and cover it with laminate. Unless you knew it was there or were actively looking for it, you wouldn't notice the repair. 'Christ Bruno, that's brilliant. Do you do fake passports as well?'

'The newer biometric ones are quite a challenge, but do-able none the less.' He smiled, then slung a tea towel across his shoulder and went back to his prep. Honest to God, I really couldn't be sure if he was joking or not.

I took the menus out into the bar and placed one on each table, leaving the remainder alongside the till. They looked a little tacky wedged between the salt and pepper shakers, but they'd do for now. At the far end of the bar stood various bottles of sauce together with the other usual condiment suspects plus the napkin-encased cutlery. I went over and double checked that everything was present and correct - not that I doubted this hadn't already been done by J.D., Janine and probably Bruno too. But I was nervous and needed something to keep me occupied. Halo was curled up in her basket under the bar, seemingly unaware of the momentous events about to take place. 'Hey J.D.; is Halo still keeping out of the kitchen?'

'Yep. Bruno says he'll shout if she shows her face in there.'

'Okay fine.' I was reluctant to keep the kitchen door shut all the time as it would make life difficult when moving stock and food through to the bar. Hopefully the new selection of treats Halo was soon to be spoiled with would keep her glued to the dining area. I did another scan of just about everything; and all was precisely as it should be. What a team I was part of; all with such enthusiasm and a real passion for getting quality into every detail of the service we provided to our beloved townsfolk and visitors. Even if they did rip the piss out of me all the live long day, they were superstars in my eyes. We were ready; properly ready. God I was nervous, but at the same time, fiercely proud of how far we'd come. Okay Pulton; come and get fed. The moment warranted some guy from NASA starting a countdown. Or the bloke that did the "Thunderbirds" intro. And then something popped loudly in the kitchen.

Concerned, I rushed for the door to investigate, but was met with the sight of J.D. carrying a tray bearing a bottle of champagne and four flutes.

'Woah easy tiger! Thought we'd have some celebratory fizz before the masses arrive; give the new venture a proper send-off.' He set the tray down and filled the glasses then handed them out to me, Janine and Bruno who'd wandered through to the bar, no doubt in on the surprise. 'Cheers one and all - here's to Pulton's newest and best eaterie!'

'Well played J.D. - I should have thought to do this.' Glasses clinked all round. 'Good luck everyone! Here's to a new chapter in the story of "The Pulton Arms". God bless you all; and please don't spit in the sandwiches, even if the customer is a colossal dick-head. Cheers!'

Lunchtime went well. Ridiculously well in fact. We were helped by a glorious, Spring-like day that encouraged more passing trade than we might usually expect at that time of year and nearly everyone that ventured into the pub gave the menu a look, even if they didn't order anything. But many did, and come half-twelve, we were a good three-quarters full and over half of those present were enjoying something from Bruno's kitchen. Although we didn't currently offer anything terribly high-end, every plate that emerged from his steam-filled domain looked classy and bloody tasty, and all I saw were satisfied faces as the dishes landed and got tucked in to. We hadn't really discussed roles beforehand as the volume of food business was an unknown quantity so we mostly made it up as we went, but it worked just fine. Whoever was closest to the kitchen door when Bruno proclaimed an order to be ready and wasn't already busy serving would play waiter, or waitress. Food orders were taken at the till, so there was little overhead there, but I took the thought away to look into table service proper.

It was all good. We received nothing but praise from the punters and also pleasant surprise that we'd broadened our offering. And the biggest seller? Bruno's chili. I snuck a small bowl myself in the kitchen - it was fabulously tasty (he adds dark chocolate to the sauce apparently); and fiery enough to banish the winter chills without burning your face off. And the second best seller? The Parma Ham and Mature Cheese Ciabatta. And throughout the session, Halo showed zero interest in the kitchen whatsoever, instead making the most of the spoils to be had in the dining area, as hoped.

By three o'clock the customers were thinning out, so I spent a few minutes taking stock of the session. In the face of my worries, we'd cracked it, no two ways about it. The team had done a splendid job and the takings bore testament to that. Even J.D. commented on the healthy till.

'Blimey. That's pretty saucy for a Thursday lunchtime this time of year.'

Saucy indeed. Yes, we had a way to go still, but I was over the moon at our successful kick-off and the way we'd got the job done. I would have hugged the lot of them but decided against it for fear of Janine telling her Dad, J.D. calling me an arse-bandit or Bruno giving me an all too intimate tour of the meat slicer. Instead, I asked J.D. if he had another bottle of champagne stashed away somewhere, which he then duly produced. At that point, with excellent timing, Pat and Tim turned up and joined in our group celebration. Fortunately, J.D.'s reserves extended to yet another bottle of fizz. Once again we all knocked glasses: I caught Bruno's eye and raised my glass again to him separately, making it clear how much I appreciated his input: and output.

'So how did it all go? Everything work in the kitchen?' Pat clearly felt invested in the new enterprise.

Bruno spoke first. 'The kitchen is a dream to work in Pat. In future I shall refuse to work anywhere that hasn't been blessed by the application of your fair skills beforehand.'

'I'll take that as a yes.' More glass raising. 'Is Chef still serving or are we too late?'

'Pat; Tim – please come with me. For you, my kitchen is always open.' Then off he went, with the two boys following him eagerly.

I looked to J.D. and Janine. 'Thanks again guys; blinding work today. How was it for you?'

'It was fine.' said Janine. 'Reckon we could get spanked in the Summer though if we don't have someone just dedicated to serving the food. If we're busy on the drinks, stuff might go cold before we get to deliver it.' J.D. nodded in agreement. Janine continued. 'I've got a mate who might be interested if you're looking to bring someone else in?'

'Maybe; if all goes well. Will she give me as much crap as you do?'

'No way! Nobody's stealing that job off of me.'

'Fine. Get her to drop in sometime for a chat.'

'Wilco guvna.'

I took a look around the bar and savoured a few moments of self-achievement. My first project at the pub had got off to a kick-ass start. And God wanted me for a sunbeam, I imagined. I thought back to this morning's meeting with the formidable Vicar Lucy Bolt. Action over inaction remember. I drained my glass, shouted a 'See you in a bit' to whoever was or might be within earshot, then slung on my jacket and headed out. There was more shopping to be done.

To traverse the channel to the SharpCrest yard, I needed a boat; a small boat that only needed to convey me and my Army surplus holdall and its contents. A dingy would do very nicely. With that in mind, I'd come to the Fishermen's Quay. I'd seen any number of suitable candidates dragged up onto the shoreline on previous visits and I was confident I'd be spoilt for choice when it came to finding a craft I could "borrow" for my mission. But the further I walked, the more that assurance was eroded.

The seaworthy vessels were secured with chunky chains as thick as my thumb, while those that had served out their days were lying there unrestrained but broken, and by no means watertight. I'd hoped to find a suitable transport, do my deed on the night then return it with nobody the wiser. No harm, no foul. But freeing a boat that was fit for purpose would require bolt-cutters or a seriously beefy hacksaw, and I'd be hurting those who'd done nothing to deserve it, unless I found some way to put things back entirely as they were. Also, it then occurred to me that even if I could liberate a suitable tub, I'd have to row the length of both the fishermen's and the yacht wankers' marinas before even reaching my crossing point to the yard. And then I'd have to repeat the same trip in reverse after completing my operation. That struck me as hard work. Okay sod it: Plan B it was.

Plan B involved a whole lot more walking. You'd think seaport shops would be packed with all the nautical equipment you could ever need, inflatable dinghies included. But you'd be wrong. First off, I tried "Archers" which was opposite the Lifeboat Station, requiring me to travel the length of the quay. This was a boaty emporium with posters in the window boasting "If we don't have it, you don't need it!'. I was tempted to ask if they stocked insulin or tampons. As for dinghies, they carried a decent range but it turned out they only held limited stock in-house and ordered most in from their far-flung warehouse. I wasn't prepared to wait two weeks. The starting price of £400 also made my eyes water; I was only crossing the channel, not crossing <u>The</u> Channel. The place appeared to mostly just stock life-jackets, charts and galley equipment, with the bulk of the latter mostly comprising novelty mugs and aprons with slogans like "My other boat's a... (something or other that meant bugger all to me).

The only other store that end of the quay was "Meghan's Trainers", a small sportswear outlet. An odd choice for the quayside to my mind. Maybe the boating crowd are more into fitness than I would have thought.

'Just heading out for essentials Sabrina - anything you need?'

'Oh Gerry yes, we need oil for the lamps, a sun hat for Porshia (you know how those gingers catch the sun; I spent all of yesterday fearing she was about to burst into flames), a new deck mop and we are getting <u>desperately</u> low on Lycra.'

I backtracked and headed into town, once more striding past "Coasters" at speed. I couldn't recall any other boating-oriented shops from previous excursions and my plod up the High Street didn't deliver any new discoveries. I guessed I'd need to visit the shops in or around the beaches of Silverbanks for the standard seaside fare of inflatable sea craft, rubber rings, boogie boards, buckets, spades and overtly sexist cardboard cut-outs featuring half-naked lovelies and Factor 50 sun lotion. Then just as the shopping centre came into view, it hit me - the catalogue shop! This was deep within the loathsome complex but I was out of other options. So, I girded my loins and charged through the door into the ghastly brightness and the legion of zombie shoppers.

Once in the store I stationed myself at an unattended, anchored to the counter, laminated catalogue - possibly one of the most efficient germ spreading devices known to man. Why they didn't have those anti-bacterial hand gel dispensers scattered throughout these places I'd never know. Right; "Home and Garden", no; "Sports and Leisure - ah-ha. After much page flicking, amidst the lilos and paddling pools, I struck gold. "Two-person dinghy with repair kit. £29.99." Bargain! It even had a safety rope and rubber oar holders built in. Inexplicably, it didn't come with oars though which was a disappointment. Still, I was pleased to read it was constructed from high-grade PVC, whatever that was. Unfortunately, that PVC was also brilliantly yellow in colour, patterned with smiling green turtles, but beggars can't be choosers. Plus, if all went to plan, I'd be the only one to see it in action anyway. I tapped the catalogue number into the gadget which informed me there was only one left in stock. This moved me to scan the room to see how many other potential dinghy buyers might be present, all the while poised to sprint to the till and claim my prize. Most of those present looked old enough not to be interested in water sports and I was reasonably confident I could best them if it came to a fist fight at the checkout. However, there was a family gathered at one station, pointing at their catalogue and smiling, with two young kids bouncing up and down excitedly. They could be a major problem: I had to move fast.

I whizzed through various different sections of the catalogue but there were no oars. Darn. Then, during an accidental browse of the "Car Winter Essentials" pages, I spied a "Travel Snow Shovel". It was oar-shaped; kind of, with a broad plastic spade end. According to the product description, it was also "lightweight but sturdy and fits into any car boot with room to spare". I was tempted; also the volume from the bouncing family was on the rise and I sensed they were getting close to settling up, having decided the sole remaining dinghy was the one for them. But I really needed to know how big the shovel actually was; I didn't want to come away with something only fit for building sandcastles or burying my Sister's Barbie because she'd stolen the flake out of my '99. Cow. Still holding my nerve, and rather impressed with my brinkmanship, I took time to check the stock and again I got lucky. Then I noticed a banner on the screen suggesting I read the on-line product reviews. Ah-ha! There could be some size clues there. I hit the button and took a quick look at the first handful of what was a surprisingly large collection of comments. Get a life people – it's just a snow shovel! That said, I was heartened by the overall rating of 4.2 stars out of 5 so perused the postings.

'Buyers should be aware that this is a travel item so the handle is considerably shorter than that of a normal shovel so you may have to bend over more than you may be used to.'

'Despite the description stating that the shovel would fit into my car boot, I was upset to find that it didn't. I do drive a Bugatti Veyron Super Sport; not a model known for its extensive boot space I grant you, but I wish these companies would carry out sufficiently detailed research before making such rash claims about their offerings.'

'Very pleased with this purchase. We recently had serious snowfall overnight and I spent several pleasurable hours watching my wife using the shovel to clear the drive the following morning while I knocked one out to "Loose Women" on the ITV.'

'I live on the south coast and we rarely get snow but it's always good to be prepared. The shovel is reasonably priced and sits nicely in the rear footwell together with the shotgun and the holy water cannon. Foot-room isn't an issue as I never have anyone on the back seat. Or the front for that matter, being single since I exposed myself in the museum that one time. Ridiculous: victimised for brief nudity in the "History of Flight" section. They didn't believe that vampire pomegranates were out to get us either. But they are, you mark my words.'

'Me and my mates used the shovel as an improvised cricket bat after a few shandies down "The Crown". It worked great with a tennis ball. Alan smashed a six with it then Toby accidentally left it on the barbecue hot plate and the plastic bit melted. Awesome!'

'Best ever purchase!!'

Okay I was sold, though slightly concerned about Keith from Nantwich, him having never bought anything to eclipse this particular acquisition; ever. Having scribbled the catalogue numbers on the ordering slip, I took off at speed to seal the deal, striding past the bouncing family who were still trying to find a mini-biro that worked: you snooze you lose suckers. A few minutes later, the transaction was complete and I was directed to collection point B. I paid cash, as I had for all my recent buys, risking no credit card activity that could be traced, just to be on the safe side. When my order number popped up, I did the same and approached the counter, curious as to why I'd been assigned collection point B specifically when collection points A, C and D were similarly empty, with a lone member of staff behind the counter walking up and down collecting items placed apparently randomly on the shelves behind her. The dinghy came in a fair-sized box, so I accepted the offer of an even bigger carrier bag to transport it in - no point in telegraphing my intentions to everyone on the High Street. The shovel easily slotted into the bag. Blimey; those super-cars really do have appallingly limited boot space don't they?

On returning to the pub, I used the tradesman's entrance to gain access, wanting to minimise the number of times I'd have to lie about what I'd bought and why. Bruno was busy in the kitchen, which looked as spick-and-span as it had first thing this morning before being fully utilised for the first time. Actually so did he, seemingly managing to complete the entire lunchtime shift without even the smallest errant splash or wipe of the hand discolouring his still gleaming whites.

He looked up from the sheets of paper laid out in front of him on the central island, all of which seemed to comprise hand-sketched flow charts of some kind. He scanned me from head to toe. 'Good afternoon Ken. A successful shopping trip I trust?'

329

'Fine thanks; just a few essentials for The Crow's Nest. Trying to make it a bit homelier.'

'Good idea. It is also common knowledge that nothing says home more than jovial green turtles.' He returned to his pages, thankfully ending his questions there.

Christ, he really did see and hear everything. That said, the carrier bag was a bit see-through. 'Oh right yes. Just keeping it nautical you know? Or should that be aquatic?' I really needed to get off this subject. 'So what are you busy with?'

'As we're discussing reptiles, might I suggest aquatic? I've taken the liberty of drafting some handling and service procedures. At some point, a Food Standards Agency inspector will drop by and expect to see the blueprint of how we operate and verify that we're working to it. I've already walked J.D. and Janine through the key points but they already possess the appropriate experience so there's not much to teach there, but it will be useful information for any new starters. I'm terribly fond of those two you know; they're what I'd call "good people".'

'They are aren't they? As are you. And thank you for this; it's a huge help. How soon do you think it will be before we get an FSA visit?'

'From my experience, I would expect sometime within the next month. But please do not fret - whenever they do decide to drop by, we'll be more than prepared.'

'Have the guys told you about the fake TripAdvisor reviews? They won't help will they.'

'Yes they did make me aware, but I wouldn't worry about those either. I understand they'll be taken down soon and I promise you, before long we will be serving food of such style, quality and originality that the only negative reviews "The Pulton Arms" will receive will come from those that have to queue around the block whilst they wait for a table to become available.'

'Amen to that Bruno. I don't doubt you for an instant.' Actually I held a small doubt, but I'd never be brave enough to tell him that. And was it that far-fetched in fact? Had he under-delivered so far? Far from it. 'You're in the right place, and we're very lucky to have you. Right; must go sort out my shopping.'

He looked around the room then back at me. 'You know what Ken? I am in the right place. I haven't felt this settled for quite some years. We're creating something special here and I'm as pleased as punch to be a part of it. The rest of the team hold you in high esteem too you know. You remain the butt of the majority of their jokes its true but all I hear when you're not around is how pleased they are to have you at the helm. Of course you didn't hear that from me, Boss.' With a wink he turned his attention back to his flow charts.

'Thanks Bruno. That's great to hear.' I was genuinely touched. I'd guessed from the day-to-day that the guys were okay with me, but hearing that they were really on-board put a proper spring in my step. Upwards and onwards.

Having dropped my shopping off upstairs, I headed back out. There was still much to be done.

Once I hit the quay, I headed straight for the sculpture and trod the steps up to the viewing deck. Work in the yard was still in full swing it appeared; Boat Bitch got a full day out of her workers it seemed, and then some. What I wanted was to see the state of play when business was done for the day, as that was the time I'd be performing tomorrow. I'd figured Friday would be the best day to choose, with nobody working the next day hopefully. I hadn't witnessed any activity over previous weekends so that stood a fair chance of being the quietest time at the yard. Also, I was getting so worked up over the mission and my need to get my life in order again, I simply didn't have the patience to hold off any longer. Tonight's recce was clearly premature however, and it was too bastard cold to wait around another couple of hours until SharpCrest shut up shop. I considered paying "Westall's" a visit, then worked out that Beth would have closed up by now. Then I thought of Jess and how much I missed her face. Stuff it; I was going to "Coasters".

Before going through the door I paused, contemplating whether I was just adding something else foolhardy to the list of foolhardy things I already had planned for the next day or so. I recalled Jess's words and her look when she'd said she didn't want to see me anymore. Then I remembered Vicar Lucy Bolt's message from this morning, thought about what Aunt Maddy would do, took a deep breath and walked into the bar.

There was no sign of Jess. I ordered up a wine then went and sat at the same table I'd favoured on previous visits, all the time scanning the room in the hope of seeing that glorious individual I'd fallen for that still made my stomach go weird whenever I thought about her. I worked my way through my drink then ordered another, now turning my thoughts to tomorrow night's adventure, walking it through to make sure there were no flaws or omissions in my strategy.

My plan was simple - row across the channel to the yard, make my simple yet direct statement, then leave. Then hope Boat Bitch got the message and ended our feud without dogging me in to the police. Not that she could prove anything. Unless I seriously cocked things up that is. I could then tell Jess that I'd worked out my differences with her mother and she'd realise I was the one for her after all, and we'd sail off into the sunset together to spend the rest of our days in deeply-tanned bliss, reading poetry to one another and braiding our sun-bleached locks between thrice-daily sessions of mind-blowing sex. With a bit of top-up fondling in between.

And some light shopping perhaps - Henna tattoos, friendship bracelets and quiche; that kind of thing. Maybe I was aiming rather high: a man can dream. Finishing my second drink, I walked over and returned my empty glass to the bar.

'Pour y'anuvva squire?' said the young lad behind the bar, sounding like a reject from "Oliver Twist". Or a young offender from "The Bill".

'No thanks; need to get going. Is Jess working tonight?' Nothing ventured....

'Na don't fink so guv. She only does lunchtimes usually and wonna the uvvas said she'd been off sick the last coupla days anyways.'

'Okay thanks. Goodnight.'

'Laters bruv.'

He reminded me of the underage drinkers who occasionally ventured into the pub, trying to style it out with what I believe the young people call "bantz":

'Yo fam! Two lagers now innit.' I could never decide whether that was a statement or a question but J.D. had their measure as soon as they walked in the door. And he took no prisoners.

'Could I see some ID please?'

'Mate you is jokin'! We is proper old enough man! You is havin' a right laugh cuz.'

'No if I were joking I'd do that one about the six-inch pianist. Or maybe a bit of Michael McIntyre; maybe his "man drawer" routine. Either way, show me some ID or get the feck out of my pub. Are ya feelin' me bro?'

I walked back to the "Sea Mood" erection, feeling mopey after trying and failing to bump into Jess in "Coasters". I wondered if she was really sick or just not able to work because her withdrawal symptoms were so severe after breaking up with me she could do nothing but spend all day crying whilst necking tequila, chain-eating Wotsits and watching "Titanic" on a loop. Not that this has tended to be my coping mechanism in the past or anything. Once more on the observation deck, I took my phone and zoomed in to what now appeared to be a deserted yard. There was nothing and nobody moving as far as I could see. The doors to the cavernous worksheds were now closed and no doubt secured with massive chains and padlocks the size of dinner plates. But the rest of the yard lay there ready for me; brilliantly illuminated by the abundant lights on poles but with the equipment and clutter providing plenty of shadow to exploit. And there sat all the boats, gleaming under the floods. Some were slung up on gigantic hoists, while their companions sat propped on stands surrounded by scaffolding or lay moored in the channel - all looking like gargantuan works of science fiction. I focused on the security cameras; they were still directed at the channel, not the yard. Maybe they didn't move after all? I spent a while with my view fixed on what I thought might be the security shed; there were lights on inside but I detected no activity. Perhaps those usually stationed within were out doing their rounds? Or maybe that was just where they kept the screws and boat polish, and the last man out hadn't flicked the switch?

I spent a good half an hour scanning the yard without picking up any movement - be that man or machine. Come the time, I'd have to be on my toes and prepared for last-minute surprises that I couldn't pick out at this distance, but otherwise I'd seen nothing to make me think that my plan wasn't workable. I just needed to be man enough to see it through on the night. Tomorrow night in fact. Blimey....

Being thorough, I took a handful of photos to study later just in case there was something I'd overlooked, then headed home. As I walked, I felt the pull of my lovely pub and savoured the thought of the company of the good people that awaited me within; and Bruno's lunchtime leftovers. Then completely out of character, I offered up a prayer to whichever deity might have been listening, asking that they look after my spectacular bunch of colleagues, friends and family and help me prevail in my quest for justice. Then I telegraphed extra special thanks to Vicar Lucy for lighting a fire under my arse.

CHAPTER THIRTEEN

So here it was. The big day. Ideally, I'd fast-forward to closing time and get the mission underway, rather than live out the hours in between, all the while watching the clock. I hadn't told Pat when I was planning to do the deed but he may have had a hunch as he'd phoned me early this morning.

'Hi mate; how's it going?'

'All good me old, all good. Starting the new contract next week so you'll have to get by without me I'm afraid. Not that there's anything you need doing unless you break something. Or someone else does. Talking of which, have you got a date in the diary for your... excursion?'

'I'm going tonight.'

'Wow - okay. You sure I can't help?'

'Thanks mate but no. A man's godda do wadda man's blah blah blah. And all that.'

'Okay. Well you go careful. Bell me and let me know how it went when you're done. Actually scratch that; I'll drop in and see you in the pub tomorrow. I know we're not MI5 but some chats are better had face-to-face if you know what I mean? Plus you'll wake the family up if you call in the wee hours.'

'Gotcha.'

'You heard from Jess?'

'Nope. I dropped into "Coasters" last night on the off chance, but no joy.'

'Ah well. Chin up mate. Go take care of business tonight, then you can think about how to get her back when that witch of a mother is hopefully out the frame. If you want her back that is.'

'Bit too much detail over the phone mate. You'd be rubbish in MI5. And yes I do; me and Jess deserve a proper go at being us.'

'Fair enough. Good luck tonight me old. And Ken....... your flies are open.'

He got me with that every time. 'Git.' He'd already hung up.

The lunchtime session was frustratingly sluggish. In reality, it was probably no slower than usual but I wanted it done and dusted. My eagerness to keep myself occupied must have been transparent to J.D. and Janine as they backed off and gave me first crack at any customer that approached the bar if I wasn't already tied up with another. Janine even commented on it.

'If you're after the "Employee of the Month" award, Halo's already nailed that.'

'No I'm playing the long game. I'm after your job.'

She looked me up and down. 'Sorry love; you 'aven't got the legs for it. Them boobs are showing promise though.'

Touché.

Although I could focus on little else but tonight's activities or the distraction provided by the immediate task in hand, I was satisfied to see the menu getting plenty of attention again and each time I scanned the tables, I was met with the sight of plates being enthusiastically cleared. Bruno had been right to start small and build gradually, as we did hit a few snags in the process here and there which could have been disastrous on a grander scale, but were easily overcome when serving relatively simple fare. There was no problem with his output, more how that combined with moving bar stock and used glasses and crockery through the kitchen. It wasn't so much the traffic, but the knock-on impact of the temperature variations between the adjacent rooms as the doors in between were frequently opened and closed. J.D. spent a while puzzling over why the real ales were misbehaving and emerging from the tap mostly as froth before he sussed this was down to the fact that the cellar was now neighbour to a fully-functioning kitchen blasting out heat and steam, so went and adjusted the chiller system. We also had to work out the most hygienic practice for bar staff doubling as waiters who were handling crates and bottles one minute, then delivering lunches the next - procedural issues of that nature. None of this was too onerous, just a bit of education we all had to go through and write into our house rules. Maybe we'd all benefit from formal training at some point but for now we got by with the FSA guidelines and directions from guru Bruno.

A pleasant distraction also arrived by way of Beth from "Westall's" who'd found some time to take me up on my offer of a free lunch. She breezed in around one o'clock when service was in full swing.

'Goodness me this place smells divine!' She took a look around the room. 'Very pleased to see you haven't changed the bar too much. Most pubs are just so sterile and characterless these days - don't you dare alter it!'

'I shan't, I promise. Great to see you Beth; really glad you got to come visit.'

'Well don't go getting any ideas; you're not without your charms son but it's really the grub I'm here for. Anyone who passes on a free meal has a screw loose to my mind. I also needed to see how big a threat the competition is. Oh and I brought you something!' She placed a string-wrapped brown paper package about the size of my fist on the bar; its contents hinted at by the several greasy splodges on the packaging. Intrigued, I went to open it but she raised her hand in warning.

'I wouldn't do that in here if I were you. What you have there is twelve ounces of Grantchester's finest Fugly - I saw you eyeing it up in my shop the other day. It's glorious stuff but would very probably clear the room if you opened it now. Enjoy it in private or give it to your Chef to do something fabulous with.'

'I shall. Thanks Beth. Now, what can I get you? I don't think we have Grappa but I can have a look through the dusty bottles at the back.'

'Tempting, but I have to work this afternoon so a small medium sherry will do me just fine thank you.'

'I'll get that Ken.' J.D. had emerged from the kitchen carrying a crate of mixers which he placed beneath the bar. All the while with his eyes fixed on Beth and his face carrying as serious a look as I'd ever seen on it.

On seeing J.D., Beth's usual exuberance fell away. Then she rallied and managed to get a smile working. 'Hi John; long time no see. How are you?'

'I'm doing fine thanks Bethany. Yourself?' He turned his back and went to pour her drink.

'Very well thank you. I've just opened a small place on the High Street. You should drop by. Ken's already a regular.'

J.D. shot me a sharp look. What the hell was going on? Placing Beth's drink in front of her, he looked at the two of us in turn.

'Bethany and I go back a way. We dated about ten years ago but couldn't quite.... make it work. Turned out we wanted different things.' He came across as stern and strained but there was no malice in his tone, just an inflection that hinted at heartache.

Beth looked at me. 'Remember that awful mistake that I told you about Ken? Well, John's the unfortunate man that regrettably paid the full price for my stupidity.'

I had no idea what to say. The two of them stared at each other, wordlessly communicating volumes I was sure. So this must be why J.D. was reluctant to talk about past relationships: it was just a reminder of painful times for him. My focus shifted from one to the other as if watching a slow-mo action replay of a tennis match. The silence and tension were bordering on excruciating and I decided the only solution was me breaking the mood by coming out with something banal or crass; as I was prone to do anyway. 'Well, I guess you two have a lot to talk about. Here's a menu Bethany. Sorry, Beth. Please order whatever takes your fancy; it's on the house.' I picked up my Fugly gift. 'I'd best get this bad boy into the fridge!' Then I clattered off into the kitchen, intrigued but also relieved to be out of the John and Bethany emotional pressure-cooker. So that's what the "J" stood for. I'd never asked. And what about the "D"? "Darko" perhaps. Or "Dracula". Bruno looked at me quizzically as I stood there with a dangling package, staring into space and silently mouthing surnames that began with "D".

'Might I assist you with that Ken?'

With a start, I was back in the room. 'It's cheese. You can cook with it.'

Taking the package from me, he then gave it a hearty sniff. 'Excellent! Grantchester Fugly if I'm not mistaken. As versatile as it is mightily pungent. Someone possesses a truly adventurous palette.' He grabbed a container to cage the beast then moved to the utility room door. 'I shall store it in the outer fridge else it will undoubtedly overwhelm everything in the kitchen. And I do mean everything.'

I was still somewhat befuddled by what had just gone down in the bar. 'It came from John's ex-girlfriend who runs the deli. I mean J.D.'s ex-deli. Westall's. The deli.'

'Oh right! The new enterprise. Splendid.' He slipped through the door then reappeared a few moments later. I was still standing there pondering the freshly revealed love story, saddened by the thwarted romance between two souls I cared greatly for. Selfishly, those thoughts also did a grand job of taking my mind off my own romantic predicament. Swings and roundabouts.

Janine then bounced into the room. 'Drop your cocks and grab your socks my lovelies. One

tuna and red onion baguette melt and one steak
sarnie with English mustard not Dijon if we have
it please. Baguette's for the chap sitting next to
the ship's wheel and the sarnie is for the lady
chatting to J.D. at the end of the bar.'

She must have been referring to Beth. At
least they were talking. Maybe there was chance
of a reconciliation? After all, she was just a girl,
standing in front of a boy, asking for an
alternative sandwich dressing. If they could work
it out, why couldn't me and Jess? Beth's call to
arms came back to me, as did Vicar Lucy's. And
Pat's. And J.D.'s. There was a trend it was true.
They'd all stressed the need for action and in a
few hours I was going to deliver. Come on
tonight, hurry up.

On re-entering, the bar I spotted Beth
now seated at a table. She gave me an
enthusiastic wave when I caught her eye. J.D.
was busy clearing plates and glasses the other
side of the bar, with Halo following in his
footsteps. Returning the wave, I wondered what
might have been said between the two of them.
I'd adored Beth from the first time we'd met, and
J.D. was (I hoped) a permanent fixture of life at
"The Pulton Arms" and I struggled to imagine
him not being around. Surely I could do
something to help these two smashing people
resolve their differences and rebuild their
relationship? Based on the current state of affairs
with Jess, most would question the validity of my
credentials to carry out such a role. I'd give it a

damn good go though; once I'd cleared the debris of my own train-wreck.

After Beth's sandwich had been and gone, I went over to her table. 'Mind if I join you ma'am?'

'Please do son.'

I had one eye on J.D. who was busy wiping the bar down; whether it needed it or not, as was his way.

'Anything else I can get you Beth?'

'Goodness no, thank you. That was thoroughly delicious and I am entirely stuffed. Please give my compliments to the Chef. I now have to spend the rest of the afternoon both looking at and serving food that I have absolutely no appetite for, whilst wearing more spare tyres than the Michelin Man. Seriously Ken, that was fantastic. More than just a sandwich – that was art.'

'Bruno's a star its true; there's so much more to come as well. I've tried some of his fancier dishes and they are to kill for, trust me. Oh, Bruno's the Chef by the way.'

'Is he married?'

'You know, I've no idea. I could ask?'

'Better not. I'd rather wait to sample what else he's got in store cooking-wise before I scare him off for good.'

I thought I'd try what I thought to be only a mildly invasive exploratory question. 'Are you and J.D. okay?'

She looked his way as he continued to cleanse the bar with forensic thoroughness. 'I think we're far from okay son but thanks for asking. At least he spoke. And I think on some level he was pleased to see me. I was certainly pleased to see him; it's been so long. He does wear well. I ...' Then she trailed off as she gazed solemnly at the man whose affections she had once carelessly misplaced, no doubt sifting through memories of happier times. Then she snapped back into the present. 'Right well, I must get back to my little shop. My assistant is holding the fort and he's just out of Uni so rather a stranger to proper work bless him so he may be flagging by now.' She gathered her things and stood up, casting a last glance at the bar. J.D. was nowhere to be seen. 'Thank you again for a wonderful lunch. We're not really in competition are we - different markets and all that I'd say. I'd be desperately sad if business came between us.'

'Not a chance Beth.' I gave her a hug. 'Friends first and business owners second. Deal?'

'Deal. Now put me down and go get that girl of yours back.'

'I'll do my utmost I promise.' I then whispered. 'Why not try getting your man back? Perhaps it's not too late.'

She backed away surprised; then her look softened. 'Maybe it is time I started to practice what I preach.' She leaned in and kissed me on the cheek. 'You're a good one Ken, don't let anyone tell you otherwise. Come see me for lunch one day soon; or else. Tell John I said cheerio.'

Once Beth had departed, I passed her farewell on to J.D. He gave me a thin smile but didn't comment further, instead turning to continue with his cleaning up. Although I felt he'd probably had enough of his history unexpectedly raked over today, I wanted to help; or at least make it plain to him that I cared. 'She's really sorry you know J.D.'

He turned to face me, still wearing the ill-fitting half-smile as the rest of his demeanour suggested loss. All of a sudden he appeared to have aged, seemingly lacking the usual spark that fired his everyday impetus. 'Sometimes sorry's just not enough. She really put me through the wringer you know?'

'Yeah she told me. And she also told me how much she regrets it; and regrets losing you. It's obvious she still cares about you. Couldn't the two of you give it another try? To forgive is divine as they say.'

He appeared to be considering the notion. 'You know what Ken, I'm not sure I've got the balls to get back in the ring.'

'I get that, it's tough putting your heart in harm's way again. But, as a very good friend and wise man once said to me; if in doubt, just think - what would Aunt Maddy do?'

Seconds passed as he mentally chewed on the idea: then he visibly relaxed and clapped me on the shoulder. 'Maybe I'll drop into that new deli. You know, just to suss out the competition.' Even glasses as large as his couldn't obscure the return of his usual good cheer. 'Seen the headlines today?' A slice of the usual banter was just what we both needed. 'Boris Johnson has failed his first training module at Clown College and Richard Branson's dumping Virgin Galactic and putting all the money into developing a fully-functional chocolate tea-pot.'

'Excellent. I'm surprised at Boris; I thought he'd have picked Barber School.'

Normal service had been resumed.

The evening shift dragged more than the day had done. I was acutely aware that I was twitchier than a virgin on prom night as I busied myself with nothing in particular. For the umpteenth time in as many minutes, I checked the clock yet again; it was only half eight. The bar was quiet, with barely enough custom to keep J.D. and Simon even remotely busy, so I headed up to The Crow's Nest to finish my prep for later.

Some of my key equipment purchases were still packaged so I set about those first. The snow shovel was pretty much as I'd expected; shorter than your usual paddle but it looked like it would do the job. Next, I took the dinghy out of its box and laid it out on the lounge floor. It really was quite yellow. Incandescently yellow actually. In fact, it was possibly a yellow of such brightness as to be viewable from space. Also, the green turtles that adorned its surface now looked as if they were leering at me in a mocking fashion, rather than smiling with any genuine warmth or encouragement. Turtle wankers. And the whole thing looked small: desperately small. I checked, and the box it arrived in still claimed to house a two-person dinghy. Okay, it would be bigger once inflated but looking at the rubber floor that was encircled by the (currently flat) sides, it was going to be a squeeze. How tiny were these two people that the manufacturer had in mind? Of a scale that fell comfortably below the minimum height restriction for theme park rides it seemed. It would have to do. I didn't have a pump to inflate the thing as I'd figured it wouldn't be a big deal to blow it up by mouth. Wrong.

After twenty minutes of strenuous puffing, all I got in return was a limp dinghy with no discernible shape whatsoever. Another twenty minutes gave it some form and endowed me with seriously rosy cheeks, providing a stark reminder that I should have quit smoking long before I did. That would do for now; wrestling it down the stairs fully inflated would have been cumbersome anyway. I'd finish it up in the yard later before go time.

Next, I grabbed the canvas bag and checked its contents - headgear, spray paint and torch; all present. I felt like I should be packing more equipment but really couldn't find a good reason to - I wasn't scaling fences or breaking into a vault. My black jeans were laid out ready to change into later, and I'd already un-picked the luminous brand logo from my otherwise suitably innocuous jacket. I was good to go. It was only half nine. What to do now? I scoured the lounge searching for inspiration then spied the video player I'd purchased the other day. Nice one! My participation in any sort of technology installation typically consumed huge amounts of time, usually because I tried to execute every task with a bread knife rather than taking five minutes out to find a screwdriver. Regrettably, I was also prone to standing on upturned plugs in bare feet. I remembered the first time I'd suffered that calamity, stepping down off a chair and putting my full weight onto the three-pronged death trap sitting on the floor below. As if drawing it from a wall socket, with considerable resistance I pulled it out, only to see the blood flowing freely from three uniformly rectangular wounds in the sole of my foot; and I powered myself down. Or "fainted" as some might call it.

However, this time around it was a straightforward and disappointingly brief exercise; all that was required was the connection of a couple of leads and within ten minutes I was up and running, with both feet bandage free. Satellite television was already available to me in The Crow's Nest, but the feed was slaved off the main box in the bar downstairs and I'd never got around to finding a remote control or working out how to change channels on the box itself. Thus my only viewing options were some European satellite sports channel where overexcited Spanish commentators shouted at football, or another terrestrial option showing documentaries about trains, and game show re-runs; something of a televisual lottery that I only participated in occasionally. Sifting through the stack of videos I'd brought down from the loft, I decided to go with whatever the "Ferris Bueller's Day Off" box yielded. It turned out to be "Robocock". Ah well; probably not a BAFTA winner, but it would kill some time.

It actually killed about thirty minutes before I decided I needed some Dutch courage for what lay ahead and headed back down to the bar. The film wasn't without merit to be fair; just rather hard work as it was a German outing with clumsily cobbled-together subtitles. Also, the plot fell short on credibility - were all criminals in whatever passed for the local equivalent of Detroit really surgically enhanced nymphos that would rather pleasure a cyborg than get a ticking off from the district attorney? Having never visited The Fatherland I was no authority mind. They'd put some work into the costumes though - I particularly admired the creativity behind the scenes where instead of drawing a gun from his leg as in the original movie, our hero's thigh panel opened to reveal a sizeable sex toy instead. His helmet was impressively shiny too. Anyway, the remainder of the story would have to wait for another day, though I was keen to see how Robo fared against "EDITH 209". She hadn't graced the screen as yet, but her name had been mentioned in the subtitles several times and seemed to be on everyone's lips; as had Robocock's appendage in fact.

Downstairs was jumping: the office crowd we'd entertained the other day had returned in force to celebrate a birthday in the team or some other achievement it appeared. J.D. seemed to be in good spirits still, having rallied from his edgy reunion with Beth earlier.

'Ah-ha! He's back. What happened up there? Tissue shortage?'

'No; just always have to be mindful of that RSI thing you know? All okay down here?'

'Yeah. Really great actually. Me and Simon have both had people asking when we're going to start doing food in the evenings. Word's getting out it seems. It's looking good for the bottom line too: yesterday and today we're up about 40% on the usual lunchtime take.'

Wow - that was blinding. 'Fab - we must have a sit-down and go through the books again. Maybe tomorrow when lunch is finished?'

'Sure.'

'Bruno's a good 'un isn't he. Nice tip J.D.'

'Toldja.'

I spent the next few hours dividing my time between chatting with J.D. and Simon and snacking on lunch service leftovers from the fridge, all of which were neatly squared away in containers with what I assumed were "best before" dates written on the lids in wax pencil. Looking inside the fridge then beyond around the kitchen, I couldn't see a single spot, smudge or smear. That Bruno was seriously clinical. And then we were closed; finally. We then went through J.D.'s meticulous end-of-session procedure that ensured we were fully prepared for opening tomorrow. By midnight we were done. I let J.D., Halo and Simon out the back door, poured a drink and gave my plan a final run through.

Then it was time.

CHAPTER FOURTEEN

Now wearing my dark, featureless outfit, I grabbed the floppy dinghy, the snow shovel and my bag of essentials and dropped them all in the yard, then went and turned the lights off in the bar and locked up.

Fifteen minutes or so of laborious blowing saw the dinghy brought fully to life, much to the cost of my already well-tested lungs. Damn; even fully inflated it really was bloody small still. I opened the gate and carried my diminutive transport out into the alleyway, then gathered the snow shovel and the bag. Having made sure the gate was firmly shut behind me, I walked to the end of the alleyway and scanned the quay. Apart from a giggling and decidedly wobbly couple clambering into a taxi at the rank down the way, all was quiet. It was a cold night; hopefully sufficiently nippy to keep the late-night walkers to a minimum. In four or so months' time, the quay would still be heaving at this time of night as the sunburned tourists and the equally toasted locals made the most of the mild evenings and extended opening hours to get plastered under the stars, without the need for several layers of insulation. I looked forward to that balmy time but for now, silence and solitude were my preferred companions. The street lamps put out enough light for me to see what I was doing, but without being bright enough to throw anything into sharp relief. And the clouds were keeping the moonlight out of play. Perfect - time to get going. Just then, on returning to my equipment stash, I caught the low rumble of a car approaching. Looking back to the quay, I saw the headlamp beam that confirmed its proximity. With my heart rate getting all sporty, I turned back to my gear, wondering how visible it might be from the road as I waited for the vehicle to pass. But it didn't. It slowed instead. Then with a subtle squeak of its brakes, it stopped right outside the pub. Now panicked, I span around, only to witness a reflection of brake lights on the wall at the end of the alley which then promptly disappeared, together with the engine noise. Shit!

For a minute I was paralysed, with no idea of what might constitute a sensible next move, apart from sprinting from the scene. My covert op had been blown wide open before it had even begun. There was the sound of a car door opening, a brief snatch of radio chatter, then the clunk of the door closing. Then a spear of torchlight infiltrated the alleyway opening. I needed to stow my kit; and fast. I couldn't remember the key code for the gate, having only used it once or twice. It was stored somewhere in my phone but God knows where. A figure appeared at the top of the alleyway, back-lit by the street lamps, with the torchlight sweeping the alley floor only a few yards from my feet, and closing that distance awfully rapidly. Grabbing the safety rope fixed to the dinghy, I swung the whole thing up and over the gate to the yard and then followed it with the shovel. The torchlight was only centimetres from my feet. I booted the bag as hard as I could back into the darkness of the alley behind me, hopefully deep enough in shadow to avoid detection.

The torch bearer came within a few feet and as the silhouette gave way to a more three-dimensional view, I picked out a policeman's uniform.

'Good evening: it's Mr Trickett isn't it? I was here a few days ago; after the vandalism? I'm P.C. Simmonds.'

Crap; was I nicked already? It's a fair cop, slap the bracelets on. 'Yes of course, call me Ken; please.' I shook his hand, way too enthusiastically, but adrenaline was my puppet-master right now. 'I was doing a final check round before turning it in for the night. Best to be vigilant and all that.'

'Absolutely. And do call me Andrew. No problems since I hope?'

'No none. Hopefully the last episode was a one-off. Just a few kids overdoing the cheap white cider probably.'

He flashed his torch at the gate, then back at me. I shuffled from side to side, hopefully blocking the view of the alley behind me. 'You're probably right. Well I shan't keep you. I do drop by the odd evening since you called in the first incident. But it looks like you've got it covered tonight. Any more problems, you know where we are.'

'Thank you Andrew. Good to know you're keeping an eye out; much appreciated.'

'No problem, that's our job. Goodnight now.' He turned and headed back to his car, driving off a few moments later.

Having nearly fallen before the first hurdle I was somewhat rattled, but at least I was still in the clear, and the game was still on. A few deep breaths later, I'd regrouped and was back on mission. With the key code at last retrieved from my phone, I punched in the numbers and opened the gate to the yard, finding the dinghy thankfully still fully inflated. Fortunately, I'd managed to hurl it high enough to avoid the spikes it appeared. The snow shovel had fared less well; it was missing its handle after bouncing off the concrete on landing. Not a biggie; I could work around that. However, I would be sure to leave a product review on the catalogue store's web site later: I'd hate for other consumers to make a purchase, blindly assuming they could toss the shovel willy-nilly over any barricade of their choosing with no fear of damage. Having once more made sure the gate was shut behind me, I hoisted the dinghy onto my shoulder and grabbed the shovel. Right; let's try this again.

On reaching the street, I looked left and right a few times. There was nobody in sight. I dashed across to the quayside and located the steps that led down to the water's edge, all the time catching glimpses of the glowing yellow entity humping my shoulder, with the turtles' laughter acting as a backdrop to the whole nervy drama. It was a dry night but blowy; more than once a sharp gust caught the dinghy or the shovel, propelling me sideways a metre or two each time. With one last furtive glance to each end of the quay, I carefully made my way down the steps. The top half of the flight was dry and grippy as the tide never rose that high, but the lower steps became increasingly treacherous as I descended, covered with harbour greenery made slicker by the oil and fuel residue from the armada that travelled this stretch of the channel every day. After dropping about twelve feet, I reached water level. Maybe a wet suit might have been more appropriate attire; we were still mired in February after all, and getting a soaking in the current temperature did not appeal whatsoever. Plus, that would have been much more of a fitting, James Bond type look. Or that Milk Tray fella, whose career of breaking and entering into sleeping women's houses remarkably never seemed to attract any interest from the police. I guess you can get away with a lot when you're packing Hazelnut Swirls, even if you're potentially a bit rapey.

Fortunately, at this limited distance into the harbour, shielded by both sides of the channel, there wasn't much in the way of a current and very little chop so it would hopefully be a smooth crossing. That said, the water looked terribly uninviting, lapping lethargically and darkly at the bottom steps, like treacle that fell out of love with its job some time ago. I knelt down and slung the dinghy into the water, gripping the safety rope along its sides so it didn't float off without me, then tossed in the shovel. I looked across the channel to the floodlit SharpCrest yard. Christ, was I actually doing this? I carried out a swift reality check; this was a criminal act - was it worth risking everything I had to get even with Boat Bitch, with only a slim chance of possibly winning Jess back in the process? Thoughts of soap retrieval and Donkey Alan popped into my head as I recalled Vicar Lucy's highly unorthodox prayer from yesterday. Then I remembered her other words, championing action over inaction. And then I pictured Jess and my stomach did its usual flip. Was it worth it? Damn right it was.

With one foot in the dinghy, I stood there wondering how to fit the rest of me into its limited capacity. It remained as teeny as it was vivid. Then the water decided to climb a step and sloshed over my anchored foot. The wet and the cold soaked into the canvas of my trainer and sock in double-quick time. I took a second to shout 'Bollocks!' into the night air, then half jumped and half fell into the boat. This manoeuvre was followed up with a variety of other (quieter) expletives as I worked to remove the snow shovel from the arse crack in my jeans, also managing to dunk my one dry foot in the water during that process so it wouldn't feel left out. By the time I got myself back to rights and stopped thrashing, I had drifted a few yards to the right of my destination across the channel, that being the pontoon at the base of one of the walkways that led up to the yard. It wasn't ideal, as the walkway emerged right alongside the timber shed I'd spotted on my recce, the purpose of which I hadn't been able to determine. I'd already entertained the idea that it was security HQ, or somewhere the workers went to pot seedlings when on a break. Or perhaps it was where the SharpCrest yard manager spent his day, planning where to deploy his resources by pushing mini caricatures of his troops and equipment across a 2D map of the place with a stick, like some sort of war-mongering croupier.

On the plus side, there was a large motor yacht moored alongside the pontoon at the foot of the walkway so I'd be able to stash the dinghy in its shadow, out of sight from both sides of the channel. I needed to get paddling. Due to the size of my vessel, I couldn't just sit on its floor and row; I did attempt it but with my legs protruding over the front, I kept sliding down onto my back as I tried to keep my feet out of the water. In the end, I managed to very gingerly ease myself into a kneeling position which worked well enough; sort of. The snow shovel actually performed credibly as a paddle but due to its width, it was necessary to reach out quite far when I took a stroke to keep the "blade" from catching the sides of the dinghy, which rendered my stance all the more precarious. Something else I made a note to mention in my product review. I also regretted the missing handle and my lack of gloves, as I drove a fresh batch of splinters into the palm of my hand with every few strokes. Having spent so long arseing about, I had drifted even further off course, so I put my back into the paddling with as much vigour as I could without capsizing and bit by bit, I got myself back on track.

The half-way point arrived quickly, and the yard was now looming light and large in front of me. I didn't check behind to see if I was being watched from the quay; I was too committed now. Also, being perched as unsteadily as I was, had I tried to turn around I'd no doubt have fallen into the harbour, leaving my transport drifting off to unknown shores. The rowing was hard work, not just because of the required over-reaching but due to its span, the shovel end took a lot of pull to draw it out the water, and my unfit shoulders were starting to complain about the exertion. Additionally, each stroke doused me with a generous shower of spray. But; I was making surprisingly good progress now and I was in high spirits. In fact, I felt bloody great - I was doing something positive to change the course of my destiny. I'd spent way too many years of my life complaining about my lot whilst doing naff all to improve it but those days were gone. At that moment, I felt like I had life by the balls, and it was an awesome sensation.

The floodlights in the yard were growing ever brighter and I could pick out the security cameras in some detail. From the quayside, the channel had looked protectively dark across its full width but now I was nearing the other side, I felt the need to cover up so reached down for my bag to fish out my balaclava. I'd do my best to keep out of the light and out of the cameras' eye-line but I figured that even if I did get snapped, there'd be no way to tell it was me and I'd be long gone before the police arrived. I was a planning genius and the world was my lobster! Or was that oyster? Either was fine. My waggling hand couldn't locate the bag. Then the reason why dawned on me; accompanied by that awful icy feeling that you get in your gut when you realise you've cocked up big time. The bag wasn't in the dinghy because I'd neglected to retrieve it after kicking it into the obscurity of the alleyway just prior to my impromptu exchange with P.C. Simmonds. With a ginormous effort of will, I managed to suppress the colossal howl of frustration that I had an almighty urge to unleash into the silence. What a prick! After my chat with the constabulary, I'd been somewhat flustered and hadn't thought further than the dinghy and the shovel. What a monumental toss-pot!! I ran through my options as I bobbed and drifted further away from my intended landing spot on the pontoon. There was only one choice; I had to go back and get the bag.

Another forty-five minutes found me back in the channel, nearing the opposite shore: again. I was feeling rather less gung-ho than during my first crossing attempt, having screwed up rather royally. It was all the more annoying because I had nobody to blame but myself for forgetting the bag. Well, maybe P.C. Simmonds should take some share of the responsibility. How dare he serve the community in such a conscientious fashion and put me off my stroke? I was also a whole lot damper due to the extended paddling session, and my recently donned balaclava was already sodden. And my shoulders ached like hell. No wonder Sir Steve got a bucket-load of medals and a knighthood - this rowing game was proper tough. Mind you, I bet he'd never had to contend with a miniature inflatable and a broken snow shovel. In your face Redgrave. All of a sudden, the brightness of the floodlights was intercepted by the waterside wall and I bumped into the pontoon in darkness, at the stern of the moored cruiser. I anchored the dinghy by grabbing one of the timber slats that formed the pontoon's decking, then dumped the bag and paddle up there using my free arm. My over-worked shoulders then mutely shrieked their protest as I dragged myself up and out of the dinghy. I lay there on the pontoon with one hand clamped around the boat's safety rope as I enjoyed a few moments' recuperation, whilst marvelling at how long it had taken me to cover about fifty metres of calm water. And gaping at the hugeness of the mega-yacht I was staring up at, rather awestruck. Like all the SharpCrest craft, it comprised several, no doubt luxurious decks of gleaming white, formed from fibreglass I'd guess but was more likely a composite of space-age plastics, carbon fibre and rhino horn, dotted with black tinted windows, chrome handrails and a plethora of other gleaming accessories. This finery was topped off with a vast array of radar devices and other tech, all more than capable of detecting the weather a thousand miles away or bringing down a satellite I'd imagine. For a moment, yes; I was jealous of those that got to spend their days visiting the world's beauty spots in vessels such as this. Then I threw off that thought, needing to be in a wholly alternate frame of mind. Okay: I was wet through, I was exhausted, but I was here. With my joints popping and creaking audibly, I got to my feet and pulled the dinghy from the harbour. All the water that had collected inside it during both voyages so far emptied itself onto my jeans in the process. I cursed to myself, even though I was already close to saturation point.

As planned, I dragged the dinghy a short way down the pontoon into the blackout offered by the sea wall and the moored cruiser. In spite of its lurid paint job, nobody would see my assault craft unless they tripped over it - something I managed to do when I turned it over to help the remaining water drain out. I dropped the shovel on top, grabbed my bag then headed up the walkway at a crouch. Game on.

Once I'd reached the top of the ramp, I'd left the security of the shadows behind me. Alarmingly, I was also looking straight through the window to the side of the potting shed. There was a light on inside, and I caught a brief glimpse of someone with their back to me dressed in a puffa jacket and some sort of cap before I swiftly ducked down and headed back into the darkness, whilst double-checking I hadn't soiled myself. Bugger. It appeared the potting shed was security HQ after all. Somehow, I was going to have to get past it undetected. Still at a crouch, I inched my way back up the walkway. Wanting to see which way the nearest cameras were pointing before exposing myself further, I looked up to the nearest mast and inadvertently stuck my face directly into the nearest floodlight's full luminance. This triggered that weird sneeze reflex you get when suddenly exposed to bright light. The first one blasted out of me before I could even attempt to mute it. 'Whachooooo!!!' Sprinting back down the walkway, I followed up my first explosion with another four that I silenced as best I could, but with meagre success. Unfortunately, covering my mouth to reduce the volume brought my veiled nose more into play and once I'd finished venting, the inside of my balaclava felt like a slug's yoga mat against my face.

Back in the shadows, I stood with my back pressed against the sea wall, ready to grab the dinghy and paddle to Mexico as soon as I got sign of the inevitable gaggle of torch beams announcing the arrival of the security posse. But they didn't come. I waited a few more minutes, mostly to give my heart time to get back to a steady rhythm but also to be sure there were no more sneezes pending. Then I headed back up the walkway yet again and cautiously raised my head above the parapet. Still seeing no activity, I crept higher and peered into the potting shed window once again. The guy in the jacket and cap was still there, but he didn't appear to have moved. There was no way he hadn't heard that first sneeze surely? My eyes gradually adjusted to the glare and I caught sight of the security cameras on the nearest tower. They were directed at the water, and stationary as far as I could see. Crouching even lower, I moved directly beneath the window of the potting shed, then straightened sufficiently to take another look. To my relief, I discovered that the jacket and cap hadn't changed location as they were hanging from a row of wall hooks and mercifully not being fashioned by a beefy security guard who'd tear me limb from limb then feed my remains to his pet alligator. There was little else of note in the room, just a desk covered with paperwork and a lone mug. It was still unnerving: okay, the puffa jacket was now less of a threat now I knew there wasn't anyone in it, but why were there lights on in the shed if it wasn't functional to some degree? I stayed where

I was, eyes still fixed on the interior, anticipating the sudden activity that would confirm my fears.

Several minutes later, all was still calm. And then my thighs started shouting at me for relief so I crabbed left of the window and stood up straight, with my back to the wall, leaning against an enormous "No Smoking" sign. To my left lay the two hundred metres of boat yard obstacle course that I needed to cover to reach my target; that being the gigantic super-yacht that would bear my message to Boat Bitch. It was perched on a massive ramp, towering above everything in its vicinity. Even the worksheds behind seemed of inadequate volume to ever house it. Mounted with its bows pointed towards the channel, the leviathan looked as if it was ready to launch itself into the harbour at any moment. Or outer space - it would be equally at home in either arena by the look of it. I scanned the yard again, looking for any signs of life but also plotting a route through the many and varied obstructions. Christ this place was a muddle. Sure, it had looked "busy" from across the channel but up close it resembled my bedroom when I was thirteen. Only with more multi-million pound boats dotted around and fewer dubious tissues. I'd observed the cranes, the other bits of hardware and the various tarp-covered mystery stacks during my previous survey, but now I could see what lay in between. There were several gangways that threaded their way through the jungle but all other space was bristling with barrels and other canisters bearing an impressive array of hazard symbols, packing crates, hoses, ropes and all manner of other accessories apparently necessary for building a big yacht. It actually reminded me of the Fishermen's Quay, with the various tools of the trade strewn around, but with gas bottles in place of crab nets. And the smell was worlds apart - paint stripper and plastic instead of mullet and whelks. Now I'd calmed down from my earlier exertions, I was breathing steadier and taking in more air, and the atmosphere was abundantly chemical. Although having been filtered through my nose-less balaclava to a limited extent, it still caught the back of my throat, even though I was in the open air. Bloody hell; people worked in this environment? I'd be sure to send an anonymous, strongly-worded letter to SharpCrest's Health and Safety personnel to complain about the noxious working/sabotage conditions. I'd have plenty of time in prison to get the wording just right. No wonder the smoking ban was so high profile as soon as you set foot in the yard; one match and you'd blow the whole place. As it was, Pat's original plan hadn't been too far removed from that very scenario, but I couldn't bring myself to go that far. Not yet at least. And no wonder Boat Bitch favoured the pub for her sales office more than a location on this site: celebs don't like being papped wearing nose plugs. A shiver ran through me; the damp and the chill were seeping into my marrow. I'd spent more than enough time fretting and playing the pansy. Time to move.

I picked my route across the yard, a path mostly in shadow, hidden from the lamps and hopefully the cameras too, as long as they stayed looking out to sea. Sliding sideways, I took one last quick peek into the hut window then grabbed my bag and headed across the yard at a low run, with my shoulders and thighs still grumbling about my prior lack of exercise and my long-time love affair with grilled cheese.

My journey wasn't unlike traversing the lounge in The Crow's Nest when I'd first moved in. It was just clutter to be navigated through, and quietly sworn at as it leapt out of the dark and smacked me on the knees and elbows or subtly tried to snag my clothing. These minor skirmishes aside, I did suffer a more serious knock however. As I ducked under the arm of a mini-JCB, a floodlight popped directly into my line of sight. Momentarily blinded yet still moving apace, I smacked my forehead on an unyielding metal edge with a mighty thump. If I'd have been featuring in an animated movie, I'd have had small birds circling my head tweeting while my tongue lolled out of my head. Dizzy, I dropped to my knees, letting the bag fall to the deck with a loud clatter. Thank goodness for the balaclava; that had surely saved me some damage, but when I touched my fingers to the area that the pain was coming from, they came away covered in blood. Bugger it.

When the fog had lifted some, I pressed on. I could feel the blood from my head wound slowly working its way down to the eye socket below, but I did my best to ignore it. James Bond doesn't jack it in and go home just because he breaks a nail or simply "feels a bit peaky". I bet the Milk Tray guy would have quit by now though, especially if he had to deliver an actual tray of milk: that would go everywhere. He wouldn't have even made it into the dinghy without losing most of it. For some reason, the random thought of slopping milk combined with the acrid air and the knock on the head caused me to pause; then throw up all over an innocent sack truck standing nearby. I apologised to it but went no further to make amends. Someone would come across the scene and clean up in the morning hopefully - otherwise rust could become a real issue. My throat now felt even more raw but thankfully I'd managed to keep almost all of the vomit outside the balaclava. Almost all. Other than keeping your face warm and hidden, they really were frightfully impractical garments. Mine was now populated by an ever-growing collection of personal emissions.

The closer I got to my target, the greater the already substantial portion of the sky it ate up. This was a monster yacht; I estimated something like 120 to 130 feet long. And the height! Jesus - with the hull exposed, it was like seeing an iceberg out of the water. After a few more yards, I was there; still pretty woozy from my intimate contact with the crane but functional, and determined to finish the business I'd come here for. Although I had revised the plan rather.

Initially, I'd planned to mimic Boat Bitch's graffiti attack on the pub by carrying out a similar act but on a grander scale, leaving her a clear message sprayed across the doors of each of the SharpCrest worksheds. Then whilst traversing the channel for the second time, I'd decided that the mega-yacht was a far more impactful choice of canvas. The base of the hull was surrounded by a complicated network of scaffolding and ladders; the only way the workers could access such a behemoth in the dry. After a quick look behind me to ensure I wasn't being pursued by giant guard dogs with head-mounted laser cannons, I started up the nearest ladder. After climbing another couple of levels, I was alongside the first black strip of tinted windows; probably the lower saloon or something. This would do - I had the entire, considerable length of the hull on which to craft my masterpiece. I walked the scaffold from end to end to get my bearings; the light was poor so I had to tread carefully. The towering mass of the yacht's superstructure blocked out all the floodlights from the yard beyond, and none from this side shone directly at the area I was currently sizing up. The torch was an option, but I'd decided against it for now as the beam would be seen from a mile off if it truly was as powerful as Birdman had claimed. Having got a reasonable feel for the available workspace and acclimatised to the limited illumination, I got down to business.

Taking one of the paint spray cans from the bag, I removed the cap from the aerosol and felt for the nozzle to make sure it was pointing in the non-me direction then faced the humongous hull, feeling like a toddler stood in the shadow of an aircraft carrier. Holding my breath, I pointed at the saloon window and pressed the button on top of the can whilst sweeping my arm from waist height to its fullest extent above my head, in as straight a line as I could manage with ever-stiffening joints and a concussion. But my only rewards were a damp flatulent hiss from the cannister and a couple of blobs of paint dripped onto my trainers. I tried again, with the same result. What the hell? Crap - I must have got a dud. Pulling the second aerosol from the bag, I repeated the same manoeuvre. Again, no glorious swathe of red across my acutely monochrome canvas. Then a thought found its way into my cotton wool filled brain and I gave the can a vigorous shake. This action did nothing to alleviate the spikey hurt building steadily in my head and also generated a high-volume rattle that echoed across the yard. From my elevated position, I surveyed the area, once more expecting company at any moment as I nervously rattled up a storm. Thankfully, as the paint mixed, the noise lessened. After a few minutes of shaking; and with a now firmly-established headache reverberating throughout my head, I attempted another spray. And this time I was rewarded with a streak of crimson as tall as I was. Yes! I was off and running. The rest of the letters just flowed as I moved gracefully from left to right along the narrow platform, being as careful to not get my spelling wrong as I was to avoid falling to my death. Yes, it was only graffiti, but quality presentation mattered a great deal as I felt the message would lose its impact if it contained even a single typo or the spacing was off in the slightest.

The first aerosol ran empty just as I started the second "B". I gave the second an energetic shake; gritting my teeth as the metallic clicking bounced loudly around the yard once more. My shoulders were really killing me now as I stretched to get maximum height on the remaining letters. But then I was done. My fatigued and bashed brain failed me momentarily as I went to take a step back to get a more panoramic view of my handiwork, but luckily some part of my reason pulled the communication cord and stopped me short of stepping back into the void that beckoned behind me. Walking the length of the scaffold, I was pleased with the work on show - it looked tidy: and tall. Really tall. This was how Michelangelo must have felt on completion of the ceiling in The Sistine Chapel; or Rodin when he forged "The Thinker". Or Tracey Emin when she did that bed piece that looked like my bedroom did when I was thirteen. Only with fewer suspicious tissues. Walking back to the bow, I was left with a few square metres of free space that begged to be filled: I'd been a little conservative with my spacing it appeared. After pondering what I could add to maximise the overall impact of my creation, I decided to go with a classic. With a few more sprays, I was done. Time to go.

Several ladders later, I was happily back at ground level with my bag over my shoulder. Before heading for the exit, I did a quick sweep to confirm that all remained peaceful. A light still burned in the potting shed but there were no signs of life. The floodlights blazed on, but seemed to have no designs on me other than affording me a higher profile should I run out of objects to hide behind. Then I clocked the nearest of the security camera towers. Both of the devices mounted thereon were pointing into the yard; and one was aimed directly at me. Shit! I ducked behind a nearby clump of barrels. So, the cameras could swivel. My reconnaissance had been seriously lacking. How long had they been directed my way? How much of my boat-spoiling had they captured? Now those few hundred yards that lay between me and my escape seemed like a very real minefield. I struggled to wrestle my brain out of its haze while I weighed up my options. Fact was, if I'd already been caught on camera there was nothing I could do about it, so now it was all about minimising further exposure. I had half-thought about taking off the balaclava once the spray-painting was complete as it felt like it was gradually fusing with my face and I was concerned that it might become a permanent fixture. But not now - that slimy ghastliness was staying put.

Keeping as low as possible, I retraced the route I'd first taken that kept me in the shadows and now out of the cameras' field of view for most of the way. There were the occasional short stretches where I was forced to break cover, but I negotiated these at a sprint while turning my face away from the light just to be on the safe side. This meant I wasn't looking directly in the direction that I was running so ended up off-course a few times, collecting fresh bruises as I cannoned off different elements of my surroundings.

Within several minutes, I was only a few yards away from the potting shed, catching my breath behind a huge shipping container, once again trying to determine if there was anyone around to intercept my exit. I just wanted to be home now: I was completely worn out, with limbs that wanted to quit and a headache that was threatening to go nuclear. At that point, my need to get back to the pub and my bed cut across any thoughts of stealth and low-risk strategies, so throwing caution to the win, I sprinted directly for the walkway then ran its length down to the water's edge. Once I reached the pontoon, I kept on running until I was back within the seclusion offered by the sea wall and the starship moored alongside it; stumbling over the dinghy for the second time in my haste but fortunately; and miraculously, just catching the snow shovel before it flew off into the harbour. I righted myself and stood with my back to the wall once more, rallying the last dregs of my energy for the paddle home while savouring thoughts of warmth, a double brandy to wash down some paracetamol, and a lengthy lie-in. And, I had all but completed my mission; just me, doing man stuff, all on my own. Go Team Ken; you beauty.

Flushed with accomplishment, I extracted the heaviest paint aerosol from my bag, gave it a thorough shake, then sprayed another creative work on the hull of the yacht in front of me. True, it was on a much lesser scale than my last masterpiece but would still attract some critical attention I was sure. Then it struck me that I hadn't taken the opportunity to properly critique my evening's achievements myself. Over-confidence was deaf to good sense so I headed back up the walkway, pausing when I was sufficiently elevated to see above the parapet and view my showpiece. Even at that distance and in semi-darkness, "BACK OFF YOU CRAZY BITCH!!" sprayed in six-foot-tall scarlet letters really stood out. Also, I was particularly pleased with the proportions of the cock and balls I'd added as an afterthought. In daylight, the whole piece would just look awesome. And it would take a monumental effort to get rid of - I thought back to the hard labour that me and Tim had put into getting The Gents' back to rights at the pub, and chuckled at the prospect of someone having to do the same to this very pricey and very tall boat.

Returning to the pontoon, I sniggered again on seeing my latest offering to the art world. Okay; "CLEAN ME!" wasn't terribly inventive, but I was a somewhat overwhelmed by the day and my head wound. Right: Home James! With my bag slung, I collected the shovel then grabbed the rope on the dinghy, ready to drag it to the starship's stern and slide it into the water. Then I heard a distant beeping sound; something electronic had woken up. And then came the unmistakable sound of someone coughing. I froze: caught somewhere between my flight or fight impulses. After a few minutes of suspenseful silence, there came the creak of a door opening - the potting shed no doubt. That was enough for me. Dragging the dinghy indelicately, I headed towards the bow of the yacht as fast as I could move, trying to put as much distance between myself, the coughing individual and the scene of my crime as was possible.

Thirty or so metres after the bow ended, so did the pontoon. I looked across the channel to the quayside which right now could have been a foreign country that I hadn't visited for many years. This was as far from my potential discoverer as I could get this way - all roads now led to the harbour. With the dinghy back in the water, I resumed my woefully unsteady kneeling position on its floor and paddled away as swiftly and stealthily as I was able. The preferred, direct route straight across the channel was no longer a possibility, as there was a healthy chance I'd place my luminous boat directly into the line of sight of whoever might be looking out from the yard. Be that the person that had emerged from the potting shed, or the army of police that had no doubt already been summoned on discovery of my evening's creative efforts. I had to work my way along the channel keeping close to the sea wall until I was well clear of the extremities of the SharpCrest yard before I turned for the opposite shore. This was further torture; what should have been a quick to-and-fro from one side of the channel to the other had turned out to be a long-winded tour of the locale, and I was struggling to keep myself upright. The thought of giving in to the fatigue and slipping over the side to embrace never-ending slumber actually felt quite appealing for a moment. But then I thought of Jess and my friends, gritted my teeth and kept paddling.

After what felt like hours, thankfully without further excitement, I arrived at the foot of another flight of steps that led up to the quayside, just short of the yacht wankers' marina. I dragged myself out of the dinghy and onto the lower step, neither knowing nor caring how much more sea water I took on board in the process. Perhaps I'd dried out some during my antics on land, but the return trip across the channel had done a grand job of reversing that and I was once again wetter than an otter's pocket. Having painfully clambered a few steps higher pulling the dinghy with me, I then removed the plug to deflate it. With a sigh of resignation, it started to fold in on itself, with the creases in the rubber contorting the turtles' faces into some very random and rather grotesque expressions. When it was done breathing out, I squeezed it against my chest to force out the remaining air. With its job done, I wedged it under my arm then grabbed the rest of my accessories and trudged up the remainder of the stairs.

As my head crested street level, I stopped and reviewed the scene. It must have been late; or early, depending on which way you looked at it. There was nobody in sight and few lights showing in windows. With great relief, I gently peeled off the balaclava, wincing as it pulled away from the patches of my face it had been glued to with blood, mucus or puke, then dropped it into a nearby rubbish bin. I felt a draught on my forehead; an indication that I'd managed to open my recent wound again. In spite of that, I was thinking relatively clearly courtesy of the sharp sea air. Looking back to the SharpCrest yard, I saw none of the half-expected flashing lights and commotion. Indeed, there was nothing to indicate I'd ever set foot in the place. Apart from the super-scale graffiti that was, which I could still vaguely make out even at this distance. I took out my phone: most of the display was misted up on the inside as a result of sitting in my sodden trousers for the last few hours but I could just make out the time – 4:15. Although it was extremely doubtful I'd run into anyone at that time of the morning (even the ever diligent P.C. Simmonds), I chose to take the back street home to the pub rather than walking the quay. En-route, I passed a series of wheelie bins on the pavement outside the various apartment blocks I walked by, indicating it was collection day tomorrow. Or today rather. After verifying as best I could that I wasn't being watched, I checked a couple of bins and finding one with some room, I unloaded anything that might incriminate me into it. I had to snap off part of the shovel bit to fit it in, then stuffed the dinghy in afterwards. That little boat had actually served me pretty darn well bless it. But master criminals such as I couldn't afford sentimentality. Farewell my turtle friends. I kept the still-unused torch, but the bag and its other contents went into the bin too. Then as an afterthought, I took off my jacket and rammed it into the remaining space. I immediately felt the drop in temperature and my damp top was steaming in the cold but if I had indeed been caught on camera, I figured I had to rid myself of anything that might help to identify me. My only jacket. What would I wear to go and buy a new jacket? I'd figure that out later.

A short while later, I arrived at the back gate to the yard, shivering and trying to bring up the entry code on my cloudy phone with frozen fingers. And minutes afterwards, I was in the bar reaching for the brandy bottle with shaking hands, not knowing if that condition was due to reduced core temperature or adrenalin running riot in my system. I took a large swig, which I almost coughed straight back up as the strong alcohol caught the back of my throat, scraped coarse by salt air and boat yard chemistry. Managing to keep it down, I followed up with another hearty gulp. The bar had been empty for hours and was far from warm, so I topped up my glass and headed upstairs, leaving a series of small puddles behind me as I went. Once in The Crow's Nest, I turned the heating thermostat up as high as it would go without breaking it, then dropped my clothes in a soggy pile on the bathroom floor and towelled myself off. I took a couple of headache tablets from the bathroom cabinet and studied my war wound in its mirrored doors. It didn't look too bad; a cut of an inch and a half or so above my left eyebrow; but it had swelled up to a generous bump which I felt compelled to prod, then immediately wished I hadn't. I cleaned it up as best I could with hand soap and a flannel, then put on my bath robe, still feeling beaten-up but gradually heading back to the normal me. And no doubt that normal me would be feeling it much more tomorrow. Brandy in hand, I turned out the lounge light and looked through the still curtain-free window. The SharpCrest lights continued to shine but there was no action beneath that I could make out. Now back in my familiar surroundings, tonight's events were already feeling somewhat surreal. Had I really been there? The string of towering red letters sprayed on a super-yacht's hull that I could just about make out were telling me yes, but was I the only person that could see them? Did I really make that journey? I didn't do things like that did I. Did I? My physical damage strongly hinted at yes, though the medication and the alcohol were beginning to blunt the edges of that thank God. Unable to tear myself away from the scene, I continued looking on, increasingly bewildered by the lack of attention my handiwork appeared to be receiving. It was strange - I didn't feel anything like the triumph I'd revelled in briefly after the act itself. Instead, I was actually rather empty inside; my mood trending more towards guilt than victory if anything. With the brandy finished, I headed to bed. As the exhaustion washed over me and I let go of the day, I muttered 'Sorry Jess.'; not really knowing why.

CHAPTER FIFTEEN

'Ken.'

...

'Ken!'

...

'Ken!!!'

Unwillingly, I was abruptly snatched from my dormancy and thrown into the reality of the day. 'Jesus! What's up?'

'Sorry Boss, it was getting a bit late, even by your standards, so thought I'd pop up and check you were still alive. I did shout up from the kitchen but you must have been spark out.'

Still blurry from recent sleep, I looked up to see J.D. standing there holding a steaming mug.

'Christ what happened to you?' He must have noticed my war wound.

'I whacked it on the door last night. Too much medication.' I pointed at the empty brandy glass on my bedside table. 'Does it look bad?'

'Ow can I put this down its bloody roasting. Sorry; dropped quite a bit on the stairs.' He placed the mug next to my glass, then leaned in and studied my forehead whilst blowing on his fingertips.

'Well it's a fair old lump. Not full-on John Merrick, but you're going to need a bigger hat.'

'Duly noted. Thanks for the tea.'

'No problem. Hope Earl Grey's okay.'

'Well if he is, he's got quite a dig ahead of him.'

He smirked and moved to the window, pulling a curtain aside.

'Bit of business over the road this morning. More coppers than we've got in the tip jar.'

With that news, I spat my first mouthful of tea across the duvet. J.D. turned and looked at me enquiringly.

'Tea's not that bad is it?'

'I think the milk might be a bit off.'

'Early Grey always tastes like that.' He turned back to the window. 'Fair few cop cars over there and a lot of people standing around looking at one of the big boats. Looks like it's got something painted on it. Probably Greenpeace protesting about carbon footprints; or diminishing bees or something.'

'Maybe they've run out of trees to marry. Right well; much as I appreciate the room service, I need to be up and doing so unless you're hankering after seeing me naked, you'd best toddle off.'

'On my way. I had a big breakfast and I'd hate to see it again.'

He made for the hallway but then stopped in the doorway and turned back to face me.

'I forgot to say; the alarm wasn't set when I came in this morning. Did you forget last night or do I need to get the guy in to check it? Might be on the blink.'

'Oh crap, my bad. I stepped out into the yard to get a bit of fresh air after I saw you guys out and must have forgotten to set it on my way back in.'

'Numpty. That'll be it then.'

He didn't look at all convinced by my story but didn't press it further and continued on his way downstairs. No doubt that was just the first lump of bullshit from the huge mound I'd have to shovel out today to cover up last night's events.

Vacating the bed was a long-winded struggle; I didn't appear to have a single muscle group that hadn't endured a serious workout as a result of my escapade. My arms and shoulders were so stiff and sore, they refused to lever my body weight off the mattress, so I only managed to progress to a sitting position on the side of the bed by rocking backwards and forwards until I'd built up sufficient momentum. Even my arse ached. Then all that was needed to get into a standing position was a series of obscenities and other noises as my over-exercised thighs and calves joined in the protest. Christ, I was a wreck. If there'd been a priest handy, they'd be reading my last rites without invitation or hesitation. Moving with all the fluidity of someone in a full body cast, I winced and hobbled my way over to the window. It was another leaden morning, with the rain that was hitting the window panes and hanging in the air offering only a hazy view of the SharpCrest yard. However, I could pick out the bright blue and yellow patchwork on the sides of the four police cars I could see in the car park. Instinctively, I then carried out a hurried, rather panicked survey of the quayside below in fear of seeing a convoy of like-coloured vehicles heading my way. Relieved at observing nothing of the sort, I returned my attention to the yard. I could make out a group of twenty or so figures close to my primary masterwork, some sporting high visibility jackets which I assumed were the police. There were also people up on the scaffold; possibly testing out how hard it was to remove the paint. Or taking photos for evidence perhaps. The thought of someone having to officially capture images of giant, hand-drawn genitalia did raise a smile briefly. Then I was back to fretting about my undoubtedly imminent arrest. I was sweating. Mind you, the central heating had been on full blast for several hours.

I needed to get a grip - if I spent the whole day twitching every time the front door opened, expecting to get my collar felt, I'd be a permanent wreck. And eventually a willing confessor when the pressure broke me. Also, it was imperative that I appeared as normal as possible so as not to fuel suspicion. Not that I thought anyone other than Pat would consider me remotely capable of such an act; psychologically or physically. And, I had to remember that there was nothing to connect me with the raid. Even if the cameras had picked up my every move, there was no means of identifying me, cloaked as I was in my entirely nondescript clothing and crusty balaclava. Any other physical evidence would be heading for the nearest land fill site in the back of a garbage truck by now. My alibi would be tough to disprove too: if questioned, I would claim I was alone, fast asleep in the pub, as I would be at that time of night every day of the week, and there was nobody to refute that. I didn't think Boat Bitch would grass me up and bring the police to my door, as she'd know I'd tell them the full story of her intimidation campaign. I could provide no more solid proof than she, but surely there was no way she'd even risk being implicated in such dodgy goings-on. After my short spell of rationalisation, I relaxed a little and tore myself away from the window and got prepped for the day ahead, still moving at glacial speed.

After groaning my way down the stairs, I emerged into the kitchen shortly after midday. Bruno was already in full flow with several orders in play, judging by the order slips queueing tidily in their slot by the door. The whole room was full of vapour, organised clutter and wonderful smells. Right, remember Trickett - business as usual.

'Afternoon Bruno! Blimey what happened? Did TripAdvisor publish a full page apology in The Times?'

His focus was on his workbench as he prepared his ingredients. 'Good afternoon Ken. Not as far as I'm aware. Janine informs me that we have a coach party in the house and it appears that they neglected to pack a luncheon. I'm pleased to say.' He looked up and grinned then his face dropped and he looked at me anxiously. 'That's a rather major contusion Ken - how did you manage that?' He came closer.

I was rather touched that having seen my wound, that immediately became his primary concern above the multitude of pots and dishes that begged his attention. At the same time, I was worried that he was ruining a good few quid's worth of stock in the process. However, as usual he was doing my thinking in addition to his own.

'Worry not; I shan't spoil a thing. Now, do let me inspect your injuries.'

'I'm afraid I overdid the nightcaps and got rather too intimate with the edge of the bedroom door in the dark.'

He leaned in and surveyed my forehead from a few different angles. 'Really? That's interesting; the shape of the bruise and the angle of the laceration suggest a horizontal contact.' I didn't think he disbelieved me as such, more just being his usual surgical self. 'Well, the cut appears to be clean and I have something that will alleviate the swelling and help anaesthetise the wound site.'

He went over to a small backpack sitting on a chair in the far corner. After fishing around in one of its side pockets, he returned and handed me a small, unlabelled clear glass jar with a blank white screw top. It contained a murky green compound of some sort. 'Smear a little of this on the lesion twice a day and you'll be back to rights in no time.'

Unscrewing the cap, I peered inside the jar, somewhat put off by the non-branded nature of the container and also by the God-awful stench emanating from it which caused me to jerk my head back sharply after an exploratory sniff. It reminded me of the Hull's Bay marina at low tide.

Bruno laughed. 'Go ahead, it will help enormously trust me. It's my own recipe, concocted during many years of needing to heal multiple tissue injuries as rapidly as possible. Alas it is a trifle overpowering; as you've noticed.

But do apply some now. I would assist but I've been handling chili's which will reduce the benefits of the ointment.' With that he returned to his workbench and his lunchtime labours.

'Thanks Bruno. So you used this for scrapes and cuts in your pro kitchen days?'

'Something like that.'

This didn't really help to allay my misgivings regarding his homemade remedy. At that moment, Janine breezed into the kitchen, turning to slide another order into the queue.

'Two more of your delish smoked salmon sandwiches please Chef; one without the orville though; whatever that is.'

Bruno turned to her and smiled, knife in hand. 'Chervil. Think of it as posh parsley Janine.'

'Gotcha.' She then noticed me. 'Ken! Thought you were having a duvet day after a few too many sherbets last ni.... Holy fuck what have you done to your noodle?'

'Bashed it on a door last night, it's no biggie.' Maybe if I repeated the lie often enough I'd start to believe it myself.

She hurried over and checked out the damage. 'Hmmm - doesn't look too bad. Anyway, chicks dig scars you know.' Then she suddenly backed away and pinched her nose shut. 'Christ on a bike; what's that whiff? Is that you?'

I held up Bruno's jar of unguent. 'It's this. Bruno made it. It's for cuts.'

'Oh right. Well put some on sharpish and put the bloody lid back on. And then stay downwind of me.'

I dangled a finger tentatively over the top of the jar; still unsure. Yes, this was me, the fearless have-a-go hero that takes down oppressive business magnates using little more than spray paint and turtle-patterned PVC, but was too much of a wimp to slap on a bit of home-brewed Vaseline.

'Oh for God's sake you complete nonce; give it here.' She grabbed the jar, then smeared a finger-load of its contents across the damaged area of my forehead; a move carried out with great enthusiasm and absent delicacy that caused me to wince; though not as much as I'd have liked to. Pulling a face that re-emphasised her disgust at the smell, she replaced the cap and handed me the jar. 'There; all done.'

'Have I got a green forehead now?'

'Nope, it goes on clear. Right - must go; can't spend all day applying your cosmetics.' She washed her hands then returned to the bar as I shouted a thanks after her. Actually the cut did already feel less painful when I raised my eyebrows a few times as a tester.

'Cheers Bruno. I'll go see if they need any help out there.'

'You are more than welcome Ken. I doubt you'll be in need of another jar before you're fully healed but if so do let me know.'

From the activity in the kitchen, I'd gleaned the bar was busy but wow: it was standing room only busy, with every table and chair occupied by an elderly lady or gent talking excitedly with their neighbours or flicking through pamphlets and guide books. J.D. came straight over, looking purposeful.

'Glad you're here; I need to change the barrel on the Fosters and Janine's been busy on the tables and helping Bruno. You okay to hold the fort for a minute? Your bonce looks a bit better.'

'Yeah sure. And thanks - Bruno gave me some stuff. And before you say anything, that's what you can smell.'

'Didn't notice any difference to be honest. Back in a mo stinky.'

It was great to be back behind the bar; sure it was only yesterday that I last was but it felt like so much longer. And it was fantastic to see the place so well populated. Mugs of tea and coffee seemed to be the beverages of choice for all but the devil-may-care handful that favoured a port and lemon or a brown ale. And the food was obviously selling extremely well. I entertained the thought that we could potentially be this busy every day once word spread even further and we introduced Bruno's higher-end fare to the menu. We were going to need a bigger boat.

'I do hate to interrupt, but I wondered if I might trouble you for another cup of tea?'

The word "tea" put me on full alert. Mastering the mammoth device that was the coffee machine was on my to-do list, but I'd failed to apply any serious time to it yet. The thing sported so many knobs and levers, it wouldn't look out of place in the cockpit of a jumbo jet. Well, maybe a bit, what with the various glass jugs and the steam and that. Mind you, aircraft of that size probably boast a Starbuck's on each deck these days; I hadn't flown for a while so couldn't be sure. I'd only used the beast of a device once when I was left alone without adult supervision, and it didn't go well. I came away with a cup half-filled with liquid of dubious quality and taste, and a broad selection of second degree burns.

'Hello? Sort of new Ken? Are you with us? Or has your head trauma left you vegetated?'

Breaking away from my thoughts, I came to focus on the purple jumper, dog collar and all-round sprightliness of Vicar Lucy Bolt.

'Vicar Lucy! Fabulous to have you here!' I'd never been so pleased to see a member of the clergy before. Maybe it was the residual guilt from last night's activities and I felt penitence was due.

She looked at me shocked. 'Goodness my boy, what a welcome. That bump on the noggin must have dislodged something. And it's just Lucy; please.'

'No I'm fine it's just... really good to see you. My head's fine; it looks worse than it feels honestly.'

'Well thank Our Lord for that: you look like you might be growing another head. Tea please!'

'Yes; yes of course.' I turned to face the coffee machine with mounting trepidation. It faced me stoically; all piano-red steel and chrome with an endless array of spouts and nozzles that gave me no indication of what purpose they might serve, or how they intended to injure me. 'I'll just be a minute.' I grabbed a clean cup and saucer, thus fully exhausting my knowledge of the process at that point. I stared at the contraption, hoping for some divine intervention (what with the present company and all). Fortunately, that intervention arrived in the form of J.D.

'Want me to sort that Ken? I think you've sustained enough injuries for the week. And you wouldn't want the poisoning of our good Vicar on your conscience as well would you. Afternoon Lucy.'

'Good afternoon J.D.; lovely to see you. It would also be a pleasure to have you in my place of business occasionally. Halo would feel at home, seeing as her namesake features on several of our stained glass windows.'

'Like I've always said Lucy, fix the heating and put in a bar and I'll be there.'

'I'm working on the former: the latter may take some time to get approved by higher authorities.'

'What? You need God's approval for a bar?'

'No. Bill; our Treasurer. He's tee-total.'

'Well, keep me informed of progress. I'll get your tea.' They exchanged warm smiles, clearly well known to each other. Then J.D. turned and started pushing buttons on the beast, which in turn started issuing steam and noise to indicate the fuel rods were dropping into its reactor.

'So what brings you here Lucy?' I said. 'Other than the charming bar staff and homely ambiance?'

'These marvellous people are from several local nursing homes and from time to time they join forces and arrange a group day out. Today's lovelies are museum and history nuts so they're on a bit of a tour. When they get to the Pulton stop, I pick up the party and show them around St James', after which we go and visit The Lifeboat Museum, and then have a nose around the main Pulton Museum just down from here. Then we stop somewhere for lunch, after which I put them back on the coach. They then fall smartly asleep until they're woken later by the need for a pee stop, or by Jenny at St Aldhelm's in Weymouth who takes the baton from me. Works awfully well. We usually do it on a week day but had to postpone because of Nancy's knee op. She organises it all you see.'

'Oh right. Is she with you today?'

'Lord no! She's still recuperating - she's 82, not Superwoman. Plus, she can't stand old people. So anyway, I remember you voicing your concerns about your fledgling lunch service when you came to see me so I thought we'd drop in today to share in your success. Either that or embrace the catastrophe as it unfolded.' She took in the room then looked back at me. 'Seems to me it's going rather well. Bravo sort of new Ken, bravo. Oh thank you J.D., I'll settle up when we're all done.' She picked up her tea.

'Well drop by any time Lucy; you're always welcome. And it's just Ken.'

'I shall, just Ken. I'm rather busy playing minder to my coach posse today but we must have a proper chat. I need an update on how you're progressing with your various other endeavours; and soon please. Look after that head. I assume it was due to something that I wouldn't approve of so I shan't ask.'

How right she was.

The grey army kept us busy till around two at which point Lucy announced to the room that the rain had stopped for now and it was time

to return to the coach. This was followed by a
unique symphony of scraping chairs, jangling
crockery, coughs, groans and excited murmurs
as the party all got to their feet, grabbed their
belongings and prepared themselves for the next
stage of their adventure: the first priority for
most being a trip to the loo before departing.
Lucy headed off the many inevitable questions
from the male folk by broadcasting the fact that
The Gents' could be found down the side alley on
the way to where the coach was parked. Once the
last of her charges was out the door, she waved a
goodbye then was off.

Now that's what you call a good lunchtime
session; nigh on everyone in the group had
ordered food, apart from one chap who informed
me that the menu was 'seriously lacking' as we
didn't offer lasagne; it was a false teeth thing
apparently. I suggested chilli as an alternative
but was abruptly informed that he didn't fight
two World Wars in order to be forced to eat
American food. What with them turning up late
to the scrap and all. To be honest, I held
opposing views on the USA's participation in
both conflicts but chose not to voice them there
and then, especially as the chap in question
swore blind that lasagne originated in Coventry.

I couldn't wait to find out how much we'd
taken and I did the rounds to thank everyone for
their grand efforts. My muscles had loosened up
a bit, helped by a fair amount of stretching and
bending during service. Also, Bruno's jollop
worked wonders: so much so I'd completely

forgotten about my injury until I wiped the back of my hand across my forehead during J.D.'s steamy and sweaty coffee machine induction training session. I wouldn't say I'd mastered the contraption, but I was far less intimidated by it. I walked into the kitchen, expecting to see devastation, but there was no such scene; again Bruno had managed to keep his house in order whilst serving a small army - the guy was indeed a machine. He was busy wiping down the worktop of the central island and I could see a sheen of sweat on his forehead. The machine had worked hard.

'Bloody well done Bruno - fantastic job.'

'You're too kind; all happy campers I trust?'

'Not a bad word said. Just one guy a little disgruntled as we didn't do denture-friendly lasagne.'

'Duly noted.'

'Look, if we get this busy regularly, you'll need some help in here won't you? Come the Summer we'll potentially have twice the customers with the tables outside as well. Janine's got a friend who might be interested in helping out; she'll be dropping in at some point.'

'That sounds like a notion worthy of exploration. Whatever we can do to improve the service is agreeable but fear not, I can manage perfectly well in the meantime.'

'I don't doubt it. But you might like to take a day off at some point.'

'Perhaps. They do say The Devil makes work for idle hands however.' Again the wicked grin which made me think he was part culinary genius, part serial killer.

'Yes well; thanks again for a grand job today.'

Walking back into the bar, I narrowly avoided colliding with Janine who was en-route to the dishwasher carrying a stack of plates and bowls. 'Beep beep! Coming through my lovelies.' J.D. was moving around the room gathering empty glasses and straightening tables and chairs to his usual exacting standards, whilst swapping gags with the handful of regulars still seated nearby. Halo followed him round, still with some appetite in spite of the few hours of pampering and high calorie intake she'd enjoyed at the hands of our very dog-friendly customers. I stood for a moment and took in the room - God I loved this place. I was Aunt Maddy reincarnate; no wonder she rarely left the place. Making out the rough shapes of the SharpCrest yard through the front windows, I inwardly reaffirmed my intention to never let "The Pulton Arms" fall into enemy hands. Then Jess popped into my head and I let out a sigh: I needed to keep busy so left the bar to help J.D. collect the empties.

By three o'clock we were back to rights, other than the sizeable collection of glasses and cups on the end of the bar that were awaiting the next free dishwasher cycle. J.D. was totting up the lunchtime take which looked extremely healthy judging by the wedge of notes he was holding. Bruno was tweaking his procedures, with the kitchen already back to a pristine state. Halo was sleeping off her lunchtime excess in her basket. All was well. Janine appeared from out back with her coat on.

'Right chaps; I'm outta here. Off to the dentist! Can't miss it as they only do Saturday surgery's once in a blue moon and it's a bitch to find a slot that works in the week 'cos of here and college.'

She looked incredibly up-beat. 'I never get that fired up about my dental appointments.' I said.

'Well your dentist probably isn't a slammin' hottie like mine is. I get to spend twenty minutes looking into his eyes while he puts his fingers in me; kind of. Why do you think I just eat chocolate and never floss? Laters potatas.' With that, she bounced out the front door as if her prince was waiting outside, glass slipper in hand.

'Fancy a drink J.D.? Think we've earned it.'

'Sure. Brandy ta.'

I shouted to the kitchen 'Can I interest you in a drink Bruno? We're all done out here and the bar's empty.'

'Thank you Ken but no; once I've completed my paperwork perhaps.'

I poured two generous brandies and knocked glasses with J.D. 'Here's to us; things are on the up my friend.'

'We need a proper review of the books but it's looking that way. Cheers.' More glass chinking. 'In other news, your head seems to be regaining its shape. Soon you'll be back to just plain ugly instead of looking like Quasimodo's twin.'

I reached up and patted my wound; surprised by how much this morning's golf ball sized protuberance had receded. 'I'll drink to that!' Just as I raised my glass once more, I jumped as the front door was flung open with sufficient force to slam it noisily against its stops.

Two large, black-suited men entered the bar, both wearing white shirt and black tie; and both wielding baseball bats. We'd only crossed paths once before but I recognised them instantly as Boat Bitch's gorillas. For the first time today, I actually wished the police were on the premises. The smaller of the two closed the door behind him, then stood with his back to the entrance; arms at his side but tensed. He tapped his leg with his bat, clearly prepared to let nobody in or out. His beefier counterpart walked towards the bar, hefting his bat in his hand as he went. Both suits had faces like thunder; I couldn't see anything but a brutal end to this scenario. I looked across to J.D.; he had his eyes fixed on the advancing muscle as he reached below the counter for his cricket bat. I didn't want him taking these guys on; not that I was at all keen to take his place.

'J.D.; I wouldn't.'

He looked at me then returned his focus to the approaching threat. He didn't pull out the bat, but neither did he move his hand away from it.

Gorilla One spoke as he neared the bar. 'I have a message from your neighbour. You're done, shit-heads.' With that he swung his bat and blasted an empty pint pot on a nearby table to smithereens. The shower of glass flew towards the bar, connecting with J.D.'s face. He swore and put his hands to his eyes, ducking behind the till. My mood instantly switched from startled and fearful to completely incensed and I flew over the bar, taking the most direct route to the main antagonist who was winding up his next swing, looking to level the stack of lunchtime empties awaiting their turn in the dishwasher. I say flew; I clambered over the bar in an ungainly fashion and dropped to the floor the other side, then forced my knackered legs to drive me upwards and in the right direction. With the red mist descended, I rushed towards Gorilla One who was now fully wound up to demolish the glassware mountain. In my periphery, I could see J.D. still bent over, clearly struggling, and to my right I sensed Gorilla Two moving away from the door and heading in my direction. Fearing further injury to J.D., I launched myself at

Gorilla One, aiming to dislodge him enough that he'd have to take time out to find his aim again. After he'd caved my head in of course. Braced for the impact, I was only a metre or so away when I heard a strange whooshing sound like a boomerang in full flight, followed by a metallic thud, as the centre of Gorilla One's forehead got forcefully introduced to the edge of two and a half kilos and twenty-six centimetres of bright red "Le Creuset" cast iron frying pan that appeared to have flown in from the kitchen (I remembered ordering that one on-line; bloody expensive; bloody heavy too). The pan then fell, sending several stone chips flying as it dug into the floor on landing. For a moment, Gorilla One just stood there, incredulously wide-eyed and stunned; then the bat slipped from his hands and he toppled like a felled oak. I was still in motion and due to the head of steam I'd built up, I was unable to stop myself so collided with him as he dropped, giving my head a hefty whack on the corner of a nearby table as I went down. I ended up on my back on the floor alongside him, struggling to catch my breath. Gorilla Two loomed over me, baseball bat half-raised, but with a confused look on his face as if his orders and expectations hadn't even vaguely encompassed this scenario. He didn't strike immediately; and whilst he stood there wondering what to do next, he was treated to a shower of wood-chips on the lapels of his suit jacket as two large kitchen knives fizzed through the air and embedded themselves in the timber of his weapon, just above the grip. He brought the bat down slowly and studied its impalers, looking increasingly bewildered by the second. As I tried to lever myself up, there came a shrill whistle from the direction of the front door that caused Gorilla Two to spin around, aware that he'd abandoned his post and interlopers were now making an entry. He must have had a fraction of a second to regard the intruder before his head snapped back and he went down, with no attempt to break his fall; seemingly out cold. He landed on me, the back of his head connecting with the fragile front of mine as his bulk squeezed out what little air I had left in my lungs. My vision blurred; then I caught a smeared glimpse of Chef's whites and shortly after, a weight was lifted. Blinking, my view gradually returned. Pat was looking down at me, wincing and flexing the fingers of the hand that must have downed Gorilla Two.

He blew on his knuckles. 'Fuck me; that boy's made of brick. What the hell happened here? You're a frickin' disaster magnet me old.' He reached down and pulled me to my unsteady feet.

By my side, Bruno spoke. 'I feel I had matters comfortably under control Pat, but many thanks for your assistance.' He looked more like he'd just whipped up a trifle rather than taken out two seriously hefty assailants bent on destruction. Looking at both of my saviours in turn, I managed a weak smile. As I was forming the words to thank them, Bruno said something

about my head bleeding; and then everything
went black.

'Ken. Wake up.'

The arm-wrestling contest with Bob Dylan
wasn't going well. I had the height advantage and
he was mid-seventies so I'd assumed it would be
a walkover but not so; I was in trouble. As I
strained to keep my knuckles above the table-
top, Pamela Anderson continued to bring me
bowl after bowl of ice cream that I had no
opportunity to eat. They were really piling up,
and I was beginning to fear her wrath as much as
I feared losing the competition to Bob. Also
didn't she do a sex tape once? No stranger to
public spectacle that one.

'Ken.'

Wasting food was also one of my pet
hates, especially when it was rum and raisin
flavoured.

'Ken. I need to talk to you.'

It should always be spelled rum and
raisin: where that whole 'n' convention came
from I'd never know.

Same with fish 'n' chips. It's "and", you
heathens.

I might make an exception with "Mum 'n'
Dad" but that's it. It would be a costly court

battle with Walkers Crisps over Salt and Vinegar; I might have to sell my neon tiara to fund that litigation.

'Ken this is important. Please wake up.'

Why isn't there fish and chip flavoured ice cream? Must get my Dragons' Den pitch ready for that one: 'I'm looking for a £20 investment in return for 150% of the company.'

'Ken!!'

Someone was shaking me with a purpose, forcing me to reintroduce myself to the real world. I did so slowly, remembering my middle school swimming class, rising lazily to the surface in my pyjamas after retrieving a brick from the bottom. The pool's bottom that is. Frozen desserts and physical challenges with iconic troubadours gave way to the present day. When the fog cleared, my view was Jess; perched on the edge of my bed, looking more troubled than I'd ever seen her. Woolly as I still was, I figured that look wasn't purely born out of concern for me: this wasn't some warm and fluffy reconciliation. I had to say something.

'Morning Jess. Good to see you. Sorry, I'm not terribly up together; I've been a bit, poorly.'

'It's eight in the evening. J.D. told me your Chef and a friend of yours carried you up here about four hours ago after you passed out.'

'I might have bumped my head a bit.'

'You look bloody awful.'

'Oi - I haven't had chance to put my face on yet.' My lame attempt at humour begat similarly poor results.

'Look, Ken; I know everything. I know it all; from your first conversation with my mother to you being laid out here after she sent her goons over to smash the place up. Even that bloody model.' She pointed at the shelf. 'But I know what you did too; the retaliation. Last night. Everything. I told my mother she'd never hear from me again if she didn't tell me the truth. And I meant it. This is.... bloody ridiculous!! Mature adults don't behave this way!!' She looked mortified; close to tears even. 'I know I didn't believe you when you told me your story in Westall's, but now I do. But it doesn't make what you're doing right!'

'Jess; look I'm only trying to save my business here. Just fighting fire with fire really. And she did start it.'

'Oh right! Playground politics it is then! I'll go call teacher! You two should be fucking ashamed of yourselves!' Her voice cracked; now she was crying.

'Jess I'm sorry. The last thing I wanted was for you to get dragged into this but that bi... your mother won't take no for an answer. Can't you talk to her? Get her to see sense and persuade her to leave me and my business alone? People depend on me and this place you know. And I want you back.'

'Oh I've tried! But she's as ridiculously stubborn as you are.' She wiped her face as best she could with the back of her hand. 'Where's your loo? I need to clean my face.'

'First door to the left as you head out the lounge.' She took a major sniff then left the room, as I tried to piece my thinking and some kind of strategy together. When she returned a few minutes later, I was no closer to a solution. She retook her seat on the edge of the bed, appearing to have calmed down somewhat.

'Look: I like you Ken. In fact, I like you more than I've liked anyone in a very long time. And I'm sorry for calling you a liar. But for us to stand a chance, you have to sort out this crap you've got going on with my mother.' I went to interject but she cut me off. 'And, I've said the same to her: if she doesn't stop her nonsense then she'll be minus a daughter. If you two can't agree a permanent ceasefire, then you can join hands and jump into the same bloody volcano as far as I'm concerned. Just make sure its active.' Then there was a half-smile which I echoed; something of the old us that gave me a flimsy glimmer of hope.

'Jess; you mean the world to me and I promise you I'll do my very best. And I promised Vicar Lucy I wouldn't be a dick and it's never wise to offend the church; just ask Galileo.'

She looked down to her shoes, then back at me: solemn again. 'Don't let me down Ken. Be as smart as you're funny and we might just stand a chance.' She stood to leave. 'Don't get up; I think you need your rest. Call me when everything's sorted out; but not before.' She went for a dramatic sweeping out kind of exit but then paused in the doorway to the lounge. 'That painting: what do you know about it?'

'What, the boat one? Nothing; it was here when I moved in.'

'It just looks familiar is all.' She must have moved to investigate closer, as her voice faded. 'It's rather grand. And I don't think it's a print.'

I didn't have an educated answer, knowing as much about art as I did about changing the head gasket on a 1995 Ford Probe. 'Maybe you attended the same car boot sale that my Aunt bought it at?'

She popped her face around the doorway. 'I'm going now. Be that good guy again Ken. Please.' Then she was gone.

I laid back on the bed, wondering if there was any way on earth to stop the seemingly unstoppable force that was Boat Bitch. I had to somehow; I wanted Jess and I wanted to keep my pub and my friends safe, more than anything. Then my grogginess gave way to anger and I sat up, scanning my surroundings for an appropriate object. Finding I had none to hand, I tugged off my shoe and hurled it with all the energy I could muster at the shelf on the opposite wall. My aim was true - the ghastly wannabee SharpCrest sales office disintegrated into a gratifying shower of white card and plastic.

CHAPTER SIXTEEN

Despite Jess's instructions to take it easy, I felt the need to check out the situation downstairs; I couldn't assume I was the only casualty from today's ruckus. Still dressed, all I had to do was roll out of bed and head down. A quick inspection in the mirror en-route revealed a blood-speckled bandage occupying the opposite side of my forehead to the original gash. Why did I always get it in the head? This whole G.I. Joe thing clearly wasn't for me - I felt like I'd spent the last few days repeatedly falling off cliffs onto poorly poured concrete, strewn with angle-iron and Stegosaurus tails. The stairs creaked less than I did on the descent.

As I hobbled into the bar, there was none of the chaos I'd been expecting to find. Looking around the room, everything was unremarkable. There were a few customers in, and the room felt rather upbeat. J.D. came over as soon as he saw me appear.

'You should be in bed; you look rougher than a badger's arse.'

'I'll live; I just wanted to check you guys were still in one piece.' J.D.'s left eye was predominantly red and looked bloody sore. 'Is your face okay? I saw that glass hit you.' Over his shoulder I could see Janine who was busy serving a customer, but kept looking my way intermittently, clearly anxious.

'Yeah it's okay. I got a splinter in it which hurt like all hell but Bruno flushed it out and gave me some drops to put in. I'm hardly feeling it now.'

'Christ that guy's a one-man field hospital. What happened after I um... checked out?'

'You were out cold, so Bruno and Pat carted you up to The Homo Hangar while I kept an eye on the suits, who were also out for the count. We had a bit of a one-to-one with them when they finally came round; or rather a three-to-two, just letting them know they'd get the same reception if they showed their faces in the pub again. There wasn't any resistance; they looked shit-scared to be honest. Especially when Bruno wrenched his knives out of the baseball bat and started explaining in great detail how he goes about butchering a cow and why the process isn't that much different when it comes to a human man. Gave me the willies as well. Oh and I officially barred them too.'

He looked like he was suffering rather more than he was letting on, but his good humour seemed genuine enough. 'Well played. So nobody else was hurt? No more damage to the bar either?'

'Well; me, Bruno and Pat are intact but there's a picture needing fixing.' I followed his look over to the entrance, to the print of a rather majestic three-mast schooner, noting the impact damage to its bottom right corner. 'The guy that Bruno took out with the frying pan was especially doolally, so Pat went to help him out the door but the bloke stumbled and twatted the picture with his bonce. Don't think that helped his headache at all.' J.D.'s smile was positively diabolical.

'Thank Christ everyone's okay. And thank you J.D.'

'I didn't really do anything. Bruno and Pat sorted them out.'

'Did you know Bruno was so... handy?'

'I didn't know he was that blimmin' handy! Did you see the knife stuff before you flaked out? Also, once the bad guys had gone, he finished up in the kitchen then made a couple of calls to suppliers to change tomorrow's orders after we got cleared out at lunchtime. Then he went home. He was completely nonplussed. Like nothing had happened I mean. Or something had happened that he was no stranger to.'

'Yeah I caught his act. What do you know about his time in the Army?'

'Nothing really; he never seems keen to talk about it so I don't push it. Whatever he did, I'm thinking he must have been damn good at it though. Oh and Pat said to say hi and he'll call you tomorrow. Oh and he also said to let you know your flies are undone.'

Yes, I looked. Even second-hand he'd got me. And then I was suddenly pinned as Janine flew my way and wrapped her arms around me with such energy I almost missed being the filling in the gorilla sandwich from earlier. 'Erm - hi Janine.' She didn't move for a while; stood with her head pressed against my chest while she continued to exert the same magnitude of pressure as those Jaws of Life cutters that firemen use do. 'Bless you, but that kind of hurts.'

When she looked up, her eyes were weepy. I was surprised and genuinely touched. Then she eased her hold a little; and it was good to feel my blood circulating once more.

'You complete dick! You might have got yourself locked up!' Then she lowered the volume. 'Messing with them posh boats? You're a fucking clown.' Standing back, she wiped her tears with the back of her hand then broke into a laugh. 'You've got some balls though our kid.'

No way; I'd been rumbled already? I looked to J.D. who gave me a half-knowing, half-apologetic nod.

'Wasn't too hard to figure out Ken, what with the neighbour being your Nemesis and all. Plus when I brought up your tea this morning, all I could smell in The Crotch Nest was chemicals and the sea. I talked with Pat and Bruno too. Pat dropped some heavy hints; he wasn't trying to drop you in it - think he was proud of you mostly. Then Janine came in tonight, full of the story from the local paper so I had to fill her in, if only to get her to pipe down and change the subject in front of the punters. It won't go any further; you know that. And like Janine said; serious balls my friend.'

They both looked at me ashamedly. But there was no way I could be remotely aggrieved at either of them. 'Well thank you for the ball comments, and your ongoing support. So I'm in the paper? I mean, <u>it's</u> in the paper?' We were talking quietly but I still took a quick look around to make sure there were no customers within earshot. Loose lips sink ships and all that.

Janine reached under the counter and brought out the local daily rag and held up the front page. The headline shouted "Pulton's Industry Under Attack!!"; a proclamation that I deemed rather too sensationalist, probably penned by a rookie journo keen to impress with their first piece, or a jaded long-timer that habitually drank Scotch with their Cornflakes. It was only a bit of paint after all. Okay, rather a lot of paint. Twice.

Taking the paper from Janine's animated grasp, I speed-read the first few paragraphs of

414

conjecture. The available "evidence" apparently pointed the finger at competing businesses in the luxury motor yacht industry or recently sacked SharpCrest employees with an axe to grind. This was somewhat reassuring. Looking at the first couple of photos, I actually felt a twinge of pride viewing my artwork once more - I really did nail the presentation. Really not too shabby for my first effort. I was a Banksy of sorts; just a bit edgier. Maybe in time I'd end up sharing a cell with him. Reasonably confident that I was in the clear for now, I didn't feel a need to read any further so handed the paper back to Janine. 'Bless you for being you folks. Let's have a drink.'

A few hours later, I was back upstairs, lying on the bed with my arms folded behind my head, conjuring up faces from the swirling Artex patterns above. Everything still ached, but Janine had insisted on (forcefully) applying sufficient of Bruno's potion to grease a tractor engine, so I wasn't feeling too much pain from my forehead injuries and nothing else hurt too much unless I moved. Or breathed. I'd hung in behind the bar for a while, keen to be there for my team but I'd flagged quickly and J.D. sensitively pointed out that I looked so crap as to scare the customers off. So since then, I'd been on my bed and inside my head, thinking of some way to bin the witch, keep the pub and reclaim the girl. Today's visit from Boat Bitch's heavies left me in no doubt that this debacle hadn't run its course. My raid on the yard had just served as further incentive for her to progress her expansionist plans; I'd just poked the hornet's nest with a stick, nothing more. And if Jess had outed me as her love interest, then I was no doubt doubly screwed. Even if Boat Bitch had no interest in the pub, she'd probably have still sent her muscle to warn me off dating her daughter. At least she now knew there was some serious resistance ready and waiting if she decided on a similar assault in the future. But what if that came after hours? And what if she sent twenty guys next time? Or just despatched some missile-laden drone to accelerate my home's make-over? Apparently, they're not that difficult to manufacture. I remembered watching a YouTube clip of a guy called "Tony XTreme" assembling one from a kit in a shed in Colchester. He knocked his tea over at one point, but otherwise it looked like a pretty straightforward build.

I couldn't remember the last time I'd felt this helpless. I liked to think of myself as a resourceful guy but I just couldn't summon the bright idea I so desperately needed; that killer blow that would put Boat Bitch in her place once and for all. And keep her there, while I got on with enjoying my life with Jess. We'd probably still have to invite her mother to the wedding if only to boost the funding, but I could learn to live with that idea. Possibly.

Another hour passed; and I was no closer to a breakthrough, though I'd made a serious dent in the bottle of red I'd brought upstairs with me. Yes I know: the new healthier regime would start tomorrow, I promised myself. Unable to find any new faces in the decoration above me, and not feeling ready to sleep, I decided to watch a bit of telly. Emitting all the now typical noises and groans, I levered myself up off the bed then grabbed my bottle of medication and its accompanying glass and tottered into the lounge; eventually plonking myself down into the armchair. Having replenished my beverage, I shuffled around the chair, searching for the two remotes that I needed to fire up the telly and the video player, wishing I'd refreshed my drink last as I continued to throw a decent portion of it over myself as I delved between the chair cushions. Then with both remotes retrieved, I sat back, ready to experience the first-class entertainment that was the finale of "Robocock". Perhaps poorly-scripted adult entertainment with questionable production values would be the solution to all that ailed me.

As it turned out, I was left disappointed with our main man's much-anticipated consummation with "EDITH 209". True, I'd never before seen a robotic police officer with prosthetic genitalia as expansive as his vocabulary wasn't get it on with a love interest that resembled a tumble drier, but it was a truly lack-lustre "love scene". Also, Edith was faking it I was sure. Reasonably confident I'd seen the money shot, I took a sip of my drink and reached for the VCR's remote, ready to swap the world of foreign porn for the world of foreign sports that I didn't understand and couldn't interpret. However, while my thumb hovered above the

"Off" button, a buxom young woman in a lab coat way too slight to contain her chest or conceal her underwear, entered the scene. Maybe there was more to come (as it were). From what little I could glean from the visuals and the sub-titles, the new arrival appeared to be some senior scientist bod that had created Edith and was aghast that Robocock had shagged her into a pile of scrap-metal and sparks (Edith that is). Then her anger inexplicably gave way to horniness and she proceeded to succumb to our electronic lawman's charms. And by charms, I mean his gleaming chrome accessory. The camera moved from the impressively detailed close-up of the penetration itself to centre on the face of our sex-pot scientist on all fours, as the police hardware continued to interface with her software at an ever-quickening pace. And then it hit me; my surprise manifesting itself in the form of a high-velocity torrent of Rioja that burst from my mouth and splashed against the screen that I now couldn't tear my eyes away from.

Aches and pains be damned - the next morning I was up and moving early doors. And moving with a purpose, fuelled by Christmas-Day-as-a-kid type anticipation. I'd peeled off the bandage nursing my most recent clatter, dabbed both abrasions with Bruno's smelly ooze, then bounded downstairs with the VCR under my arm. Feeling rather wired after my discovery, I hadn't really slept last night so was somewhat sleep-deprived and possibly still concussed after my few recent knocks to the melon, but my head felt surprisingly fog-free. Intending to keep it that way for now, I fixed myself a cup of tea then got to work. After a good while searching the bar for a remote control or anything else that might wake the TV in the corner, I came up empty, so jogged around to the device itself and pressed the power button. Alas there was no picture, no sound and not even a glowing LED to indicate I'd brought it to life. Bugger. I traced the mains lead back to a single wall socket behind the bar, finding that the telly was playing second fiddle to the coffee machine and had no juice. Ah-ha! I took life away from the steam monster and plugged in the TV instead. A red light popped on to indicate proof of life but there was still no picture so I returned to the set and started playing with what looked to be the channel selection buttons. After a few random presses, I was rewarded with the sight and sounds of some enthusiastic Scandinavians engaged in a curling contest. I'd seen curling competitions before and they'd always struck me as atrociously ill-prepared events with all the frantic sweeping that went on while the game was in progress. If the organisers just took ten minutes to have a quick brush-down the night before they'd be laughing surely. Armed with the necessary connecting leads I'd brought down from The Crow's Nest and a plug adapter I'd successfully scavenged from one of the drawers in the utility room, a few minutes later I had the VCR propped rather precariously on the bar, sharing its picture loud and proud on the big screen. Satisfied, I powered it off together with the TV. Then I sent Jess a text; show-casing my freshly discovered technical prowess by rounding of my message with two lower-case "x"s.

J.D. was first to arrive that morning, as always surprised to see me up and on deck already.

'Crikey - doesn't your bed work anymore?' He dropped his paper on the bar as Halo wandered over to say hi and dribble on my shoes. Then he looked at me in a rather more studious fashion. 'You look like you lost a quid and found a fiver. What's up?'

I grinned as if unhinged, which probably wasn't a long journey from where I was at right then. 'Nothing in particular. I just think today's going to be a good one.'

'What? Another coach party?'

'Here's hoping. Have we got a remote for the TV?' He frowned as I drummed my fingers on the bar, too infused with nervous energy to keep all my extremities still.

After a moment of contemplation, he then turned and rummaged about on the back shelf behind the bar where pencils, notebooks and spiders went to hide. 'Eureka!' With that he spun and tossed me some old gadget that threw a cloud of dust my way as I caught it.

'Fab - thanks.' I pressed the biggest button I could see on the device which remarkably brought the TV back to life; again with the foreign curling and its wholly unnecessary last-minute broom-based housework.

'Christ! I don't think we've had that thing on since the last Royal Wedding. Or Coronation maybe. What are we watching?'

'Are you a film fan by any chance?' I wandered over to the VCR and powered it up, thus replacing icy sport with the grandeur of "Robocock"'s closing scenes.

'Jesus, where did you find that relic?' J.D. walked to the other side of the bar so he could fully see the screen. After a few moments of viewing, he looked at me surprised; probably no stranger to adult film content, but maybe a little taken aback to see it playing out in the bar room of "The Pulton Arms". Returning his attention to the show, he watched for a few minutes longer. Then his eyes widened to the size of saucers and he slowly turned his head in my direction, clearly flabbergasted by what he had just witnessed.

'No: fucking: way!'

'Yes way J.D. Yes way.' We shared a knowing grin.

Turning off the VCR, I swapped its plug for the coffee machine's in the socket - we'd need that for lunchtime service. There was still business to be done after all.

421

'Good Morning gentlemen! I trust we're all well.' Bruno entered from the kitchen, looking immaculate in his work attire as always.

I was over the moon to see him. 'Bruno!' I sprinted over. For the first time in memory, he actually appeared a trifle alarmed. Suddenly aware that this was Bruno, the gorilla-stopping, knife and saucepan hurling machine, I managed to brake before I crashed into him full tilt. 'I just wanted to say thank you for yesterday; you were, well.... awesome!' I reached out my hand. His look softened and he smiled like he wouldn't kill me just yet. Which was nice.

'I was glad to be of service. It was hugely pleasurable to work such an industrious and productive session - a grand test for the kitchen; and I would hope we passed with flying colours?'

'No. Well yes I mean, that was great too but I meant the... visitors, later. You saw them off.'

'Oh yes the undesirables. No problem whatsoever. Alas one will always attract the odd bad apple wherever one sets up shop. I was all too happy to help, though your good friend Pat did the leg work really. What a solid individual he is to be sure; both physically and morally. I trust you're feeling better? You looked a little peaky last evening before you took to your bed.' With that, he shook my long-proffered hand then headed off to prep the kitchen before I'd managed a reply.

'Once Janine's in, we'll have a staff meeting and I'll let you know what's on my mind. In the meantime, let's just focus on having another belter of a lunchtime service.'

'As always Ken; here's to ticking another box on Pulton's culinary wish-list.' He waggled one of his larger knives in the air without looking my way, then set about his vegetables.

I called Pat.

He answered. 'Morning fatso! You're still alive then? I'd have pulled the plug on you last night to be honest. Not that you were dying, I just needed a socket to charge my phone.'

'Stop it, you're so caring its making me all blushing and girly. Seriously though mate, thanks for everything yesterday - you're a full-on superhero.'

'No problem me old. I'm damn sure Bruno could have handled those wankers on his own mind you. Remind me never to piss that guy off: ever. You on the mend? The head I mean - I think you're stuck with that wind problem.'

'Yeah, still a bit sore but getting there. Look, any chance you could drop into the pub around half-three this afternoon? Just for an hour or so?'

'Sure - it'll get me out of shoe shopping with Lor. Not expecting more hassle from Queen Twat are you?'

'No. Hopefully the opposite. I'll see you later mate.'

'On the Ron John.'

Thankfully, it was another energetic lunchtime session; no coach parties alas, but plenty of visitors reluctant to cook their own Sunday lunch. Bruno did the honours for them instead, in his usual exquisite fashion, while I flew around all charged-up and edgy ahead of the afternoon's big event. Having removed my head dressing, and with Bruno's wonder gel healing me impossibly fast, I was comfortable I wouldn't be scaring the punters off so got stuck into service. Whilst out and about in the bar delivering food orders or collecting empties, I still had to field some concerned enquiries from many of the customers who'd noticed I'd been in the wars somewhat. After going with the bland (and false) 'hit my head on the door' answer, I set myself the challenge of coming up with a different fake scenario each time the question arose.

'Those are actually tribal tattoos, not bruises.'

'I was taking part in an extreme Frisbee display and got distracted when I heard an ice cream van.'

'Recently started to dabble with S&M - just a spot of light chafing.'

'Took a tumble playing Quidditch; no biggie.'

Things like that. Some of which raised a laugh; the remainder just confused frowning.

By three, we were done and the last of the customers were finishing up their drinks before leaving.

Pat arrived about twenty to four and I brought him up to speed, as I had the rest of the team prior to his arrival.

Lunchtime had been cleared away; tables and chairs had been straightened and every surface wiped down with fastidious attention. It was almost dark outside and I found myself longing for Summer, when warmth and sunlight would be flooding through the windows at this hour. Looking around the room, I'd never felt more proud of our little pub. And endlessly appreciative of the fabulous people that kept it (and me) afloat. But the room was tense, with little chatter; everyone charged with the anticipation of what was to come. Other than me, I think it was only Bruno that hadn't poured themselves a glass or two of resolve-stiffener. Yes, I'd been tempted, but today was a day for keeping a clear head and shelving my "wine with everything" policy. If all went to plan, we'd celebrate later.

J.D. caught my eye, holding up a handwritten notice that simply stated "Closed for Private Function". I nodded, and he went and taped it to the front door. We didn't want anyone in attendance other than those present and those that I'd invited. I unplugged the coffee machine and plugged in the VCR. It was two minutes to four.

Pat stood with his back to the till on the other side of the bar. Ranged behind him, also facing the door stood me, J.D. and Janine, with Bruno positioned just outside the kitchen door with his arms folded, showing none of the tension that the rest of us were no doubt exuding in buckets. Still fixed on the front door, I addressed the room.

'Remember, none of you need to be here guys. I gave you the option because you've been part of this journey and you've all been superstars. Bless you for being here, but if you'd rather wait out back and eat crisps then go for it. This is all on me.'

Without turning around, Pat just raised his arm and flicked me a 'V'. Nobody else budged an inch. Halo grunted in her basket.

'Okay then.'

On the dot of four o'clock, the front door opened, and in filed enough suits to stock a small branch of "Top Man". Behind the first row strode Boat

426

Bitch, similarly dressed for business, wearing a sharp outfit and her customary stand-out red lipstick and a look of unbridled self-satisfaction. She couldn't have looked any more smug; clearly savouring the moment, as she would if she'd knocked a toddler's ice cream out of its hand into the dirt. The suits were all predictably hefty blokes; more steroid-fuelled mobsters. Two arranged themselves to one side of Boat Bitch when she reached the bar, two the other, alongside Pat. Another three formed a row behind her, then another pair stationed themselves near the entrance. These last two were familiar to me and didn't appear to share the over-confidence that flowed from their colleagues, instead looking nervous and furtive, especially when they caught sight of Bruno and Pat. One sported an angry-looking bruise that bisected his forehead, and the other wore a puffed-up cheek and black eye. Presumably they'd both been forced to show up today as punishment for failing in their previous mission. Pat reached behind him and grabbed his glass then took a sip and raised it in the air.

'Nice to see you again lads! Didn't you bar these two clowns though J.D.?''

Bruno took a step further into the bar. Both his and Pat's previous combatants took a backward step, looking increasingly panicky. The two new gorillas just to Pat's left turned to face him. For a moment I thought it was all going to kick off again but Pat, still with glass in hand, just faced them down. 'What?' They stayed where they were, apparently baffled by Pat's lack of concern for their bulky presence and potential for violence.

Then Boat Bitch spoke. 'If you could all keep the testosterone and the show-boating in check for now, that would be greatly appreciated.' She fixed her look on me; still smiling and oozing superiority. 'Obviously I received your message via my daughter; hence my presence here. You invited me to "make the peace" did you not? I assume this means you are finally ready to see sense and capitulate without reservation. Or even better, simply fall on your sword here and now. That said, I do relish the thought of administering the killing blow myself after the damage you wrought in my yard, and your misguided pursuit of my daughter's affections against my clearly-expressed wishes. As yet, I haven't passed your name to the authorities, but I do still have that option available should you be anything less than fully compliant during the process of signing your premises over to me. Oh, and I'm afraid the opportunity to "sell" me your business expired the moment you decided to vandalise a multi-million-pound cruiser and fuck up my delivery schedule. So: no business; and no girlfriend either. What's the phrase? Oh yes - it sucks being you. Before you drop to your knees and weep Mister Trickett, I'll have a large gin and tonic. By way of celebration of your capitulation.'

Expressionless, I studied her for a few moments before I responded. 'Goodness; you do like the sound of your own voice don't you? That must be tiresome, right guys?' I scanned the muscle in the room; more than one of whom rolled their eyes in quiet affirmation. 'As for the drink, no; sorry. Unless J.D. disagrees as co-licensee, I choose not to serve you. This is still our business you see. <u>Our,</u> business. Maybe next time; as long as you don't turn up with your squad of bruisers in tow. No offence lads. Though Angie, you really must drop by for lunch when we've got our full menu on the go; Bruno will dazzle you I swear. Oh and if any of your guys are thinking of starting a scuffle, bear in mind that Chef might well finish them before they have time to blink. He takes down well-built thugs just as expertly as he cooks don't you know.' I swung my arm to point in Bruno's direction and he responded with a low, self-deprecating bow; then straightened and shared a "butter-wouldn't-melt" type smile with the room as he unhurriedly opened his knife roll on the bar counter.

'My mate Pat's a bit handy too, as those nearest the door will testify to.'

Pat took another sip of his pint, still clearly un-fazed by the many beefed-up adversaries he was surrounded by. He didn't move or make eye contact, just continuing to stare past them out the window. After another sip he just said 'Gym wankers.'; and no more.

The suits shuffled their position, now obviously with far less confidence in their numbers. Those flanking Boat Bitch took half a step back, wanting to put some space between themselves and Pat and Bruno, but without too blatantly leaving their Boss undefended.

I continued. 'As for the police, I read in the paper that your night watchman was asleep during the "incident", so I doubt you have any evidence you can pass on to them regarding who may have carried out the raid. Had you managed to capture the perpetrator on video, I imagine he or she would have been very publicly brought to justice by now.'

Boat Bitch's aura of smugness dissipated a little and now somewhat confused, she looked at J.D. then Pat. With no response from either, she looked back to me, clearly agitated. 'You do realise you're being both insulting and obstructive?'

'Yes. I'm multi-tasking. It seems that's not solely a female talent after all. Who knew?'

'Look, this is over - do you understand? You invited me here to accept your surrender, so go ahead and offer it up and stop wasting my time. Your dignity is far beyond saving, so at least do what you can to spare yourself further humiliation, you pathetic excuse for a man.'

'Oh. Are we down to name-calling now? Isn't that a little below us?'

Pat chimed in with 'I always go with Queen Twat now; seems to fit.'

'Thanks mate. Good shout. I reckon we can come up with something better though.

Hmmm... let me think on that. Actually, I could do with a drink myself now.' I slowly and deliberately poured myself a large Gin and Tonic whilst appearing to be in deep thought crafting another title for Boat Bitch. Standing directly in front of her, I took a long draw from my glass whilst looking her in the eye. She appeared to be slowly unravelling mentally, as she struggled with the unfamiliar feeling of not having absolute control of the situation. It was time to go for the throat. 'I've got it! From now on I think we'll call you "Angel Stark". That's terribly catchy. Almost a film star name. What do you think Janine?'

'Sounds like a colossal tramp to me Ken. Spot-on I'd say.' Janine stared at Boat Bitch, radiating disgust.

Boat Bitch was clearly dumbfounded. Her mouth opened and closed as she tried to formulate a fitting reply; but she'd just had the rug of all rugs pulled out from under her, and the words wouldn't come. I had no such problem, and pressed on.

'Actually that name rings bells. In fact, I'm pretty sure I've seen Angel Stark in action. What was that film?' I stood there tapping my fingers on the counter as I deliberated with a far-away look. 'Game show maybe? Some reality trash? Costume drama perhaps - maybe a Downton spin-off? Oh God of course! It's this one!' Grabbing the TV remote, I powered on the set. The screen in the corner came to life, showing men in leotards grappling with each other. 'Gosh, as huge a fan of Belgian Catch Wrestling as I am, this isn't quite what I had in mind.'

Boat Bitch stood there in silence, apparently still struggling to reclaim her voice while her goons switched their confused attention to her, then me, then the screen, understanding less and less of what was going on with each swivel of their heads.

Turning on the VCR, I then treated the room to a large-screen showing of an entirely naked Angel Stark, a.k.a. Angelique Sharp, getting rear-ended by a cyborg policeman.

'I've watched this one a couple of times. Not a bad movie; I just wished they'd spent more of the budget on set design. Some of it looked a bit thrown together. Especially that scene where you do the guy in the workshop after you erm, "drain his oil".' I froze the scene. All eyes in the room gradually drifted back to mine. Boat Bitch seemed to be struggling to breathe, and the flush of her cheeks was now far more prominent than the deep tan she'd acquired from her numerous jaunts to The Middle East.

Finally, she found her voice. 'You won't get away with this. Give me the ta...'

I cut her off. 'Oh no no no.' I wagged my finger in front of her face. 'You don't get to tell me what to do ever again. And I mean <u>ever</u>. But sure, you can have the tape if you outbid your beefy colleagues here; they seemed quite interested in your "performance". But, I'm afraid there's no way I'm parting company with

"Mannequim" or "Steel Shagnolias". Classics both, and might I say, your finest work to date. Or Angel's finest work should I say; whatever - you're interchangeable; and clearly one and the same person. Angel must be what, about twenty in the video? You have worn well I must say; good bones and a decent skincare regime work wonders don't they? Would it be too clichéd to ask for an autograph?' I grabbed a notepad and pen and slid them across the bar towards her. 'Could you sign it as Angel? I'm just like, her hugest fan. I'm a little star struck, truth be told.'

All eyes were now on Boat Bitch; even her bemused henchmen, though a few still gazed at the TV, either transfixed by what they'd witnessed or hoping for an encore. After taking several deep breaths, she spoke again: softly, with her previous arrogance a fading memory. 'Might I trouble you for a glass of water?' She looked mentally broken, and seemed to have physically withered since she first rode in on her wave of seemingly unassailable supremacy.

I saw little point in twisting the knife now that it was so firmly embedded. 'Sure.' I passed her a glass and she drank deeply, then stood there with her head bowed, seemingly trying to regroup. After some time, during which nobody else in the room moved or spoke or seemed to breathe, she looked up at me.

'So what do you want?'

'I want you to cease and desist any and all activity concerned with getting your hands on

433

"The Pulton Arms", and indeed any activity that carries even the most infinitesimal risk of pissing me or my friends off. And you'll tell Jess that me and you have patched up our differences, because I am in love with that spectacular girl and I am going absolutely nowhere. You don't have to invite me to Sunday dinner every week and we don't need to feign mutual adoration when we do meet, but unless I give you good reason to, you won't mess with our relationship or even look at me in a disapproving way unless you really do want your turn in "Who Screwed Roger Rabbit?" all over social media, supplemented by a few choice stills the tabloids can run with. Maybe a few copies on eBay for good measure as well. Deal?'

She raised herself up and stuck her chin in the air defiantly, apparently working at mustering the energy to go back on the attack. But then she appeared to realise she was devoid of offensive options, and her shoulders slumped. Then she turned and left without another word. Her hoodlums still looked baffled, but without further orders, they dropped in line behind her and trudged out. When the last suit had left the room I turned and looked at the tensed but expectant faces of Pulton's finest. Nobody seemed to want to jinx the moment and speak first, so I took the plunge.

'J.D. - got any champagne left in your secret stash? I think we just slayed a dragon.'

Then the room disintegrated into relieved shouts, cheers and hugs as we collectively exorcised the anxiety and tension that had accumulated over the last few hours, days and weeks, and celebrated what looked to be a promising future. I was right with my earlier forecast - today had been a good one.

CHAPTER SEVENTEEN

Come on - sleep. There's nothing to get up for right now. Treat yourself, I kept telling myself. But no matter how many times I rolled over and tried to nudge my brain in the direction of the whimsical and a decent doze, I remained indecently awake. In the end, I decided that was okay because today I had naff all to fret about. Well, not immediately at least. For the first time in a good while, I had high hopes that this would be a normal day, minus the craziness that had become typical of late. I wanted the normal that meant no heated confrontations with guys that had biceps wider than my thighs wanting to beat lumps out of me, and no feisty exchanges with neighbourhood captains of industry wanting to run me out of town. Just normal. Maybe a cup of tea first. Then ideally a pleasurable and prosperous shift behind the bar without the need for any knife or pan throwing. Perhaps the sun would shine and I could spend a few blissful hours revisiting the gloriously non-fresh air of the Fishermen's Quay. Yep - that would do very nicely. Up and at 'em...

I swung my legs off the bed and sat upright, still somewhat rigid and creaking from my out of character "doing my own stunts" sessions from the past few days, but feeling less like the physical derelict I'd been the last couple of mornings. After a few stretches, some clicking joints and a shower, I was bar bound, and feeling generally in good sorts, yet carrying some nagging uncertainty regarding my professional and romantic future. Had Boat Bitch truly backed off? Would Jess give me another chance?

When I reached the bottom of the stairs, I was surprised at the hustle and bustle going on around me. Then the kitchen clock let me know it was 12:30 already and the day was fully underway. Man, I must have needed that sleep. Deciding to pass on the tea, I strolled through the kitchen then out into the bar amongst the tables which were already populated by a decent clutch of eager early birds, all of whom were scanning the menus with enthusiasm or already tucking into something. En-route, I engaged all the usual faces as per the daily routine I'd come to cherish. This was my realm; and I couldn't imagine myself being content anywhere else.

'Hey Bruno. Are we all set?'

'Ken, we are more than set. I have in fact already served two Grantchester

Fugly quiches and I hear the plates are being rapidly cleared. If I may be so bold, I feel we're ready to expand our menu - I have a few creations in mind that I believe will establish us well and truly on The South's culinary map. Might I discuss further with you when service is complete?'

'Bravo. And absolutely!'

'Afternoon J.D. What's new in the world?'

'Well, according to the local rag, the SharpCrest Head of Security has been sacked for snoozing on the job. Turns out he wasn't working the cameras 'cos he was asleep on duty so he's history, and they've no idea who made a mess of the yard. In other news, I've been invited to dinner, by Beth. Think I might accept; everyone deserves a second chance don't they.'

'They sure do; Aunt Maddy would approve. Give Beth my love when you call to confirm.'

'Hi Janine. Still stalking Bieber on Twitter? Or your dentist perhaps?'

'No way, that is so last week. Turns out my dentist hottie has a boyfriend but OMG I would so get on that.' She thrust her phone at my face; the screen showing a buff young chap in a gym setting. 'Maybe I can turn him?'

'I don't doubt it; go get him.'

'Oh and you got flowers; again. No vase I'm afraid since you royally effed-up the last one.' She pointed to the far end of the bar which was obscured by an ice bucket that struggled to contain an impressive display of bright white flowers. 'I think they're poppies. Oh and the shitty TripAdvisor reviews are gone too by the way.'

It was quite the bouquet; enormous. The flowers' variety and colour weren't lost on me; this was someone waving a flag. I walked over and pulled out the card that sat between the stems which was simply addressed to "Mr. Trickett". I opened the envelope and pulled out an exquisitely penned, hand-written note.

'Dear Ken.

I appreciate that we have had our differences of late but hopefully we are beyond those now and can look to forge a convivial relationship moving forward. You have a wonderful property there on the quayside but in spite of my previous advances regarding its purchase, I must now confess that I've decided it sadly not to be a good fit for my portfolio and must reluctantly advise you that I shan't be continuing down that particular avenue. Of course, I wish your own business well for the future. Your inaugural "Film Night" event that I attended last evening was certainly an eye-opener, but might I politely suggest that you put that idea to rest and refrain from widening your audience? I would also ask that you do not share that particular film or similar content with my daughter, as that kind of "entertainment" is very much not to her taste. In fact, she was born shortly after that particular era came to a close and has no knowledge of any association I may have had with it. Indeed you might say her arrival triggered that very closure. I trust you'll do the decent thing, for the sake of both of our sensitivities.

Respectfully yours,

Angie.'

I looked across the bar and beyond: through the windows where early Spring was heralding its arrival on the calendar by beaming in and lighting up the room. I read the note again, then folded it up and slipped it into the back pocket of my jeans. There was an urge to crumple it up and toss it into the trash as a triumphal flourish, but I held back. If The Devil gives you a "gimme", it's always wise to preserve the proof, just in case. But it was a result none the less. I bunched my fists and shook them before me whilst treating myself to a silent "Yes fucking yes, you beauty!!" I leaned in and sniffed the flowers which didn't smell of a whole lot but which triggered a major sneezing fit that seemed to last for hours.

Janine passed me a length of kitchen roll which I was fairly confident would reach around the planet at least twice. After a few hectic minutes, I was done sneezing and wiping. 'That must have been some sort of record!' I looked around and raised my arm for a high-five but there was nobody in range that looked even remotely interested. After one last wipe, I threw the bunched-up tissue into the bin. Pinching my nose, I held position whilst taking a couple of serious sniffs to make sure the nasal storm was done with. My eyes pooled a bit, so I had to blink a few times before my focus returned. And when it did, the sunshine was back in the room: and so was Jess.

She stood a couple of feet from the bar, with the sunlight framing her from behind. She wore her red woollen coat with its matching accessories; and a cautious smile. Christ, she looked fabulous. My old nerves returned as I stood there, not knowing whether this was the longed-for reconciliation or the final goodbye. Then she spoke.

'Bless you.'

'Thanks.'

'Are you busy right now?'

'I was just going to have some iced tea and split the atom, but that can wait.' (Damn you "Bridges".)

She nodded in the direction of the flowers. 'Serious flowerage. New admirer? Anyone I know?' She walked up to the bar and fingered some of the petals, intermittently switching her look from the floral display back to me, then back to the flowers again as if stalling before dropping a bombshell.

'You might say so. Maybe not an admirer; more an ex-adversary perhaps.'

'I'd heard you've been making friends.' She looked at me fixedly whilst running her hands through the poppies. 'I don't care how, you know. I just need to know you fixed it.'

'I said I would; and I did.'

'Mum still looks cross when your name crops up; but she says you're okay.'

'So do we have her blessing?'

'I wouldn't go that far.'

'But she's called off the hounds?'

'It would seem so.'

'That's good to know.' Still unsure which way the conversation was headed, and having possibly started to grow a pair as a result of my recent exploits, I decided to steer the dialogue myself. 'Any chance you're free for dinner sometime? I know of at least two places that'll do you decent fish and chips. Or three even, when we update our menu.'

Then it seemed as if a heavy weight she'd been burdened with for way too long just dropped from her shoulders and she launched herself across the bar, planting a passionate smacker of a kiss on my mouth as she sent the drip trays and towels flying: also narrowly avoiding propelling the flowers floor-wards. When we eventually untangled, she leaned back and beamed at me, with the mega-watt, no holds barred smile returned to her beautiful face. 'Goodness; even a better kisser than I'd remembered. Room for improvement though - hope you're up for some practice. And defo dinner.'

I could see Janine to my left doing the silent but rapid hand-clapping gesture whilst grinning from ear to ear. I looked back to Jess with mock sincerity. 'I could possibly find a few free minutes; let me check my diary. Pubs of this calibre don't just run themselves you know.' Then I vaulted over the bar, this time managing to stay on my feet and not knock myself out, instead grabbing Jess on landing and kissing her right back, while squeezing her as close to me as I could without fracturing anything. 'Christ I've missed you.' I said with heartfelt sincerity, partly drowned-out by the cheers, whistles and applause from all those in the bar enjoying the scene.

'You too. The fish send their best as well. So; might you be able to spare a girl some of your precious time? And possibly pour her a drink too?'

At that point J.D. wandered into the bar with Halo at his heels and stood next to the still effervescent Janine. 'Go on Ken; take some time out. There are other people I can call on if we get low on limes or we have a need for would-be heroes that do little more than fall over and smash their head into things. Hi again Jess.'

After giving Jess another hug, I walked back behind the bar, bowing to those punters who offered some follow-up clapping in appreciation of my earlier romantic and gymnastic display.

Once I was back on-station, Jess looked at me determinedly then pitched her look upwards to the ceiling, as if focused on something far beyond the illustrious walls of "The Pulton Arms". Then she swung her gaze back to me. 'There are two, no; three things you need to do to secure your future happiness: and mine. Number one was the reconciliatory snog which has already passed muster so we can tick that box; well played you on that one. Extra credit for the bar leaping too. Second thing is never looking twice at another woman again regardless of how hot she might be: that is doubly true of bridesmaids at our wedding which is a long way off yet but is still hopefully a possibility but nothing I wish to rush into because my ex stuffing one of the aforementioned bridesmaids was the principle reason we broke up when I found out long after our "Happiest Day". Sodding Judy Benson. Stick thin, micro-arsed, no-tits barfaholic that she is. Plus I lent her my GHD's that I never got back. The cow.'

'I'm kind of scared to ask what number three might be? Do I need to go and kill Judy Benson for you? Or just buy you new straighteners?'

Jess shook herself out of herself, then stretched across the bar again to get the closeness back. 'Actually there's four. Three is a large glass of dry white please.'

I went to pour her drink; my back to her. 'And four?'

'Four is a trip to Prague. Have you been?'

I placed her drink on the counter, rather thrown by number four.

'No. Why Prague?'

Clearly rather excited, she reached into her coat pocket, then unravelled what looked to be a print-out of a web page article and flattened it out on the bar. Then span it around so I could read. 'We need to see a man about a painting.'

Also curious, J.D. and Janine crowded at my shoulder; keen to get a look-in. Still clueless, I looked at Jess dumbly, then returned to the print-out. "Hunt for stolen masterpiece continues." announced the headline. Below that was an image that struck me as being awfully familiar - a seascape picturing several brawny sailors wrestling with sails and rigging, getting battered by a nasty-looking storm whilst their counterparts just sat around and chewed the fat. Idle gits. 'Hang on, that's...'

'Yes it might be. Come on, I'll help you pack while I explain. After we make up for lost time that is.' She picked up her glass then grabbed my hand and pulled me towards the kitchen and the stairs that led aloft to The Crow's Nest. 'Not having one yourself?'

'I'll share yours - trying to cut down don't you know.'

I followed her up the ever-creaking stairs. 'Just one thing - where's Prague?'

THE END

Before you go....

If you enjoyed 'The Quay' and you'd like to read more of the series, you can find more information here:

https://quaywordsblog.wordpress.com/

And feel free to leave a comment too....

Thanks to...

Huge thanks to all those that braved some or all of the first draft of 'The Quay' and shared their thoughts with me; you helped me make a better book.

As this is a work of fiction, any resemblance to actual persons is purely coincidental. But thank you to those colourful characters I have in my life that just might have inspired some of Pulton's finest. You know who you are. x

23264324R00270

Printed in Great Britain
by Amazon